HAUNTED REMAINS

The Possession Chronicles #6

By

Carrie Dalby

For Lee Ann Ward,

the first member of Team Alexander.

And Benjamin Eidem,

for inspiring visuals of

the many moods of Alexander Randolph Melling

One

Alexander Melling looked away from the pleading letter, crinkling it in his hand as he thought about the mess he was in. The shabby furniture he had worked at the past year and a half, along with the depressing view of the brick alley from the tiny window, further grated his nerves. He needed help, and his mind instinctively fell to Claudio. Having his best friend back in town as of last month was a blessing. Often, Alexander needed to bare his transgressions and gather Claudio's advice—and the situations requiring that assistance increased as Lucy's belly swelled with their growing child. With a sigh, he tucked the envelope into his briefcase as a knock sounded on the office door.

Straightening his navy suit with high-quality tailoring like he wore when he worked with his father, he sat to his full height in the gray room. "Come in."

Ms. Trigg, the office secretary at Mr. Connell's law firm, entered. "Excuse the interruption, Mr. Melling, but there's a sister here to see you."

"Sister?" Visions of Eliza's cheeky smile and sparkling blue-violet eyes caused a cloud of unease to settle on his countenance.

"Sister Prudence."

He brushed off the memory of his deceased sibling and forced a smile. "A nun? Of course, I can make time for a sister in need. Send her in."

"Without an appointment on Friday afternoon?"

"A servant of the Lord would not seek a lawyer without great need."

"Yes, Mr. Melling." Returning a moment later, she made quick introductions. "Mr. Melling, Sister Prudence." The secretary immediately stepped out and shut the door.

The nun's smile held brightness behind her reservations, and Alexander offered his gloved hand in the humble space. "Come in and have a seat. Would you like some coffee?"

"No, thank you, Mr. Melling. I'm sorry to come unannounced, but I didn't know what else to do."

Her brown eyes followed him as he took his seat, causing a tug of familiarity to tickle Alexander's thoughts.

"I'm happy to help. Did Claudio send you?" Seeing her puzzlement, he clarified, "Father De Fiore?"

"No, though I hear he is kind."

"If you ever need assistance, he's the priest to see." Alexander lifted his gold pen and held it over the notepad on his desk. "What brings you here today?"

"Hazel and Consuela."

He felt the color drain from his face as the image of his regular prostitute from years back filled his mind. Petite, dark, and daring—Consuela was his to conquer until he set his sights on Lucy.

"You must have seen the newspapers." The nun wrapped the rosary at her thick waist around her finger. "Hazel Kline's been arrested for murdering her client. The newspapers make her sound like a heartless killer, but it was self-defense. You were always kind to us girls, and I knew you would be the one to ask for help."

"Are you saying—"

"Yes, and you were the best client of all, Mr. Melling. All you asked for was brandy and to see the pleasure in my eyes. I felt like I should have paid you for the experience."

Alexander dropped his pen and leaned back in his chair. "Show me your hair."

A smile creased his cheeks as she removed her head covering and displayed a mane of well-kept blonde hair. "I remember you, Prudie. Consuela's stand-in when she was indisposed. You were delightful."

"Consuela picked me because she didn't think you'd crave me over her. But you made me feel special—the only man to accomplished that. Except, of course, my Lord and Savior." Prudie crossed herself. "Forgive me for saying it, but I'd lay with you right now if you promise to help Hazel."

Only when she went to open her habit did Alexander realize he was standing before her. He ran a hand through his hair and stepped back. "No, Prudie. That won't be necessary." The disappointment in her eyes brought strength to his posture. "I'll see what I can learn from the police in regards to evidence and interview Hazel."

"Bless you, Mr. Melling."

Alexander cupped a gloved hand on her round cheek. "And Prudie, you needn't offer yourself. We can't dwell on the past, no matter how enjoyable it was." His leather-covered thumb wiped the tear that escaped. "Pray for strength, for both of us."

Prudie's arms went about him—warm and comforting. "You were our fantasy. We both wanted Alexander the Great, but Consuela made sure she was center stage whenever you arrived. I dreamt you'd come back after our times together and tell Consuela you were there for me instead of her. When word reached us of your death after the hurricane, I couldn't stand the thought of my one hope being gone forever. The priest coming for Consuela gave me the idea to join the convent to escape, but the memories of my hours with you never left."

"Sweet Prudie." Alexander's fingers trailed to her jaw, and then her lips were on his.

Feeling the rosary beads at her waist sobered him with sickening clarity. He stepped away. "I'll see to Hazel, but you must leave."

"I brought some personal things to the jail this morning to keep her comfortable." She accepted her head covering from him. "It was sinful of me to lust for you. I know you're married now, and I with the Lord. Forgive me, Alexander."

Her penitent stance in her habit churned his stomach. *God, what have I done? She's a nun, and my Lucy's at home!*

"We're two imperfect people, Prudie."

He escorted her to the front room with a hand on her arm, past Rupert Lyons coming out of Mr. Connell's private office. Alexander quickly turned back to his own space, but Rupert followed.

"Visiting with old friends, Melling?" Rupert closed Alexander's door behind them. "What would your gorgeous wife think of you meeting with a prostitute you used to enjoy the company of?"

Fists clenched, he turned on the one who'd purchased his father's law firm after the supposed death of both Melling men six years previous. "She's given her life to God."

Rupert lit a cigarette and offered one to Alexander. "She was always too fleshy for my taste, though I remember you boasting how her form allowed—"

"Stuff it, Lyons."

Rupert laughed. "Come on. I see that grin. You enjoyed it. Is she paying for legal services with favors?"

Alexander took a long drag and refused to respond.

"You can take the girl out of the red light district, but you can't take the red light out of the girl." Rupert perched on the corner of Alexander's desk. "Your secret's safe with me. Once a Dardenne brother, always a Dardenne brother. Why was she here?"

"She wants me to represent Hazel Kline. Prudie says the murder was in self-defense, and she thinks I can get Hazel out of jail."

"It's the case of the decade, my friend. Complete with sex, scandal, and a murdered banker. Your talents are wasted in this little office." Rupert pointed his cigarette at Alexander. "Take it, clear the whore's name, and return to your old office. It'll save me the trouble of changing out the sign. I was going to drop the 'Melling' at the end of the year now that your dear mother is no longer with us."

Alexander shook his head and blew smoke, aiming at Rupert's crooked nose.

"Why not, Melling?"

"Lucy."

Rupert laughed. "So our wives have never gotten along. *I* don't even get on with Kate. That doesn't mean we have to end our friendship."

"No, your actions against Lucy and Magdalene did that."

"Says the man who pointed me back to Magdalene Jones to finish what I started."

"That was a lifetime ago." But the doubt that had crept in after he'd kissed a nun made Alexander think he wasn't so changed after all.

"You're rivaling Davenport these days for Pious Man of the Year." Rupert looked down at Alexander. "I bet his muscular build primed Lucy to take anything you're able to—"

Cigarette dangling from his lip, Alexander swung at Rupert but was blocked. He ground the smoke into the ashtray on his desk. "Don't *ever* speak of my wife!"

"I crossed a line that's been painted since we lost our friendship. But think about being back at the office fronting Bienville

Square, with a pretty secretary of your choosing always at the ready and your name on the sign out front. Prudie came looking for you there. I heard who was seeking your help and had to follow up on what I knew would be a tantalizing story. I remembered Connell offered me a cigar earlier this week and thought it the perfect time to claim it." Rupert gazed a moment at the faded wallpaper and fingered a gash in the desk. "Alex, you belong where your forefathers set your legacy—at Lyons, Melling, and Associates."

Pain burned through him at the thought of all his father had done. "The Melling name is nothing to me."

"Then why did you take your parents' mansion after your mother died this spring? I know you can't be making enough in this place to support a household that size." Rupert smirked around his cigarette. "Are you dipping into your parents' money to cover the bills, or is Lucy paying for things? How does it feel to be married to a woman more successful than you?"

Alexander straightened the suit Lucy bought him last month, compliments of her most recent royalty check. "I'm her muse and take pride in her accomplishments."

Rupert laughed and put out his smoke. "Your father must be turning in his grave. Maybe it's best you stay here until you rediscover your masculinity."

Alexander opened the door and motioned him into the hall.

Rupert rose from his perch. "Think about it, Melling. You're better than this."

Alexander collected his briefcase and drove home. Expecting the Davenport girls to be in the back yard that late September afternoon, he parked in the porte-cochere on the side of the house rather than pulling to the garage to allow a few extra minutes to collect himself. He dropped his case, jacket, shoes, and gloves in the marble foyer. Undoing his tie, he stopped at the vision of tenderness in the front parlor: brunette hair swept into a loose bun, blouse half open to allow access for her baby to suckle, and her homey skirt fanned about her lap. Having Prudie thrust before him the previous hour, he'd forgotten the Campbells' planned visit. He hadn't seen

Magdalene since Darla and Henry's wedding, and he fell to his knees before her.

"Magdalene, please tell me I'm not a horrible person."

Her radiant smile brought him back to their time in Seacliff Cottage. She raised a hand to his stubbly cheek. "I've always spoken of your bravery. You've shed your past and are blessed with Lucy. Now turn away a moment so I can get myself situated."

His roaming eyes studied the nursing baby with a sparse crop of russet hair. "Don't interrupt the tyke on my behalf. I watched Lucy nurse Bethany many times, even before we wed. I found it fascinating."

Magdalene laughed. "I'm sure you did, but now isn't the time for you to indulge your curiosity. In another few months, you'll have the pleasure of watching Lucy once more."

Alexander sighed and turned away. "I've behaved abominably today. I feel myself shattering and fear I'll be left a shell of a man."

"It can't be all bad, Alex. And thank you for sending the Scotch this week. You're always generous. Here, you can turn now." She held out her son. "Meet Simon Claude Campbell."

He took the three-month-old into his arms. "Welcome to the fine city of Mobile, Simon Claude. But Claudio now has two children bearing references from his family. When do I get one named after me?"

"I'm sure Douglas would frown on that, but you'll have a chance with your own, and Claudio won't." Magdalene's brown eyes watched him as he swayed her child in his arms. "Lucy swears your baby is a boy. Will it be Alexander Randolph Melling the Second?"

"I refuse to be hopeful for a boy over a girl, though it would be nice not to be so outnumbered."

"Since when do you mind being the minority among females?" she teased.

"You're right." He laughed, handed Magdalene back her youngest, and kissed her cheek. "He's a fine boy, and I'm glad you'll be able to return to visiting the city regularly. I've missed you. Did you find your rooms adequate?"

"Everything's lovely. We'll be more than comfortable the next few days."

He collapsed on the sofa beside her, resting his head on her lap and curling to his side. "I won't be able to unwind until I speak with Claudio. I'm turning into my father."

Supporting her infant in one arm, Magdalene dropped her other hand to Alexander's shoulder. Running fingers across his shirt, she focused on the area of his chest covered with scars. "You released your sins long ago." Her voice was soft, full of affection. "And you're *nothing* like George Melling."

The memory of Prudie's lips on his blended with the sensation of Magdalene's touch, leaving him swollen with the need to experience more from those who adored him.

"Magdalene, I can't handle your attention today, even when offered in friendship." He raised her hand to his lips, kissing each knuckle. "I'm not safe to be around."

"Yet you make no effort to move." She placed her hand back on his shoulder.

"It's taking all my strength to stay where I am rather than falling upon your luscious form."

A door slammed in the back of the house, followed by the sound of running feet.

"God bless Phoebe," Alexander muttered.

His oldest stepdaughter raced into the room, followed by Kade Campbell. Phoebe's blue dress was streaked with dirt, as were her rosy cheeks.

"Mr. Alex!" She leaned over him, kissing the smooth spot on his cheek above the shadow of a beard that hid his burn marks. "Welcome home! Kade and I caught a toad, but Momma said we had to ask Miss Maggie if we can keep it."

Phoebe brought her hands within inches of Alexander's face, displaying the lumpy amphibian.

"That's a great find, Knight Phoebe." Alexander sat upright, resting a hand on Magdalene's knee.

"Can we keep it, Mama?" Kade took the spot beside his friend, straightening the knot on the sailor's kerchief about his neck.

Magdalene smiled. "Return it to its home before you come in for supper."

"Thank you, Miss Maggie." Phoebe turned back to Alexander. "Are we going riding tomorrow? Kade wants to see me on the pony!"

Alexander grinned with the knowledge Phoebe enjoyed her riding lessons as much as he found pleasure in teaching her twice a week. "I'm not sure with company here, but I'll discuss it with your parents."

She squealed and ran for the back, Kade on her heels.

"They have such fun," Magdalene remarked. "I'm glad our families are friends."

"Our bonds are strong, Maggie. Never leave me."

Two

Melissa Davenport stopped at the mirror in the front hall of her house, "The Old Easton Homestead" as her husband liked to refer to it. She tucked a loose strand of copper hair behind her ear and straightened the shoulders of her green dress.

A moment later, a horn sounded. Crossing the yard of the Queen Anne house, Melissa went toward the automobile rolling slightly in the oyster shell drive. Darla Adams perched behind the wheel in a purple striped suit, which looked beautiful against her pale skin and dark hair.

"Hop in fast, Melissa!" Darla reached across to open the passenger door. "I'm not sure I can get it going again if it stalls."

Falling in, Melissa dropped her purse on the seat and pulled the door closed. She smiled, happier than usual to see Darla after her day alone. The only thing she enjoyed more than time with Darla—no children, no husbands, just womanly camaraderie—were the rare hours she spent one-on-one with Freddy.

"It's my first time driving without Henry," Darla said as she pulled away from the house. "But as he's riding to supper with Mr. Davenport, I'll have him with me on the way home."

"I told you the *Mr. Davenport* needs to stop unless you're going to call me Mrs. Davenport." Melissa held onto the dashboard as Darla swung wide onto Government Street.

"I can't call him Freddy after working for him."

"Some people call him Frederick. That's a step away from his formal title."

"*Some people* like Lucy. She's the one I hear use that most often."

"And Claudio and Maggie. It's a fine name."

"I'll try my best. Have you talked him into giving you driving lessons yet?"

"He insists the girls not be in the automobile, and it's rare they aren't."

Darla chanced a look at her. "Surely you could work something out with Lucy and Alex."

"He doesn't want to burden her while she's expecting."

"She's perfectly capable of watching her *own* children a few more hours a week. Do you want me to speak to him for you?"

"No, but thank you. I think I'll wait until next year, once she's settled with the baby."

"I don't see why you need to do that, but it's your choice. Hold on when I pull into the driveway. I hope there'll be room for *Frederick* to park behind us."

Melissa jumped out at the Mellings' house as Darla set the brake. "There's plenty. And you're even—no tires on the grass."

Taking the lead, Melissa rang the doorbell. Douglas Campbell opened the door.

"Captain!" Darla's arms were about her friend from Dauphin Island. "Your beard is gone!"

"I shaved it off for the summer and haven't started it back yet." He hugged her in return, raising an eyebrow. "How is Henry treating you? Do I need to rough him up after supper?"

"He's wonderful, every bit the doting husband."

"Good to hear." Douglas turned to Melissa and hugged her as well. "And you're looking prettier than ever, Melissa. Being Mrs. Frederick Davenport seems to agree with you."

Her cheeks flushed. "Thank you."

"Most are gathered in the front room."

Darla rushed ahead and cooed over the Campbells' newest arrival. By the time Melissa greeted Maggie and Tabitha, Darla had Simon unwrapped and examined his reflexes like the seasoned medical professional she was.

"He's handsome, Maggie." Darla tied on his gown and swaddled him back into his blanket. "Every bit as strong as Kade and as smart as Tabitha. And those blue eyes like the captain's hold an old soul, to be sure. Claire was right about him."

"Pass Simon to Melissa when you're through." Maggie turned to her daughter. "Could you check on Papa and the other kids? Maybe see if Miss Lucy needs help with Bethany."

Tabitha nodded and slipped off the plush sofa.

"Before the others join us," Maggie said as she leaned closer, "both of you tell me about married life. The last time we were together, Darla was full of questions."

Darla's joyful face turned crimson, and she nestled the baby closer to her chin. "It's everything you all said. I never thought I could love Henry more than I did when we were engaged, but we're closer now. I ache for his arms by the end of the day, and when I'm out late birthing a baby, I only want a hot shower and to lie in his arms when I return."

"And any news for either of you on that front?" Maggie asked.

"I'm trying to wait until the end of the year. I learned a few tricks from research and speaking with knowledgeable people through the years on preventing things." Darla handed Simon to Melissa. "Henry and I are so busy with work, I'd like as much time with him as possible before having a baby, but I wouldn't be upset if something were to happen."

Darla and Maggie turned to Melissa. While she envied the younger newlyweds their privacy, she wouldn't trade life with Freddy and his daughters for anything. He was almost as alluring as he played with his girls as he was when they were alone. But to have him to herself more than one regular night a week would be bliss.

"Nothing yet, but I'm older, and it could take time if it happens at all." She paused, reminding herself to check her calendar when she got home because she believed her monthly was due soon. Baby Simon gripped her finger, causing her to smile. "It's a good thing, too, with my contract to keep up. I'd hate to disappoint Mr. Noble if I were to get sick during pregnancy and fail to turn in my features. I'm two months ahead for now, even with the trip we took with the girls to Yellowstone in August for Freddy's birthday. That helps ease worry on my part. I'm still learning about mothering Phoebe and Bethany. That takes a good deal of effort, even though Freddy's an excellent father to them and a teacher to me."

"And what has he taught you?" Maggie giggled and looked to Darla, who blushed deeper.

Fortunately, Douglas, Lucy, and the four children came in, allowing Melissa to remain mute on the topic.

"I hope we didn't interrupt anything." Lucy lowered into a gilded armchair, her red evening dress draping her curves as only she could accomplish.

"Not at all," Melissa was quick to reply as Bethany climbed beside her to look at the baby. "We were admiring Simon."

"His friend will be along in a few more months." Lucy patted her belly and looked to Darla. "My midwife assures me all is well."

"Aye, and where's the proud father?" Douglas asked.

Maggie straightened. "He sat with me a few minutes when he arrived. As soon as Claudio came, Alex whisked him into the den."

"Claudio is here, too?" Douglas folded his arms. "I see where I rank with those buggers."

"Alex needs time with his adviser," Maggie said.

Lucy stood. "What's wrong? Shall I go to him?"

"He needed a listening ear, but I'm sure it's nothing major." Maggie motioned to her baby. "Would you like to hold Simon now? Melissa can bring him to you."

Lucy nodded and returned to her chair.

Melissa sought to calm Lucy as she passed her the baby. "Thank you for hosting us for supper. You look lovely, and I'm sure Alex will greet you with kisses before long."

Phoebe perched on the arm of her mother's chair and examined Kade's little brother with him looking on. Tabitha was on her father's knee, and Melissa kept her arm about Bethany as Douglas, Maggie, and Darla spoke of their mutual friends on the island.

Ten minutes later, Phoebe rushed to answer the door, coming back with Freddy and Henry, both freshly showered after their time at the gym. She led her father directly to Simon, and he greeted Lucy with a kiss on the forehead and shook Kade's hand before turning to the other Campbells and Darla. Finally, he came to Melissa and Bethany. He lifted his youngest over his head before pretending to drop her, cuddling her to his chest as she came down.

"Daddy."

"Love you, Beth." He kissed her cheek, catching Melissa's eye with a wink over his daughter's shoulder. "Let me see to Sissa now."

Bethany snuggled on his far side as he sat beside Melissa, tucking her under his firm arm. After a kiss on the lips, he pecked her ear. "You look divine, Beloved."

She was sure he could see the want in her countenance because his brown eyes shone in response with a curve of his lips amid his trimmed beard. He leaned in to kiss her neck and whispered, "Tonight."

Melissa rested against his side and made the mistake of glancing at Maggie, who winked at her. Darla saw the exchange and hid a laugh.

Freddy cleared his throat. "Henry, would you like to tell Lucy the news, or shall I?"

"I will." Henry turned to their hostess from his spot beside his wife. "Eddie bested two boxers this afternoon and nearly beat me as well."

"Good for him," Lucy remarked on her brother's improvements. "Be sure to tell him how proud I am if you see him before I do. He was top of the ring at school. I'm sure he's coveting that position again."

"He's a better weight-match for me," Freddy said. "I hope to take a full round with him next week. We've only gone at play this summer, but he's ready for more. He's thinking about entering the tournament next month."

Douglas joined Freddy and Henry in boxing chatter until Claudio and Alex appeared in the doorway. Claudio—ever striking in his priestly frock—went to Douglas and Alex to Lucy.

"See how happy Momma is with the baby," Phoebe declared. "Simon makes her smile, so he's on our team, Mr. Alex."

With reserved movements, Alex pressed a kiss to Lucy's cheek. Then he ruffled his stepdaughter's blonde locks. "So he is, Phoebe."

When Naomi called the group to supper, Alex stopped Freddy and Lucy. Freddy took Melissa's hand to involve her in the conversation sure to revolve around the girls, a tender gesture that cemented what he always told her—they were a team, though she still didn't feel like much of a mother.

"Phoebe asked if we'll still have our lesson tomorrow. She wants to bring Kade so he can see her ride. Do you think that will be fine, or are there other plans?"

"We've agreed for you to have her Saturday mornings since her fifth birthday," Freddy said. "I see no problem."

"I don't have plans unless Maggie needs to shop," Lucy said as she pressed against her husband. "But that could easily be done in the afternoon."

Alex nodded. "Phoebe will probably ask before the meal is over, so I'll ask now. Do you wish for the girls to spend the night to allow them more time with the Campbells?"

Freddy held tighter to Melissa's hand. "If she asks, that's fine. We can pick them up in the afternoon."

"Thank you, Frederick." Lucy smiled and followed Alex's lead to the dining room.

Using their window of privacy, Freddy took Melissa into his powerful arms. "And whatever shall we do with no Pancake Time entertainment in the morning?"

"Make our own commotion, of course."

After supper, they said goodnight to the group, and Melissa settled beside her husband in the automobile, a hand on his knee that migrated up his muscular thigh under the cover of night.

"Did you notice Alex behaving distant?" she asked. "He hardly gave Lucy any attention when he's typically all over her."

"I've given up trying to understand the man, but horses are all he and Phoebe talk about these days. With Henry and his vast knowledge, there wasn't much room to discuss anything else. As for his attentions with Lucy, thankfully, that's not my concern. Nor should it be yours. We needn't involve ourselves with their marriage drama. Our only concern is the well-being of our daughters when they're at the Mellings' house. Do the girls appear neglected or unhappy?"

"Not at all."

"Then don't fret. We'll have the house to ourselves, and you're all I crave tonight."

At home, Freddy walked the main floor as he did before retiring each day, then he chased Melissa to their room, falling in a tangle of clothes upon their bed. Her previous concerns were swept away as their passion mounted, and in the hour that followed, she thought only of her husband and their shared experience.

But after midnight, when her head rested on Freddy's chest in the quiet darkness, Melissa couldn't help but think of the man who wore his scars like a warrior. Something serious had to be going on for one ruled by passion to neglect his true love.

Three

After the Campbells were in their rooms for the night, and Phoebe and Bethany tucked into their beds across the hall, Alexander denied Lucy's advances, claiming she needed her rest after the busy evening playing hostess. He'd held her until she fell asleep while his sins circled his soul with tornadic activity—not unlike the demonic wind that moved him to sin within Seacliff Cottage.

Like a fairy bell, the bedroom mantel clock softly chimed one. Feeling Lucy's curves against him brought his moment with Prudie to mind, causing a wave of nausea to envelop him. Claudio had assured him he would visit Sister Prudence and advise her to allow all correspondence between her and Alexander to go through him from now on, but that didn't undo what had already happened. On the eve of six years of righteous living, he was viler than ever.

Not even my father would touch a nun.

Alexander shifted away and turned his back to Lucy's silk-clad form, curling into himself as his discolored hands rubbed the scar lines on his chest.

I created these to save Magdalene, but this afternoon, I was ready to indulge with her as well.

Claudio had told him to cast aside his sins and cleave to Lucy that night, but he couldn't get over the fact that he'd betrayed her.

Betrayed himself.

Lucy's cool hands on his back returned him to the present.

"Happy re-birth day, Alexander," she murmured. "I love you and all you've done for us."

"I fear I'm no better for you now than I was when you left me."

Lucy's movement was sudden as she tugged him around. From his back, he looked up at her ethereal form in the darkness. Her hair hung down in golden rays, the deep cut of her white gown showcased the shadowed valley between her breasts, and her luminous green eyes shone with concern.

"Never speak like that, Alexander Randolph Melling. You've proven yourself worthy, and while neither of us are perfect, we're perfect for each other."

A primal moan escaped his parting lips. "I need you desperately, my queen, but I don't wish to harm you or the baby."

"You won't, my angel." Her loose hair trailed over his skin as she kissed his scars. "I'm here for you. Here to share myself with you, always."

Reflecting on Rupert's words—four years of being with Frederick primed Lucy for a powerful partner, and the fact that Frederick himself told him that spring that he didn't have to abstain while she was pregnant—the desire to hold nothing back pulsed through him like it hadn't since her pregnancy was visible.

He pulled her close and nuzzled into her chest. "Lucy, my everything, may I take you?"

"I'm yours. Do with me as you wish."

His hands and mouth went to her smooth skin as her fingertips, toughened by hours at the typewriter, traced every line of his body. The mutual pleasuring lasted the better part of half an hour.

Then Alexander took command, finding new positions to best accommodate the swell of her middle while allowing the depth he craved. He didn't worry over their impassioned sounds. He only cared about fulfilling the yearning that sought to ruin his life by acting upon it with Lucy.

"My queen, you give me life each moment we're joined, each time I recall your erotic words. 'The sweat and sounds we created together,'" he recited as he took a moment to savor the build.

"'Salty and sweet awash in my mouth

Your hands over my skin

Mine on yours

Your scent all around me.'"

"'In me.'" She ran a hand through his hair and kissed him deeply before continuing.

"'Your impassioned words as I cried out

You showed me much

But there is more to learn

Know that I'm forever yours.'"

Alexander's focus was too intense for a reply as the passionate moment continued.

When the clock struck half-past-two, he lay in the middle of the bed, sweaty and exhausted, while Lucy washed in their bathroom.

"Are you all right?" he called when the water shut off.

"Never better!"

Seeing her wrapped in a towel in the bathroom doorway brought back memories of their first times together—both the good and the bad. He mustered a smile from his prone position as Lucy returned to their bed in a fresh gown, pale pink and lacy. She curled against his side, fingering his scars from jaw to hands.

"I heard you were upset this afternoon. If you need more, I'm here for you," she whispered.

He rolled to face her, tugging her into his arms as they kissed.

"Lucy, you're my everything, but you've given me more than enough tonight. Did you enjoy yourself as well?"

Her kisses followed his neck. "You always thrill me, Alex. I want to keep sharing moments like this with you always."

"We shall, my queen. You own my heart."

***

"Momma! Mr. Alex!" Phoebe's knocking accompanied her calls. "It's Pancake Time!"

Alexander moaned and reached for his pants. "Don't tell me Freddy is here to create that racket in our kitchen."

Lucy laughed. "I asked Naomi and Sharon to cook a hot breakfast today. Melissa only has Sharon three days a week, and I know she could use the money."

Preferring to run the household entirely with his income— though it had been impossible to do since they moved into the mansion—Alexander turned fully to Lucy as he buttoned his pajama pants. "Miss Sharon is Freddy's hire, not ours. She's not your responsibility."

"But she's Naomi's cousin, and it's no trouble. I take her pay from my account."

"I need to understand what it's taking to run things here so I can better plan my career to upkeep our home. If you keep pulling from your account for extras, I'll never be able to balance a budget." *Not to mention stop relying on my parents' savings.*

"I'll try to remember." She tied on her kimono and smiled in her flirty way that set him craving her touch. "Do you want to shower before you come down for breakfast?"

"It might be best." He pulled Lucy into his arms and nibbled her ear as his hands roamed.

With a laugh, she wriggled out of his grasp and opened the door to her daughters. Phoebe bound straight to him, but he watched Bethany wrap her pudgy arms around Lucy's legs as he lifted the oldest.

"We get to go riding today, Mr. Alex!" Phoebe kissed his cheek. "And Kade and Mr. Douglas are coming to see how good I am!"

He hugged Phoebe, grateful she didn't shy away from his scarring like other children might. "That's correct, and all knights are excellent riders."

"And Melling Militia!"

"I've got a good cavalry unit in my army of one." He set her back on the floor. "I'll be down in half an hour. Save some food for me."

Phoebe ran out, and Lucy motioned to Bethany, who was still clutching her legs. "Would you watch her while I dress?"

"I'd rather watch you undress." Alexander winked as he scooped her daughter into his arms and fell on the bed with the nearly two-year-old. Bethany bounced on his stomach, giggling as she pounded his bare chest. "Oof! Your leader taught you well. Hurry back, my queen, before Bethany clobbers me."

A few minutes later, Lucy emerged from the walk-in closet in a stunning red dress. Alexander left his stepdaughter on the bed and crossed the room to his wife.

"Bethany, your momma is the prettiest woman in the world. I can't help but want to dance with her and make love—"

"Alex!" Her indignation was short-lived as he swayed against her suggestively.

She still tasted fresh from her middle-of-the-night shower, and his lips teased until he settled at the base of her throat. He massaged her hips through the silky dress. "Tell me you'll need a nap after the girls are picked up this afternoon. I could nap all day with you, my queen."

"I think we need to stop indulging in front of Bethany. She's getting too big." But as she said the words, she moved closer for a provocative kiss.

Alexander pulled away to prevent taking Lucy in front of her daughter.

As though reading his thoughts, Lucy smiled as her hand trailed down his arm, inciting a racing heart. "Go take a cold shower. I'll see you downstairs."

Dressed for the riding club, Alexander entered the dining room half an hour later after Lucy, the girls, and the Campbells assembled for breakfast. His eyes swept the table and settled on Magdalene's appreciative stare. She took in the length of him, from his tall brown boots to the pale riding pants, and up to the earthy vest over his white shirt, ascot knotted at his neck.

"I never thought you'd look better than you do in a tuxedo," Magdalene said, "but I have to say I prefer this style."

He took the riding hat from under his arm and dropped it on his head with a wink. "Now you have something new to dream about me in."

"Enough of that, Alex." Douglas's brogue sounded as thick as molasses while he cracked his knuckles.

"But the vision of me on Janus rather than the rugged stable hand could have done wonders for me and Maggie back then." Alexander crossed behind Lucy, pausing for a kiss before taking his seat beside her.

While the two families ate, Naomi held little Simon, clucking over him as she paced the hall. When Magdalene finished, she collected her son on the way out. Alexander went in pursuit a minute later. He found her in the morning room, an open blouse revealing more of her than the midnight blue gown from years past. Before he could enter the room, a strong arm hooked around his neck.

"If you think I'm not on to your games, you have much to learn." Douglas tightened the headlock. "Maggie told me of your exchange before Claudio arrived yesterday. You need to keep your distance, do you understand?"

Alexander nodded as well as he could in the grip, and Douglas stepped away. Turning to the other man, he appraised the captain's strength. Douglas wasn't as large as Frederick, but his lifestyle made him just as robust. Having been at the receiving end of his strikes, he didn't wish for a repeat performance.

"My apologies, Douglas. Might I claim the stress of becoming a father on my poor choices?"

Douglas crossed his arms. "My warning's been given. Next time, there'll be no hesitation from my end. Maggie can hold her own as well."

Remembering the enraptured moments he'd shared with her within Seacliff Cottage, a leering smile crept out. "Don't I know it."

Alexander found Lucy on the back patio, watching over the four children playing in the yard. He embraced her wondrous body. "I'll need that nap with you after the girls are picked up this afternoon."

"It will happen if you behave." Her hand trailed his belt.

"But I need you even more when I'm naughty."

Her fingers played across his back like kisses from enchanted sunbeams. Accepting her lips, he shifted to the side so they could get closer without the barrier of her swollen womb. He fought the urge to whisk her to their bed by resting his hand upon the life growing within and was rewarded with a gentle movement beneath his palm.

Lucy's smile was just a beautiful as the sensation of feeling the child he waited seven years to have with her. Wrestling the rise of emotions threatening to spill over, he leaned his forehead against his wife's. "I'm trying to do right for you and the baby."

"It will be enough, Alex. It always is." The kiss from her satin lips sealed his peace—at least for the moment.

Ten minutes later, Alexander left with Phoebe, Douglas, and Kade for Spring Hill.

"Miss Darla and Mr. Henry came to see me ride two weeks ago, but I'm even better now," Phoebe told Kade as they jumped out of the backseat at the riding club.

Alexander had spared no expense on riding clothes for his stepdaughter. She had three complete outfits, plus two pairs of boots, so there would always be one clean despite the laundry or shoe shine schedule. He'd bought the same for himself, though he felt guilty tapping into the money for his pursuits. Alexander pulled on brown leather gloves and situated his hat before showing Douglas and Kade to a shady spot near the ring Phoebe would practice in. Across the property, a group of men prepared for a polo match that would take place that afternoon. A flare of jealousy over the other men lit Alexander. He longed to return to the sport he excelled at during his youth—the hours spent on the field with Janus and twice as many on the trails, pushing their limits.

Upon signing in, Alexander was free to take Phoebe to the stable. He walked her through preparing her borrowed pony for riding. She was a fast learner, and he only needed to reach things she wasn't tall enough to handle on her own. Then he jogged to the ring beside Starlight as Phoebe rode.

Alexander held the gate to the ring open, and Kade clapped as Phoebe rode in, her smile outshining the sun. Remembering Frederick's annoyance at supper the night before over Kade's constant attention on his oldest, Alexander began to get an inkling of what he imagined when he saw the boy with his daughter. After all, Frederick himself loved Lucy since childhood, and the doting father must think the worst.

Four

As soon as Freddy turned off the automobile in the Mellings' driveway, his daughters and the Campbells' children could be heard in the backyard. More specifically, Phoebe and Kade.

Smiling, Melissa accepted her husband's hand after he opened her door. "I have a feeling Phoebe will put up a fuss about going home."

Freddy nodded. "We could invite the Campbells over, but I wouldn't want Lucy thinking we're trying to steal her house guests."

"She might appreciate the respite with Alex focused on Maggie and horses."

"Not your concern," he reminded her as he steered them for the back gate.

"But surely it should be yours, with you wishing to protect your best friend from her scoundrel of a husband."

His arm muscles tensed beneath her touch. He opened his mouth to speak at the same time the front door of the mansion was thrown wide.

"Freddy!" The excitement in Lucy's voice carried down the veranda to where the Davenports passed through the porte-cochere. "Come in, please!"

In a swirl of red silk, Lucy tugged her ex-husband into the parlor. Melissa, happy to see the joy on Lucy's face, released Freddy's arm and settled across from the two as Lucy pulled him onto the sofa beside her.

"I know you can keep a secret, and I have to tell someone before I burst!"

Freddy leaned his head against Lucy's and patted her torso. "You've got a few more months before that happens."

She laughed. "Alex is feeling the baby move every day. He's happy, but I know he's worried. He's been stressed lately, but he doesn't tell me everything. After he gets back from riding with Phoebe, he's much improved. I talked to Henry a few weeks back, and he watched one of Phoebe's lessons and chatted him up to get a feel for what Alex would want in a horse of his own."

Freddy leaned back, looking upward with an exasperated expression.

"Henry's spoken to his father, and it sounds like there's a great match for Alex at his stables. He's going to Chatom next weekend, and if the horse is everything his father says, he'll buy it for me, secure transportation, and set things up at the riding club for boarding so it will be here in time for Alex's thirtieth birthday."

"Goosy—"

She ignored Freddy's tone and pulled a check from under her sash, placing it firmly into his hand. "I need you to pass this to Henry on Monday."

His mouth set straight amid his beard as he looked it over. "It's much too extravagant."

"That's for the horse, as well as Henry and Darla's travel, the delivery, boarding at the club for the rest of the year, and a bit for Henry's efforts. A finder's fee of sorts. I trust his judgment, and he isn't expecting the extra, but you make sure he doesn't repay the difference."

"You're about to have a baby, Goosy." Leaving the check on his lap, he took her hands into his. "The last thing you need is the trouble of a horse, not to mention Alex's time and attention being split between work, home, and the riding club even more."

Melissa shifted in the chair, an ache over the concern on Freddy's face playing at her chest. *Somedays, Lucy is no better than another child demanding his attention.*

"I'm scared, Freddy," Lucy whispered. "I'm scared he's slipping back into darkness. I need to be sure when he's not home that he's somewhere safe. The riding club—especially when he's with Phoebe—is a haven for him. It's healthier than the other establishments he used to frequent, you know it is. And if it costs boarding and grooming fees each month and a handful of afternoons without him, that peace of mind is worth it."

He kissed her cheek. "Of course it is, Goosy. I'll be sure to give the check to Henry and tell him I'm happy to help with anything he might need to see this fulfilled. Phoebe loves riding as well. I'm glad she and Alex are bonding over it rather than the wars."

"I was hoping you'd say that. I want to discuss getting Phoebe a pony for Chris—"

Freddy groaned. "Another day, Goosy. Wait and see how this purchase goes before you run off spending hundreds of more dollars. And to think I used to proclaim your sensibilities with expenses."

Her bell-like laughter filled the room, and then she kissed him before standing. "I've strayed in my time away from my sensible numbers man. Let me collect the girls for you."

***

The following Tuesday, Melissa was preparing breakfast when Phoebe bounded into the room. Melissa turned in time to see the girl staring at the wall calendar. She'd already pulled yesterday's page off, and the new page clearly read OCTOBER 1.

"I can plan my Halloween costume now!"

"Good morning, Phoebe. Wait until after breakfast before setting loose with costume ideas." Melissa flipped the ham slices in the cast-iron skillet. "Is Bethany up as well?"

"She's with Daddy."

Freddy was more capable of readying for work with his daughters underfoot than she was of cooking breakfast with her attentions divided.

"Would you mind setting the table and getting Doff's milk?" Melissa asked so she wouldn't accidentally over-cook the eggs.

"I can do it!" Phoebe's eagerness to prove she was a big girl never waned.

By the time the last piece of toast was buttered, Phoebe had the table ready. Bethany pushed through the kitchen door, immediately tugging on Melissa's skirt.

"Sissa, I hungry."

Freddy joined them at the counter by the stove. "I'm hungry too, and only a kiss will satisfy me."

His musky cologne was subtle, though his kiss was anything but. Using his broad shoulders to shield his actions from the girls, he dipped Melissa backward as he tasted of her.

"Careful, Freddy. Breakfast won't be as filling after a display like that."

His brown eyes shone with friskiness he usually kept for the bedroom as his hands circled her waist. "Then I'll have to come back for seconds."

"You know where to find me." Smiling, Melissa thought of the days Freddy came home for lunch—and other fulfillment—but knew nothing would happen that day because she kept the girls with her Tuesdays.

"How about coming to town with the girls to eat at the diner with me midday? Come to the office any time after eleven-thirty."

"That sounds wonderful." She teased across his biceps and winked. "But be sure you keep things respectable, Mr. Davenport."

After breakfast, Freddy pulled her into the study while the girls were in the parlor. "I'm back for more, Melissa," he said as he locked the door.

Laughing, she looked at the twin desks for each of them, as well as a small library table for the girls in the functional workspace. "There's no longer a chaise in here if you haven't noticed."

The way he lifted her off the floor brought to mind the times he'd held her during their passion, communicating that they didn't need a bed. Her nobleman, with the strength of a Greek God, was capable of many things—including shifting her attentions with his well-placed caresses.

"Freddy …"

Their kisses went deeper.

Her hand was at his belt when the knock sounded.

"Sissa, storytime." Bethany's little voice barely carried through the oak door.

The passion drained from her in an instant, leaving her flushed.

Pressed against her, so she knew how much he was planning for their moment as well, Freddy kissed her with fierce attention. "I can never get enough of you, Beloved."

"Early bedtime for the girls tonight?"

"I'll change all the clocks in the house if needed to convince Phoebe."

Freddy saw Melissa and his girls settled on the sofa before he left. Gone were the frilly Victorian items that Lucy had filled the parlor with. In their place were sturdy furniture pieces from Freddy's old house and a few new things he and Melissa chose together. Before opening the book, Melissa looked at the boxing trophy on the mantel and smiled over the memory of the spring day that brought them closer. Now that they'd spent months sharing the ultimate in physical togetherness, it humored her to think she'd been satisfied with necking on his sofa back then.

Melissa and the girls passed the morning reading, discussing Halloween costumes, and tidying the house before heading to the streetcar. They took the Government Street trolley up to the loop at the west end of the line and then back around Royal Street—passing both the Mellings' house and the ornate courthouse. At the same time, Phoebe gushed about her stepfather to the delight of the other passengers when they passed each location. Once they got to the north side of the road, they disembarked at Hamilton Street. Melissa held each girl by a hand as they walked a block north to Davenport Allied Accountants.

"There isn't a brighter day than one when the Davenport girls stop in," Ms. Neves said as soon as they entered the office. "And that includes you, Mrs. Davenport."

"Thank you, Ms. Neves. That's a lovely color on you," she remarked over her blue suit.

"I'll have you know, after reading your article on New Orleans, I've decided I must see it for myself. I talked my cousin and her husband into going with me. We're booking train tickets and hotel rooms for November. That Dauphin Island bit in August was interesting but too rugged for my taste. What's the feature to be for this month?"

"Atlanta."

"From when you went to visit Mr. Davenport's sister over the summer?"

"Yes, we don't always take the girls, but Angela was good enough to entertain them while we saw more of the sights."

"Where are you off to next?" Ms. Neves asked.

"The Point Clear Hotel and Fairhope this weekend."

"It must be nice to have an excuse for all these getaways." The secretary smiled and pulled a peppermint out of her desk for each girl, motioning Melissa to her husband's office. "I've got the dears."

Freddy sat at his desk beyond the open door with his eyes focused on the pages before him as his right hand punched numbers into an adding machine on the corner of his desk. She waited until he pulled the lever to denote the end of a line before making herself known.

Closing the door behind her, she lifted her skirt to her knees with a motion much like a dancer at Moulin Rouge in Paris, showcasing her stocking-less legs. "Still savoring a taste of me, handsome?"

"More than you'll ever know." He swept her into his arms and went at her lips before hugging her tight. "I look forward to our trip across the bay Friday afternoon. Get your work done as quick as possible because I'll demand much of your attention those two nights at the hotel."

"There are a few places I'll need to see by moonlight to make my article well-rounded. Business before pleasure, Freddy."

"My business is complete for the morning." He fell into the chair in the back corner, pulling Melissa on his lap. "What pleasure will you indulge me with?"

She ran her fingers through his thick, brown hair as she kissed him. Electricity from his hand creeping under her skirt brought immediacy to her cravings. She grasped the tie at his neck as his hand went higher, and their kiss deepened.

Shifting towards him further, she leaned back enough to take a breath. "Would you, Freddy?" Expectancy crinkled her voice. "In your office?"

His smile reminded her of Alex for a brief moment. "Not with the girls here."

"Ms. Neves gave them peppermints and wanted me to come back for you."

"Looking for a fresh bit of gossip, I'd say. Should we rumple our clothes a bit, loosen your hair?" He winked at her.

"Only if we go through with it. Nothing just for show."

"My fiery redhead." He squeezed her thigh and then trailed his hand down her leg. "You'll just have to wait. For now, let's collect the girls and head to the diner before the lunchtime crowd arrives."

Five

Alexander's inquiry at the police station the previous day afforded him a glimpse of the situation Hazel Kline was in. After his Tuesday morning appointments, he went to the jail to secure a meeting with her. She had refused her court-appointed defense, and Alexander was unsure if she would accept him. That would be revealed when he returned at two o'clock.

At his office, he nursed a cup of black coffee and three cigarettes while he made a list of questions to ask Hazel. He had advised a few men in jail during his time in Louisiana, but nothing he ever had to go to trial with. All of his court appearances to date were for non-criminal matters. Could he handle the pressure of a high-profile murder case? Rupert seemed to think so, but maybe it was payback for breaking his nose, and the beating Douglas gave him all those years ago. But it still didn't make up for the pain Alexander went through with Twila because of him. The man had been nothing but trouble the past decade, but knowing Rupert felt him capable of handling the case gave Alexander a sense of pride.

At one o'clock, he telephoned the diocese and asked for Claudio.

"Father De Fiore," the voice came through the line like a calming breeze.

"Pray for me, Claudio. I see Hazel at two."

"May I meet you at the cathedral afterward?"

"I'm not sure how long it will take." Alexander exhaled a tight smoke ring. "She could refuse me in the first two minutes."

"What woman refuses Alexander Melling? I thought they all begged for you."

He smiled at the memory of the one who mattered most offering herself to him their first time in a carriage. "True, but there's no longer enough of me to go around. Lucy consumes me."

"Then you are in luck. I shall be at the cathedral at three. If you cannot make it by five, I shall call on you at home this evening."

"Thank you, Claudio. I owe you much."

"And for the love of God, do not touch her."

"I've learned my lesson."

"I sincerely hope you have."

Alexander donned the derby that matched his new charcoal suit and took his briefcase in his gloved hand.

"I'll be at the courthouse the rest of the day," he told Ms. Trigg on his way out. "Take messages. I'll be in tomorrow."

"Yes, Mr. Melling. And here's your mail."

He tucked the envelope into his briefcase without looking at it and walked to the courthouse to displace his nervous energy. Pausing on a bench outside the side entrance, he took another smoke, keeping his hat low to prevent eye contact that would lead to small talk with those passing by. After signing the visitor's log at the guardhouse, he waited to be called to a conference room.

Sheriff Paul appraised him. "I hope you know what you're getting yourself into, Mr. Melling. Your father never would've tangled himself in a case like this. He was too smart to get involved with someone accused of murdering one of his peers."

"Thank you for your concern, Sheriff, but I'm no longer with my father's office."

"There are more than enough odd circumstances in your own life. Faking your death, taking a divorced woman, and then that business with the stalker your house guest encountered earlier this year. Didn't your father teach you how to avoid being gossiped about? How to not be written up in the newspaper?"

Alexander gave him the Melling stare to remind the sheriff he was speaking to someone above his station. "He tried many times, but I was too stubborn to listen. Thank you again for your concern."

A guard arrived, pausing to search Alexander's pockets and briefcase before leaving him in a windowless dungeon of a room. Alexander took the scratched seat on the far side of the rickety wood table facing the door and arranged his notebook and pen before him.

Minutes later, two wardens escorted in a brunette woman more ragged in appearance than the meager furniture. Her hair was snarled and the cotton dress filthy behind her cuffed hands. She kept her head down as the guard on the left, a burly man with tobacco-stained hands, released his grip and slapped her on the backside before walking out.

"Fifteen minutes," the other deputy barked. "That should be more than enough time. I hear she takes things quick and hard."

With a bawdy laugh, he pinched her rear and shoved her toward the table. Hazel stumbled for balance without the use of her arms.

Unable to stand the injustice of her treatment, Alexander was on his feet in an instant. A gloved hand gently took her elbow—her body rigid beneath his touch—and his other pulled the chair out for her.

"Here, Ms. Kline." Hoping Claudio would forgive him the contact because it was the gentlemanly thing to do, he crossed himself on his way back to his chair.

Alexander sat. "Now, Ms. Kline, did they explain to you why I'm here?"

Her head rose with deliberate purpose, and she glared amid a blackened eye. Her lip was split, and her face lined, showcasing several decades of hard living. A hint of beauty lay beneath her unkempt appearance, but the anger in her eyes masked it.

"I can only assume you're here to try me out like the others who've stopped in since I've been jailed."

He grimaced. "No, Ms. Kline. I'm here to offer my legal services."

"I should have known you were a lawyer by your expensive suit. I've no need for your kind. I've known too many in my line of work."

"I've prepared a list of questions, and if you would be so good as to answer truthfully, you'll see that I'm here to help." He reached for the gold pen he'd placed by the notebook and found nothing. "Ms. Kline, my pen, please."

He laid his hand palm up on the table and held her intense gaze. She stood and raised her bound arms, gripping the pen like a dagger above him.

"Who sent you?"

"I'm Mr. Melling and—"

Hazel spit on him, arms beginning to tremble. "I should have known by your penetrating stare and flashy suit. The offspring of George Melling, are you?"

With his left hand, Alexander flicked the handkerchief out of his breast pocket and wiped the saliva from his jacket. "I am, but I'm not my father."

"Another lawyer who spends his time in whorehouses? No, not the same at all."

"I haven't entered the district in over six years." He dropped the soiled handkerchief onto the table.

"I know your game." She continued to stare down at him in his seat. "You may not have darkened the doors, but you sent a priest to collect your favorite when you left for Louisiana. Yes, Mr. Melling, I can put two and two together. When you were back from the dead, and the newspaper recounted the fire and the timeline of you hiding away in Monroe, I remembered the Italian priest bound for Monroe. He came for Consuela after the hurricane. Did you keep her to use as you liked and toss her away when she was past her prime? Is that why you came back to Mobile because Consuela was used up, and you decided to settle for that society tramp?"

It took all his effort to keep his hand on the table exposed beneath her make-shift weapon and hold back the anger from his voice. "You may say whatever you like about me, Ms. Kline, but you must not insult my wife."

Hazel threw the pen and crumped to her chair. "I can't deal with chivalry!"

"Then you'll not wish to hear the story of Consuela." A smile showed at the corner of his lips. "I'm here because of Consuela and Prudie."

"Prudie is dead to me." Hazel put her face down on the table. "She came the first day I was here and promised to get help, clothing, and supplies but hasn't returned. I've been in this sack, unbrushed and repeatedly raped since Thursday."

"Prudie came to my office Friday afternoon seeking help for you. Had I known your dire situation, I would have come sooner. Ms. Kline, I fear you are suffering in this jail because of your station in life. I do not doubt Prudie brought everything you requested, but I believe it's being kept from you. Accept me as your lawyer, and I'll see you receive the care you are due."

Face wet with tears, her cracked lips managed a smile.

"I'd offer you my handkerchief," he said, "but it's used."

"It's no bother to me. I'm a wretched creature now." She maneuvered her cuffed hands to pick it off the table and blew her nose. "I remember Consuela and Prudie gushing about your soft touch, but having spent more time with your father than I cared for, I thought they were lying in hopes of getting someone else to take you off their hands."

"Their very capable hands." He winked at her like they shared a private joke, and Hazel laughed. "Yes, I did send the priest for Consuela. I wanted her to tend my wounds and then marry her, to help her escape the hell she lived in as I had escaped mine. I paid for her room and board several weeks—a private room, mind you—but then caught her with a client when I stopped to see if she wanted an afternoon out with me."

"Men like her because she makes them feel large and powerful, but she's petty and jealous. I hope you sent her packing."

"I did, but I'm sorry to say she passed away a few years back." Needing a reprise from the heaviness of the conversation, Alexander removed his gold cigarette case from an interior pocket. "Do you smoke?"

"Yes, please!" In her excitement, she grabbed his free hand. "I'm sorry I was rude. It's been hell for me."

"I'll find what happened to the things Prudie brought you and see that you get cleaned properly before I leave." He placed a cigarette between her lips, then his own, and lit a match to light both. "Then we can focus on what happened the night Mark Wayne died."

"I did kill him, Mr. Melling, but I was trying to get away."

Alexander released a ring of smoke at the gray ceiling and pushed away the thought of lifting his father to the flames inside Seacliff Cottage. "I know the feeling, Ms. Kline."

"I'd been with him before and never cared for the man, but that time he was barbaric. He was strangling me, and I think I passed out for a time. When I next opened my eyes, he'd drunk the rest of the whisky. I was able to get to the edge of the bed before he noticed. He punched me in the face, so I grabbed the bottle off the table and swung. It shattered on his head, but he didn't stop. I jabbed it into his stomach. I only meant to stop him."

Alexander moved to snuff out his half-used cigarette, but Hazel reached for it.

"May I have it? I don't know how often I'll get the luxury."

"Of course, Ms. Kline."

She took it with her dirty hands and set it beside hers, bringing them both to her lips. "Call me Hazel, Mr. Melling."

"Were you examined by a doctor?"

"I've received no medical care or even a shower since I arrived."

Alexander stood to retrieve his pen from the floor and paced the room twice before returning to the table, writing notes on what she'd shared to that point. "You were booked into the jail last Thursday morning?"

"Yes, the attack happened over Wednesday night."

"Much of the evidence of your struggle could be gone."

She sucked on her twin smokes. "I still have bruising on my neck and other locations."

He winced, remembering the marks he'd left on twenty-year-old Lucy during one of his drunken encounters.

"I know this case isn't ideal, but I can pay. I was planning to retire when I turned forty-five and have saved accordingly. Two years to go, and this had to happen."

"Don't worry about that just yet." He slipped his pen into his pocket, placed his notebook in the briefcase, and went for the door. "Guard, I need Sheriff Paul and a police officer right away."

"Is the prisoner misbehaving?" the man with the stained hands asked with a smirk. "I can handle that one just fine."

"Not at all. Major infractions against protocol have been committed that need to be addressed. Get the sheriff and an officer promptly if you wish to keep your job."

"In case you ain't noticed, this here's the jail, not the police station."

"Simpleton!" Alexander roared. "There are always a handful of policemen in the halls of the courthouse. Send a man up to fetch one! And don't forget the sheriff. I know he's here."

"Yes, sir." He scrambled down the hall.

Feeding the bluster he needed, Alexander lit another cigarette and stomped around the small room. Minutes later, the sheriff and an officer arrived, accompanied by the guard.

"What is it, Mr. Melling?" Sheriff Paul frowned. "I don't appreciate being interrupted, and I'm sure this detective has other things to do."

"I'm here to address the mistreatment of my client, Ms. Kline."

The sheriff chortled and slapped the policeman on the shoulder. "A prostitute taken from the whorehouse with the dead body in her chambers, covered in the man's blood. It doesn't take a genius to see the guilty party."

"As everyone is innocent until proven guilty in our fine country, I'd have to point my finger at Mr. Wayne, who was indulging in adultery." Alexander made a show of puffing a few smoke rings. "But I'm not here to judge a dead man. I leave that for the Lord. My focus is on the mishandling of this case and the mistreatment of Ms. Kline."

"You've got some nerve, coming into my jail and accusing my staff of—"

"What happened to the personal items Sister Prudence delivered here Friday morning to help Ms. Kline meet basic levels of hygiene and warmth? Protocol is to sign in items on a ledger and have the deliverer initial, correct?"

"Don't tell me how to run this facility!"

"If I'm shown Friday's ledger, I should see a list of items brought for Ms. Kline by Sister Prudence that have yet to been given to her."

"I haven't had reason to inspect the ledger lately."

"She's a goddamned nun! Does the sheriff's office steal from the church? I want those items brought to Ms. Kline in the next hour, or I'm filing a theft report."

"It was a misunderstanding of sorts, Mr. Melling." The sheriff wiped his face with a handkerchief. "No need to involve the police."

Alexander, eyes burning with righteous anger, turned to the detective. "Even if Ms. Kline's items are found, I still have a complaint to serve the police department. My client told of her attack by the deceased, yet no medical examination was done nor care given to her wounds before she was processed into the system. I demand a doctor to see to Ms. Kline before five o'clock and that she be given shower privileges immediately afterward."

"Of all the—" The sheriff silenced the guard with a glare.

"And if your men do not desist with molesting Ms. Kline, I'll be filing reports of harassment against each and every one who has had contact with her the past five days. Starting with the two who brought her into this room, as I witnessed their groping hands." He ground his cigarette into the table and blew his last mouthful of smoke at the guard.

"I was wrong, Mr. Melling," the sheriff said with a sneer. "You *are* your father's son."

Six

Alexander strode the streets of Mobile to collect his automobile from his office, riding the high his mighty legal skills afforded him. He had rescued a damsel in distress—securing her health care, proper clothing, and enough cigarettes to hold her comfortably through the night—had the case of the decade in his grasp and the sheriff's office seeking to please him.

At home, he slipped in the kitchen door with a light step.

"Good evening, Mr. Alex," Naomi said.

"Yes, it is." Alexander went for his den.

"Alex!" Lucy called when he passed the dining room.

He paused, leaning an elbow on the doorframe and feeling every bit as arrogant as he looked. His gaze lingered over Lucy and Claudio sitting across from each other at the middle of the massive table.

"I was worried about you." She came toward him with the fluidity of the rolling surf. Her fingers brushed his cheeks as her satin lips planted a kiss on his mouth. "You've never been this late before."

"I started a new case today that will occupy much of my time. I need to work on some things in my den."

"You need to eat, my angel." She undid his tie. "Claudio's been here since five, so I invited him to stay for supper. We waited until six-thirty, but I was beginning to feel faint, and he insisted we eat. Join us. It's all still warm. I'm guessing you skipped dinner because you were consumed with the new case."

Seeing her green eyes wide with concern tugged him off his pedestal of power. "You're exactly right, my queen."

He set his briefcase by the wall and dropped his gloves on top of it. He tossed his suit jacket over the back of an empty chair. Before helping Lucy to her seat, he held his wife close, relishing her clean scent and shining hair.

"And how were you and the baby on your quiet day?" He leaned over to caress the swell of her middle before taking his seat beside her.

Smiling over his attentions, she pressed his hand into her belly until the baby pushed in return. "I sat on the patio for a while and jotted ideas in my journal for possible stories. I napped after dinner and then tried to figure out the best place for a bassinet in our bedroom. Much quieter than your day, I'm sure."

He pressed his lips to her forehead. "But every bit as important as you nurture the one within."

Pleased to see Lucy glow under his attention, Alexander kept his conversation light and directed toward her as they ate. He ignored Claudio's harsh stare until they all stood after the meal.

Alexander offered Lucy his arm as he nodded to the priest. "Claudio and I have a few things to discuss. Shall I see you settled on a sofa or upstairs?"

"How long will you be?"

"No more than an hour." His arm went about her waist, fingering the bow at the back of her sash as he leaned closer. "I feel the call of your soul to mine and must indulge soon, my queen."

Lucy clasped his hand. "Then bring me to the morning room so I'm nearby."

He left her with a stirring kiss that almost distracted him enough to fall upon her. Instead, Alexander collected his things from the dining room and went to his father's old lair, where Claudio waited for him.

Much like Mr. Easton's study that Lucy took over in the other house, George Melling's den was wood-paneled and filled with shelves, though done in mahogany rather than oak. Alexander's blue chaise was in one corner, but Lucy didn't brave the smell of his smoking habit to enjoy the space with him. He planned to air the room properly when the weather cooled, and he could light a cozy fire in the hearth. As for now, Lucy kept to the morning room where she had her desk by the window overlooking the back gardens so she could watch the girls play.

Claudio had him by the shoulder as soon as he was within reach. "What manner of sin did you entertain that had you looking like a stuffed peacock upon your return?"

"Merely pride, Claudio." Alexander pushed him away and set his briefcase on the massive desk. "I did a great service and gloried in my legal prowess, but I wish I hadn't missed our time at the cathedral. I know it would have humbled me to be in that space."

Claudio smiled and settled in the leather armchair across the desk from him, accepting the offered cigarette. "And what did you accomplish?"

"Justice for a mistreated woman." He expelled his first puff with a flourish. "She was in a wretched state. They'd denied her everything from medical care to the personal things Prudie brought last Friday."

"Sister Prudence," Claudio corrected him. "You must not be as familiar with her as you are with me."

"Why not? After all, I have known her in the Biblical sense."

Claudio slapped the desk as he stood, causing Alexander to laugh.

"I tease, Claudio, though it's true."

"Do not make light of your grievous sins, especially after your actions with her as recently as four days ago."

Alexander's smile dropped, and he nodded penitently. "I was a gentleman today—all righteous anger against the molestations and denied care Ms. Kline has suffered since her arrest. I stayed late to see she was able to shower after the doctor saw her."

Claudio took a sharp drag on his smoke. "And how did you accomplish that without the guards lying, as I assume they lied about other things they have done?"

Alexander propped his feet on the desk and leaned back in his chair. "A stroke of brilliance on Hazel's part. She made me attend her showering."

"Have you gone mad?" Claudio threw his cigarette into the ashtray, but it bounced out and rolled across the desk.

Alexander dropped his feet to catch it and snuffed it out, avoiding the rage on his best friend's face. "She's the only female in jail at the moment, and there are no matrons on staff. She would have had at least one male guard in attendance, and they've been abusing her. Hazel insisted I go into the shower room to make sure she wasn't accosted."

"I will not sit by while you openly place yourself on the front lines of temptation!" Claudio paced before the desk. "Have you no decency, no thought for your wife or child?"

Alexander took a slow drag before answering. "After all my bluster on calling out their abuse, I couldn't walk away when she asked for help."

Claudio's gaze softened. "And I suppose you had to watch her."

"More like kept my eyes on the two guards leering at her while she washed. One was so worked up he—"

"*Silenzio!* The sins of another man are not my concern at this time, but I suppose the woman is pleasant to see, and she had no trouble disrobing before Alexander the Great."

He laughed and leaned back further in his chair as he looked to the ceiling, remembering the way Hazel caught his eye as she dropped her dress. "She hated me at first. Spit upon me even. Ms. Kline thought me to be like my father and believed the other girls lied about me being the best lover. With all the degrading remarks she's suffered, I felt obliged to acknowledge her with an appreciative eye when she looked to me in the shower. It was the least I could do to give back some of her self-respect."

"No!" Claudio trilled in Italian so rapidly Alexander couldn't catch more than a few words during his tirade. They weren't kind. Then the priest lay his hands on his friend's shoulders and leaned in. "You have coveted that which is not yours."

Alexander couldn't help smirking because he knew Hazel could be his—was already as she made her devotion known that evening through glances and subtle contact.

"You must pray!" Claudio roared with indignation over Alexander's flippant attitude. He shoved a rosary at him. "On your knees!"

He did what was commanded because he knew Claudio was right, though he preferred his friend's listening ear to his priestly rage.

"Now confess your sins before the Lord."

"Bless me, Father, for I have sinned. It has been four days since my last confession. I have allowed pride and lust to seep into my life."

After going through confession and reciting "Hail Mary" dozens of times, in both English and Italian, Claudio prayed over him.

"See me to the door, Alexander, and then cleave to Lucy, your one true love."

"Will you visit with Lucy while I sort a few papers? Only ten minutes more, Claudio."

"You needn't push me to her. I spent nearly two hours with your wife before you arrived. She is pleasant company, something you need to remember and not allow to be taken for granted."

Alexander rubbed his discolored jaw. "I'm unworthy of her, though she tells me otherwise."

"You are blessed, *amico*. Remember, you waited years for the right time to return to her. Ten minutes or we will come for you."

Upon opening his case, he found the mail Ms. Trigg handed him on his way out of the office. Reading the return address for the first time, he sighed.

Opal. Again.

He'd replied to her last letter on Friday and wasn't thrilled with the prospects of a bonus correspondence.

September 27, 1912

Dear Alexander,

I want to thank you, once again, for agreeing to help me with my transition. When Mother and Father next come, I will let them know you have been most brotherly in your efforts to secure the best experience for me as I move on from this home of mine for the last eight years to the unknown of adulthood when I come of age in a month. Surely your valiant efforts seeking my comfort will show them you are just as helpful to the family as Frederick Davenport ever was.

I have enclosed two photographs so you may see for yourself how much I improved. The smaller is a picture the hospital took on my last birthday for my file. The larger is from this summer, wearing the Easter dress Mother and Father brought me this spring. I am sure it is a shock to see me all grown up. I was such an angry child when we last met, but I will happily greet you with a kiss on your cheek as my newest brother-in-law, though it is long overdue.

Sincerely,

Opal Loraine Easton

Alexander stared at the photographs. The two-inch one was Opal with her waist-length hair brushed but veiling her face in a wild manner, mouth straight, deep-set eyes haunted. She appeared to be wearing a robe and couldn't look more like a witch if it was Halloween.

The new one, touched with rose and gold tones, was a different young woman. Immaculately dressed in a tasteful gilded gown, a wide sash cinched below her bust showcasing a lovely hourglass shape—so much like Lucy's. Her hair was done up in a simple, modern style with a fashionable Art Deco headband. She didn't smile, but her Easton chin was high, and there was a sense of knowing behind her gaze. It reminded him of Eliza's fifteenth birthday portrait she went along with to please their mother—a placid countenance but venomous eyes. He studied it with curiosity until a knock sounded on the door. Then he tucked the correspondence and photographs into his briefcase and grabbed a few mints on his way out.

Smiling, he put an arm around Claudio's shoulders and the other around Lucy. "I'm done for the day. Thank you for seeing us this evening, Claudio. It's always a pleasure."

In the foyer, Claudio kissed Lucy's cheeks. "Continue to rest when you can. You must retain this healthy glow the whole nine months."

"Thank you for keeping me company."

As Alexander embraced his friend, Claudio whispered, "I will call the office tomorrow."

He nodded and locked the door behind the priest. Turning to Lucy with an impish gleam, he linked their fingers together and led her upstairs.

He waltzed her around their room before slowly lowering her to their bed.

"My glorious queen, how may I honor you tonight?"

Her previously happy face darkened, reminding him of Opal's picture. "You've worked too long today and need more from me than what you're able to give." A finger traced his brow. "I want to help. What concerns you, Angel?"

Deflating, he dropped beside her and curled against her soft form. Her warmth brought immediate calming, and he nestled the side of his head on her breast, an arm below her swollen middle. She traced her fingers over his back, a murmur of touch that evoked all the tender passion they shared when they first explored each other. He fought to remain motionless, to savor the warmth of Lucy's arms rather than rushing to experience the thrill of sex.

He angled his chin up a few inches so his whispered voice would carry to her ear. "You are my everything, you always have been, but sometimes life tries to edge out all the good. Being the brightest star in my life, you suffer the most."

She turned to him, his head falling to her arm as she settled on her side. Blinded by her beauty, he closed his eyes as her lips went to his. More warmth and softness, sweet and full. Tired of battling the visions of those who sought his attentions the past week, he opened his eyes to cement the reality of being with his wife. His luscious Lucy, forever showering her devotion on his errant self. She was on her knees opening his shirt when he liberated his desires.

"The power you have over me is undeniable, my queen."

Her eyes brightened with the attentions of his well-placed hands. "I fear you no longer find me attractive as my body continues to change."

"Your glory expands with your motherhood, a miraculous wonderland I want to taste of daily." He gently followed the curves of her torso, tugging down her neckline so he could leave a passion mark over her heart. "You're my one true love, though the darkness threatens to take you away."

"I left once, Alexander Melling. Never again."

Seven

Friday morning, Melissa sat on the rug in the girls'
room fixing Phoebe's hair after breakfast while Freddy loaded his
daughters' suitcases into the automobile for their weekend with Lucy
and Alex.

"Sissa, could you come to the riding club next week and take
photographs of me riding Starlight and Mr. Alex on his horse? He
usually rides a big chestnut called Ranger."

Thinking of Alex's approaching birthday and the fact that
Lucy would appreciate photographs, Melissa smiled. "I'm not sure
which day I'll be able to come, Phoebe, but I promise I'll come one
day in October."

Phoebe's arms went around her neck, and she kissed
Melissa's cheek. "Thank you, Sissa! You have a good time with
Daddy. Momma says the hotel is beautiful. I want to see the pictures
when you get them."

"You will, Phoebe."

The five-year-old gathered Rummy and Pinky—her cherished
toys—and hurried for the door. Without being asked, Bethany
plopped herself before her stepmother. Melissa brushed through her
brown hair until it was smooth.

"And a blue ribbon for you to go with your pretty dress."

"Sissa, come home."

"I'll be here when you get back from Momma's on Monday." She kissed Bethany and walked her downstairs.

Freddy met them on the porch. "I'll be home around noon. Alex will be here at three o'clock to drive us to the docks. Three hours should be plenty of time for us to finish packing." Freddy left her with a kiss and a flirtatious smile.

Laughing, Melissa gave Doff a hearty rub on his perch atop the railing. Then she went inside and straightened the parlor. She couldn't help but think how she had judged Lucy's and Alex's yearnings when she stayed with them that spring. Now she knew she and Freddy would be just as active if they had more alone time. She often felt starved for affection as she wrangled her stepdaughters more often than she indulged with her husband. They had after the girls' bedtime and the early mornings—not to mention Wednesday nights when the girls slept over with their mother—but any extra privacy during their nearly five months of marriage was well occupied with impassioned encounters.

Melissa spent the morning going over her itinerary for the weekend and packing the remainder of her things. She was over a week late for her monthly cycle, and while she hoped it held off until after the trip, she packed cloth strips, just in case.

At eleven-thirty, she stopped to prepare a midday meal for her and Freddy—an omelet and pancakes to use up the rest of their milk and eggs. She packed a small picnic basket with the remainder of their fruit so they'd have snacks should they need them on the ferry or in their room at the hotel.

As she flipped the final pancakes, Freddy came up behind her, kissing her neck. He wrapped his arms about her loose-fitting house dress. "Smells wonderful, but I look forward to dessert even more."

They kissed until the smell of burnt pancakes permeated the room. The final batch was a lost cause, but there was more than enough for the two of them. After washing the dishes with Freddy,

Melissa double-checked Doff's food supply to be sure it was easy for Sharon to find, as she would stop in daily to check the cat.

"Enough of that, Melissa. The house is neat as a pin, and we're down to two hours before Alex arrives."

"Count to ten!" She dashed for the stairs.

She closed their bedroom door with a bang and then stole quietly into the guest room she'd stayed in when she was there on assignment with the Mellings. Melissa locked the door, removed her clothing, and slipped under the blankets.

"I don't want to use our time on games today," Freddy called as he opened the master bedroom.

Smiling, Melissa propped her head on her arm, listening for when he learned she wasn't in their bedroom. It took him a minute before he checked the door, then he laughed as he opened it. Freddy was an impressive sight in his underdrawers.

"And here you are, once again opening my locked door and boldly entering in nothing but your undershorts."

"But this time, I can achieve what I only dreamed of that day."

"You never told me your secret to unlocking the door," Melissa said as he joined her.

"Not now." He pulled her to him, and they lost themselves in the joy of sharing their full selves with each other.

At a quarter to three, Melissa sat in the armchair by the front window. Freshly showered, she wore a feminine navy dress with lace details at the chest and cuffs. Frederick disappeared into the study, closing the door for several minutes before he reemerged.

"I telephoned and added Sunday night to our reservations. With the girls staying with Lucy until Monday evening, there's no reason to rush back. We'll take the Monday morning ferry, and I'll only miss an hour or two of work. I've already spoken to the office and Sharon."

Melissa stood. "I'll need more clothing."

"Oh no, you don't." He caught her waist and swung her around. "I know you always pack an extra set. And if you are worried about becoming threadbare, we can save our clothing by staying in bed when you're not on assignment."

"Then I'll need another nightgown."

Freddy kissed her hard and swayed with her. "I want you as you were this afternoon. Just you and me, no fabric to get in the way."

They kissed until the clock struck three and then brought their luggage to the porch. Alex still wasn't there at five after. Freddy rang the law office ten minutes later and stomped out the door.

"To the automobile." He lifted their cases, leaving Melissa her handbag and basket.

"What's wrong? Where's Alex?"

"Apparently, he's been at the jail with a client since noon. Must be about that big case Lucy says he started this week. He probably forgot us. I don't want to risk switching streetcars to get there when we're short on time. We'll just have to leave the automobile at the dock."

When they drove past Alex's house on Government Street, Freddy shook his head. "At least Lucy has her head on straight these days. God keep our girls safe this weekend."

***

Ecor Rouge loomed to the left, a haunting sight in the setting sun. After steaming south from the Montrose pier, Melissa pointed to the remnants of a dock at the base of the red cliff.

"You think that's it, Alex's property?" she asked.

Freddy glanced at it and nodded, fists tight. Taking his hands, she kissed his taunt knuckles until he relaxed.

"I wasn't there, but I remember that day." The sadness in his eyes was acute.

"The fire?" Melissa whispered.

"No." He sat rigid for half a minute. "The day he brought Lucy there and took her innocence."

He stalked to the railing at the back of the ferry, gazing at the sheer wall of red earth blazing in the reflection of the lowering sun. After a minute, Melissa linked their hands and leaned against him.

"Would you like to talk about it?"

"There isn't much to say. I knew what had happened as soon as I saw her, but Eddie was blinded by Eliza at their side. He didn't see the glow of womanhood Lucy exuded, the weight of guilt in her eyes, or the way she hung pathetically closer to Alex. I wanted to rip his head off, but because Lucy already told me she'd offered herself to him at a different time, I knew he wasn't solely to blame."

"Your love for her was admirable."

"Like a fool, I allowed her to drag me along."

"Like a devoted friend and later husband, you walked beside her, often carrying her when she was too weak. Your willingness to serve her isn't pitiable. It's a testament of your nobleness."

Freddy took Melissa's face in his hands and kissed her like he hadn't done in public since their time in the hallway after the boxing tournament when they'd infuriated Judith Smith.

"You're my sun, Melissa." His voice was breathy and hot in her ear. "My girls made the passage worth it, but you … you illuminate each day as a magical journey. It's a blessing to love you, for you to love me in return."

"I feel the same, Freddy." She hugged him. "I never knew love could feel this good."

"This kind of love is everything." He led her to a bench, and they nestled together.

As the ferry approached the Point Clear Hotel, Melissa went to the railing to snap a photograph of the shimmering lights reflecting off the bay. They saw their luggage on the transportation but opted to walk the manicured path to the hotel to stretch their legs and enjoy the mild evening.

"Welcome, Mr. and Mrs. Davenport," the concierge greeted them. "We are honored to host you."

Their luggage was already in the second-floor suite when they were shown in. As soon as they were alone, Melissa turned to Freddy. "I don't like it when hotels upgrade my accommodations to try to impress the travel writer. I feel guilty to experience more than the average vacationer."

Freddy hung his jacket on the coat rack by the door. "I upgraded to a suite when I called to extend our reservation. Are you impressed now?"

With a smile, her hands trailed his broad chest. "Knowing it was your planning, I'll be able to enjoy every bit of luxury this weekend affords."

"Two nights of supper in the dining hall, and then room service in the privacy of this lovely space our final night." Freddy kissed her with a tenderness she didn't expect after his fervor that afternoon.

"I didn't think I could enjoy my assignments more until I married you. Now I can't imagine visiting a new location without you by my side. You're the perfect assistant."

He brought his cheek to hers as he held her closer. "And what can your assistant help you with now?"

Melissa shifted against Freddy as she stared into his brown eyes. "I need to change for our supper reservation. You may assist in disrobing me."

She savored his gentle touch while he unbuttoned her dress. Then she artfully removed his shirt and tie. Playing back and forth with controlled passion until nothing was between them, they surged together.

Afterward, when they were dressing for their formal supper, Freddy wrapped his arms about her silk underdress. He caught her eye in the dressing mirror she stood before and gave her a wistful smile.

"You know what I enjoy most about you?"

She shook her head, afraid her voice would break the mood.

"The way you look at me when we make love." He kissed her neck as he gently turned her toward him. "To see your excitement, yearnings, and release shining in your eyes is tantalizing, but your mutual love and attention for me are provocative to no end. I'll never tire of sharing moments like this with you. Beyond caring for my family, your devotion is all I need in this life."

From his remarks on the ferry, Melissa knew his thoughts were on Lucy. She could imagine that Lucy—pining after her lost love—would have been a detached wife and lover to true-hearted Freddy. *Did the woman not know what she was missing by spurning him?*

"I love you with all my soul, Freddy."

He held her against his broad chest. "I know, and it means the world to me."

 Eight

When Alexander unlocked the backdoor
Friday night, the dining room was lifeless. The house quiet. After
dropping his things in the den, he grabbed a handful of mints from
the bowl and strolled the back hall to the morning room.

Dark and empty.

He took the stairs two at a time, anxious over Lucy failing to
greet him. Just as he paused in their unoccupied room, the door
behind him opened. Lucy quietly shut the girls' bedroom, the white
of the door a stunning backdrop to her colorful kimono.

"Lucy, my queen, I'd forgotten the girls were here for the
weekend." She felt stiff as he kissed her. "Allow me to tell them
goodnight."

"No." She blocked the entry but kept her head down.
"They're already settled, and if Phoebe sees you, she'll be riled up in
no time."

"Then may I see you to our room, or would you like to sit
with me downstairs?" He offered his arm.

"No, thank you." She brushed past him, pausing inside the bedroom. "I suppose Freddy and Melissa got to the ferry all right. Taking the time to bring them must have put you behind schedule the rest of the afternoon."

The smile slid off Alexander's face, settling in a pit in the middle of his gut. "Oh, sh—"

"How could you?" Lucy met his gaze—every bit as venomous as the photograph of Opal.

He ran a hand through his hair, remembering he was in the jailhouse with Hazel at three, awaiting her shower time. "I completely forgot."

"Freddy never asks for favors, and this *one* time—"

"I'm sorry, Lucy. This case has me busier than anything, but they must have made the ferry, or we would have heard something by now. I'll telephone the hotel to be sure they checked in."

She slipped off her robe, revealing a red gown as silky as the covering. "No, go eat. Your supper is in the icebox."

"I'm not hungry." He fingered the tip of a tendril of hair that curled halfway down her back.

She turned to him in a flash. "Is that because you've partaken elsewhere?"

The meaning of her words was evident in her pain-filled eyes.

"Lucy, I—"

"Before you say *anything*, you might want to read the note on your pillow. It arrived for me this afternoon by courier. Imagine how I felt reading it while your child moved within me. If there's any truth to it—" Her words broke with a sob.

Alexander snatched the envelope from the bed, remembering the one she handed him in March telling of her attempted affair with Frederick.

Mrs. Alexander Melling,

I thought you should know that your husband is consorting with fallen women he had shared experiences with several years ago. Though the guise of legal advice might be sound, it does not bode well—especially when the women appear all too pleased when they leave meetings with him. (And he's looking a mite pleased with himself these days if you haven't noticed.) Gossip will begin as the details of the trial emerge. I found it my duty to warn you first so it does not come as a shock to you for the first time while in public.

Sincerely,

A concerned friend

He dropped the paper as though burned. *"Always a Dardenne brother," my ass!*

Alexander exhaled and paused before meeting his wife's teary gaze. "It's not like what it says, Lucy." *But it is, in a way.*

"Is this about your new case?"

He nodded, not trusting his voice as he felt himself splintering from the pain on her countenance.

"Is your client a whore?"

He nodded again.

"Don't tell me it's that woman who murdered the banker last week."

Alexander's eyebrows pulled together, and he pursed his lips as he nodded.

"Why haven't you told me? It's been on the front page of the newspaper every day!" As she stared at him, understanding washed her face with the clarity of grief. "You laid with her back then!"

"No!" He clung to her arms, happy he could refute one of the vile thoughts she had. "She knew my father and hated me because of him when I first showed up at the jail, but I didn't know her."

Lucy sneered at the mention of his father but didn't brush him off. Alexander took the moment to pull her into a hug.

"Then why did you go to her, and why do you stay?"

He kissed her soft hair above her ear, inhaling her calming lavender scent. "It's complicated."

"I'm not a fool, Alexander Randolph Melling! I went through this with the attentions of Mrs. Smith on Freddy, and that tore me apart. I know you've changed, but I also know you've been under stress. Imperfections are magnified when life is less than ideal. There's too much you've hidden from me lately, and you're taking private talks with Claudio. I'll not stand by while you're playing hero to a prostitute while I'm neglected at home, wondering when you'll return because you haven't telephoned to say you are running late or where you are or who you're with!"

He felt her tears dripping onto his shoulder and hugged her tighter. "I'm sorry, my queen. I do the best I can, but I often fall short. It's your love that pulls me through."

"But why did you go to her?"

"Someone came to me and asked. I would never have thought to go. I've never worked a murder case before."

"Who came to you? The longer you wait to speak the words, the more I'm left to think the worst."

He didn't know if he could say it after believing he'd atoned for the sins associated with Prudie, which made him wonder if he had truly repented. Acknowledging all he'd indulged in during the past three days since seeing Claudio made him wince.

"A nun came to me last Friday, asking me to see to Ms. Kline's legal needs. She believed Ms. Kline acted in self-defense, and after speaking with the accused and seeing the evidence, I believe it as well."

Lucy pulled away to look at him, the way she studied him communicating she was searching for the whole truth. "A nun? Someone Claudio knows? But how did she know the prostitute?"

"No, not Claudio. She knew Ms. Kline because she used to work with her. She came because she trusted me." He felt his cheeks burn with shame. "She was Consuela's stand-in when she was indisposed."

Lucy paled.

"You know how I was back then!"

"No." Her voice was a whispered stab. "You're not telling me everything."

Alexander clung to her, nudging her back until she was against their bed. He lowered her as fear rose in her eyes. "I've confessed already. The sin is forgiven. But I need you now, Lucy. Always and forever."

"You took her when she came to you? A nun!" She looked at him the same way she did the night of The Battle House fire.

"I'm not that wretched. I'm not!" He knelt on the bed beside her, a finger effacing the remnants of her tears. "Don't think that of me. I'm stronger!"

Her pain shifted to anger. "What did you do?"

"She was scared for her friend and found comfort in remembering our moments together. She clung to me and kissed me. In an attempt to soothe her, I returned the attentions. But when I felt her rosary beads, I sent her away."

Below him, Lucy trembled with silent tears.

"It was a shock to see Prudie there, and it brought my old life back to me. I was out of my mind but a moment. When I confessed to Claudio, he set things for my communication with her to be done through him so we'll never need to meet. I won't see her again, Lucy."

Grasping for something to say to help her understand, he grabbed at what first came to mind. "I didn't do half of what you and Freddy did together this spring, yet I forgave you."

"I was possessed! Oppressed by a devil from my sin with you! Do you claim the nun was affected as well from your shared sins?"

He reacted to her fire with a fuel of his own. "The only taint I left with Prudie was by being too good. She was never able to find another lover that lived up to my expertise. She left her profession when I supposedly died because the hope for me ever coming back was gone."

Hysterical sobs consumed her, but Alexander felt no pity over her double standards Frederick always spoke of. A moment later, Alexander knew nothing but fear as Lucy clutched her round belly.

He smoothed a hand across her silk-clad middle. "I'm sorry, my queen. Should I call Darla?"

She shook her head and caught her breath. "She's in Chatom with Henry."

"Dammit, Melissa and Freddy are gone, too. Should I call Naomi or your mother?"

"No. Leave me." She rolled to her side, facing away from him.

He came around and tucked a pillow between her knees, handing her his old handkerchief that was underneath. "I'll never leave you. I'm sorry for my anger and imperfections, but some credit is due. Prudie was willing to lie with me, but I didn't allow it. This body is only for pleasuring you, Lucy."

"I didn't mean to doubt you."

"You have every right to. I'm no saint, but I'm the best man I can be when with you."

His lips played against her salty cheek until she turned to him. Her kiss—like her will—was malleable as long as he kept her the focus of his everything. And she was, more than he wanted to admit because he was on the verge of losing her by his actions that week. He probed deeper, and his caresses inched her nightgown up her legs. Grasping a hip, her moan of pleasure was music to his ragged soul.

"Let's heal each other's hurts." Her hands worked down his buttons.

Alexander's went to the swell of flesh under her gown. "But the baby."

"He didn't like me being upset, but we're fine now."

"I'm happy to hold you tonight if you're—"

"You need me, Alex. I know you do. And I'm more than willing to indulge."

***

Alexander woke at midnight, hungry and craving a glass of brandy. Remembering he hadn't eaten supper, he eased out of bed, making sure the blanket was snug around Lucy's slumbering form. He pulled on his pajama pants, stepped into his slippers tucked under the foot of the bed, and made his way down the hall. At the top of the stairs, he heard a door behind him.

"I'm just getting something to eat, Lucy," he called back. "Do you need anything?"

Through the carpeted darkness, Phoebe emerged into the light of the stairwell like a phantom in her pale nightgown. "Mr. Alex, how come you didn't come home? I missed you."

Alexander sat on the top step and opened his arms to his stepdaughter. She settled on his knee. "I'm Sorry, Knight Phoebe. I worked too much this week, but you know what that means?"

She shook her blonde head.

"It means I get to play extra tomorrow. How about we stop somewhere fun after the riding club? Maybe find a special treat to bring home to Momma."

"Yes, please, Mr. Alex." She laid her head against his bare chest and hugged him. "Mr. Alex?"

He smiled at the way she tugged his heartstrings. "Yes, Knight Phoebe."

"I don't want to call you 'Mr. Alex' anymore. Beth and I call Miss Melissa 'Sissa', why can't I call you something nicer too? Kade calls his daddy Papa like I call Momma's daddy, but you aren't as old as a Papa."

He laughed. "Douglas only has a couple of years on me, Phoebe, but you pick a name you like, and I'll love it as I love you."

"Poppy!" She brightened like the noon sun but then grabbed his frowning face. "You said you'd love it!"

He laughed, and Phoebe jabbed her fingers into his dimples. "It might take some getting used to."

"I'm hungry, Poppy. May I go with you?"

"Of course, but we have to be quiet." They descended the stairs hand-in-hand, but the quietness melted away as soon as they were in the bright kitchen.

"Cookies, please!" Phoebe bounced around the tiles.

Alexander pulled out his supper plate. Still craving a hard drink, he spied a bottle of Naomi's cola she kept in the back of the ice box and took it for something out of his ordinary.

"We'll have to buy Miss Naomi a new one tomorrow. Would you like some?"

"Yes, Poppy!"

"Get two glasses." He transferred his food to a skillet to warm on the stove while splitting the fizzing cola between the glasses.

Once they were both at the corner table, he led them in prayer. Phoebe dunked a cookie into the drink and happily munched the soggy treat. After she took a gulp of the cola, she let out a small burp.

"You can do better than that. A knight needs to belch! Here, watch this." Alexander took a mouthful and swished it around before making a show of swallowing quickly. A moment later, he cupped his hands around his mouth to amplify what surfaced.

Phoebe giggled and tried the same. Laughing over her efforts that seemed to echo in the cavernous kitchen, she repeated the trick. "Thank you for teaching me, Poppy."

He belched in reply.

Lucy walked in as Phoebe ripped another and then laughed at her mother's startled face.

"What's going on here?" Lucy's hand went to her curvaceous hip draped in her red nightgown.

"Poppy taught me how to belch like a knight!"

"Poppy?" Lucy asked.

Phoebe smacked a kiss on Alexander's cheek. "My new name for my special daddy!"

A lump of tears threatened to rise in his throat as Lucy's pretty face broke into a divine grin. He took a bite of green beans to help swallow his emotions.

"We're all lucky to have him in our lives. Now finish up and clear your dishes."

Lucy stood behind Alexander, hands massaging his shoulders. "Do you want tea or anything?"

"No, thank you. We took Naomi's cola, but I'll bring a replacement home with me tomorrow."

She ruffled through his hair before taking the seat across from him.

Phoebe pushed her plate with one shortbread cookie left to Lucy. "I'm full. Goodnight, Momma. Thank you, Poppy." She left him with a hug and a kiss.

"Make sure you brush your teeth," Lucy called as Phoebe skipped out of the room. Her eyes settled on Alexander, dropping from his face to his scarred chest and arms as he finished his meal. "I'm glad you had company for your midnight supper."

"But *Poppy*?" He laughed.

Lucy's bare toes found his legs under the table and trailed them until he trapped her foot between his knees.

"You know you love it." She took a bite of Phoebe's leftover cookie.

"I love your girls. I'll answer to anything they call me because I've probably been called something worse." He rubbed her foot a moment before releasing his catch. "But my favorite names by far are the ones that come from your lips."

A smile lit her eyes, a vision of sensuality with tousled hair. "Alex?"

He nodded.

"Alexander." It rolled from her tongue like a thousand caresses.

Standing, he rounded the table and kissed her collar bone.

"Alexander Randolph Melling!" Her tone of mock outrage made him laugh.

He pulled her to her feet and snuggled against her.

"Husband. Lover. Soul mate." Lucy kissed him after each pronouncement, and then she brought his hand to her round middle. "Father."

Eyes closed, he spread both hands across her belly, feeling the wonder of life. Fear of becoming a father like his own kept him from growing too excited for the approaching day, but sensing his child safe within Lucy allowed him the assurance that he couldn't yet do wrong to the baby.

"I love you, Alex." Her breath tickled across his face. "I know you'll be the best you can possibly be, for all of us. And it will be enough."

Nine

After a busy Saturday around Fairhope and Zundel's Wharf, Melissa and Freddy dressed for their eight o'clock supper reservations. Melissa watched him adjust his white bowtie, and then he stood back as she pulled on her gown. She'd never worn it in front of Freddy—an over-the-top tea gown she preferred to use in the evenings. It was the dress she carried with her on her cross-Atlantic travels and often wore when invited to the captain's table during voyages. It had caught the attention of several fleeting men, but nothing prepared her for her husband's admiration.

Freddy's gaze turned from pleased to sultry as he came at her, mouth on her neck and lowering with each kiss until he was at the décolletage of the deep U-cut of the emerald gown. Touching the embroidered peacock details on the trim, he straightened.

"Perfection, Beloved. May I help with the fasteners?"

"Only if you promise to help me with them later as well."

"I'm at your service." He kissed her lips, leaning in a second time for a longer one. "Tell me again what's left on the day's itinerary. Once it's completed, I'll bring you back here."

"Dancing after supper so I may report on the hall and musicians," she said as he closed the back of her gown. "Maybe a moonlit stroll on the Bayfront."

"We did that yesterday."

"And it was lovely. I wouldn't mind another walk tonight." Feeling the last clasp closed, she turned to him. "Thank you."

Freddy's smile was teasing. "Just don't be upset if I Turkey Trot you out of the ballroom and straight to bed."

"You want to get me banned from a hotel for the first time in my career?"

"Didn't I tell you I'd show you many new adventures?" he countered.

She laughed. "I'll be ready as soon as I set my hair."

Hair twisted into a soft bun and tuxedo tails donned, they strolled respectfully to the dining room on the main floor. Freddy's requested table in a corner wasn't an option that night. They were brought to a table on the main aisle to the kitchen. The additional noise and traffic kept their conversation sparse while she jotted thoughts in the little notebook she'd stashed in her beaded reticule.

She allowed Freddy to order for them as she had chosen their food the previous night. When he requested an entire bottle of wine rather than two glasses, she raised an eyebrow at him.

"Are you trying to get me drunk?"

"Just loose enough to Turkey Trot in the grand ballroom."

Her laughter turned several heads, including the group arriving at the table across from them.

"Fancy running into familiar faces in the off-season," Rupert Lyons said as he approached their table. "How are the Davenports today?"

"Just fine. Thank you for enquiring, Mr. Lyons," Melissa said.

He nodded to her notebook and motioned to Freddy. "Mixing business with pleasure, Mrs. Davenport?"

"Whenever I possibly can, Mr. Lyons. I'm blessed to have a job I enjoy and the flexibility to incorporate my family with my research." She inclined her head toward his table where his wife, Judith Smith, and an unknown man sat. "I believe your group is waiting for you."

He turned to Freddy. "You might want to look at the newspaper today, even if you're on vacation. You should know your ex-wife's husband is representing the prostitute Hazel Kline for her murder trial. Dear Lucy might need a strong shoulder to cry on if the company Alex is keeping turns him to old indulgences."

Rupert smirked his way across the aisle.

Melissa held her tongue but looked sideways at her husband.

He sighed. "That explains why Alex forgot us yesterday."

When the bottle of wine arrived, Freddy insisted on handling it rather than the waiter. Once the glasses were poured, he smiled at Melissa. "To another great article."

"Thank you, Handsome." She squeezed his knee under the table.

When their supper came, Freddy kept his eyes on their food or Melissa, but her gaze continued to wander the room. She often caught Judith and Kate studying Freddy.

"It makes no sense," Freddy muttered in exasperation after he'd finished his stuffed crab.

"What's that?"

"Alex playing criminal defense, and for the likes of her no less." He wiped his mouth with the white linen napkin and dropped it beside his plate. "Unless he knew her from—but no. Even he wouldn't put himself in that situation."

"At least he sent the telegram to say he was sorry for forgetting us. He went out of his way to do that."

Freddy's fists tightened. "Lucy probably made him."

"But he did it, and that shows he felt sorry enough to show his concern." Melissa's hand went to his biceps, giving his hard arm a squeeze. "I know what you need."

He looked at her with annoyed amusement.

"You need a few dances with your wife to help clear your mind."

Freddy kissed her. "Sounds perfect."

The dining room manager stopped by as Melissa finished her food.

"Was everything to your satisfaction, sir?" he asked Freddy.

"No, not everything. I requested a corner table when I booked our reservation last month. As you can see, we were placed on your main thoroughfare, even when I reminded the staff when we arrived."

"My apologies, Mister …"

"Davenport."

The manager's eyes widened, and he looked to Melissa. "A thousand apologies, Mr. Davenport. I hope this mistake does not shadow your article, Mrs. Davenport. What can I do to make this up to you both?"

"Crepes with fresh fruit and cream plus champagne sent to our room at nine in the morning would give us something to look forward to."

"Of course, Mr. Davenport. May I offer you both a sampling of our fine desserts?"

Melissa shook her head, allowing Freddy to finish with the manager.

"I've promised to take my wife dancing, but thank you."

When they stood to leave, Judith Smith and the man from the other table came over.

"Mr. and Mrs. Davenport, it's good to see you. As you probably heard, I was married in July and now reside in Atlanta with my husband, Andrew Larrabee. We're here for the weekend on our way to New Orleans. Andrew, this is Frederick and Melissa Davenport."

Freddy was good enough to smile and shake hands, as well as offer his congratulations before they entered the ballroom.

"She shaved a few years off from her previous husband, but that one's still got at least a decade on her. Better him with her on his arm than me." He gave a faux shiver.

Melissa laughed and hugged him. "She appears happy—even though she kept looking at you while we ate. Not that I blame her. The only thing you wear better than a tuxedo is a pair of boxing shorts."

"You naughty woman."

"Does that mean you won't grant me a private audience in your shorts this tournament?"

"Before or after?" he asked as he led her onto the floor.

Melissa held his gaze as she took his hand and placed her other on his firm shoulder. "Both."

"I believe that may be arranged." Freddy pulled her against him for a kiss before guiding them in the Viennese waltz.

They danced for half an hour. When the music offered no variations, they decided to call it a night.

"You know," Freddy said, "I'd happily walk the grounds with you."

"I think you had the better idea of quick-stepping back to our room."

When they reached the second-floor hall, Melissa and Freddy Turkey Trotted to their suite.

***

After a romantic Sunday that started and ended with meals and recreation in bed, Melissa and Freddy were up before dawn Monday to catch the morning ferry across Mobile Bay. The automobile was just how they left it, and they stopped at the grocers to buy a few essentials before continuing home. Feeling renewed—like only a stay at a fine hotel could accomplish—Melissa went to her typewriter when they returned. Freddy saw to Doff and then readied for a late start to his work day.

The doorbell rang.

Melissa reached the front door first. "Alex, what a surprise."

He stood on the porch, hat in hand and blue eyes doing their best to look sorrowful as his lips curled into a half-smile at Melissa. "Do you forgive me?"

"Of course. Come in if you have time."

They were in the foyer when Freddy hurried down the stairs, pulling on his suit jacket. "And the errant man arrives two and a half days late."

"Forgive me, Freddy. I was at the jail and didn't arrive home until after eight. Phoebe was quite put out by me not coming home until after she was in bed, and I was sick when Lucy asked if you'd reached the ferry on time."

Freddy frowned. "And what of your wife? What does Lucy think of you spending your hours counseling a prostitute while you neglect your family?"

Alex ran his gloved hand through his dark-blond hair. "We had a bit of a misunderstanding when I got home Friday. Someone had inferred my client was a woman I was familiar with and told Lucy as much—which is false, mind you. Ms. Kline knew my father, not me. She was too old to merit my attentions when I was in that neighborhood."

Freddy crossed his massive arms. "It's good to know you have some limits, though I don't think Melissa needs to hear of your adventures in The Tenderloin."

"Melissa's seen a lot in her travels. She might find my stories fascinating." He ducked by reflex, though Freddy didn't bother to throw a punch. "I'm glad you knew I was teasing, but it was you who brought it up. Lucy knows my past, my scarred body, and my stained soul. We straightened things out that night, so don't worry about your Goosy."

Melissa smiled at the complete Alex-ness of his information. "If you start gyrating your hips, I'll have to ask you to leave."

Freddy turned to Melissa with a straight face, but Alex doubled over with laughter.

"What?" She turned to her husband. "I've seen him do it before, as if we need the visual with all the things we're subjected to in our time with the Mellings."

Freddy cracked a smile but pointed to the door. "Go, Alex. And don't wiggle your hips or anything else on the way out. I'll see you when I pick up the girls after the gym."

Once they were alone, Freddy took Melissa into his arms, pressing their bodies together. "This weekend was great, especially yesterday."

"Why, Mr. Davenport, are you wiggling your hips against me?"

He caught her smile with a kiss. "If I wasn't already late for work …"

They tasted of each other as they teased with their hands. Gazing at him, she smiled once more. "We might have indulged too much yesterday, but we'll survive until tonight."

"You underestimate the power you have over me, Beloved. And now that I think of it, the staff is already expecting me late."

He scooped her into his arms and carried her to their bed. His attentions were precise, his motions thorough.

Over too soon for her liking, Melissa clung to him in her breathless state. "And now I don't want you to leave."

He traced her lips with a fingertip, trailing the path down to her torso. His smile stirred her heart to soaring as he brought her hand to his chest. "I keep you in here everywhere I go."

Once they were redressed, Freddy saw her to the study, where she typed with Doff sleeping on the corner of her desk until Sharon arrived at noon. Melissa took a cup of coffee and a sandwich with her before returning to work.

While she was in the middle of typing about the elegance of the dining room at the hotel, the telephone rang. "Davenports'."

"Melissa," Lucy said with her breathy voice. "I hope Alex made amends for his neglect."

"Yes, he stopped in this morning after we arrived home, but it was unnecessary after his telegram Saturday."

"He sent a telegram? He must have seen to it while out with Phoebe. He does care for you both and was upset about forgetting. Do you have a moment to talk?"

"Of course, Lucy. Is everything all right?"

"I'm not sure, but I need your help. When you come for supper Friday, could you talk to Claudio for me?"

Assuming it would be something about Alex and his case, her surprise was evident in her voice. "Claudio?"

"I'm worried Alex is speaking with him about matters he should address with our priest, but Claudio is treating him as a friend. I don't think Alex is receiving the necessary spiritual care. Yes, he needs a friend, but I think Claudio is unintentionally leading him astray by being too soft with him. I fear it will do him harm in the long run."

Shocked, Melissa stayed silent as she thought back on Alex and Claudio's hijinks in the short time she'd known them—mostly involving the Mellings' supper parties, including flamboyant dancing and miniature opera scenes with Alex playing the part of the love-stuck female while Claudio's rich voice belted out Italian lines. It made sense Lucy might be worried over the casual ways of the priest, but not knowing what pain caused her to come to that conclusion made Melissa's stomach churn.

"Could you help me, Melissa? I thought it might be better coming from a woman than Frederick. You don't have to accuse Claudio of mishandling things. You can say a wife needs her husband to discuss his concerns to help them stay connected during stressful times. That you're worried Alex speaks of everything to him and leaves nothing for me. You may say I look shut-out, and you know how much it helps you and Freddy when he talks to you about his day in the evenings."

"Of course, Lucy. I'll speak with Claudio, but I'm not comfortable mentioning confessions. That's not my place to advise someone else on their religion."

"Thank you, Melissa. I knew you'd help, and you get along well with Claudio."

"How were the girls this weekend?"

"Fine as anything once Phoebe got over Alex coming home late. And Henry and Darla are supposed to stop in this afternoon with news of the horse."

"I hope everything goes well for the birthday surprise."

Her tinkling laughter brightened the mood. "As do I. How was the hotel? Did you see everything you needed to?"

"Yes, it's a lovely location. The only unpleasantness was Saturday's supper when the Lyons and Judith and her new husband sat across from us."

"How is her husband?"

"Mr. Larrabee seemed nice. Average looks, close to forty in age. Freddy's glad to be rid of her attentions."

"I'm sure you give him everything he needs."

Melissa felt her cheeks heat—glad the conversation was over the phone. "Lots of romance this weekend, but that's all I'll say."

Lucy giggled. "Freddy always valued his privacy. I'm happy for you both, and the girls will be overjoyed to see him this evening. Stop in one day this week if you want. Naomi always has cake or cookies at the ready."

"Thank you, Lucy. I'll talk to you soon."

Ten

Alexander paced his office at two o'clock, hoping the telephone call from Claudio would come before he had to leave for the jail at the bottom of the hour. Lying in bed with Lucy after their passion Friday night, he knew he had to stop being the one to guard Hazel while she showered. She might be safe, but continuing to look upon her—even when he tried not to—wore him thin, especially when her body language welcomed more. The thought of having nuns attend her came to Alexander during Mass the day before, and Claudio was supposed to speak with the bishop and find out if it could be arranged.

Twenty-four hours later, still silence.

Must I sacrifice my peace for the safety of another yet again?

But he knew he would because no one deserved the treatment Hazel would get without protection. Alexander lit another cigarette and stared out the window overlooking the alley. The thought of his old office brought his mind to Rupert. Anger over him sending the note to Lucy pulsed through his tight limbs. Rupert hadn't outgrown his Dardenne ways and needed to be stopped before his list of misdeeds grew longer.

A knock at his door had him rush to it.

"Telephone call, Mr. Melling," Ms. Trigg said.

"Put it through."

He picked up the receiver on his desk with the first ring. "Alexander Melling."

"Alex," Lucy's soft voice filled his ear, calming him for an instant until he feared trouble because she didn't make telephone calls lightly.

"My queen, is something wrong?"

"I have a craving I hope you could help me with."

"I'd be happy to after the girls are picked up." He was sure she could hear the smile in his voice.

She laughed—the silvery sound that haunted him during their years apart. "That would be lovely as well, but the baby wants chocolate pecan fudge. I was hoping you could buy some for us on your way home."

"Anything for my baby and queen. If I can't make it to the candy shop before closing, I'll pick it up first thing in the morning and bring it back to you before going to work." He puffed out a smoke ring.

"Thank you, Alex. I'm sorry to be a bother."

"You, Lucille Amelia Melling, are never a bother. You've brightened my afternoon considerably."

"Thank you for telling me."

The pure joy in her voice made him feel wretched. *Have I been so neglectful of her she doubts her importance to me?*

"Would you like to go out to supper tomorrow night, my queen?"

She hesitated, but that was her way of not wishing to be gawked over. "Could you request a corner table?"

"If that's what you'd like, that's what it shall be. Did the girls nap?"

"Phoebe is up, but Bethany is still sleeping."

"Tell her I'll try to be home before six so I can see them before Freddy comes."

"I will, Alex. I love you."

"And I love you, more than you'll ever know, Lucy."

Smoking the remainder of his cigarette, Alexander jotted down RESERVATION and FUDGE on the notepad on his desk. If he had a personal secretary like Ms. Renna back in his days at Melling and Associates, she could see to both things so he would be sure not to disappoint Lucy. He glanced at the clock and decided he had time to call for supper plans.

"Battle House Trellis Room, please," he said when the operator picked up.

Reservation secured for seven the following day, he rushed to his automobile.

At the jail, he waited in the worn conference room for Hazel. She came in wearing a black dress with her head high and a sly smile on her lined face, radiating confidence. *She knows that I'll do all in my power for her, that my capable hands will protect her.* Alexander's posture squared, and he blew smoke toward the nearest guard.

"Leave us until her shower is ready."

"You're supposed to save the cigarette until afterward," one said, and the other guard chuckled as they left while Alexander lit one for Hazel.

"Did you have a pleasant weekend?" Alexander asked once she was seated.

"Prudie came to visit Saturday. Brought me this dress and a bar of rose soap, which I look forward to using." She balanced the cigarette between her lips as she pulled the soap from her pocket. "Would you help me lather, Mr. Melling?"

"You know I'd never touch you with the guards looking on, Hazel."

"Then now?" Her hand went to the button at her throat.

"I'll not do that which I seek to protect you from while you're within these walls."

Hazel eyed him from head to toe as he stood opposite her, a wicked smile on her face as her hands lingered at her chest. "So much restraint. Either that or I've lost my appeal."

Alexander's lips curled around his cigarette. "You're pretty, Hazel, and it's good to see your confidence, but I'm a professional."

"As am I." She winked. "I could take care of you in a minute without removing a stitch of clothing or make it last as long as you want. You're my legal savior, Mr. Melling. It's the least I could do."

The primitive man within heaved with the thought of release. His languid gaze returned her proposition with an appreciative grin before he returned to pacing. "Your pretrial is set for Wednesday morning. A judge will hear the basic evidence, take our complaints of you being mistreated upon arrest, and decide if bail will be set or you will remain in jail until the trial takes place."

"Could the charges be dismissed?"

"Don't get your hopes up for that."

"Thank you for being honest with me, Mr. Melling. When Prudie was here, I spoke with her about securing my money. She's supposed to bring your payment to the office this week. I figured one hundred dollars would be a good starting point, as we've yet to discuss fees."

"That will be enough for now. I'll be sure to send you weekly expense reports so you can keep track of my fees."

"Good. I want to know that every hour you're spending with me is compensated. You appear to enjoy yourself, but I can't be sure without proper contact." She shifted in the chair so her legs straddled it beneath her skirt.

The door opened, and a guard called, "Show time!"

Alexander walked with the others though isolated in his despair. He took a rigid stance facing the open shower area with a cigarette in hand. The guards needed to see him as the ultimate in power, not shying away from the woman's figure, but without ogling her either. Hazel needed to be seen as someone beneath his appeal, though he couldn't appear repulsed by her. As the man in control, he would look on her all he wanted but strike down anyone who attempted to molest her.

Halfway through Hazel's shower ritual, the sheriff walked in. "Everyone out except Ms. Kline."

Alexander waited for the guards to leave, then paused near the door. He stared at the sheriff, who stepped to the side and motioned someone in the hall to enter. Prudie and another nun joined them. Her eyes went from Hazel to Alexander and back as her cheeks colored.

"Sisters from the convent will arrive between two and three in the afternoon to attend Ms. Kline as she showers. Their escort and guards will remain in the hallway until they emerge within fifteen minutes." The sheriff stared at Alexander. "Does that meet your satisfaction while Ms. Kline is within these walls, Mr. Melling?"

Alexander took his briefcase from where he left it by the door. "That will be sufficient."

Wanting nothing more than to crumple into a chair, Alexander kept his shoulders back and chin high as he stepped into the hall. Hoping to see Claudio, Alexander was met with the placid face of a priest who worked with the convent. He managed a curt nod, then paced the hall until his cigarette was spent.

When the women emerged from the shower room, Alexander approached Hazel. "I'll arrive tomorrow afternoon to go over what I prepared for the pretrial. You may make a list of everything you believe should be mentioned, and we'll compare."

"Thank you, Mr. Melling."

In his office, he spent an hour compiling his notes before packing everything into his briefcase to bring home.

"Don't forget your mail, Mr. Melling," Ms. Trigg said on his way out.

"Thank you." He paused to collect it from his basket behind her desk.

A hand-delivered envelope and a mailed one from Opal. He tucked the envelopes into the breast pocket of his jacket and headed for the candy shop.

***

"Poppy's home!" Phoebe squealed as soon as Alexander was in the door.

He had to balance four gift boxes as he set down his briefcase while his stepdaughter bounced around him.

"Presents for us, Poppy?"

"Yes, Knight Phoebe, if you were a good helper today."

"I helped fix dinner and set the supper table for you and Momma!"

"Excellent. Would you hold the boxes while I remove my jacket? You'll have to stand still."

"Yes, Poppy." She held out her arms with complete concentration.

He removed his suit jacket and tie, hanging them on the coat racket—something too functional for his parents ever to display as they had a servant waiting to take away their outerwear. His gloves and shoes were off before he took the boxes from Phoebe.

"Where are my beautiful queen and Knight Bethany?"

"In the morning room." She lifted a finger to her lips. "Momma's been writing."

"Then that proves you've both been wonderful helpers." He offered a hand to Phoebe, and she squeezed it as she smiled up at him, blue-green eyes shining.

"Your daddy's going to have trouble in another ten years," he muttered.

"Why Poppy?"

"Never you mind."

Alexander twirled Phoebe with his free arm as soon as they were in the morning room. "Good evening, ladies. I come bearing gifts for my lovely queen and her cherished daughters."

He dropped to a knee and offered one of the small boxes to Phoebe. Bethany raced over on her pudgy legs and received one of her own along with a kiss. "Now, my knights, you may go to the kitchen table to open and enjoy them."

"Chocolate!" Phoebe grabbed her sister's hand, and they hurried out of the room.

Laughing, Alexander sauntered to the sofa with several flamboyant moves that brought a curving smile of appreciation to Lucy's radiant face. He set the remaining two boxes on the coffee table and knelt beside her on the sofa.

"Still have a craving, my queen?" He left a lingering kiss on her lips.

"I'm always hungry for you, Alexander Melling."

The next kiss was deeper, and he let his defenses down as her hand teased under his shirt. He was upon her—though gently in her state—and tugged the red skirt of her gown upwards.

"Alex, the girls." But she played with his buckle.

"I need you, Lucy, like never before." He didn't care that he sounded desperate. "I'll keep it quick."

He brought her to the blue chaise in his den because it was the only downstairs room with a lock. Alexander shed his clothes but kept Lucy in her silky tea dress because he loved the texture and color beneath him. Doing what he needed for release kept him from seeing to her needs, but he planned to make it up to her that night.

As he rested beside her a moment to catch his breath, she kissed his forehead. "I'm glad you're home. Don't ever shy away from me, Alex. I need you, and I need you to need me in return. You know you can tell me anything, don't you?"

He curled against her, burying his head in the lavender scent of her hair. "Yes, my queen. We'll talk over supper."

Kissing her neck, he savored the moment as long as he dared before helping her stand. Alexander pulled on his pants and reached for his shirt, but Lucy stood upon it.

"Leave it off. It will help you remember what we shared and what I expect after the girls are gone."

"Are we returning to a love affair?" Alexander's grin caused her to blush. "Naughty Lucille, what shall I do with you first?"

"Give me fudge and bring me to bed."

"Gladly." He escorted her to the morning room, set the large sampler box on her lap, and then saw to the girls with the final package in hand.

Phoebe and Bethany were up to their pert little noses in milk chocolate.

"Get a wet cloth for those faces before Mr. Frederick sees you've spoiled their supper." After stirring the contents of a pot, Naomi turned to him. Her good eye briefly widened, but she shrugged. "I see how it is. Occupy the sugars with chocolate so you two …. Mr. Frederick won't like that one bit. I'm not sure I do either."

"You're a good sport, Naomi. So good you get tomorrow evening off because I'm taking Lucy out." He set the chocolate box on the counter and kissed her cheek. "And I didn't forget you."

"You're the best type of rascal, Mr. Alex."

After washing the girls' faces, Alexander danced them down the hall to Lucy. Bethany curled in her mother's lap, gently patting her round belly while Phoebe kept hold of Alexander's hand and led him to the loveseat in the corner.

"Miss Darla and Mr. Henry stopped by today," she whispered.

"They did?"

"Miss Darla played with us in the yard while Momma talked with Mr. Henry. Darla told me they rode horses all weekend, and she'd like to take me to the farm sometime if Daddy and Momma would let me go."

"I'd like to see it myself. Be sure to ask if I'm invited next time you see her."

"I will, Poppy. You love horses as much as me!"

When the doorbell echoed through the house, Phoebe ran for the foyer. "Daddy!"

Alexander reached the front hall after Phoebe already hung upside down from Frederick's massive arms.

"Look at me, Poppy!"

"Poppy?" Frederick set Phoebe on the marble floor.

"My special name for Mr. Alex, like Sissa has one."

"Well, how about that?" He smoothed over his immaculate beard before slapping Alexander on his bare back. "It's like you're a real member of the family now."

"Can I see your photographs from the trip tonight?" Phoebe asked as she led her father down the hall.

"I dropped them off for developing this afternoon, so it will be a few days. We can tell you all about it over supper, though."

Seeing Lucy's eyes brighten as much as Bethany's when Frederick walked into the room reminded Alexander how blessed he was that Lucy chose him despite his many weaknesses when she'd had a man like Frederick Davenport.

He hugged Bethany and lifted her onto his back before kissing Lucy's cheek. "You look content, Goosy."

"We enjoyed our weekend with the girls."

"You rest tomorrow, and I'll see you Wednesday morning."

Alexander saw the Davenports out the front. Returning for Lucy, he found her at her desk in the corner.

"I thought it was play time." He kissed her earlobe. "But if you're working on a poem for me, go right ahead and finish."

"This one will take time, not like how you can make quick work of things."

"Is that a challenge, my queen?"

"Write a poem for me," she countered. "See if you're a poet on the run like you are a lover. Some sort of modern highwayman, perhaps."

"Challenge accepted." He held out a hand, and Lucy placed a pad of paper and pen in it. Alexander fell back on the sofa and mulled over a few ideas. Settling on one, he jotted down the following and handed it to his wife.

There once was a woman named Lucy

Whose ex-husband called her Goosy

But she was all mine

And much too fine

For a name as silly as Goosy.

Her eyes sparkled as she looked to him. "Nice for a first attempt, but try not to reuse the same word. That's too Edward Lear."

She handed back the paper. Alexander felt her eyes on him as he wrote. Minutes later, he passed it back to her with his second and third attempts.

There once was a lover named Alex

Who lived in a great marble palace

He took on a blonde

Of whom he was fond

Though it brought on her ex's malice

There once was a sexy mother

Who I came to claim as a lover

She runs hot all night

Never dulls my light

Even when wrapped in the covers.

Lucy laughed as Alexander pulled her to her feet, swaying with her. "Did I do well, my queen?"

"You write the best limericks out of anyone I know, Alex of the Marble Palace." Her hands roamed his back as she kissed his scarred chest. "I'm adding them to our poetry book."

He narrowed his eyes. "You wouldn't."

"My first love's first poetry for me, I have to. But I think I need a few more to round out the collection. May I inspire you tonight?"

"Always, my queen."

Naomi found them in each other's arms. "Supper's ready, but I'll hold the dessert."

Eleven

After supper, Alexander brought Lucy back into his den. He opened the windows to the cool night air, the curtains billowing behind him as he sat shirtless at his desk. Copying the talking points of Hazel's defense onto a fresh legal pad, he crinkled the edges of each page so it would be easy to turn the pages with his gloves on. Lucy worked on the chaise, happily recording his ridiculous limericks into their book of poems she kept tucked in a hidden drawer in the base of the lounge chair.

"It's nice having you in here with me."

Eyes widening with intrigue, Lucy's smile beckoned him to the island of blue within the dark space. "I love being with you, Alex. I know you're stretched thin with this case, but I'm here for you."

He turned off the overhead lights, leaving only his desk lamp on. Curling beside her, he gazed into her green eyes.

"Jot this one down." He cleared his throat. "A novelist named Olive Kent/whose heart I kicked until dent—"

"Really, Alex!"

"Write it down, my queen. You'll like the way it ends." He smiled mischievously to spur her on and then waited until she had the first two lines written before continuing. "Took another chance/when I asked her to dance/now I mount her like a good gent."

Lucy giggled and straightened. "I should spank you for that."

"Just write it down." Watching her handwriting roll across the page and the smile light her face, he craved those hands and lips upon himself.

Catching his gaze when she finished writing, Lucy eyed him with interest. "I suppose now you want to mount me 'like a good gent.'"

"Not yet. First, I need the book." He caressed her from shoulder to hand when he took the leather journal from her. After kissing her with a seductive air, he backed toward his desk with a smile. "Do you trust me, Lucy?"

"With all my heart."

Alexander settled at his desk, book before him. He lit a cigarette—the first one he'd smoked in front of Lucy in he didn't know how long—and took a drag while he thought of one last rhyme for her. He wanted to reach for a brandy but retrieved a pen instead. Directly into the book, he wrote the following:

My beautiful and loving queen

Moves like in a dream

I take off my gloves

And make lots of love

Until in passion she screams.

The previous few attempts at poetry from this hopeless limerick-maker are for

Lucille Amelia Melling.

He snuffed his cigarette in the full astray and stood. Taking a few mints from the bowl, he smiled playfully at Lucy, who watched his every move as he rolled the candy with his tongue.

He returned to her with the book. "Do you want to hear it from my lips or read it?"

"Both. Indulge me, Alex. I've been good."

"So good and beautiful." He kissed down Lucy's neck as he handed her the open book. Alexander recited the poem as she read, then he was silent while she read his note, studying the way her lips curled into a smile.

"You still know how to romance me, Alexander. And how to make me cry out in passion."

"You're my everything, Lucy. I'm going to pleasure you now and always."

Her hands went to his waistband as his traveled up her legs. Already her breath was near-panting with expectancy, encouraging him along. All clothing removed, Alexander stretched the length of the chaise, enjoying Lucy's rhythm and their complete oneness in his private room. He wanted to close the windows to capture her scent forever within those walls. Once belonging to his vile father, it was now transformed to a place for passion and longing with his wife, and all was right with his world.

***

Wednesday morning dawned cloudy and cruel. Alexander snuggled beside Lucy and clung to the memory of them dancing scandalously after their supper the night before. It was considered disgraceful because women in the family way weren't supposed to dance in public. But he'd caressed Lucy, swayed against her, and even kissed while they waltzed and tangoed, not caring about the whispers that raced around them.

"Lucy, think of me today." He nibbled her ear until she squirmed against him. Then he followed the curve of her hips and trailed his hands over the rise of their growing baby. "I'll be thinking of you and our child, doing my best to be honorable."

"You'll do well, Angel." She kissed him hard and deep as her fingers followed his burn marks down his arms. "If I didn't have the girls today, I'd be there."

"A murder trial is no place for you, my queen." He nestled into her bosom, complacent to stay in her arms all day.

Dressed in a hand-tailored charcoal suit, crisp shirt, and blue silk tie, Alexander hugged Lucy by the backdoor after their quiet breakfast.

"Whatever happens, you'll have my love." Her voice struck his soul.

He kissed her lips and then the swell of her dress. Lucy touched her left breast where he'd created a passion mark over her heart the night before. "I'm blessed to be yours, Alex."

He returned the gesture with a gloved hand over his own heart and hurried to his automobile so he could escape before the girls arrived. He didn't have the focus to give Phoebe and Bethany what they deserved, so he kept away rather than slight them.

At the office early, he settled in for what he hoped was a quiet hour before he had to go to the courthouse. He lit a cigarette and leaned back in his chair, court notes before him.

A knock sounded on his door a few minutes later.

"Come in!"

Ms. Trigg opened the door. "One of your relations is here to see you, a Mrs. Davenport."

"She's not a relation in the traditional sense, but I count her as family nonetheless. Send her in, alone is fine."

Melissa looked savvy in a navy pinstripe suit. In general, he didn't care for the masculine style of day dresses for women in recent years, but Melissa was feminine and professional enough to display the look to its best advantage. Standing, he reached toward the ashtray to put out his smoke.

Melissa stilled him with a graceful hand. "Don't stop on my account, Alex."

"Well then, would you like one?"

"Yes, please." She took the seat across from him and smiled in her broad, easy way, causing Alexander to envy Freddy for having regular access to a mouth like that.

He raised his eyebrows as he went for the case in his pocket. "And what does Frederick think of you indulging?"

"I haven't had one since we've been married." She tucked the cigarette between her lips and leaned forward while he lit it. "I never smoked in my apartment, but I did at the office. Another way to blend in with men in the career world."

Alexander sat back with an amused smile. "Did it work?"

"They often discussed baseball scores, boxing matches, and their previous night's exploits without shame, if that says anything." She exhaled a smoke ring that rivaled one of his own.

He laughed, which did almost as much for him as Lucy's calming touch. "I miss our conversations, Melissa. I had fun when you stayed with us, but why did you never come outside and smoke with me?"

"It seemed like you sought solitude when you were out there. I didn't want to intrude."

"My time to reflect on the day or worry over Lucy, but you would have been welcomed, as you are now. Your presence is great—another adult to converse with, witty exchanges, and a fine figure to gaze upon as well." He watched her take another drag. "Do you have any idea how attractive you are?"

Her laughter gave her even more of a glow. "I didn't come here to talk about my looks, Alex, but thank you for the compliment. I need your advice on something."

It was his turn to smile around his cigarette. "If you're thinking of leaving Frederick, I'll be happy to put you up at our house. I wouldn't ask for much in return." He winked to let her know he was teasing.

"If only it were that simple." Her chest heaved as she sighed.

"You're happy, aren't you? I won't be as dim-witted to ask if he's treating you well as it is Frederick Davenport we're speaking of."

"I couldn't ask for a better husband, but I must apologize for my judgment of you and Lucy when I first came to town. Had I known ..." She looked at him with a slight blush. "Had I known all the wonders of married life, I wouldn't have faulted your exuberance in love-making."

"The lucky bastard! How did a world-traveling career woman that looks like you never take a lover?"

"Such flattery today, Alex. I had admirers and several would-be lovers, but none of them felt right." She balanced her smoke between her lips and fiddled with her giant emerald and diamond ring. "While I experienced much, complete consummation was never part of the relationships."

Alexander shifted in his chair and adjusted himself. "And what would your dashing husband do to me if he knew what we are discussing right now?"

"If you promise not to speak of my smoking, I'll not mention the liberties you're taking in conversation."

"Fair enough." He snuffed out his cigarette and took a fresh one. "Now, what's bothering your intelligent soul today?"

She put her elbows on the desk and drew closer. "How do you do it, Alex? How do you balance your passion for Lucy with Phoebe and Bethany running around? I find myself jealous of Darla and Henry. They only have themselves and their work while I'm doing good to get an hour of private time with Freddy a night, and often I'm too emotionally exhausted to want to do more than lay in his arms."

Alexander chucked her under the chin and gave her a wry smile. "You've got it rougher than I do as the girls are there most nights, and when they're gone during the day, so is Frederick."

"He often comes home for lunch."

"I don't blame him. I do that on Tuesdays when you have the girls." Alexander laughed. "Listen to us comparing schedules! I'd offer to take the girls another night during the week or even on Saturdays as I already get Phoebe those mornings, but I'd have to discuss that with Lucy and then see if Frederick would agree to it. You and I are powerless when it comes to deciding for the girls."

"I know, Alex, but thank you for thinking of ideas. It seems silly to want to work things to satisfy my personal needs, but I'm worried because more changes might be coming."

"Sexual satisfaction means a lot to sensual people like us. You waited thirty years and deserve to enjoy it all." He sucked on his cigarette. "What change are you worried about?"

"I'm nearly two weeks late with … you know."

"And have you spoken to Darla or told Freddy?"

"Not yet. I don't want to get people worked up over something that might not be true." She put out her cigarette and gazed at him with her big, brown eyes. "I'm not even sure how I would feel about it if it is happening. I wanted to go to Antarctica and Australia this winter, though I knew those things might not happen when I married Freddy. But if I am, then those things surely won't happen for years."

He nodded his understanding. "I'll see what I can do for you on my end. But for now, take it whenever and wherever you can get it, Melissa. I'm sure Freddy won't mind, but if he does, you come to see me."

Laughing, she stood. "Thank you, Alex. I feel better just talking about my worries. You're excellent company, but I won't keep you. You have court today, don't you?"

"Yes, I'll be glad when it's over. Criminal cases are new to me, and I'm barely treading water." He came around his desk and hooked his arm through hers to escort her out.

"You'll do great." She kissed his cheek. "I'll see you Friday at supper."

"All right, Melissa. In the meantime, try to wear out your boxing champion before the girls wear you out."

With a lighter mood, Alexander gathered his papers and briefcase. He drove to the courthouse, pleased to use the front entrance rather than slinking through the underbelly of the building like he had to do to see Hazel.

"Melling, hold up a minute."

Alexander bristled under the familiar voice and turned with a deadly stare. "I don't have time, Rupert."

"Sure you do. The pretrial isn't for another half-hour."

Alexander set his briefcase on the floor, lit a cigarette, and leaned against the wall. "What do you want?"

"To wish you luck. I look forward to seeing if you've still got what you once had in court. I have special permission from Judge Troy to sit in as you and I might be partners soon."

"I never agreed to that."

Rupert lit his smoke and smiled. "But your name's on my sign. It's practically a done deal. Everyone thinks so."

"I don't, and I'm the only one who matters."

"You're as full of yourself as your old man. Relax, enjoy the spotlight, especially away from that little wife of yours. This case will set you apart as your own hero."

"Is that why you sent Lucy that note, to try to drive a wedge between us? Would that make more of a headline than the trial: DEFENSE LAWYER SEPARATED FROM WIFE, IS THE WHORE TO BLAME FOR KILLING THEIR LOVE AS WELL AS THE BANKER?"

"That's not half-bad. I bet I could sell that scoop to the paper."

"You make me ill." Alexander shouldered past Rupert and directly into a swarm of reporters.

"Mr. Melling, would you care to give us your thoughts as you head into the pretrial?"

"Is it true Ms. Kline has been abused?"

"How do you feel about going up against Solicitor Herman and his tough track record of getting the death penalty for ninety percent of his cases?"

"Do you have a statement for the Wayne family as you seek to let the killer of their husband and father walk free?"

As other such questions were hurled, Alexander tightened his grip on his briefcase and continued through the crowd. "I will not go on record with anything until after court."

He paced the far hall until it was time to enter the chambers. Solicitor Herman, with decades of experience, was already at his table but offered Alexander a smug smile.

Hazel arrived with her hair solemnly fixed in a tidy bun, black dress buttoned to the neck, and a set face—exactly as he counseled her. Alexander nodded as the guard brought her to the defense table.

The crowd was considerably smaller than he expected, and he noticed a doorman checking a list before allowing people inside. A closed court. He recognized the priest from the convent and knew he was there to find out if Hazel would be moving in with them or not.

His former friend took the seat directly behind Hazel. When Alexander caught his eye, Rupert looked to Hazel's back and leered. Obviously, she was more his style than Prudie, but to see him behave that way in court was despicable.

Once Judge Troy entered, Solicitor Herman wasted no time laying out the evidence of Hazel's deadly force against Mr. Wayne. "She's not safe to let loose on polite society while she awaits trial."

Alexander approached the bench. "I am not here to say what happened to Mr. Wayne was not a crime. I am here to clarify that Ms. Kline reacted in fear for her life. What resulted in deadly injury to Mr. Wayne was a direct result of *his* crimes against the accused. She was beaten and strangled within an inch of her life and fought to survive with the only thing at her disposal—an empty whisky bottle. It was not premeditated nor done in anger. It was self-defense, pure and simple."

Alexander went on to describe Hazel's wounds and her neglect at the hands of the police and sheriff upon arrest and booking. Then he called out the official regulations.

"In this year's August 20, 1912 printing of 'Rules and Regulations for the Government of the Convicts of Alabama,' Rule number thirty-two clearly states 'Male and female convicts shall be kept always in such a manner as shall prevent improper intercourse.' I would like it noted that the rule should also apply to employees and officials as my client has been subjected to vile solicitations, physical molestation, and forced sexual conduct from numerous men on staff within the jailhouse." He paused several seconds and then plunged ahead with his demand. "And because of her mistreatment and harassment, I deem this location an improper fit for any member of the fairer sex. As Ms. Kline is currently the only female prisoner, I ask that she be granted bail and sent to live with the nuns at the convent until the time of her trial. Her safety would be assured, and her welfare cared for so she would not need to rely on unseemly professions to make her way in the world. Thank you for your time, Judge Troy."

Banging the gavel, he cleared his throat before speaking. "Court adjourned until one o'clock."

Alexander rushed out of the building, not stopping until he was on the riverfront. There he paced and smoked for half an hour as his gloved hands trembled, feeling only a drink would calm him. A splash of brandy would be like a comforting kiss from Lucy to his anxious state—warm, wet, and filling—though leaving him craving more. He yearned for the liquid to soothe his nerves.

To relieve what symptoms he could, he walked to the nearest diner and ordered a coffee at the counter.

"Alex, my little brother." A hand went to his shoulder and squeezed. "You're tense. Ah, court day. How'd the pretrial go?"

Maxwell Easton slid onto the stool beside him, looking concerned—and more like his father than ever.

Alexander offered him a cigarette, which he accepted. "We hear the results at one."

"And how's my kid sister? It's no fun when you two skip the monthly family dinner. Does she look ready to burst?"

"We had company from the island the other week, but she's as ravishing as ever."

"I heard how you couldn't keep your hands off her at the Trellis Room last night. A 'shameful display of sexuality with a woman already swollen with child' is how I heard it put."

Alexander laughed, freeing a bit of the weight that held him down.

Maxwell lightly punched his arm. "I thought you'd appreciate that."

"As she's already filled with my child, it shouldn't be a shock that I find my wife appealing." Alexander stirred a splash of cream into his steaming cup. "How are Lottie and the kids?"

"Fine as anything. I'm headed back to the office now, but it was good to see you. Let me know if you ever want to take lunch together. I'm good for it anytime."

"Thanks, Max. I'll see you later."

Navigating a fog, Alexander finished his coffee and struggled back to the courthouse. Rupert was already in the seat behind the defense table with Alexander's current boss, Mr. Connell.

When the judge set things in motion, waves of uncertainty crashed against Alexander. His ears seemed to clog with water. Drowning in confusion, Hazel smiled at him. Mr. Connell and Rupert slapped him on the back.

Solicitor Herman stopped to shake his hand. "I'll see you back here in a few months, Mr. Melling, and I'll be none too kind to your client as I expose her true character."

"How about a cigar, Alexander?" Mr. Connell asked.

"Raincheck, please. I need to go."

Alexander felt someone behind him as he reached the courtroom door. Grasping at the familiar face, he sought to understand. "What happened, Rupert?"

"What, so you can gloat as you hear it again?" Rupert put a hand on his shoulder and pushed into the mass of reporters in the hall. "Mr. Melling has secured bail for his client, Ms. Hazel Kline. She will be tucked away in a convent until the murder trial begins."

Alexander freed himself from Rupert's side and absconded down the front steps of the courthouse—leaving his Dardenne brother to the reporters. He drove to the cathedral and threw himself onto a back pew, praying for the urge to drink to disappear.

Minutes.

Hours.

Still, his tremors continued.

The sun lowered on the horizon when he stumbled onto the portico. Alexander managed to drive to the rectory and collapsed on the front steps until Claudio arrived after dark.

The priest went to his knees beside his friend. "*Amico*, what is it? I heard the good news about Hazel's bail."

Alexander gripped his black cassock and stared through his soul as the world spun around him. "Let me drink, Claudio, but make sure I don't do anything stupid."

Twelve

Melissa clicked off the light in the study at ten-thirty. She'd come down to check her article on the Fairhope area one last time before sealing it and the photographs into an envelope for Mr. Noble. It would be her December feature, the final one for her six-month contract on the "Southern Charm" column for *Noble Travels.*

When she reached the stairs, the telephone rang. Confused at receiving a call so late, Melissa picked it up with a question in her voice. "Davenports?"

"I need Freddy!"

Melissa's heart lurched to her throat. "Lucy, what is it?"

"I need Freddy's help, and you must take the children!"

The line went dead.

"Freddy!" Melissa called as she mounted the stairs in her robe. "Get dressed! Something's wrong with Lucy."

He refused to take the time to change out of his pajamas, racing down to start the automobile while Melissa pulled on a black skirt and buttoned a blouse over her nightgown.

Freddy didn't question anything until he was driving. "What did she say?"

"That she needs you, and I need to take the girls home. She was frantic."

"I never thought it would come to this."

"What?"

"The son of a—" Freddy struck the steering wheel so hard Melissa thought it would fall off. "I told her when they were first engaged that if Alex were drinking, it wouldn't be safe for her. She was to call me no matter the hour, and I would come for her."

"But he doesn't drink. Claudio told me my first day with them that they kept a dry home."

"He's been sober six years, but what else could it be with him acting differently the past few weeks? And the pretrial was today. I wouldn't put it past him."

They came to an abrupt halt in the Mellings' driveway. Freddy raced to the front door and barged in, fists clenched. He held a crying Lucy in his arms at the bottom of the staircase when Melissa entered. Closing the door behind her, she watched as Freddy smoothed Lucy's hair and kissed her forehead.

"I'm here, Goosy. Are the girls safe?"

She nodded and clutched her middle.

"Did you fall?"

She shook her head as the sound of Alexander howling in rage thundered from the back of the house.

"Did he hurt you?"

"No, but I feel like I won't last another minute like this." Lucy's breathy voice caught on itself as she buried her face against Freddy's chest.

"Is he drunk, Goosy?" Lucy nodded, and—still holding her—Freddy turned to Melissa. "Call Darla. See if Henry can take you and the girls home."

Melissa used the kitchen telephone. "I'm sorry to bother you, Henry, but there's an emergency at the Mellings. Freddy and I are here, and we need you and Darla. Can you come as soon as possible?"

"Of course, here's Darla. Let her know what to expect."

"Melissa, what's going on?" the young woman asked.

"We're not quite sure, but Alex is raving drunk, and Lucy's hysterical and holding her stomach."

"God help you. We'll be there soon."

Freddy had moved Lucy to the sofa in the front room, where one faint side table lamp lit the massive space.

"They're coming," Melissa whispered.

Freddy nodded and continued to rock Lucy. Melissa's heart sank seeing him so intimate with his ex-wife.

"I'd blame the new case, but it started before that," she choked out between sobs.

"Did he bring something home with him after work?" Freddy asked.

"He didn't come home at all! Phoebe waited for him in her riding clothes. He's usually here by three on Wednesdays, but when he still wasn't here at five, I had her change back into her dress because it would have been too late to make it to the stables. She cried straight through supper and her bath and cried herself to sleep. Poor Bethany didn't know what to think. After they fell asleep, I waited down here for him. Claudio brought him in after ten."

"Claudio?" Freddy stiffened.

Remembering what Lucy had asked of her regarding the priest, Melissa focused on the conversation rather than the closeness between Freddy and Lucy.

"Alex couldn't walk straight, so Claudio brought him to the den. When I went to him, he started yelling about pain and suffering. He pushed me away, and then Claudio."

Anger clouded Freddy's countenance, and his knuckles tighten though he kept hold of Lucy. A moment later, Darla and Henry arrived in rumpled clothes. Freddy released Lucy and stood.

"Darla, please see to Lucy. Henry, I need you to bring Melissa and my girls home." He marched toward Alex's den.

"I might need you to hold him back," Melissa said to Henry as she rushed to follow.

Henry caught her elbow and walked with her into the paneled room.

"I want to know what happened!" Freddy stood before Claudio, arms crossed.

The priest—blocking Alex on the chaise from the vengeful Freddy—took a step forward. "He was a wreck on my front porch when I arrived. He said he was about to go to a bar but preferred to drink with me so I could be sure he did not do anything he would later regret."

"What do you think is happening right now if not regret?" Freddy yelled. "Why didn't you see to his spiritual needs, remind him of his family, and bring him home?"

"He had already made up his mind to do it. I thought it best to sit with him."

"No man of God would allow someone to self-destruct like this!" Freddy's clean punch struck Claudio in the face, and he went down. Then Freddy moved to strike again, but Henry took him from behind. "Let me go, Adams. He deserves more!"

"Leave it, Davenport." Fear crossed Henry's face because he knew what Freddy was capable of, but his hold didn't slacken. "You need to see to Alex and Lucy."

"This is all on you, Priest, just like when Alex came back, and adultery was in the air! You're not helping but hurting him. Not to mention destroying Lucy!" Seeming to have gotten what he wanted off his chest, Freddy's fists relaxed.

Henry dropped his hold and went to Claudio, offering his handkerchief for his bloodied nose.

Alex heaved upright, pushing off the curved, upholstered footrest of the chaise. "I didn't mean to hurt Lucy, Freddy. I meant to protect her as I've felt myself losing the battle against my demons the past two months. No one but Claudio knows what I've been dealing with. I'm in over my head and needed release."

"There are other ways! Your friends are here to help, but you must open to us. Riding helps you, and it was your day to go to the stables. Not to mention the release and healing you and Lucy claim to have with each other. Did you not dance with her last night, showing the city how much you adore her? And Phoebe cried for hours when you didn't arrive. Lucy had to handle the girls alone while worrying about you, and in her state, that's not a good thing."

Alex swayed. Melissa reached out to catch his arm and helped him to the chaise.

"I don't deserve their love. I'll cause nothing but pain for them. My choices today prove it. I need to cut them all loose, starting with your girls. They don't need me when they have Frederick Lionel Davenport for a father."

"You self-centered bastard!"

Henry rushed to Freddy, but he held his ground. "I'm not low enough to strike when he can't stand on his own."

Claudio ambled forward. "Now is not the best time to discuss—"

"Get out of here, *Father* De Fiore," Freddy commanded. "Get out of this house, and don't return until you're summoned. Go and confess your part in Alex's relapse and pray for him—and yourself!"

Henry escorted Claudio out, and then Freddy's attention was back on Alex. "And you, Alexander Melling, are the lowest of low if you think walking away from my daughters will serve them well. They adore you. You've molded Phoebe into a cowgirl, and I wouldn't know the first thing how to encourage her at the stables. And Beth doesn't know life without you. Who's she to pounce upon in battle if you're no longer here? They have Lucy's heart, and they love and accept you as you are, scars and all."

Melissa didn't realize she was crying until she saw the tears on Alex's face and reflexively wiped her wet cheeks. She sat beside Alex and put a hand on his knee. "We're all here for you. Our lives wouldn't be the same without you, Alex."

The pained look in his blood-shot eyes switched in a blink to a hungry leer. His trembling hand reached for her face. "I know how you feel about me, and I think it's time for me to try out a red—"

Freddy grabbed Alex's collar. "Melissa, please get the girls ready. Coats over their nightgowns should be fine. Tell the girls I love them but need to help here for a while."

Melissa nodded and stepped for the door.

"And Henry, I won't be at work tomorrow. You and Mr. Peabody can take any of my meetings possible. Otherwise have Ms. Neves reschedule them."

"Of course," he replied.

Melissa and Henry went to the front room. Lucy was curled on her side on the sofa, a pillow between her knees and one under her head.

Darla embraced her husband. "It's like it was two years ago when Alex returned. She's all right, but some days I hate him."

Melissa put a hand on her shoulder. "Will you help me bring the girls down?"

Darla nodded, and Melissa linked their arms. When they reached the upper hall, Phoebe stood at the bedroom door with a scared look on her face.

"Where's Momma?"

"She's resting downstairs," Melissa said as she took her hand. "She's not feeling well. Daddy and Momma want me to take you and Beth home so your momma can have quiet time tomorrow."

"How come Poppy never returned?"

"He's here now, Phoebe. He's not feeling good either. Find your shoes and coat."

Darla saw to Bethany, wrapping her in the crib blanket, and carried her downstairs. Melissa, hoping to reassure Phoebe by holding hands, smiled down at her stepdaughter.

"Why didn't Poppy take me to the stables today? He promised."

"He had a very busy day in court, and then he didn't feel strong enough."

Phoebe stopped halfway down the stairs. "Why didn't he come home and go to bed?"

"Everyone is different, especially when they're not feeling good. But we all love you, Phoebe. You'll get to ride the pony another day. You may kiss Momma goodnight. She's in the front room."

Phoebe skipped ahead when they got to the bottom of the stairs. Another one of Alex's anguished cries echoed down the parquet floors. Phoebe turned, eyes wide.

"Poppy!" She dashed for the den quicker than Melissa could reach her.

Thirteen

Alexander was on his knees in the middle of the Oriental rug, discolored hands raking through his hair.

Phoebe bound through his den's door. "What's wrong, Poppy?"

She kissed Alexander's cheeks and hugged him before her father could keep her from the monster.

Alexander swayed slightly on his knees and slowly lowered his hands to his sides. Her little arms were chains, anchoring him to his family.

"You didn't come for me, and you promised!" Her words punctured his heart with each breath. She clung tighter when Frederick tried to pick her up. "No, Daddy. Poppy needs me! Are you sick? Are you sad? I love you, Poppy!"

Her tears mixed with his as her warm cheek pressed against him, but Alexander didn't trust himself to speak.

"Phoebe, you need to go home." Frederick's hands were under her arms, but he didn't yank her away.

"But here's home too, Daddy. My home with Momma and Poppy. We all love each other, Sissa said so. Do you still love me, Poppy, even when you forget your promises?"

Alexander's arms went around Phoebe, and Frederick took a hesitant step back.

"I love you, Phoebe Camellia. More than I ever thought possible. I'm sorry for disappointing you." Grateful for the time to apologize, Alexander seized the tiny spark of relief as Phoebe forgave him. Maybe Lucy would too. "You need to listen to your daddy and get home and back to sleep. Keep Bethany safe, all right?"

"Will I see you soon, Poppy?"

He gave a little smile. "I hope so."

As soon as Melissa whisked Phoebe out of the room, Frederick had him on his feet. "Go wash up, and then we're relocating to the kitchen for food and coffee."

Alexander planned to slip out of the bathroom to find Lucy, but Frederick was waiting for him in the hall and took him by the arm when he emerged.

"I need to see Lucy."

"She saw enough of you when you arrived home stumbling over yourself and pushing people around."

"Lucy! I'm sorry, my queen!" he hollered before Frederick shoved him through the kitchen door. He thought he heard her soft voice in response but couldn't be sure in his dizzy state.

Frederick brought him to the table in the far corner. "Sit and don't move without my permission."

When the room began to spin, Alexander laid his head on the table and closed his eyes. What seemed like a second later, Frederick gave him a powerful nudge. Raising his head, Alexander smacked his mouth open and shut, trying to rid it of the pasty film coating his tongue.

Frederick pointed to the puddle of drool on the table where he'd rested. "Now that's attractive." He tossed a towel at Alexander and brought coffee and a sandwich to the table. "Eat, drink, and will yourself to sobriety."

He ate silently, Frederick watching with arms crossed.

"Thank you for not beating me, Freddy. And this sandwich is the best I've ever had."

"Don't try to soften me."

"I haven't eaten since breakfast. All that alcohol on an empty stomach." Alexander groaned. "But I did drink a cup of coffee on my lunch hour. And cigarettes. I've been carrying two cases with me a day to make sure I don't run out. One gold, one silver. Did you know?"

"No. And I don't care what you do to yourself as long as it's not something that could harm Lucy or our girls. I didn't want you to see them tonight, but Phoebe was too quick when you cried out. Eddie's done great cleaning himself up this summer. Have you seen him recently?"

"It's been over a month, but he looked healthier." Alexander stared at the half-eaten sandwich and grabbed the coffee. "I need a cigarette."

"Not in the kitchen." Frederick leaned forward. "Eddie's close to besting both Henry and me in the ring. He's almost to the level he was at more than a decade ago. You could train with us, Alex."

"Hang out in a gym full of sweaty men? No, thank you."

Frederick laughed. "I don't think they'd let you into a women's gymnasium."

"*That* I could go for." Alexander stood, one hand on the table to steady himself as he fumbled with the buttons on his shirt with the other. "Bring me all the beautiful women, and I'll win them, one by one. Or maybe two by two. My stamina and prowess are legendary. Just two weeks ago, a nun offered herself to me in my office. A nun!

She loves me more than God. Does that make me a deity? A sexual champion, at least. You can hit in the ring all you want. I'll take my strokes in the boudoir."

He pulled his shirt off then felt himself falling, but he never struck the ground. Frederick had him around the waist, holding him upright with one arm.

"Come on, we're walking to the sink. Don't make this any more awkward than it is. And since you removed your shirt, you can't complain that I'm going to get it wet."

"You want me wet, Freddy? What would Lucy say? To hell with it, let's dance. I'll even let you lead because you're such a big, strong man."

Alexander felt up Frederick's biceps, causing him to let go. He landed on a heap on the tile floor, laughing. "Lucy! Help me, Lucy!"

"Leave her out of this."

"But I need her." Alexander rubbed his hands over the scars on his chest and moaned. "I need Lucy. Oh, how I need her cold hands and hot tongue. Lucy, my queen, I need you!"

Frederick yanked Alexander off the ground, shoved his head into the sink, and turned on the faucet as the door opened behind them. Screaming and flailing, Alexander managed to grab Frederick's arm so that he loosened his hold. He took the opportunity to straighten himself but knocked his head against the spout, spraying cold water everywhere. Frederick turned off the faucet and held Alexander's dripping head over the sink.

Henry crossed the room, laughing. "Lucy wanted me to make sure you weren't killing him."

Alexander started tremoring. "Kill me, Freddy! Put me out of my misery. Save Lucy and the girls from my weakness."

Frederick motioned for Henry to throw him a towel from the counter. "That would be too easy, and I prefer a challenge. Tonight's challenge is getting you sober. Do you want more water on your head or coffee?"

"Coffee and a cigarette, please. I promise I'll be good. Bring me to the den or the backyard so I can smoke."

"The fresh air might be good."

Henry walked with them to the den to gather Alexander's smoking supplies and then out the French door onto the patio. Once he was seated and the cigarette lit, Frederick handed Alexander his coffee and turned to Henry.

"Is Lucy stable?"

"Yes, and Melissa sent a fresh change of clothes and shoes for you so you wouldn't have to venture out again in your pajamas. She said to call anytime, and that goes for Darla and me as well."

"Thank you. If you need to get home, I've got things here."

Henry smiled and shook his head. "Darla's not leaving you alone with the Mellings. She'll stay until morning. I'll pick her up around seven so she can ready for her nine o'clock appointment."

"Thanks, Henry."

They clasped hands. The friendship they shared reminded Alexander of himself and Claudio. Frederick claimed Claudio wronged him—wronged Lucy—for doing what he had asked, but in the moment, it seemed like the right thing. The brandy tasted good and soothed his troubles. But now, he felt worse than he did before, coupled with the buzz in his head and giddiness that came and went. He was unstable. Unfit. Unlovable.

Seeking redemption, Alexander said the first good thing about himself he could think of. "I got my client free on bail until her trial. A bit of a victory for my first criminal defense, don't you think?"

"You were always a good lawyer." Frederick leaned back in the wicker rocker. "I heard she's to live in the convent. Is that something to do with the nun you bragged about earlier?"

"I told you about that? No bother, I told Lucy last week. Yes, Sister Prudence, known to me as Prudie during her time in the district. She was friends with Consuela. She came to beg me to accept Hazel's case and begged me to take her as well. She used to fantasize about me. Never could find my equal." Alexander sucked his cigarette and paced, a hand absentmindedly stroking his chest. "After all I've been dealing with, I almost gave in. She was a monthly treasure to me. She was so solid I could do anything with—"

"Details aren't necessary, Alex."

"Claudio lets me tell him everything." He laughed and took another drag. "Maybe it's because he's not getting anything for himself these days. I lived without for over four years, but I could never do that again. Lucy has me spoiled. "

"She's an amazing woman, one that deserves a man who'll cherish her and their vows."

"I do, I do, I do!" Alexander focused on Frederick, eyes burning clear. "Prudie put *her* arms around me. Kissed *me*! I didn't chase her. Yes, I kissed her back and returned her touch—but then ended it and sent her away. Lucy knows and has forgiven me."

Frederick shook his head. "I don't know what to think of either of you. She was fire and ice for me, but maybe she needs that from another."

"She's the only woman who understands me except Magdalene, but she's off-limits." The spark of want caught flame in his core. "Douglas was very dutiful in watching her during their last visit."

"You're shameless."

"What am I supposed to think when I come home to Magdalene with her blouse open in my front room? I watched her nurse Simon as she reassured me I wasn't completely wretched, for that was the day Prudie came to me. I needed Maggie's kind words, and when I curled in her lap, she blessed me with her soft touch as she caressed the scars I created for her." Cigarette dangling from his lips, Alexander swiveled his hips as he rubbed his wounds.

"And here I thought you'd be subdued after the watering down you got," Darla said from the doorway.

"I'm afraid we've yet to see the best show from him tonight," Frederick replied.

Alexander laughed, tossed his cigarette in the ashtray, and went at Darla with his actions. "Come here, you fresh young thing. I'll make a wild woman out of you."

"Touch me and die—whether from my hands or Henry's is yet to be seen."

His laugh was bawdy, his spirit high. "Then bring me to my wife. I don't think I can abstain much longer. There's too much love in this body of mine screaming to get out!"

Darla ignored him. "I'm going to help Lucy upstairs, Frederick."

"Not until I see to her!" Alexander pushed past Darla and dashed through his den, sliding in his socks down the hall to get to the front room. "Lucy! Don't let them keep us from each other!"

On his knees before her, he brought a hand to her cheek. Immediately she leaned into his touch, green eyes softening in the half-darkness.

"Get away from her," Frederick warned as he came at them.

"Freddy, leave him a moment."

Lucy's hands were cooling relief as she trailed down Alexander's torso. Focusing only on him, she kissed so deep he thought she'd choke him with her tongue. His hands went to her hips, and he nudged her to the edge of the seat as he kissed down her neck.

She arched against him. "You still love me, Alex?"

"You know I do, my queen. I weakened, made a mistake, but for you and our child, I'll do better." His hands went to her sides and then surged together at her breasts. Lucy moaned in pleasure, and he felt her all the more through her kimono.

"Time's up, Romeo." Frederick pulled him away.

"Let him stay," Lucy begged. "Or let us go to our bedroom."

"Don't you remember what he did to you after heavy drinking, not once, but twice before?"

"He's different now, and I know my limits." Lucy clung to Alexander's hand.

"He could be just as vile as he was back then. You called me for help, and I'm going to do whatever I can to be sure you don't end up like you did back then—broken and fearful."

Alexander grinned in defiance. "I'll be gentle with her."

"You can't promise that, not in your current state. A minute ago, you were ready to go at it with Darla."

Lucy caught her breath, and Alexander turned back to her. "That's why I ran for you, my queen. When I knew how much I needed release, I came for my soul's true love. Heal me, Lucy."

Her curving smile said it all, and he struggled to free himself from Frederick's grip.

"You can't be trusted!" Frederick shouted. "What would it do to Lucy if you lost control? She's in her final months of pregnancy, Alex. There's too much at stake just so you can gratify your sexual cravings while drunk."

Alexander's smile felt like it would shatter his face—it was that huge. "You can watch to make sure I'm not too rough with her."

"You're disgusting, an absolute disgrace!" His grip tightened.

"Frederick Lionel Davenport, unhand my husband!"

"I'm here because you called me for help."

"Now I'm asking you to step down as my knight." Her eyes blazed with passion as she boldly confronted the one keeping them apart.

"Do you not remember the risk?"

"Alex didn't hurt me half of what I made you believe back then," Lucy said haughtily. "I played up my physical pain to cover my emotional wounds so you wouldn't leave me. I needed you then, Freddy, but right now, I need my husband."

"You're both pathetic and deserve each other!" With a flurry of pain behind his glare, Frederick stalked out of the room, taking Darla's arm on his way.

The fact that there was no door to the parlor gave him pause for half a second. Then Alexander was upon Lucy with dozens of kisses. Gone were any inhibitions and stress. The moment was all he knew—Lucy's cool hands roaming his back and feathering across his ribs. The sensations heightened his already aroused state.

"I should have drunk of your sweet nectar rather than the bottle. Forgive me, my queen."

"Don't stray from me, Alexander Melling. You're all I need in this life."

***

"Alex. Alex, wake up, please!"

He groaned and tried to roll away from the light but found himself on the floor.

"Freddy!" Lucy cried out. "Freddy, if you're still here—"

"Just because I didn't want to watch doesn't mean I abandoned you, Goosy."

"I'm sorry for chasing you away. Alex passed out. When I tried to wake him, he fell off the sofa. Will you help him?"

It felt like he jerked Alexander up, such did his head loll. His pants dropped to his ankles as Frederick maneuvered him to the sofa.

"At least your drawers are up," Frederick said as he stepped back, "but you couldn't button your pants when you were done?"

Lucy blushed. "How did you know we were done?"

Frederick crossed his arms and looked at his ex-wife with an amused expression. "I sat on the stairs in case you should have called in distress, but you were eerily silent."

Alexander laughed until he had to clutch his aching head as Darla walked in. "Her mouth was full," he managed to say.

Lucy smacked his arm with her legendary backhand. "You don't have to tell him anything!"

"He's obviously curious and went to the trouble of listening while you expertly took care of me."

"Lucy!" Darla gasped. "Go wash your mouth with antiseptic or something!"

"Ah, to be at that stage again where things still shock you." Alexander sighed.

"You were never at that age," Frederick countered.

Alexander smirked. "Maybe in grammar school."

Fourteen

Melissa and her stepdaughters were eating breakfast when the telephone rang at eight o'clock. She hurried to the study in case she needed to close the door for privacy.

"Davenports'."

"I wish I was in your arms right now, Beloved." Freddy sounded exhausted.

"I hated to leave you last night."

"You had the most important job of all. I hope the girls were able to get back to sleep."

"Phoebe took some coaxing, but they slept in until seven-thirty to make up the difference. They're eating grits and apple slices right now." She straightened her typewriter on the desk. "How about you? Is everyone still in one piece over there?"

"Yes, and thank you for the forethought of sending my clothes with Henry. I feel half-human now that I'm out of those pajamas. Lord willing there isn't, but if there's another emergency, force me to dress before dashing out like a madman."

Melissa laughed. "I'll try. How's Lucy?"

"Still sleeping. Darla got her to bed after two. She sat with her until seven when Henry picked her up." Freddy sighed in exasperation. "Alex passed out a few times, but he's been snoring in the front room since one, wearing only his underdrawers. I threw a blanket over him, but it's still a bit seedy, especially after his displays last night."

"I can imagine."

"He opened up a bit to me about what's been weighing on him, but I hope to talk with him more today. He needs friends, good people to lean on. Claudio, well, I'm not sure what to think of him right now."

Not wanting to betray a confidence, Melissa nonetheless thought it best to be said while Freddy was on the topic. "Lucy called me about Claudio on Monday."

"What did she say?"

"That she was worried Alex shared too much with him. She was afraid Claudio was acting like a friend when Alex saw him as a priest, so he was giving him worldly support when Alex sought spiritual. Lucy wanted me to talk to Claudio when we're over Friday and ask him to encourage Alex to discuss things with her so she wouldn't be isolated from his worries. That a husband and wife need to lean on each other."

"Sometimes she's so right, while other times she's a goose. Stay level-headed, Melissa. It does me a world of good to experience your love and support. I'll call after they're all up and hopefully decent. If Alex isn't a monster, maybe you and the girls could stop in if you think they'd like to, and you're up for it."

"Of course, whatever is needed. The only thing I have to do today is get to the post office to mail my assignment."

"Have you decided about signing a new contract?"

Melissa closed her eyes. "It might not even be offered. Mr. Noble probably wants to see how my book sales do the first month."

"How many days now?"

She could hear the smile in his voice and loved him all the more for it. "Eight days. My copies should be here tomorrow."

"I look forward to reading and, more especially, to seeing you hold it. All your hard work comes to fruition."

"You're the most supportive man I could ask for. I wish I could hug you right now."

"Hug the girls for me in the meantime. And be thinking about where you want to travel next. Articles or not, I've grown fond of our ramblings together. I'll want to see how Alex does for a few weeks before deciding about leaving the girls with Lucy, so choose a place that would be suitable if the girls are with us. We could go at the end of the month or early November."

"You don't know how much that means to me, Freddy. I'll go over my list and see what sounds right."

"I'll call later."

"Take care, Handsome."

Melissa returned to the kitchen with a smile and hugged Bethany and then Phoebe. "Daddy called. He sends you both hugs."

"Is he coming home soon?"

"Later today. He's still helping at Poppy's house. We need to clean up the breakfast dishes so we can go to the post office."

"Nana and Papa live near the post office! Can we stop and see them?" Phoebe bounced in her seat.

"I think we could try while we're out. Be sure Doff gets his food."

At nine o'clock, the Davenport girls were at the streetcar stop. In her mint green dress, Phoebe sparkled in the warm sun as she held Melissa's envelope and chatted with a neighbor. Bethany clutched Melissa's finger, her other hand wrapped within the hem of her blue dress.

Knowing they didn't get out much with Lucy, Melissa stopped in Bienville Square to allow the girls to feed the squirrels after they mailed the package. Then it was the Eastons' quaint house.

"We can't stay long," Melissa told Mrs. Easton as soon as she opened the door.

"I'll take what I can get, but James is golfing with Maxwell right now. You know you can stop by any time, Melissa. I haven't seen the darlings in weeks because Lucy hasn't made it over lately. But I did hear she and Alex created quite a spectacle on the dance floor the other night."

"Momma and Poppy love to dance!" Phoebe did her best ballerina twirl across the snug parlor.

"Poppy?" Mrs. Easton mouthed to Melissa as she carried Bethany to the settee.

Melissa nodded.

"They've always been a handsome sight. Those first months of courting, they were the golden couple during Carnival season. That dazzling grin of his." Mrs. Easton looked to the ceiling. "I knew he was trouble, but Lucy loved him, and he managed to charm even me. I still can't believe she wore her chosen wedding dress from their broken engagement to his mother's funeral. That girl and her symbolism were nearly the death of me back then. I'm happy she and Alex are doing well this time."

After their grandmother showered the girls with attention and cookies, Melissa gathered them to say goodbye. As they came down the front walk, Maxwell parked at the curb. He lifted his father's golf bag from the back of his automobile and came around with hugs for his nieces and a kiss on the cheek for Melissa.

The girls followed their grandfather into the house for yet another treat.

Melissa smiled at Maxwell. "It was supposed to be a quick stop while we were in town on errands."

"When the kids are with me, I've never been able to escape in less than two hours. How long have you been here?"

She checked her wristwatch. "Fifty minutes."

"Impressive! Give them ten more, and you've still bested my time by half."

Laughing, Melissa went through the door he held open for her. Maxwell put away the golf bag and then kissed his mother, who watched over her husband in his armchair, a granddaughter on each knee.

"Thank you for stopping by, Melissa," Mrs. Easton whispered as she took her hands into hers. "Time is precious, especially when they're young. I'm glad they have you—all three of them. Though I had wished Freddy with Lucy for always, he's never been happier than he is now. Thank you."

Maxwell nodded. "And word from the gym is that he's stronger than ever. Is he participating in the tournament at the end of the month?"

"He plans to."

"I might have to place a bet this time. Not that I'm a gambling man, mind you." He looked to his mother and winked.

"Just don't bet against our Freddy," Mrs. Easton replied.

***

On Friday, Freddy took Phoebe and Bethany to stay the day with Lucy on his way to work. Melissa studied a book on St. Augustine she'd checked out from the library when her delivery arrived at eleven o'clock.

With a huge smile, she signed the invoice and accepted her case of books—*Memoirs from the Globe: Confessions of a Female Traveler* by Melissa Stone Davenport. The sturdy blue covers were embossed with a gold globe on the front, a size slightly smaller than average to make it easier to fit in a purse or travel bag. Melissa picked up a copy, smelt the pages, and hugged it to her chest.

Giddy with excitement, she rushed to the telephone to share her news. After giving the number to the operator, Melissa tapped her fingers as she waited for the call to be answered.

"Davenport Allied Accountants."

"Hello, Ms. Neves. Is Freddy available?"

"His ten-thirty appointment just left, Mrs. Davenport. Let me transfer you."

After a short pause, Freddy came on the line.

"They're here, Freddy! Is it okay if I come and show you, or are you filled with appointments after missing yesterday?"

"I don't have anything until one. Why don't you meet me at the diner for lunch in half an hour?"

"That sounds great."

"And how's the quality?" His voice was teasing.

"As fine as Lucy's last book."

"Top of the line for Mr. Noble's excellent travel writer. I can't wait to see it, Melissa. And you, of course."

Melissa rushed to her dressing table and set her hair into a chignon. She pinned her cameo from Freddy at the throat of her blouse, smiling over the fact that the woman with the globe was more her than ever now that her book had the same icon. After packing two copies of the book into her larger handbag, she hurried to the streetcar for the second day in a row.

Though she was ten minutes early, Freddy already waited outside the diner. His hug was electric, but she cut it short to retrieve his book. She bounced on the soles of her shoes as she watched him admire the spine and cover, his finger carefully touching the scrolling *Davenport*. Realizing she'd given him something Lucy never could—a published book with his name she'd taken at marriage—Melissa smiled all the more.

Freddy took her arm to still her and planted a kiss on her lips. "You're like an over-grown Phoebe springing around with excitement, and for good reason. It's wonderful, Beloved. Is this my copy?"

"Yes." She opened to the signature page.

October 11, 1912

For Freddy,

my favorite travel partner.

Thank you for the unconditional love and support

you've showered me with since the beginning of our relationship.

You mean more to me each day

and I'll forever be awed to share this adventure called life with you.

Love for eternity,

Your beloved Melissa

He gazed at her—eyes dewy with joy—kissed her again, then spun her around as he held her to his firm chest. "Thank you for sharing my life with me."

"Careful there, Mr. Davenport," a man remarked in passing, "or you'll have all the ladies on the block swooning."

With a hearty laugh, he set Melissa on the sidewalk and looked at their audience. "My wife's first book!"

Freddy held it over his head like a trophy, and those around them clapped. After a kiss on her cheek, he led her into the diner, where they received another round of applause from those who'd watched from the windows.

Freddy went for his coffee cup at the end of the meal. "And where are we off to for our next adventure?"

"St. Augustine, Florida. I think it will only be one train transfer in Jacksonville, and the beaches, fort, and all sorts of old buildings to look at should keep everyone occupied. I've heard wonderful things about Hotel Ponce De Leon as well."

"I knew you would find the perfect place. The girls and I have never seen the Atlantic Ocean. So why don't we take them no matter what?"

She forced her voice to sound perky. "They were excellent on the Yellowstone trip. Give me dates to work with, and I'll do more research."

After a few more minutes and a rousing hug and kiss, Freddy left her outside the bookstore before heading back to his office.

"Good afternoon, Mr. Lloyd," Melissa said as she entered the shop.

"Why, Mrs. Davenport, it's good to see you. I ordered two cases of your book for its release. I'm promised they will be here by next Wednesday. Would it be all right if I call you when they arrive so you could sign them at your leisure?"

She couldn't help the silly grin on her face. "I'd be honored, Mr. Lloyd. And I have a treat for you." She pulled the book from her bag. "I thought you'd enjoy an early copy so you can familiarize yourself with it."

"And talk it up for more sales?" he asked as he accepted it.

"That wouldn't hurt either of us, now would it?" she countered.

He laughed. "It's good to have a woman who's forthright with her writing business. Readers will be pleased to see a notable Mobile family name on such a handsome book."

Melissa's face tightened. "Lucy had very good reasons for choosing a pen name when she did, Mr. Lloyd. Now that she and Mr. Melling are together, she's more open about things, but with a solid readership across the country, changing her writing name to Melling at this point would be counterproductive to all parties involved, from publisher to respected bookseller."

"Very true, though I wish she were more willing to reach out to her readers."

"I've seen her sign books when asked, Mr. Lloyd. Have you ever approached her with the offer of signing stock or doing a reading?"

He sighed. "No, I suppose I'm still feeling put out for the times she came in here playing me for a fool, asking after Olive Kent books she couldn't remember the title for."

Knowing how Lucy played the publishing staff in New York, Melissa had to stifle a laugh. "I'm sure it did her a world of good to hear your kind words about her books. She never had the opportunity beyond immediate family tell her directly how much they enjoyed them."

"You're ever so gracious, Mrs. Davenport. Much like your husband. How would you suggest I contact her?"

"By post, most definitely. I bet she would come to you both now and when her new book releases next month."

"Isn't she very much in the family way?" Mr. Lloyd's cheeks reddened.

"Yes, but she's as good as ever. Just be sure she has a comfortable seat, and there shouldn't be an issue."

"Thank you, Mrs. Davenport, for both the book and advice. Now, do you need anything while you're here?"

"Do you have any books on St. Augustine?"

Fifteen

Alexander drove back to his office after taking a quick dinner break at home with Lucy and the girls. He smiled over the memory of his plans nearly eight years ago when they prepared for their vows to go to Lucy at the duplex for his midday break. After being driven by lust most of his life, he was pleased their relationship had proven to hold more than mere physical attraction. Though he would have made love to her if the girls hadn't been there, he received almost as much fulfillment seeing her smile as he did when they expressed their carnal desires.

As he walked into his office, his mood dropped. He patted the envelopes in his pocket—his mail from Monday that he'd left in his other suit jacket. When Naomi gathered the week's laundry, she always left loose items from his clothes in his den. Not wanting Lucy to potentially see the letter postmarked from Opal's mental asylum, he brought it back with him—along with the unmarked mail—to review in the privacy of his office.

He began with the unknown. It proved to be one hundred dollars with a handwritten note.

Alexander the Great,

He frowned and balled the note, tossing it into the trash can. Prudie cautioning of Hazel's possible entanglements if she was out on bail, which she was now, disturbed him. She could have been speaking out of jealousy—for she did allude to their moment in his office, and she didn't like Hazel's body language toward him when she first arrived at the jail for shower time—but it could have been a righteous warning from a saintly nun.

Alexander laughed to himself as he lit a cigarette. *Calling Prudie a saint is like calling myself the Pope.* He reluctantly opened Opal's latest correspondence, afraid of what news might be included.

Your devoted little sister,

Opal Loraine Easton

Mr. and Mrs. Easton went to visit with Opal last weekend. Alexander expected to hear directly from them as Opal was sure to broach the subject with her parents. From her earlier letters, he knew Opal was trying her best, and she sounded sincere on paper about making amends with her family, but he questioned her intent.

At two o'clock, he met with a gentleman experiencing trouble with tenants not paying rent. Then at three, it was an elderly woman seeking to update her will who all but drained his patience with her slowness. He managed to keep a smile on his face the two hours it took to get everything accomplished, and his client rewarded him with a pinched cheek and compliment on his charming ways.

Not until Alexander parked his automobile in the garage and went for the backyard did he remember they were hosting everyone for his birthday eve. Wanting to change into a color more suitable for a supper party than his somber black suit, he didn't care if he scuffed his knees. Crouching, he silently entered the side gate from the driveway and stalked toward Phoebe.

He roared like a lion and grabbed at her sides. She jumped but turned to him with a finger to her lips. "Momma's hiding in the labyrinth. I'm supposed to find her."

"May I go in your stead, Knight Phoebe?" he whispered back.

"Only if you carry her to captivity."

"That's something I haven't attempted while she's growing a baby. I'm not as strong as the king of Davenport."

She crossed her arms and pouted. "The militia is weak."

"Yes, but we are mightier with our cavalry. I shall trample Kingdom Davenport under my horse's hooves tomorrow!"

Her blue-green eyes brightened, and she hugged him. "I'll give you five minutes."

"Challenge accepted." He tucked his gloves into his pockets, removed his jacket, and set it around her shoulders.

Bethany came over from where she'd played with her doll across the lawn. He handed her his watch with Phoebe looking on. "No coming for us until the big hand is on the number four, right there."

Phoebe saluted him, and he dashed into the path between the bushes, oyster shells crunching beneath his feet. He slowed enough to muffle the sound but pressed on until he came to the center. Seeing the empty bench, his playful smile faded.

From behind, soft hands went about his eyes as a kiss landed on his jaw. "Guess who."

His hands caressed the length of her arms as she reached around him. "With graceful limbs, a stimulating kiss, and the fragrance of an early summer morning, it would have to be a spectacular woman. Radiant with love and sex, abounding with wit and intelligence, and seductive enough to seek pleasure in all sorts of ways. My queen, my Lucy, my everything."

Her arms dropped, and he took her into a secure embrace. "We have three minutes before Phoebe chases us out. How shall we spend it?"

She smiled, tongue playing between her teeth for a tantalizing moment. "Kissing, like we did while when we found alone time in our youth."

"Naughty necking, coming up."

Alexander led her to the bench and took a dominant stance, one knee on the seat beside her as he leaned over with an air of conquering. He felt his gaze soften as her smile healed the stress of his day. When their lips met, all his clients were forgotten. Only he and Lucy existed, two impassioned lovers amid the green walls of the camellia bushes. His hands were in her silky hair, around her voluptuous breasts, and finally to her round middle, where they paused to feel the life moving within.

"He's happy you're home." Lucy's breath was heavy in his ear as she teased her lips on his neck.

Alexander pulled her into his lap and nestled into her chest. "I'm scared."

"Whatever for, Alex?" The softness in her voice matched the curves of her body.

"I'm not proper like Freddy. What if I ruin the child with the wrong upbringing? What if I turn into my father?"

"You have too much love for that, Alexander Randolph Melling. Too much love, compassion, and joy in your life for you to turn cold, selfish, and unethical. But remember, your son will be part you, so the potential for spoiling will be ripe."

"How do you know, Lucy?" His hands roamed the swell of her belly. "How do you know the child is a boy?"

"I've known since taking tea with your mother."

Alexander softly kissed her lips. "Melissa never said the Jamaican differentiated the child a boy or girl."

"Maybe it was something the demons whispered to me as I lay overwhelmed."

His fingers trailed her face. "No more demons for you, my queen. You're safe now."

They were locked in another kiss when their time came to an end.

"Ah-ha!" Phoebe jumped into the clearing, sword raised in one hand, Bethany's fist clutched in the other. "The militia didn't follow orders, but he captured the queen!"

"She captured my heart many years ago in this very spot. On a cold winter night, she made me hers forever."

"Kiss her, Poppy! Kiss her once more, and then we need to get ready for your supper party."

"My party?" His mouth opened in surprise.

"For your birthday!"

"Birthday!" Bethany echoed.

"I suppose I better. Knight Phoebe isn't one to be ignored." He kissed Lucy long and deep until he felt her yielding in his arms, craving more. With a wicked smile, he helped her stand. Then Alexander was pressed against her length, nibbling her ear. "Tonight, my queen."

***

After taking a cigarette in his den and changing into a sky blue button-down shirt and navy pants, Alexander joined his family in the front room. The girls wore matching red dresses he'd never seen—all ruffles and satin trim—and Lucy displayed a new scarlet evening gown.

"My ravishing beauties." He smiled over them, kissing Bethany and Phoebe on their foreheads before leaving a lingering one on Lucy's lips. "You three are the best presents, all dolled up in your red ribbons."

"I mail-ordered theirs from a catalog. I'm glad they turned out so fine."

"And yours?" His hand roamed Lucy's gown as he settled beside her.

"Mademoiselle Bisset, of course. She always has things at the ready for me."

"Her favorite customer to dress." In her ear, he added, "And your beautiful clothes make it even more fun for me to undress you."

Bethany climbed onto his lap, quieting any further mischief. When the doorbell rang a minute later, Phoebe rushed to answer it.

"Sissa and Miss Darla! Come in for Poppy's party!"

"Hello, everyone." Melissa crossed the room to where they lounged on the love seat, the electric lights catching on the sheen of her green peacock gown. Leaning over, she kissed Lucy's cheek and then took Alexander's chin in her hand. "You look well and happy today, Alex. Happy early birthday."

"Thank you, Melissa. And thank you for the lovely view." He glanced down at her décolletage and winked.

"I was going to kiss you," she said as she straightened, "but not after that remark."

Bethany reached for her stepmother to lift her, freeing Alexander to give more attention to Lucy, who was ready with a kiss.

"That's all right, Melissa. My Lucy never disappoints."

"I'll say my greetings from here, Alex." Darla took the far armchair, placing one of the decorative pillows against her chest like a shield. "Henry is bringing your present."

"My thanks to you and Henry." He winked at her. "And I'm sure he thinks you're scrumptious in lavender."

She threw the pillow at him. Alexander put up his arms to defend Lucy and caught it while laughing.

"Is it battle time?" Phoebe couldn't hide the excitement in her voice.

"No." Lucy was firm. "No battles tonight, please."

The doorbell rang again. Phoebe went for the foyer. "Uncle Eddie!"

Alexander straightened and looked to Lucy. She smiled. "It's time to further heal old wounds."

Phoebe pulled her uncle into the front room.

Edmund looked about the place and sighed. "I haven't been here since the inaugural Christmas party."

Alexander got to his feet and offered his hand. "You're welcome anytime, Eddie. It's good to see you."

Edmund accepted the handshake and slapped his back with his other. Then refusing to let go, he held his gaze. "You're treating my sister well, aren't you?"

It seemed like everyone in the room held their breath.

"I'm not perfect, but I'm doing my best. Ask her yourself if you'd like."

Lucy's warm smile showed not an ounce of mistrust or shame. "We're good, Edmund, as it appears you are as well."

Edmund ran a hand down his significantly flatter middle. "Freddy and Henry are trying to talk me into signing up for the tournament."

"You should, though I'm sorry to have to miss this one. I don't want to risk the heat and crowds. I wish you all well and would love to host supper afterwards."

Alexander took her hand and moved beside her. "Yes, let's host supper as we did in the spring. Maggie and Douglas are coming that weekend, aren't they?"

"Yes," Darla said. "They're trying to talk the Walkers into coming as well."

Frederick and Henry were soon there, and everyone settled around the large room in the relaxed atmosphere. Henry passed Alexander a box containing a handsome pair of leather riding gloves. Then Frederick sent both Bethany and Phoebe over with boxes.

"For you, Poppy!"

"Thank you, Knight Phoebe." Inside was a necktie of scarlet and blue in a diamond pattern. "This is perfect to match my girls tonight. I think I might have to wear a tie to supper after all."

He buttoned his collar and knotted the silk at his throat.

Lucy ran her fingers over it. "Very handsome."

As Bethany handed Alexander her box, Melissa spoke up. "One is for you, and one is for you and Lucy. I'm sure you'll be able to decide which is which."

Lucy clung to his arm to watch over his shoulder as he removed the lid. She squealed and snatched the top book. "It's gorgeous, Melissa!"

"Don't I get to see it first as it was in my box?" He nipped a kiss at Lucy's cheek as she handed it over. He turned to the inscription and read aloud. "'For Alex'—see my name is first—'and Lucy. Thank you for allowing me into your lives and supporting my travels and work. This book wouldn't be here without Lucy's forethought and kindness. Maybe there will be a big adventure somewhere exciting for the Mellings and Davenports in the future. Love and thanks, Melissa.'"

Alexander helped Lucy stand so she could hug Melissa. Only when she was safely across the room did he uncover the next book from a layer of tissue paper. With a hearty guffaw, he looked to Frederick, who shrugged and pointed to Melissa.

"Ladies and gentlemen, I'm now the proud owner of *The Twentieth-Century Gentlemen's Guide to Manners and Sexuality*."

"Frederick Lionel Davenport!" Lucy put her hands on her hips. "And you let Bethany deliver that!"

"It was Melissa's idea, though I fully agree it's something that might be useful."

"And it was a special order from New York, mind you," Melissa added. "That's not something Mr. Lloyd would ever stock at his bookshop."

Darla was as red as an apple, and Alexander couldn't help himself. "Don't worry, Darla. I'll allow Henry to borrow it. Eddie, are you interested as well? Maybe we should start a gentlemen's book club."

That got the men laughing, though it earned Henry a sharp stare from Darla.

As though forgetting they were missing a member of their party, the group startled when the doorbell rang. Phoebe tore for the front door, and Alexander rose to follow. By the time he was halfway across the room, Phoebe had led Claudio in. His olive countenance was humble, his dark eyes subdued.

"I am not sure if I am still welcome, but I would like to wish my dearest friend a blessed birthday on the morrow, and then I can be on my way."

Alexander offered his hand. "I was the fool. You only did as I asked."

He could feel the stares from the others—especially the anger rolling off Frederick—but Lucy came before Claudio, kissing his cheeks. Seeing the one most wronged by his actions forgive the man who helped him in his sin brought Alexander to the edge of euphoria. Swallowing the lump in his throat, he smiled at the sight of his wife comforting the priest.

"We love you, Claudio, but please remember Alex sometimes needs you as a spiritual leader, not a friend. Don't be afraid to be hard on him—he often needs it."

"I have let down too many people this week. I promise to do better, Lucy. You are most gracious."

"I'm pleased everyone could be here," Alex said as he took Lucy by the hand. "Now, let's gather in the dining room as family and friends."

Sixteen

"I'm proud of you, Freddy." Melissa wrapped her arms about his middle as she gazed up at him after they put the girls to bed. "You held your tongue when you wanted to tell them both off."

"Lucy's a goose to put up with Alex, but Claudio was right in calling out her graciousness. She was lovely, the perfect hostess. I can't stay mad at her even after what they subjected me to the other night."

Melissa smiled. "But you stay mad at Alex."

"What can I say? He's not nearly as pretty." Freddy gave her a teasing smile.

"Oh, but he is," Melissa countered. "His scars give him a rugged edge, but he is attractive."

"And I suppose that manners book will give him even more charm, won't it?"

She laughed. "I hope not, for Lucy's sake. She's powerless before him as it is."

Freddy's hands roamed down Melissa's back as he pressed her against him. "And do I have that effect on you, Beloved?"

"Quite the opposite." Her hands traveled his muscles and contours in return. "You make me feel powerful, as though I could take on anything, including your body's colossal strength."

He lifted her until she was a head above him and kissed her collarbone before lowering his lips to the sweep of her neckline. Freddy's attentions brought her to the edge of ecstasy, but hovering above her were thoughts of her book she'd held that day for the first time and the look of admiration on Freddy's face when he saw her name on the cover.

Then he was unfastening her dress, hands touching the skin of her upper back as the sleeves lowered. His big arms went around her waist, and he kissed her exposed shoulders.

"Melissa, I only got to read the first chapter in your book this afternoon." He moved her hair aside and kissed her shoulder blades. "It was glorious, like a secret window into your wonderful mind allowing me to get to know what makes you the woman you are. Would you mind if I hold you tonight while I read more?"

Her laugh was the truest of her whole life. She turned to him, gaging his attentive expression. "Freddy, nothing could be more romantic, more sensual than you seeking to understand me better."

He cupped her cheeks, his thumbs tucking into her smile lines. "You're glorious, Beloved. Are you sure you're mine—that I'm yours?"

"I've never been more sure of anything in my life, Freddy. Read all you want. I'll not sway you to other matters."

His hands lowered to her hips. "You can be very persuasive when you feel powerful."

"But tonight, my power lies within the pages of my confessional."

"And you'll own me, Beloved."

***

Melissa woke nestled in Freddy's arm. Her book was face down on his stomach, and the bedside lamp still burned though the sun began to peek through the drapes. Beneath her cheek, his breathing was even. She shifted into him, leaning up to kiss his lips amid his beard. Freddy reached for her but struck the hardcover instead. Eyes opening, he smiled at her.

"Morning, Beloved. How did you sleep?"

Her hand went under his shirt, teasing across his abdominal muscles. "Perfectly content in your embrace. Should I be offended you fell asleep reading?"

He lifted the book to check the page number and set it on the side table, clicking off the light. "I read halfway, though. After finishing the Tuscany chapter, I set it down because I wanted to ask you about it, but you were sleeping. I closed my eyes a moment to think, and that's the last I remember."

"And what did you want to know?" She stretched a leg over him. Immediately his hand was running the length of it, nudging her cotton nightgown higher.

"There was an undercurrent of warning, almost like a cautionary tale of what not to do."

"You're a perceptive reader."

He took her by the hips, tugging her atop him. In the dim light of daybreak, his brown eyes were intense. "Who was he?"

Melissa gazed down at Freddy with a faint grin. "Antonio Rossi, the eldest son of the vineyard owner."

"An Italian lover, complete with wine and windswept landscapes. Is that why you're so fond of Claudio?"

"I named Claudio's accent the first night I met him. And yes, his voice and handsome features brought me back to that journey, but I remember why I stopped things when I did with Antonio. I still don't regret anything, either what was done or left undone."

Freddy's hands went under her gown until his warm hands were on the bare skin of her waist—the ultimate sensation of both stimulation and comfort. She caught her breath, and he shifted to let her know he was ready for more.

"I don't want to leave anything undone this morning, Melissa."

"I wouldn't have it any other way." She kissed him deeply as he worked at freeing their clothing.

After an hour of shared passion, the sound of Phoebe making her way to the hall bathroom forced them to meet the day out of bed. Melissa and Freddy exchanged a few more touches as they dressed, taking their time as they helped each other with buttons. Melissa went for the door, but Freddy hugged her once more.

"Falling asleep with your words on my mind and you in my arms was wonderful, but so was waking to your stimulating touch. I love you and what we share, Melissa. Thank you for giving me hope every day."

The warmth in her chest spread south as her desires flared. Between roaming hands and probing kisses, Melissa nudged Freddy toward the bed.

Then the banging on the door started to the rhythm of Phoebe chanting, "We want pancakes! We want pancakes!"

Freddy stroked Melissa a final time. "What I wouldn't give for another hour with you."

"But we want pancakes!" She slapped his firm rear. "We want pancakes!"

"I see how it is. You want me for sex and cooking, but I'll give you what you want, Melissa." He pinned her arms behind her back with one hand and winked before releasing her. "I love it when you blush."

Their Pancake Time was as lively as ever, coupled with more innuendos and flirting than typical between the couple. By the time Alex stepped in the front door, the kitchen was cleaned, and the family ready for their day.

"Happy Birthday, Poppy!" Phoebe jumped into Alex's arms.

Melissa studied their smart riding clothes and the glow they both carried over their shared adventures. Then she realized stalling Alex would give Lucy a jump on reaching the stables before him as Henry and Darla were picking her up as soon as Alex left home.

"May I take your photograph with Phoebe before you leave?" she asked.

"Of course."

"How about by your automobile? Freddy and I are on our way out too. A few errands, but we'll be back before you return with Phoebe."

In the driveway, Alex posed with a boot on the running board, his arm on the ledge of the door, and a thumb looped in the pocket of his riding pants.

"You're a natural, Alex. The camera loves you. And Phoebe as well."

The five-year-old had climbed into the automobile from the opposite side and rested her elbows on the door, propping her chin in her hands. Melissa took two pictures, and then Phoebe called out, "Come see me ride, Daddy and Sissa!"

"We will if we have time. I'll even bring the camera with us." Melissa, closer to them than Freddy, stepped to the automobile and leaned in to kiss her cheek. "Have fun, Phoebe. And you enjoy your birthday, Alex."

Bethany sat happily between Freddy and Melissa on the front seat, watching the trees and houses go by as they drove through Spring Hill. Freddy stayed half a mile behind Alex on the way to the riding club and parked in the back of the clearing after Alex and

Phoebe headed for the office. Placing Bethany on his shoulders, Frederick took Melissa's hand.

A minute later, Phoebe ran out of the office building toward the stables, Alex following with an easy stride as he pulled on his new riding gloves. Phoebe ran back out, waving her arms. She clutched Alex's hand as she bounced.

Henry led a black stallion out of the stable, Lucy riding sidesaddle on its back like the Queen of Hearts in one of her red tea gowns.

Freddy gripped Melissa's hand. "She shouldn't be on there!"

"Look, Darla is on the other side, and Henry has a steady hand. It's just for a moment, Freddy."

Freddy's fists were white while Melissa took a picture of Lucy on the horse as Alex approached her.

"Happy thirtieth Birthday, Alexander Randolph Melling."

Melissa took more pictures as Alex helped Lucy down and embraced her with his typical flourish. Then he was in front of the horse, gloves off as he rubbed its neck.

"Poppy got a horse for Melling Militia!"

Darla took Phoebe's hand and led her away from the horse so her bouncing wouldn't spook it.

"His name's Apollo," Henry told Alex, "the finest in my father's collection. I picked him out for you on Lucy's command."

"He's perfect, and my other horse was Janus, another Roman deity. You did well, Henry. And Lucy," he said as he turned to her again, "I don't deserve such a gift."

He kissed around her jaw before settling on her lips, making Darla turn away and Freddy cross his arms.

"But when you're good, you're *very* good." Lucy smiled as though she was full of all the light in the universe. "I want you to be able to ride at the end of a stressful day, ride to enjoy the seasons, and play polo if you'd like. The fees are paid through the end of the year, as well as Phoebe's rental charges. I'll cover for next year at Christmas. Come as often as you like, Alex. Happy Birthday."

He buried his face in her loose hair, hugging her to him. "I don't deserve you, my queen."

"Don't say that, Alex. Ever. We were created for each other."

"Come on, Birthday Boy." Freddy nudged him. "We came to see your present and watch Phoebe ride. We'll bring her home today so you can spend more time here if you'd like."

"I'll help Phoebe saddle up," Henry offered. "You ride Apollo to the ring, and I'll watch him while you instruct Phoebe."

"Thanks, Henry. Phoebe can do it all herself," Alex said. "She only needs help reaching some of the tack off the wall. Starlight, stall three."

Alex turned to Apollo, stroked the muzzle, and spoke softly in its ear. Then he caressed down its side until he got to the stirrup. With fluid grace, he swung into the saddle.

"Look over here a moment," Melissa called to him. He flashed a smile for the camera and then set off at a gallop. She laughed. "He's as handsome as anything on that horse and knows it."

Lucy sighed. "What I wouldn't give to ride with him like that."

Freddy took Lucy's arm. "A horse is not the place for you in your condition."

"I tried to talk her out of it," Darla said. "She swindled Henry into the plan."

"I figured as much." Freddy shook his head. "Lucy's as heedless to common sense as her husband."

"But you love me." Lucy kissed his cheek and allowed him to lead her toward the practice ring.

In the shade of an oak, Freddy lowered Bethany off his shoulders, holding her a moment so she could kiss her mother. Then he set her beside the fence in a soft bit of grass, a pretty dash of yellow against the green. Melissa squatted beside the brunette and took a picture that captured her profile—chubby cheeks and all.

When she straightened, Freddy caught her eye and smiled. "I look forward to seeing that one, Beloved."

Lucy linked Melissa's arm. "Thank you for coming and taking photographs."

"It's my pleasure, Lucy."

Henry jogged beside the pony as Phoebe rode Starlight into the ring. She paused before the camera and grinned in a way that made her look exactly like her stepfather.

"Watch me, Daddy and Momma!" she called before she set off at a trot once more.

Alex still wasn't back, but Henry stayed in the center of the ring and called instructions. Melissa settled on the grass beside Bethany and Darla. Lucy leaned against the white-washed fence as her eyes followed her daughter's progress. Placing a friendly arm about her, Freddy joined his ex-wife.

"I always wished to learn to ride. Alex was supposed to teach me at Seacliff Cottage, but fate only sent us there once."

"And how is the progress on the new house?" Freddy asked Lucy.

"It all but stopped over the summer with the rain, but it picked back up last month. Alex is supposed to go over one weekend to check, but he doesn't want me traveling that far until after the baby is born."

"It's good to know he's sensible about some things."

"I still haven't been across the bay since that time, Freddy. That terrible, wonderful day."

"Those memories will have no power over you in the new house, Goosy, just as you've found happiness in the mansion. But feel free to spend the day with us when he goes, if you'd like."

"Thank you. Alex was all set to build a cottage—a real one, small and quaint—but I insisted on two master suites. I want it large enough so we can all go. A suite in each wing on the second floor, with four small rooms and two baths snug in the middle for the children or other guests."

"You needn't go to all that expense."

"It's no trouble. I'm paying the difference from my account."

"It's none of my business, Lucy, but how are things working out since you moved? I'm sure the monthly expenses are above Alexander's income at that rag-tag law firm."

"That's been part of his worries of late, I'm sure." Lucy paused to smile and wave at their daughter.

"You're a real cowgirl, Phoebe!" Freddy shouted as she passed.

"He keeps all the books, but I think he's using from his inheritance, which disturbs him because it makes him feel like he's relying on his father. That's why he escaped to Louisiana, to get out from that." Lucy twisted her wedding ring. "That's one of the reasons I wanted to take over the expense of the riding club. He wouldn't have allowed it unless it was a present. The mansion is above his means, but not if he let me help. I want to help him, Freddy."

"A man is brought up to believe that the only way to have true success is if you keep your household running by your own merits. It would be a blow to his esteem to acknowledge he relies on your money to keep things as they need to be, even if you aren't showing off for society like his parents did."

"But it's already cutting at him because he's using his father's money. Isn't my money a better option?" Lucy's green eyes were misty.

"Would you like me to offer my accounting services to him?"

"Would you, Freddy?"

He smiled and handed her a handkerchief. "You know I would, Goosy."

The man himself galloped into view. Alex jumped Apollo over the fence into the ring. Melissa tensed as the stallion barreled toward the pony, but Alex reduced his speed to a trot to match Phoebe's pace.

Henry slapped his hat on his leg and went for Freddy and Lucy. "That was completely reckless! Alex should have dismounted at the gate and walked Apollo in. The pony could have been spooked and Phoebe thrown."

Freddy's knuckles whitened over the railing, but Lucy put a hand on his. "He knows Phoebe's skills and Starlight's temperament. He wouldn't have done it if there was a chance of injury. He wouldn't do anything to hurt Phoebe. They've been out here for months, twice a week. He knows them, and more importantly, he loves her."

Freddy pulled his hand away, fists balled at his sides.

"Look at how well she's doing, Frederick."

Melissa went to Freddy's other side, hands clasping around his fist. She kissed his cheek, making sure her chest brushed against his arm in an attempt to refocus his attention. "All is well, Freddy. Look at her joy and be happy for her. And Alex and Lucy, too."

He turned fully to Melissa and pressed his lips to hers with a force that took several seconds to soften.

"Now who's flaunting their relationship?" Lucy teased. "Darla, do Alex and I look half that fetching?"

"I'd rather not discuss that," the young woman said with a clipped voice.

Freddy smiled and leaned his forehead to Melissa's. In a whisper, he spoke as his hands caressed her back. "Thank you for talking me down from my anger, Beloved."

Melissa grinned. "I believe that was more action than words."

"Whatever it was, it was most successful. Feel free to try it again sometime."

Seventeen

The others were two hours gone by the
time Alexander dismounted at the stables. He saw to Apollo's
grooming himself and gave specific instructions to the stable hands
and office staff for his horse's care. Never had he received such a
perfect gift—not even one of the automobiles from his father. Lucy
was overly generous. His drive to town took forever as all he could
think about was reaching her. He'd been selfish to send her home
when Frederick and Melissa left, but it would have been worse for
her if she was stuck on an uncomfortable bench as he rode the trails
around the club.

He left his gloves, ascot, and hat in the entry hall and
searched for Lucy. He found her sleeping on the chaise in his den,
French doors open to air the room. Her hands, folded on top of the
swell of their baby, rose and fell evenly. Creamy skin, rosy lips, and
golden hair against her colorful kimono and the blue of the chaise
pulled on his carnal desires. He locked the door and studied her,
watching the breeze ruffle her loose hair across the folded velvet
blanket she used as a pillow. Unable to control himself a minute
more, he removed his boots, belt, and vest, unbuttoning his shirt as
he approached Lucy's sleeping form.

"I've returned, my queen."

Her eyes fluttered open, and a curving smile found her lips as she took in the sight of him undressing. "There's never been a more handsome man in all the world. When I saw you mount Apollo, I wanted nothing more than to ride away with you."

"Mount. Ride." He kissed each cheek after the words. "We can share that right now."

Lucy giggled as he straddled her thighs. She wasted no time opening the rest of his buttons and running her hands over his exposed skin. Then she kissed and licked the scars across his chest. He shuddered and caught his breath.

"Happy Birthday, Alex. I'm ready for you—all of you."

"My delightful queen, you spoil me."

Alexander gently rocked his pelvis against her, thinking of their time in bed that morning, how he dominated her in every possible way as she flushed and moaned with pleasure. Lucy brought his hands to the sash about her waist. The sight of his damaged hands upon her unblemished skin always shocked him, but the gasp of delight she rewarded him with each time made it bearable. It was his turn to kiss, lick, and caress.

Looking down at her, his heart swelled with emotion. "I know your body is changing, Lucy. Don't be shy about telling me if something no longer feels good or you need more. I'm here to fulfill your every desire."

"I love you more with each moment we share. Promise me after the baby is born you'll tuck me on Apollo with you and gallop down some pretty trail."

"I'll ride you to a secluded spot in the woods where we'll share passion like never before. You were beautiful riding him." He trailed his fingers through her hair. "If we were alone, I would have taken you in a bed of hay within the stables."

"You have me now."

In her eyes, Alexander saw the power he possessed. The pale green shone pure in her devotion to him, but he knew all too well the pain of letting her down. Of injuring her and breaking her trust. He'd seen the horror on her face before and never wanted her to suffer under his mistakes again.

He kissed her perfect lips. "This year, I'm going to be a superior husband for you, Lucy. I'm going to better provide for us—all of us—even if it means switching law firms. I'll not entertain the people and thoughts that seek to drag me back where I was before. And I'll see you satisfied before satisfying myself."

"Knowing I have the means for your release fulfills me as much as anything."

"Not as much, my queen." He kneaded her hips, delighting in the little sighs and gasps. "I see and hear the difference. You don't enjoy it as much when I don't give you any control. With the baby coming, I want to see that your needs are met, both before and after. You deserve complete release and attention as well."

"But today is your day." She fingered around his waistband.

"And I want to see bliss on my wife's face and hear her cry out in pleasure."

He stood and stripped the remaining clothing from his limbs. Then he helped her stand before spreading the velvet blanket across the chaise and lay down with a welcoming smile.

"Mount me, my queen, and ride away."

***

When Alexander woke alone Sunday morning, he was quick to seek Lucy. Upon entering the kitchen, he kissed her cheek.

"Good morning, my queen. Thank you for giving me the happiest birthday ever. Making love with you throughout the day is all I could have hoped for, but the horse was an added bonus."

"Henry did a fine job choosing Apollo."

"But not as fine as I did choosing you." He fingered her loose hair.

Lucy kissed both of his discolored hands and teased him with a smile. "If you're trying for a repeat of yesterday, I'm sorry to say there isn't another horse."

"I'd take you over a horse any day. You're even more fun to ride."

Their hands and lips were all over each other until the kettle whistled.

"I'm glad what we share isn't a sin, though I'd be willing to be consumed by fire again for you, my queen."

"You're brave and wonderful, and I can't get enough of you."

She brought the coffee to the square table in the corner. The pastries Naomi prepared yesterday afternoon were already there, and they settled together. He took her closest hand into his and eyed the deep V of her kimono pulled open during their frenzied moment.

"I don't know if I'll be able to focus enough to pray."

"But you're not wearing a shirt either."

"If you don't understand the difference between my chest and yours, I'd be happy to teach you with a hands-on lesson."

Lucy laughed but didn't adjust the robe.

Alexander led their breakfast prayer with one eye open.

"Do you feel up to going to Mass today?" he asked after they started eating.

"No, but you go if you'd like. My mother called before you came down, and they'd like to come over this afternoon. I invited them for a simple luncheon, and she accepted."

Dread pooled in Alexander's stomach knowing Opal would have spoken to them. Hoping to prevent an uncomfortable conversation in front of Lucy, he made up his mind. "Then I'll attend the cathedral and be sure they follow me back."

"You drive them here, Alex. Father hasn't been behind the wheel in a month. Mother says he's too weak and fears he'll not be able to handle the automobile. Maxwell and Edmund have been driving them around. I'm sure they'd appreciate the break if you saw them here."

Knowing the previously healthy Mr. Easton was slowing in his old age created a shadow of sadness in Alexander. He was close to seventy but still played golf and toted around his plethora of grandchildren. Lucy's parents were older than his, and he was spared going through the aging process with his parents, though seeing his mother suffering her final weeks was enough of a strain on him.

"Of course, Lucy. I'm behind in the news because we missed the last family dinner. It was the weekend Magdalene was here."

She narrowed her eyes. "And Douglas and the children."

"Yes, of course." He took a bite of his Danish and looked to the ceiling like a little boy caught in a lie.

"Part of me wants to ban Maggie from ever seeing you on Apollo, especially after what she said about your riding clothes." Lucy tried to sound stern, but her smile gave her away. "I don't know how Douglas and I put up with you two."

"You put up with us," he said as he took her hand, "because you love me. Maggie and I may flirt, but you know I'm only for you."

Alexander brought her to her feet and kissed from her succulent lips all the way to the sash belted below her voluptuous chest.

"You'll have to do better than that if you're trying to make me forget your wandering eyes."

"Now who's seeking a repeat of yesterday?" His hands were under her robe, clutching her to him. "Do you need me now, Lucy?"

Her body cues all said she did, and he led them toward one of the sofas in the morning room. Unlike Eliza's tea party all those years ago, this time, there were no witnesses as they convened on the sofa in a tangle of passion. Lucy's pale skin glowed amid the sunlight that flooded the room. Like the sun, he wanted to see her rising above him.

Alexander scrambled off her and took her place on the damask cushions. "Don't think me an old man because I want to take it lying down again, my queen."

"Never, Alex. And I do love this." She situated herself until they fit seamlessly together and brought them both what they sought while Alexander attempted to rid his mind of the approaching conversation with her parents.

***

"I can't believe she got you a horse!" Edmund slapped Alexander's back as they met on the portico before late Mass.

"How did you know?" Alexander adjusted his derby that was knocked crooked from Edmund's exuberance.

He motioned to the doors. "Henry told me. He's already inside with Darla. I can finally look at her without seeing Eliza, so that's something."

"So it is." He shook Edmund's hand and looked about. "Are your parents here yet?"

"Max is driving them today. He already dropped Lottie and their kids first."

"Lucy invited them over for dinner, so I'll bring them home."

"Father will enjoy that. Lucy's always been his favorite. I need to join Mary Margaret before she starts sulking, but it's good to see you, Alex."

"Same here, Eddie."

"There's enough room for you with the family," he called from the cathedral doorway.

Unable to speak, he raised a hand in thanks. An invitation to sit with the Easton clan from the man who professed Alexander would never be part of his family—and wanted to kill him at several points in their lives—was huge. It was almost like he and Edmund were inseparable Mystic of Dardenne brothers once more. And speaking of Dardennes, Sean Spunner climbed the steps onto the portico.

"Alex, it's good to see you." Sean took Alexander's hand in a firm grip showcasing his strength. He had mellowed as he matured, but the pain of losing Eliza still shadowed his gaze after nearly seven years.

"And you, Sean. Are you taking part in the boxing tournament again?"

His chipped-tooth grin flashed in a youthful way. "I'm thinking about it. I don't want to be known forever as the man knocked out by Henry Adams."

"There's no better way to secure a woman's hand than showing off in the ring. Freddy claimed Melissa not long after the spring tournament. You're not too old to do the same, Spunner."

"I'll be hard-pressed to ever find another woman as bold and brilliant as your sister."

Alexander's smile faded—saddened Eliza's passing still stung his old friend. "She was something special."

Sean nodded and clapped him on the back. "See you later, Melling."

Spying Maxwell and the Eastons on the sidewalk, Alexander's heart reflexively sunk further because Lucy wasn't with them. The months of waiting for her on the portico for Mass were ingrained in his fiber—one of the reasons he preferred the cathedral over the other parishes. Seeing that Maxwell had his father's arm urged Alexander to action. He met the others at the bottom of the stairs and kissed his mother-in-law's cheek.

"Good Sabbath morning, Mrs. Easton."

"Alexander, our resident charmer, you look sharp as ever in blue." She looked about as she took his offered arm. "Is Lucy here?"

"She wanted to conserve her energy for playing hostess." His grin had more to do with remembering the energy Lucy expelled after breakfast than the fine company before him. "Good morning, Mr. Easton. Maxwell, I'll see your parents to my house after Mass."

"That's good of you," Maxwell replied.

"There's much to discuss, Alex," Mr. Easton said. "You bring Evelyn in, and we'll be along shortly. Unfortunately, I'm not as quick as I once was on these steps."

Once inside, Mrs. Easton received loving greetings from Edmund and her daughters-in-law and enthusiastic welcomes from her grandchildren. At the same time, Alexander was given curt nods from the women and curious stares from Lucy's nieces and nephews. Seeming to take pity on Alexander, Edmund slapped his oldest boy on the back of the head and nodded to him.

The boy—there were too many Easton nieces and nephews for Alexander to keep them all straight—turned to him and smiled. "Hello, Uncle Alex."

"Hello … young fellow."

Maxwell reached the pew and whispered, "That one's Oscar. You need to spend more time with the family so you can learn all their names."

Throughout Mass, Alexander watched the antics of the youngest Eastons. When their parents weren't looking, there were pulled hairs, spit wads, and every other type of mischief. Would his child be as spirited as these? On his way back from walking with Mrs. Easton to partake of communion, he inclined his head to Claudio in a silent greeting.

After the service, a gathering of sisters moved out from a shadowed corner. Beside Prudie was a black-shrouded Hazel Kline. They paraded by the Eastons' pews, Edmund following their progress with an open mouth. Once they were gone, he turned to Alexander and backhanded his arm.

"That was your client, right?"

Alexander nodded and leaned closer, not counting on Edmund to be discreet. Fortunately, Mary Margaret started their brood up the nave, followed by Lottie and her children.

"Did you see that nun with her? Maybe it's because I had the district on my mind, but she looked like Prudie. That girl wasn't half bad back in the day. I had Hazel last year and wouldn't mind another go with either of them."

Maxwell snatched Edmund by the ear. "You're in the cathedral, for God's sake!"

Edmund jerked out of his brother's pinch-hold. "Being a former Dardenne, I know you're no saint."

Alexander's eyes went wide. Noticing his surprise, Maxwell laughed and put an arm around each of their shoulders. "True, but I never claimed complete innocence, only that I didn't have to go to the district to find trouble."

"Trouble or pleasure?" Edmund looked at his brother with new admiration.

"Both, but that was before Lottie. You need to make sure you don't stray from your vows again, Eddie."

Edmund looked all too pleased with the knowledge of his brother's escapades. A flicker of optimism grew inside Alexander. The fact that Maxwell was now as straight as they came—much like Frederick in many aspects—gave him hope that he could make a full transformation as well.

The cathedral was nearly empty as they approached the doors, Maxwell's arms still around the other men's shoulders. Hazel and Prudie entered—Hazel bold but Prudie a step behind, looking at the marble floor.

"Isn't this a fun reunion," Hazel drawled. "The eldest Easton, who I made a man two decades ago. Little brother, who's looking fine these days compared to the pudgy import salesman that came to me last winter. And my dear lawyer, who's seen all that I have to offer the world most recently."

Maxwell tensed at the final line.

"I've done nothing other than represent you in court. My dealings have been professional," Alexander said through clenched teeth.

"I'm a professional as well, Mr. Melling, or have you forgotten? I'm sure one of the Eastons would be happy to disclose my expertise."

"Go to Hell, Hazel," Maxwell said with a sneer. "I was a drunken eighteen-year-old at my first masquerade. I didn't even pay you."

"No, but your friends did. I bet I helped put a few hairs on your chest." Hazel motioned to Prudie. "Are you all acquainted with Prudie as well?"

"I remember every curve." Edmund winked, and Prudie reddened in shame.

"Ms. Kline, if you wish to keep me as your lawyer, you need to leave my family alone."

"Family? Oh, that's right." Her grin proved she never forgot. "What a perfect family for you to marry into. The Eastons are just as wayward as the Mellings ever were, though your father was the vilest. That's something to be proud of in company like this."

"Sister Prudence!" Claudio's voice echoed through the nave. "The others are waiting for you. Ms. Kline as well."

"Yes, Father De Fiore." Hazel sounded contrite, but her eyes told Alexander she wasn't done with him yet.

As Claudio ushered the women out, Edmund laughed.

Maxwell took Alexander by his lapel. "If you're ever unfaithful to Lucy, I'll kill you."

"I've done nothing with Hazel."

"Then what was that talk about seeing her assets?" Edmund smirked.

"She was being molested in the jail. I had to stand in on a couple of her showers to make sure the guards didn't assault her."

"Well, that's rough for her," Edmund said soberly.

Maxwell knocked both Edmund and Alexander on the back of the heads. "Go home and stay out of trouble, or big brother Max will be after you."

Eighteen

The ride home was silent, which allowed Alexander time to calm after his encounter in the cathedral. Mrs. Easton sat beside her husband in the backseat and held his hand, cementing a vision of what he wished for himself and Lucy in their later years. After parking under the porte-cochere, Alexander helped his father-in-law out of the automobile and across the veranda. Lucy met them at the door.

When he saw his daughter, Mr. Easton straightened. "Lucy, my girl."

"Father!" She hugged him and took his arm from Alexander. "Come sit with me a moment in the front room."

They settled, and Lucy curled against her father much like Phoebe and Bethany did with Frederick. Seeing the love between father and daughter brought a lump to Alexander's throat. *Bless her for loving him, but Lucy will crumble when her father is no longer here.*

"It was lovely having Alex with us, but it would have been even better if you were there too," Mrs. Easton said.

Lucy placed a hand on her protruding belly. "I didn't wish to tire myself."

"Nonsense! I heard about you dancing earlier this week. A trip to Mass isn't as strenuous as tangoing after supper."

"But dancing is more fun." Lucy's cheeks went pink, and she glanced at Alexander.

He winked in return before Mrs. Easton looked at him.

"Tell her, Alex! Tell her how important it is to make church a priority. You've been so dedicated to attending Mass and going to pray after court cases. Yes, I hear everything about the town, even if I don't get out much."

Lucy sat up. "You stop in the cathedral to pray?"

"It's a habit I started when I moved back." He saw the pain in her eyes and looked away.

"Why did you never tell me?"

"I didn't wish to sound self-righteous or pushy."

"A husband should push his wife to church if she's straying," Mrs. Easton huffed.

"Lucy isn't straying. She has her own way of expressing her faith."

"I dare say she hasn't attended Mass at St. Mary's more than twice since Easter. And when was the last time you went to confession, Lucy?"

She shrugged. "I don't remember."

"Did you ever get your membership straightened out after being baptized at Trinity?" she asked pointedly.

"No, Mother."

"So this child you're carrying is going to be raised Episcopalian like Phoebe and Bethany?"

"Don't be ridiculous, dear," Mr. Easton said. "Alex will be sure the baby is baptized and raised in the faith."

"I have no objection to raising our child Roman Catholic. You're making too big of a deal out of this, Mother."

"Too big of a deal when I'm concerned for the state of your soul and that of my grandchildren?"

"Precisely."

"At least I'll have one daughter in town for a while who takes her faith seriously."

Lucy brightened. "When is Susan coming? Or is it one of the twins this time?"

"I speak of Opal, of course. She's been diligent in attending Mass when the hospital allows it. The visiting priest there gave her a glowing report for her transfer file. Coupled with the evaluation she'll receive here in town, thanks to Alexander, she'll find a much better alternative for placement than that horrendous asylum that has almost as many missing patients as they have current ones."

It was back—the look of horror in Lucy's eyes as she gazed upon Alexander. After the exchange with Hazel and the Easton brothers, he'd forgotten his purpose in sparing Lucy the conversation about Opal.

"Lucy—" he began.

"Have you kept it a surprise, Alex?" his mother-in-law asked. "She really is so much better. Go fetch the photographs Opal sent you. She told me about them, but we never got to see them for ourselves. Oh, it will be a blessing for James to see his youngest home for her eighteenth birthday."

Alexander struggled to stand under the weight of Lucy's stare.

He had failed her.

Again.

Mrs. Easton stepped between them. "Come on, Lucy. Let's go to the table for dinner. Alex can meet us there. I don't want to keep your father out too long."

"Yes, Mother. We are dining in the kitchen today, so I don't have to carry everything down the hall."

Mrs. Easton took her husband's arm. "I quite understand. It's a difficult house to manage in your condition. I'm sure Naomi is a great help to you."

Alexander followed them as far as the kitchen and turned to go to his den. Numb with pain, he shuffled through the letters from Opal in his briefcase until he found the envelope with the portraits. Upon joining the others at the small table, he stood behind Lucy, placing a hand on her shoulder—which she stiffened under.

"Here, Mrs. Easton. The top is her file photograph from her seventeenth birthday. The other is from this summer. She said you gave her the dress for Easter."

"So I did. Why she's as lovely as you, Lucy, though her coloring favors Cora and Emma more, don't you think?"

Lucy's hand began to tremble, but she choked out a "Yes."

Alexander kissed the top of her head. "Does anything else need to be brought over?"

"No."

Alexander took his seat and asked his father-in-law to lead the prayer. Then they were passing sandwich fixings and potato salad that Naomi had prepared the day before while Mrs. Easton prattled on about their last visit to Opal and plans for her birthday.

"A week will be plenty of time to see to everything she needs done in town, including her medical appointments. Hopefully, there will be placement somewhere closer. Poor James is no longer up to the half-day train trips."

Alexander noticed Lucy took little food and ate even less from her plate. "May I make you some tea, my queen?"

She shook her head, refusing to make eye contact.

"You do look pale, Lucy," her mother said. "Maybe church this morning would have been too much. Alex can take us home as soon as we are done, so you needn't entertain us."

"It's no trouble, Mother. I'm glad you both came."

"It does me good to see your pretty face," Mr. Easton told his daughter. "Come see us more often. We got to see Melissa and the girls this week."

"Yes, on a Thursday no less," Mrs. Easton said. "I thought they were with you that day, Lucy."

"Alex and I were both feeling under the weather. Melissa was kind enough to keep them for me."

"After all that dancing and then court, it's no wonder. You've both had a busy week, though I'm not fond of my son-in-law defending a known prostitute."

Even one both your living sons have lain with? Alexander wanted to ask. "It's not my ideal situation either, but she had several injustices done to her after being brought into custody. I felt it the gentlemanly thing to do. She is, after all, someone's daughter."

"Very Christian of you, Alexander." Mr. Easton folded his wrinkled hands atop his slight paunch, signaling he was full.

Mrs. Easton took notice and spent more time eating and less talking so she could see to her husband.

Alexander rested a hand on Lucy's knee. "You haven't eaten much. Is there anything you have a craving for I could pick up on my way home?"

"No, thank you."

When everyone was done eating, Alexander and Mrs. Easton insisted on clearing the table. Afterward, Alexander helped Lucy stand.

"Say goodbye to your parents, and then I'd like to see you to bed before I leave."

"Just to the morning room, please." She turned to her mother. "Thank you for coming. I'll try to visit more often. And Father, I hope you get a good nap this afternoon."

"Take care, my girl."

"Yes, do rest, Lucy." Mrs. Easton hugged her. "You're positively pallid."

Alexander took Lucy by the arm and brought her down the back hall. "I know the information has upset you, but we'll talk when I get back. Are you sure there's nothing I can bring you?"

She shook her head, and he kissed her lips, but she did nothing in return.

The agonizing ride to his in-laws' house brought him near frenzied with fear over leaving Lucy alone. On the way back, he lit a cigarette and tried not to be annoyed at the other drivers out for pleasure cruises on the autumn afternoon when he wanted to return to his wife.

"Lucy, I'm home!" Alexander called as soon as he was in the door. He found her where he'd left her—upright on the sofa in the morning room. "Don't you want to lie down? I'd be happy to hold you, my queen."

"No." She crossed her arms and stared at him. "What else have you kept from me?"

Weakened from the pain in her eyes, he fell before her. "I keep nothing from you."

"Then why does a stranger have to write to tell me you are representing a whore? Why does my mother, who you scarcely see once a month, know your attendance records at the cathedral? Why did I not know you are helping get my sister out of the asylum? The sister, I'll remind you, who was sent away because she tried to kill me!"

"I only meant to spare your feelings."

"I can handle damaged feelings." She clutched a tremoring hand over her heart. "It's the pain of deceit that's unbearable. You promised, Alex! You promised never to hurt me!"

He gripped her upper arms and shook. "I'm not! I swear I'm up to no trickery. Everything I do is for you. I'll keep you safe, always! You possess my heart—you have since the day I saw you dancing in the fountain. You're all I have in this life, don't be mad. Please, my Lucy."

Alexander pulled her off the sofa and onto his lap on the floor, doing the thing he knew best. Kissing her so hard his lips ached, he caressed her body and ran his fingers through her blonde locks. After what seemed like hours in his attempt of winning her back, he felt her yield to him as her posture relaxed, her lips no longer as tight at the corners.

He touched a cheek with his hand, his other under her gown massaging her thigh. "All I do is for us. I didn't want you to be uncomfortable knowing I went to the cathedral regularly because it's an unhappy place for you. I know I fall short, but that's why I go so often. I need the extra guidance. I try my best, Lucy. You always told me it was enough. Isn't it still?"

"I won't be lied to or have information withheld."

"A thousand pardons, my queen." He brought his other hand under her dress, kneading her hips like he knew she loved. "I'll show you how much I love and need you right now."

"That won't be necessary."

Her cold tone chilled him. He scooted away, hands trailing down her legs as he distanced himself. He'd hurt her and gone too far in his attempt to repair his wrongs. But then Lucy managed a smile that melted a piece of his heart, spilling over from the corner of his eye.

"Go see Apollo. While you're riding, think of everything that's been weighing on you the last few months and decide which of those things could affect me. And of those items, remember which you have not been open about. When you come home for supper, I'd

like you to share that information with me. I'll do my best to be as
level-headed as you are honest, no matter how much it smarts."

"But what I've kept from you I've done to protect you. I
don't want to burden you with the stress of running the house or my
job or family drama."

"I'm supposed to be your wife, your partner. Do you think
me too dim-witted to be helpful?"

"No, of course not." He reached a hand to her knee.

She pushed it away. "I'll not be ruled over like George
Melling did to Ruth—a pretty society wife with no input without an
argument."

He felt the heat flood his face and towered over her. "I'm not
my father!"

"Then quit acting like a tyrant!" She dropped her face against
the sofa and sobbed.

Alexander's first instinct was to scoop her into his arms and
hold her, followed closely by the thought he should prove his Melling
blood by taking her right there.

*I have, after all, been called out on my disreputable family today. Any
other woman would be happy for me to bed her. Lucy doesn't know how good she
has it with me. A Melling man is to be feared and respected!*

He raked his fingers through his hair and shook his head.

No!

Tentatively, Alexander placed a hand on her back. "I'm sorry,
my queen. I didn't realize how everything looked to you. I saw my
father burn to escape his dominion. I'd never want to do anything
like him, and you know I'd never want to cause you pain. I'll go to
the riding club like you suggested. See, I can take your advice. You're
clever, just as intelligent as you are beautiful, if not more. How else
could you write those wonderful books and amazing poems?"

Her crying slowed. He traced circles on her back with a slow,
looping movement.

"Please allow me to help you onto the sofa before I change, or are you ready for bed?"

Lucy caught a sob in her throat to answer. "Here is fine."

With a gentle touch, Alexander raised her. He left a tender kiss on her cheek as he kept an arm about her shoulders—for he now knew better than to force himself on her lips or nether regions. Then he set water to boil and raced upstairs to change.

When he returned in his riding clothes with tea, he set the cup on the side table and smiled down at her. Cocky from her appreciative gaze, he adjusted his manhood and winked. "I think you wanted to see me in these pants again."

Her gorgeous smile was back, coupled with a momentary shine in her green eyes. "Hurry back to me, Alex."

"Anything for you." He kissed her lips, secure in knowing she couldn't stay mad at him.

Nineteen

Settled at her desk, Melissa poured over the book on St. Augustine she purchased from Mr. Lloyd. Deep in research about the fort, she startled when the telephone rang.

"Davenports'."

"Melissa, I'm scared." Lucy's voice came over the line.

"Is Alex drinking again?"

"No."

Melissa waited for more, but all she heard was Lucy's breathing. "What is it? I can't help unless you tell me what's going on. Do you need Darla? Freddy?"

"I need protection."

"From what, Lucy?"

"Ask Frederick to spare me a minute in the morning. I need to speak with him after Alex goes to work."

"Are you in immediate danger? He'll come to you now if needed."

"No, but please tell him to see me in the morning."

"I will, but call if something changes before then."

"Thank you, Melissa."

She replaced the telephone and went to Freddy in the parlor. He lounged on the sofa reading the newspaper—Sunday shirt untucked and the top button of his pants undone because he'd taken a second helping of roast and potatoes at dinner. His enjoyment of the meal pleased her. She hadn't felt a hundred percent and stayed home from church, focusing on the meal preparation.

"Hello, Handsome."

He lowered the paper and appraised her basic skirt and blouse. "You're beautiful yourself. Who was on the telephone?"

"Lucy. She was upset and told me she needed to speak with you in the morning after Alex leaves for work."

"What?" He swung his legs and sat upright.

"She said he wasn't drinking, and she wasn't in immediate danger. Do you want to telephone her back and see if you can understand what it's about?"

"It sounds like it can wait." He took her hand and gently tugged her until she stood between his knees. "But a beautiful woman like you needs some attention before the girls are up from their naps. What's been occupying you in the study?"

"The book on St. Augustine." Melissa sat on his knee. "I've been taking notes on the history and places to see."

"I'll ask Lucy about which week would be best for us to go when I talk to her tomorrow. How many days do you want to stay?"

"At least five, not counting travel days—if you can spare the time off work. There are a lot of sights to see, and the pools at the hotel are legendary. The girls should love it."

Freddy smiled and put his arms around her waist. "I'll take off however many days you want. That's one of the benefits of being the boss. You know what I like most about our travels?"

"What's that?" She inclined her head and watched his striking profile as he angled toward her ear.

"Because you're the boss of me." He kissed her earlobe, his whiskered chin tickling her neck.

"I recall you dominating our Sunday in Point Clear." She began opening his shirt buttons. "Not to mention Friday and Saturday nights, and that's just the last trip."

"I only take over when your itinerary has been met. So don't blame me if you're too efficient." He went at her blouse, his hands stumbling with the dainty buttons at her throat.

"So if I claim to have not completed my list for the day, I get to rule the night as well?"

"Precisely."

"May I practice now?" She trailed her hands over his pectoral and abdominal muscles.

"Yes, Beloved."

"Carry me to bed."

She rested her head against his warm chest on the journey upstairs. Once they were in their bedroom, he laid her on the green bedspread and doubled back to lock the door.

Phoebe and Doff stood on the threshold. "Is Sissa tired?"

"A bit," Freddy answered. "Is Beth still sleeping?"

"Yes." Phoebe leaned around her father. "I hope you rest good, Sissa."

Melissa was sure she was blushing, but since the girl was used to Alex being half-dressed at any time, she didn't seem to think too much of her father's open shirt.

"Thank you," she managed to say.

"Would you start on building a fort in the back guest room while I make sure Melissa is taken care of? After Beth's awake, we can have story time in the fort."

"Yes, Daddy. And Doff will be my silent helper."

"Thank you, Princess."

Once the door was locked, Melissa couldn't help smiling. "*Taken care of?* Somehow that doesn't sound too romantic."

"You demand romance?" He removed his cufflinks and slipped his shirt off, pausing to flex his muscles. "Would you settle for strength and burning passion instead?"

"Passion from you is the most romantic of all."

They managed nearly a quarter-hour of privacy before Phoebe called from the hallway. "Beth's awake!"

"Thank you, Princess!" Freddy's voice rumbled against Melissa's chest.

Melissa trailed her hands down his back. "Are you thinking what I'm thinking?"

"Drop the romance and go for gratification?"

"Exactly."

As his efforts increased, the thought of a week of sharing a room with the girls and no privacy with Freddy loomed like a black cloud over a beach day. Their two-week trip to Yellowstone was nearly unbearable for that very reason—a shared train cabin and hotel room. Thinking back on Alex's advice of "take it whenever and wherever you can get it," she pictured her and Freddy in the hotel bathroom, closet, and maybe some turret after shackling the girls in the dungeon while exploring the fort. She knew she was being ridiculous and tried to refocus on what she had at the moment—her husband's virility at her disposal.

Afterward, Freddy shifted to his side, hugging Melissa as they kissed. "Stay and rest for a bit if you'd like. I've got the girls."

Melissa wanted to be in his arms the rest of the day but knew she had to share him with his daughters. He pulled the sheet up to her neck and left a kiss on her cheek. Then he folded the top blanket to her waist, exactly how she liked the linens arranged when falling asleep, though she'd never explained that to him.

"I love you," she whispered. "And from your actions, I know you love me too."

He kissed her, slow and deep. "More than I ever thought possible."

Melissa watched him dress with a lazy smile. She was tired but didn't wish to close her eyes and miss a chance at seeing Freddy's magnificence—each athletic muscle in his body on display for her.

Alone in the closed room, her thoughts darkened. Melissa placed her hands on her stomach, recalling her absent monthly flow as worry crept higher. Freddy would be a wonderful father to any child they had together—it was already part of who he was when she met him. His devotion to his daughters was one of the reasons she fell in love with him. But she had trouble cooking a meal when the girls were underfoot, and Phoebe was mostly self-sufficient. What would a helpless newborn do to the balance in the house? True, she could bring Sharon in more days, like she was before the wedding, but she liked the control of running things in the home—it helped give her purpose. Was she the type of woman to be content raising children with no prospects outside of the family? She'd met her biggest career goal—publishing a book—but there was still so much to see of the world and write about. Clutching her middle, she curled on her side and closed her eyes.

***

A light kiss on her cheek, followed by a hand on her forehead, woke Melissa.

"Are you feeling all right? You never nap, and you had that headache this morning." Freddy settled beside her on the bed, and her body dipped toward him.

Under the blankets, she stretched her legs and realized one hand was still on her middle. She pulled her hands free, which tugged the sheet low on her still unadorned body. Freddy smiled and pulled the cover back over her chest.

"I'm fine now." Melissa glanced at the closed door before taking hold of his shoulders and pulling him to her lips. Her kiss was playful and nibbling. Freddy responded by bringing her with him as he straightened, arms around her bare back as he deepened their contact. His hands roamed, then his lips.

He gently tugged her earlobe with his teeth. "You feel and taste as good as you look."

"Freddy, some days I want you all to myself, but I'm learning to take these little moments with you whenever I can. You don't mind, do you?"

He laughed and hugged her stronger. "I treasure these moments with you."

She traced his buttons. "Do we have time?"

"I'm afraid not. I made a shepherd's pie out of the leftovers. It's in the oven for supper. The girls are playing in the fort with their dolls, but I don't know how long that will last. This afternoon pushed things enough, though I'd do it again with no questions."

Melissa ran her fingers through his hair and smiled. "Would you be able to take Wednesday off? Even just half a day? I promise I'd make it worth your time."

"You're always worth every moment, Melissa. I'll see what I can do with my schedule to make it work."

He lifted her as he stood, and she wrapped her arms and legs around him. Caressing hands coupled with his sultry gaze started her heart racing.

Freddy tossed her onto the bed and opened the buttons on his pants as he climbed upon her. "Maybe we have time if we make it quick."

Melissa laughed and shimmied his pants lower on his hips. "That's the pioneering spirit."

"Daddy!" Phoebe called through the door. "Bethany needs help with the doll carriage. I think she broke a wheel!"

Freddy let out a groan of frustration.

Melissa kissed him quickly and helped close his waistband. "After supper it is, just like you said. That's what we get for trying to sneak in more this afternoon."

He laughed. "I don't fault you for trying or myself for falling under your captivating spell. I'll be sure to try to clear time for us this week."

Twenty

Even trotting at a brisk pace, the wooded trails were calming. Alexander, refocusing his thoughts while riding Apollo, was surprised at all the things he dealt with after listing them in his mind. He decided to come to the stables every day that week so his horse would learn to trust him more and further mulled over his stresses and possible pain-inflicting situations while he groomed the horse after his ride.

I should be a diamond from all this pressure. Still, none of it was an excuse to hurt Lucy.

Stroking the horse with his bare hands, Alexander leaned against its neck. "I'm blessed to have you, Apollo, but more so for having my wife." Then he rubbed behind Apollo's ears and fed the stallion an apple before leaving.

When he entered the kitchen at home, he caught Naomi whistling while she finished preparing supper.

"Perfect timing, Mr. Alex. Get yourself and Lucy to the table in fifteen minutes. That should be enough time to shower so you don't smell like a stable hand over my shrimp scampi."

"To shower, but not dress, Miss Naomi. Would it be all right for me to be skimpy for your scampi?"

"You rascal." She snapped a dishtowel at him, and he laughed.

"I'm home!" He called out in the main hallway, hoping she heard him wherever she was. "I'm going to shower right quick. Supper's in fifteen minutes!"

When he didn't see her in any of the rooms he passed on the way to their bedroom, he assumed she was still in the morning room. After showering, Alexander pulled on a pair of sleep pants and nothing else, just to tease Naomi. On the middle stair landing, he hopped on the polished wood banister and slid down the rest of the way. Lucy stood by the tall dining room windows, gazing at the street. She wore her pink evening gown that she'd worn to the orchestra the night he came for her two years ago when she was swollen with Frederick's child. Now she carried his—the newest limb on the twisted Melling family tree.

With a quickness, he stole back to the stairs, nearly running over Naomi carrying a tray. Alexander steadied her load, held a finger to his lips, and winked before dashing to his room. Tossing his pants onto the bed, he grabbed his white tuxedo out of the closet. He pulled on the pants and jacket, skipping everything in between.

Naomi exited the dining room and tried to hide a smile. "I preferred the other outfit, Mr. Alex. At least in that one, you weren't trying to look respectable."

He kissed her cheek. "You love me."

"I'll leave you two alone."

"Don't wait up for us if you need to leave before we come out." He winked at her before closing the double doors.

Lucy turned at the noise and gazed at Alexander in surprise before a curving smile found its way to the surface. She broke into a laugh. "You're wonderful!"

"I wanted to dress for Sunday supper, but I may have missed a few steps. You don't mind, do you?"

They met beside the table, and Alexander's hands instinctively went for Lucy's satin-covered hips. Pleased to see her smile, he grinned in return. She slipped a cool hand in the open front of his tuxedo jacket, caressing his scars and then down his middle.

"You know I don't mind. And since you've been riding the past few months, your abdominal muscles are showing definition."

"A slim version of Frederick now, am I?"

"I wouldn't go that far, but you're perfect, Alex. I, on the other hand—"

"You're glorious, mothering our child all this time." He brought his hands to the swell of her middle and kissed her mouth. "I'm sorry for hurting you, my queen."

"We'll talk about that in a little while." She brought her hands to his shoulders and gazed into his eyes. "But the ride seems to have agreed with you."

He hugged her to him, kissing her hair. "Yes, thank you. I'd like to go every day this week to allow Apollo more of a chance to bond if that's all right with you. I'll try to leave work earlier, so I don't miss time with you and the girls."

"That's fine, Alex. Just don't forget Phoebe on Wednesday."

"Never again." He escorted Lucy to her chair and sat across the center of the table from her, flipping up his tails as he did so. After completing the sign of the cross, he bowed his head, praying over their food.

They ate in silence for a few minutes, but Lucy repeatedly looked to Alexander with a peaceful smile. "Where did you ride this afternoon?" she finally asked.

"West, through the wooded areas. There are some nice trails, and I'm sure I could locate a secluded spot when the time is right."

"You're incorrigible in your appetites, especially when you set your mind to something sexual." She speared a shrimp with her fork and pulled it from the tines with her teeth, all while holding her husband's gaze.

He walked to the end of the table and pulled the table cloth until their place settings were at the end rather than the center. Then he sat Lucy on the table where her food used to be.

"My craving is for you. Right here, right now. But as I was able to walk myself back from nearly taking you this afternoon, I'll regretfully step away from your radiant figure now." Alexander went for her neck, and she leaned back, bracing her hands on the table behind her as he tasted the base of her throat.

She wrapped her legs around him, silky gown cascading around her bare knees with the movement. He trailed a hand up her leg and found nothing in his path. Catching his breath, he straightened.

"You're my seductress—you always have been. It pleases me to know you want it as much as me—that you plan for moments like this. Expect them. You bless me like no other, Lucy. We're meant for one another, and I know that as sure as I know that if I didn't need to share my concerns with you, I'd be buried deep inside of you right now."

He imparted a probing kiss, then helped her situate in the chair. After pulling the tablecloth back into position, he settled across from his wife. A tear ran down her cheek as she looked at her plate.

"I don't deny you, Lucy. I never have. I merely try to wait for a better time. I want to answer what you asked of me this afternoon before we lose ourselves in passion. Sometimes it's difficult to put lasting relationship matters first rather than the fervor we have for our love affair."

She continued to stare at her food.

"Eat, my queen. Your last bite was tantalizing to watch, and you'll need energy later if I have anything to say about things."

Her laugh broke through the sob. Lifting the linen napkin, she dabbed her cheek under her right eye and finally looked to him. "As I told you yesterday, when you're good, you're *very* good, Alexander. I know you treasure me, that you have from the beginning. But sometimes your narcissism gets in the way."

"I love it when you talk dirty to me." He winked and took a bite.

No more words were said, but they exchanged foot nudges and glances while eating.

"Where would you like to talk, my queen?" he asked after the meal.

"In our bedroom." She took his arm, leaning in for a kiss.

"But we talk first."

Her luminous eyes said she wanted other things, but she nodded.

"I'll tell Naomi we're done. She was concerned we might be hours when she saw me like this."

Lucy laughed. "She knows us too well. I'll be waiting upstairs."

"And don't change a thing, my queen. You're my walking fantasy."

The billowy sleeves, much like from a Renaissance dress, encircled him as they hugged.

Alexander kissed her. "You were a vision when I saw you at the orchestra in this dress. When you walked in on Frederick's arm, it took all my control to stay in my seat. And then at your door, when you wrapped your arms around me, my whole world was filled with light once more. And now our life comes full circle as you're carrying my seed beneath this gorgeous gown."

She tucked her head under his chin and seemed to breathe in his essence. "Come to me soon, my angel."

Alexander ran for the kitchen.

"We're done and going upstairs for the night, Naomi." She turned to him from working at the sink, and he spun around. "And see, I'm still fully dressed."

"Fully dressed from half an outfit ain't nothing, Mr. Alex. Don't try to talk yourself up any." She nodded to the counter. "I've got two slices of carrot cake there for you and water keeping hot for coffee."

"I know she won't turn down that. I'll take it with me. Thank you."

"I'll lock up on my way out."

When he carried the tray into their bedroom, Alexander was surprised to see Lucy in one of the wingback chairs in front of the unlit fireplace. He expected her to be lounging seductively on the bed.

"Dessert, compliments of Naomi."

Lucy moved the books she had piled on the side table, and Alexander set the tray next to her.

"Shall I light a fire?" he asked.

"A small one. The nights are cooler, but the air through the windows feels wonderful."

He removed his tuxedo jacket, knelt before the marble hearth, and readied the logs with a few newspaper pages. "While on my ride, I did as you asked, Lucy. It surprised me to understand all that's been piling up on me since Mother died, though the stress took a month or two to build, and then other things happened since then to add to my troubled mind."

The dainty spoon tinkled against her cup as she stirred sugar into her coffee. "I knew you'd been worried. I've wished you'd come to me, but you kept going to Claudio."

He turned to her after the fire took flame, a hand going for her knee. "As I said, I didn't want to burden you. I know from the days I spent with you before Bethany was born that stress on a pregnant woman is a concern. I don't wish to harm you or our child."

"I understand and appreciate it, but not telling me is causing greater stress than the actual issues."

"That's just the thing. Some of them are so monstrous they might not be." He took his cup and sat across from her.

Lucy stretched her legs between the chairs and lifted her feet to his lap. "Start explaining from when we moved here."

"I know you loved your family's home, but I wanted to give you more. Maybe it was wrong to bring you here, to set you like a trophy in this mansion, but I wanted to prove to myself I could run a household as fine as my parents."

"I'll go wherever you go, Alex. I wanted that home for the girls, and they're with Freddy more than me. They're all happy there, and I won't take that away from them."

Alexander nodded. "It's good to hear you say that because I expected as much. I thought this property would be good for Phoebe and Bethany as well."

"And it is. We're all happy here because of you."

His smile was small, but Lucy looked pleased to see it. "The fact is I can't support this household at my current firm. The utility bills and grounds keeping eat most of my monthly income even before the grocery bill. By July, I stopped pulling from my small savings and dipped into my parents' account to make ends meet."

Lucy's gaze was steady and soft like she expected as much. "There's nothing wrong with using that money, but if you'd rather not, I'd be happy to cover the difference from my account."

He shook his head. "You're using too much of your money as it is. Paying Sharon, my new suits, the Seacliff expansion, and your overly generous birthday gift. But covering the stable fees through the end of the year eases my burden, Lucy. That was another expense coming from the Melling interest, though I like to think my mother would have found pleasure in providing the luxury of riding lessons for Phoebe, a sense of pride. You know, something only a Melling would do because an Easton wouldn't be so frivolous."

"Your mother!" Lucy huffed.

"Hopefully, she's resting in peace." Alexander crossed himself and lowered his voice. "My biggest fear is turning into my father. I'm trying to be good to your girls, much better than Father ever was to Eliza."

"You're amazing with them, just as you'll be wonderful with our son."

They were quiet a moment, sipping their coffee and looking at each other. Lucy broke the silence as she lifted a plate of cake, resting the edge on the curve of her middle.

"I told Freddy about the Seacliff house yesterday—how I wanted it bigger to accommodate both our families and other guests. He thought I was being extravagant."

"Practical Frederick, though I still can't get over that ring he bought Melissa."

"He loves her, loves her like he never loved me." A sadness settled on her face, and she took a bite of cake.

"And that's a good thing. You've wanted nothing but happiness for him."

"But it still stings. Part of me thinks if he'd looked at me the way he looks at her, my heart would have been completely satisfied by him."

Alexander caressed the top of her foot in his lap. "And where would that leave me?"

"I know, and I'm happy with how it turned out, but there's that question and—I'll admit—a tinge of jealousy."

"So you're human and not a saint." His hand traveled to her knee, shifting her gown higher.

"I'm no saint, and you know it, Alexander Melling."

"Know it and love you all the more for it, Lucille Melling." He shifted forward and tasted the sweetness of her mouth before resettling with his own plate and refilled cup. "Because I want to provide for us from my own salary, I've been thinking about switching to a bigger firm. When Prudie came to me about Hazel Kline the other week, Rupert Lyons did as well. He said if I won the case for her, he'd take me back at the office because the publicity would be excellent for business, and I'd have proven I'm as good a lawyer as ever."

Lucy's expression was one of a bad taste in her mouth, though she ate her favorite food.

"He's the one who sent you that letter, Lucy. Part of me thinks he wants me to fail, but part of me thinks he's earnest in wanting me at the office with him. He got in the closed pretrial on the pretense that we were becoming partners."

"He can't be trusted!"

"I know, but the thought of my old office and the view of the square rather than an alley is tempting. Not to mention a better clientele and income."

"You can accomplish all that without Rupert." She shoved the rest of the cake into her mouth, and the empty china plate clattered onto the tray.

"True, but sometimes the easy road is appealing."

"And often it leads to broken bridges and dead ends."

"My feisty queen." Alexander set down his dishes and rubbed her legs. "Representing Hazel has come with its baggage. Old temptations and the stress of a high-profile criminal case are among the worst of them."

Lucy shifted lower in her seat, stretching more of her leg to him. "Temptations like that nun you told me about."

"Yes." He held her gaze and knew she waited for more. He wanted to light a cigarette and take a drag from it before continuing but settled for a deep breath. "And from Hazel herself. She's offered for me to touch her—and more—during our private counsels. I brushed her off by saying I'd not do to her what I was trying to protect her from while in custody. Before I came to her, the guards were molesting her. She was denied her personal belongings and basic hygiene. The first things I demanded was for the supplies Prudie brought to be given to her, a medical examination performed, and shower privileges."

She stared, waiting for the gavel to drop.

"To protect her from further mistreatment, she asked that I accompany her to the shower room. I stood by several times with two guards while she washed. She put on quite a show, and I was obliged to watch. I was able to set it up for nuns to attend her, but I'm sorry I didn't think of it the first day." His words tumbled out quicker. "I couldn't deny her plead for protection, nor could I look away and appear weak to the guards when I was cementing myself as a powerful legal arm seeking justice for the wrongs they inflicted on her. But she's nothing to me. I didn't act on her offers, and I'll not take private meetings with her from now on, especially since her behavior after Mass today."

Though her eyes glistened with unshed tears, Lucy appeared calm. "Did you go there to see her?"

"I went to see your parents, to bring them here for dinner, nothing more."

"Nothing?"

"With the purpose of hopefully discussing Opal before coming here, to save you from finding out." Leaning forward, he took her hands. "I'm being honest with you."

"What happened at the cathedral?" Sensing his hesitation, she squeezed his hands. "I must know."

"Nothing good, and in telling you, I'll be disclosing information about others."

"You must, Alex."

"I was standing with Eddie when Hazel walked by with the nuns. Eddie recognized Prudie and made some rude comments about having another go with her or Hazel if given a chance. Maxwell took him by the ear and admonished him to watch his language in the cathedral."

"Good for Maxwell."

"Did you know he was a Dardenne too?"

She freed her hands and crossed her arms. "No, but he's a decade older. It's nothing that would have been discussed around me."

"Max warned Eddie not to go back to whoring because he'd already repeatedly broken his wife's trust. And in response to Eddie calling out his imperfect past, Maxwell didn't deny he was a cad back then but insisted he was true to Lottie from the beginning." Alex inclined his head and gave a shy smile. "That made me hopeful, knowing Maxwell was a scoundrel of a Dardenne but managed to settled into a respectable life."

"You're doing well, Alexander."

"Then Hazel came back after the rest of the Easton family had gone and said it was a happy reunion with the Easton men, seeing as how she'd made Maxwell a man at his first masquerade and had serviced Eddie this past winter."

Lucy looked nauseous and laid a hand on her stomach. "Mother would be livid, and it would probably kill Father."

"It's not my sin to disclose to them, nor even to you." Alexander kissed her cheek. "I've shared it with you to ease this strain between us. After her banter and scorn, I told Hazel if she didn't leave my family alone, I'd cease being her attorney. She told me the Eastons were as vile as the Mellings, though my father was the worst."

Lucy grimaced and reached for her coffee. "There's no blame on you for my brothers' poor choices, and your father is beyond your scope as well. You've worked hard to change your life, and it shows."

"You think so, my queen?"

"Yes, but where does all this relate in regards to Opal?"

"She wrote me at the beginning of August while Freddy, Melissa, and the girls were out west, and you were absorbed in writing those short stories. Opal said she was to be transferred when she turned eighteen at the end of October. She claimed to be doing well and wanted to be reevaluated in Mobile, away from the staff, because she feared them tampering with files to keep her in their system. Apparently, the asylum they want to transfer her to is notorious for missing patients, and whether they break out or are lost in some shady internal procedures, I've yet to find out. But Opal wanted a month at home before relocating. I talked her down to a week. And she's gotten your mother worked up about the other asylum, afraid to send her there lest she goes missing."

"She's always been able to manipulate Mother, but how did she get you?"

Alexander looked at her sheepishly. "I wouldn't have thought it possible, but after thinking it over on my ride, I'd have to say flattery. She praises my intelligence and claims helping her will prove to your parents I'm as useful to the family as Frederick. How she knows I feel second fiddle to Freddy, I don't know."

"She was always playing you two against each other when we were courting. It would be only obvious that after me having been married to the cherished family friend that you might feel inferior to him in the eyes of your in-laws. That doesn't take a genius to connect the two."

"No, it takes a shrewd schemer. And I'm sorry, Lucy, but it's set in stone. Opal will be here a week from tomorrow, on the twenty-first."

"I don't wish to see her. Those photographs were enough with her hollow eyes."

"You won't have to, my queen." He took her hands brought her to his lap. "It is a bit of a relief to get it all out between us. Do you still love me?"

"You know I do." Her lips on his were healing. "Come to me from now on for more than your sexual release. Share with me. We'll be able to grow even closer."

"I will, but for now, we can be as physically close as two people can." He kissed from her lips to her décolletage as his hands went under her gown. "Will you allow me to love you?"

"Every day, Alexander. Our everlasting love affair."

Twenty-One

"You're insatiable lately." Freddy tucked a strand of Melissa's hair behind her ear as he looked up at her.

"Do you mind so much?" Melissa shifted to lay beside him.

"It wasn't a complaint. I love that you're an early riser. Feel free to wake me like this every morning. It's a great way to start the week, just as last night was a marvelous way to end it."

They kissed until the sun was too bright to ignore.

"At least you don't need to rush this morning." Melissa stood. "Lucy said she wanted to talk to you after Alex left."

"Then where are you going?" He took her hand with his strong grip.

"To get a head start on breakfast." She allowed him to tug her back and perched on the edge of the bed. "It's better for me to cook when the girls aren't about."

"Is it getting easier with time?"

She sighed. "Not like I expected. It's difficult to balance the house responsibilities with that of parenting. I feel inferior most days, a complete failure at least twice a week."

"You're anything but a failure, Melissa." He traced her face with a finger. "I've never been dissatisfied with a meal, the house is orderly, the girls adore you, and you fulfill my every desire."

Smiling, she looked to his earnest brown eyes. "You're certain?"

Mischievousness flashed across his face as his hands went about her waist. "Do I need to show you how certain I am, Mrs. Davenport?"

She wanted to sing out with a resounding *YES*, but a flicker of thought passed through her head. It wasn't something they'd spoken of since the first few days of marriage when they'd stayed alone in his house on State Street. After their first time, Freddy had held her in his arms. His hands rested low on her stomach, and he'd whispered that if the time came when they had a family of their own, there would be room enough for all in his heart.

"Do you ever think of being a father again?"

Freddy's gaze calmed, but his smile remained. "Every blessed minute after we're joined."

"Have you been disappointed?" The uncertainty in her tone betrayed the depth of her concern.

"You're no disappointment, Melissa." His roaming hands soothed her worries. "My only plans have been to love, cherish, and honor you. Have I failed?"

She laughed. "Do I sound that ridiculous?"

"A husband has the right to remain silent so as not to incriminate himself."

"Don't tell me you're taking legal advice from Alex these days." Her voice turned playful, but his countenance fell.

"I hope he hasn't done something completely idiotic."

Melissa embraced him, leaning her head on his solid chest. "Don't worry about it until you talk to Lucy, and even then, it might be nothing."

"Beautiful *and* smart." He held her to him. "Why don't we take the girls to breakfast tomorrow morning? I might even have time to bring you all back before going to the office."

"Don't worry about that, Freddy. They like to look around downtown and ride the trolley."

"That will save you another morning of drudgery in the kitchen."

"I don't mind it, but the break will be a treat." She kissed him before standing.

Melissa dressed in a shirtwaist and navy skirt. In the kitchen, she started water boiling for oatmeal and coffee and sliced fruit. Overhead, she heard Phoebe running about and couldn't help but think Freddy asked her to stay upstairs until he was dressed as a way to give Melissa some quiet.

Fifteen minutes later, he came in with Phoebe and Bethany, all ready for the day minus his suit jacket.

"Good morning, Sissa!" Phoebe hugged her around her legs, pink ribbons bouncing.

"Good morning, Phoebe."

"Sissa, hug." Bethany came to her once Phoebe was seated.

"And happy day to you, Beth." Melissa kissed her chubby cheeks and carried Bethany to her chair in the breakfast nook.

Freddy brought the milk and coffee to the table. Like the gentleman he was, he waited for Melissa to settle before taking his seat. Then he asked Phoebe to lead the prayer.

"Lord, sit with us at our bounteous table. See us through the day. And bless our family and the food, we pray. Amen."

Freddy smiled at his daughter and gave a hearty "Amen."

The meal was like most other weekday breakfasts at their home. Phoebe chattered about her dreams, ponies, or whatever adventure she had in the works. Bethany quietly asked for help when she wanted more food. And Freddy and Melissa held their own conversations when feasible. Melissa was glad he wasn't the type to hide behind the morning paper. He told her he wasn't used to such luxuries raising the girls by himself, so he went through the paper in his office when he had quiet moments.

After they left and Melissa tidied the kitchen and eating areas, she curled on the sofa with the latest copy of *Noble Travels*. Jolted awake by the ringing telephone, she glanced at the mantel clock on her way to the hall. A quarter after nine.

"Davenports'." She couldn't help the husky sleepiness in her voice.

"Sorry to disturb you, Mrs. Davenport," Ms. Neves said, "but is Mr. Davenport caught up with family matters this morning?"

"He left with the girls an hour and a half ago. Has he not made it in?"

"No, and he has a nine o'clock that's been waiting for him." There was an edge of worry in the secretary's tone. "He's never been late without word."

"Is it something Mr. Peabody or Mr. Adams could handle?" Melissa asked.

"It's one of his personal accounts, but I'll see if one of them can help smooth things over while I reschedule."

"I'll check with Lucy to see if something happened when he brought the girls. Let me know if you hear from him, please."

"Of course, and the same for you, Mrs. Davenport."

Melissa immediately hung the receiver and picked it back up to request the Mellings' number from the operator.

After the fourth ring, the line connected.

"Mellings' residence."

"Naomi, it's Melissa. Are the girls there?"

"Good morning, Miss Melissa. Yes, they were here when I came, same as usual."

"And is Freddy there, by chance?"

"No, I usually don't see him 'til the evenings, though I miss that fine man."

Melissa tapped her fingers on the telephone box. "Is Lucy busy?"

"She's stretched out in the hammock with both girls. How she expects to get out of that contraption, I don't know, but I'd think it'll take a good five minutes at the very least if I called her to the telephone."

Melissa managed a tight laugh. "Leave her be, but thank you, Naomi. I'll see you later."

It was scarcely a mile from the Mellings' house to the office, and Melissa didn't understand what could have happened to Freddy between the two places other than an automobile accident. But he was a safe driver, and surely someone would have told her by then if that had happened.

Not knowing what else to do save walking the path he took or staying by the telephone for news, Melissa set the kettle on for tea. As she pulled a teacup out of the cupboard, there was a disjointed knock at the front door. She turned off the stove and hurried to the foyer. The familiar form of Freddy's mass could be seen through the leaded glass. Fumbling with the lock, Melissa gasped when she opened it.

Freddy leaned on the doorframe. His white button-down shirt clung to his wet body, and his knuckles were a bleeding mess.

She took his arm to steer him inside. "Freddy, what happened?"

He remained mute as she led him to their bathroom. Melissa turned on the tap and filled the sink with warm, sudsy water. After removing his cufflinks, she peeled the shirt off his sweaty body, then guided his hands to soak in the sink. Freddy winced but held them under the water. Then she took his belt and shoes and checked the rest of him for injuries but found none.

Unable to handle his continued silence, she started with questions. "Did you beat someone? Alex perchance?"

A growling sound rumbled through his broad chest. "I wanted to. Still do. He's stabbed Lucy in the back with his latest plot, not to mention he's endangering her whole family."

She plunged her hands into the water, carefully flexing and extending each of his fingers as she stood beside him.

"I went to the gym and pounded the first bag I came to until I couldn't lift my arms. Then I ran here because I didn't trust myself with the automobile."

Satisfied his hands weren't broken, Melissa dried hers on the towel. Ducking under his extended arms, she stood between him and the sink, gently alighting on his chest. The touch softened his countenance, and he looked at her with more worry than anger. Knowing Freddy would tell her when he was ready, she asked no more questions. Instead, she kissed him. His lips immediately responded with a searching kiss of his own as he wedged Melissa between himself and the counter. Then his wet hands were groping across her back, pressing her to his firm body.

Melissa had studied science and psychology. She understood the basic instincts of man: protect and reproduce. Survival of the fittest, especially when life was threatened. Freddy was unquestionably a top human specimen, and after fearing for the safety of those he loved, he needed to conquer the threat and reestablish his dominion. She'd not seen fervor like that in him before, but it didn't panic her. He would never go too far, be too rough—though she worried about his knuckles as he lifted her to their bed and grasped her hips. Savoring the moment, she urged him on. It was ardent, precise, exhilarating! And over much too soon.

Coming to his senses, Freddy pulled down her skirt and righted his clothing. "I'm sorry I was barbaric, Melissa."

She held her hand to him, and he pulled her into his arms. "It was stimulating in the best possible ways."

As his adrenaline returned to normal, Melissa noticed him flinching over his movements.

"Let me wrap your hands."

He kissed her hard and followed her into the bathroom. "I'm blessed you understand me and know my needs. I hope I care for you as well."

"You most certainly do." Melissa rewashed his knuckles and patted them dry before applying a liberal amount of ointment on the wounds and carefully wrapping them. "Ms. Neves called looking for you. She sounded concerned that you were late for your nine o'clock."

Freddy went to tighten his fists in frustration but sucked in his breath. "I don't think I can go yet, but I'll call." He pointed to her blouse. "Your shirt is soiled from my hands. Probably the bed, too."

"No worries, Freddy. It was worth it. I'd do it again without hesitation."

Melissa changed shirts and pulled off the bedspread, adding them to the laundry collection for the week. She found a patchwork quilt Grandmother Stone made for her in the top of the closet and placed it on the bed before joining Freddy downstairs.

"I don't want to talk about it right now, but I'll tell you when I see you," Freddy said into the telephone. "Ms. Neves knows it was an urgent family matter. I'll try to be in by one, but it depends on when I can speak with Alex."

He gave a bitter laugh. "Of course it has to do with him! Who else is keen on wrecking people's lives?"

"That won't be necessary, but thanks, Henry."

Melissa kissed Freddy's cheek before he could give the operator his next number and stepped into the kitchen to reheat the water, listening to the conversation.

"Mr. Melling, please." He didn't sound at all like himself in his anger. "You tell him it's urgent, about his wife. I'll wait on the line."

A pause.

"Alex, you either promise to be at my house by noon, or I'm coming to your office right now."

"I'm sure you can guess what it's about."

"Melissa is here, but if I come to your office, I'll be alone."

"Just be sure you do."

Freddy stomped into the kitchen, and Melissa reflexively opened her arms to him. She tucked against his chest, and he rested his head atop hers.

"Coffee or tea?" she asked.

"Coffee, but I'm getting a shot of brandy first." Freddy went for the dining room, where they kept a small bar inside the left door of the credenza.

They enjoyed an occasional glass of wine with supper and often toasted something silly together after the girls were in bed on a Friday night. Every few weeks, Freddy took a glass of brandy after work but never had he reached for a drink during the day. He came back to the kitchen with a half-full tumbler.

She pointed to his shirt, which had a few blood smears on it. "Do you want to change before he arrives?"

He took a swig of brandy and clunked the heavy glass on the counter. "Let him see what his actions have done."

"In that case, shall we open your fasteners? I'm sure he'd get a sense of pride over spurring along our zealous moment."

The hard line of his mouth broke into a smile, followed by a laugh before he kissed her. "He'll receive no satisfaction in coming here. Your enjoyment has unlocked a new door, though. One I hope to open again soon."

"I'm always here for you, Handsome."

"Thank you for making me smile." He drained the rest of his tumbler while she readied a coffee tray. "Are you going to pretend this is a pleasant social visit?"

"What else can I do when you've not told me his infraction?"

Freddy followed her into the parlor and waited until she placed the service on the coffee table and settled on the sofa. "He's helping Opal get out of her asylum. She'll be at the Easton's house next Monday while she undergoes testing."

Opal. She'd heard Alex mutter that name while Lucy was plagued by demons and tried to seduce Freddy. When Melissa had asked Freddy who Opal was, he briefly told her the story of the girl's attack on Lucy and subsequent hospitalization.

The doorbell echoed down the hall.

"You have every right to be upset, Freddy, but please remember violence won't solve anything."

Twenty-Two

Alexander knew he looked terrified and appreciated Melissa's smile when she opened the door. She held out a hand to collect his briefcase and jacket.

"Come to the parlor, Alex."

"You'll protect me, won't you?" he whispered as he stuffed his gloves into his pocket and handed over his things.

"You do this to yourself. But I'll do what I can." Melissa kissed his cheek. Her lips were warm and—he could have imagined it—smelt faintly of brandy, which made him crave a drink.

Frederick stood in the middle of the parlor, arms crossed, hands tucked under his biceps like he held back from attacking. Melissa touched his shoulder and inclined her head toward the sofa, and he followed her lead. Taking the adjacent armchair, Alexander sat closest to Melissa, so she was between him and Freddy.

"Coffee, Alex?"

"Only if I can smoke along with it."

"Not in my house." Frederick, arms still crossed, looked away in disgust—long enough for Alexander to wink at Melissa.

"Then may we proceed to the point where you thoroughly berate me so I can catch my next appointment?"

"Are your appointments more important than mine?" Frederick's voice rose with each word. "The news I received from Lucy this morning had me so upset I missed my meeting with Mr. Van Antwerp."

Alexander sucked in his breath. He knew that was one of Frederick's biggest accounts. "I'm sorry, though I don't see why Lucy—"

"She's scared to death!" Frederick stood and released his arms. There were dried splotches of blood on his shirt, and his hands were both bandaged. "Right in this room, Opal unleashed the hatred and fury no adult, let alone a ten-year-old in their right mind, should possess! I had to stop her—me! Maybe that means nothing to you because you weren't here. You were too self-absorbed after you had your way with Lucy that you couldn't be bothered to see her home properly. No, she had to send for me, the one who is always there to clean the messes you create with your Melling ways."

Brandy vapors flooded Alexander's senses with each exhalation as Frederick prattled on.

"You haven't a care in the world over Lucy when you know loyal Davenport will swoop in and scrape her off the floor after you've drug her so far down she can't stand by herself. I was there to escort her home after you abandoned her in the Dardenne hell. I was the one who stopped you from chasing her through your duplex when you were set on ravishing her before she could escape your poisoned clutches. I'm even the one she came to when you couldn't give her a baby."

Alexander went to his feet. "That's a cheap shot, and you know it! It has no bearing on any of this!"

"But it does! Wasn't it because you took her innocence that she became afflicted by demons?"

"I didn't take," Alexander's icy voice betrayed nothing of the fear rattling inside him. "She gave herself most willingly, as you well know."

Melissa rose between them. "I'm sure you both feel better after having boasted of your domination of Lucy, but let's stay focused on the matter affecting her at present."

"It more than affects Lucy." Frederick's nostrils flared. "It affects all the Eastons and possibly beyond. Mr. and Mrs. E would be helpless if Opal were to start on a rampage. You have no idea what evil you're unleashing by helping Opal come home."

"It's only a week," Alexander said, still meeting Frederick's gaze defiantly.

"Whole civilizations have been destroyed in less time than that," Frederick countered.

Melissa's hand went to her husband's arm, causing him to relax his guard a tad.

"We're planning a family vacation to Florida, and when Lucy told me the news, I wanted to move up our travel days so we'd be gone next week. But she asked me to wait until the following week so I'd be here when Opal's in town—not that any of us wish to see her. Keep her away from Lucy, and keep her away from our girls! Do you understand?"

"Lucy told me last night she doesn't want to see her sister, and I respect her decision, as I will yours. I wish no harm on anyone. I'm only trying to help bring peace to Mr. and Mrs. Easton over the placement of their daughter. They've suffered so much loss with the three souls who died from yellow fever."

"Spare me the melodrama, Alex. You don't even remember their names! You don't even know the names of your nieces and nephews."

Shame heated his face. "You multiply all those Easton siblings by their spouses, and you get an ungodly number of offspring because they're all single-handedly trying to multiply and replenish the Earth. I bet you don't even know who has how many and what their names are."

"Maxwell and Lottie have five, Susan and David seven—"

"Forget it! You're more a part of their lives than I am. You always have been. That's the reason I decided to help Opal—an attempt to win the graces of Mr. and Mrs. Easton. But if something happens, I'll be worse off than ever." Alexander sunk to the chair. "I'd be pleased to take that coffee now, Melissa."

"Of course." As always, she was ready with a smile.

"Thank you for your hospitality, Melissa." He caressed her hand as he accepted the cup. "There *is* one matter I need to discuss with you both."

"You're a shameless fool," Frederick muttered as he sat back on the sofa.

"You're already upset with me. I have nothing to lose."

Melissa laughed. "He has a point, Freddy."

Frederick huffed. "Go on, then."

"In one of her letters, Opal mentioned that she'd like to see the house. She was a girl when she left, and it would mean a lot—"

"I'll not have that lunatic where my wife and daughters sleep!"

"You wouldn't have to be here. I could—"

Frederick was on his feet once more. "Get out of here, and pray my bloodied fists aren't a precursor for next week!"

Alexander stood, feeling weak from Frederick's brandied breath. When he turned for the hall, his eyes swept the room, focusing on the corner where Mr. Easton used to keep a decanter at the ready, but there was no liquor.

Melissa stood.

"He can see himself out," Frederick's hard voice cut through the air.

"I'm hostess here," she reminded him.

After helping Alexander into his jacket, they held each other's gaze.

"I don't see the harm of her coming when the family isn't here, especially if it would help the girl heal," she whispered. "I'll give him some time to calm and see what I can do."

"Thank you, Melissa. You've been a great comfort to me."

Alexander kissed her cheek and then headed for the riding club rather than his office. There he signed up for polo practice on Saturday afternoons, spent an hour in the ring practicing movements and commands, and then over an hour on the trails. He kept his afternoon appointments beginning at two and returned to his home by five.

That night, after the girls were gone and supper was eaten, Alexander held Lucy without the thought of pressing for more. The feel of her silk nightgown against his chest as they lie spooned together was comfort enough. Head buried in her lavender-scented hair, he whispered in case she'd drifted to sleep.

"I'm sorry you're frightened. I wish you didn't feel the need to go to Frederick, but I understand. He's been the stalwart figure in your life. I pray that one day I can be that for you as well."

Her hand moved atop his on the curve of their child within, cool and relaxing. Then she lifted his hand to her lips to kiss the palm and then his wrist.

"I love you, Alex. I rely on you for much, but I'm sorry if it pains you that I still see Freddy as my knight. He's been there since childhood, shielding me."

"It makes me try harder, my queen. It only pains me when it's by my actions you seek his shelter."

"She won't be able to hurt me, will she?"

"You'll be safe, Lucy. I'll see to it."

***

After lunch Wednesday, Ms. Trigg knocked on Alexander's open door.

"Ms. Kline is here to see you."

Alexander frowned. "Bring her in and leave the door open when you leave."

Ms. Trigg's posture went straighter, and she turned sharply on her heels. She did as asked, and Hazel looked back at the opened door with a smirk.

"Safeguarding your reputation these days, Mr. Melling?"

"Someone has to, Ms. Kline." He lit a cigarette for her. "What do you need?"

She blew smoke at him as her gaze lowered to his lap. "I hoped for a private audience with you."

"That's not going to happen. Please share your business or leave."

Hazel's smile was eager. "Sharing my business is exactly what I've wanted to do with you since the first day you came to me. I want to know why the girls called you 'Alexander the Great.'"

"If you insist on keeping banter like this part of your communication, you'll need to find another lawyer."

"That's why I've come. I've received a note from Mr. Lyons stating that you're going into practice with him, and if there's something you aren't able to see fulfilled, I should call on him."

Alexander lit a cigarette for himself. "I have no intention of joining his practice. If you found my father distasteful, you'll find Rupert Lyons equally offensive. But I'm sure he would entertain your banter with action if that's what you seek."

She laughed. "I'm lonely in the convent, but not that desperate. The stories the girls tell of him are just as bad as those about George Melling."

"Then keep clear because he doesn't play fair, nor does he take no for an answer."

"But a note I received from him this morning said he would come for a consultation at your request."

Alexander slammed his hand on his desk and stood. "He lies! It's your choice to meet with him, but if you do, I'll no longer represent you."

"You sound jealous, Mr. Melling."

"You found out what you needed, and I have clients with appointments to see to. Please leave."

Hazel leaned forward to put out the cigarette in the ashtray. "I hear your wife is swollen with child. I can make sure you don't go without while she's unable to see to her wifely duties. You know where to find me."

While the temptation wasn't there, his mouth went dry. He instinctively licked his lips. "Go, Hazel."

"You're such a tease." Both her hands went to her chest and moved downward. Far from being sensual, Alexander found it vulgar.

Stoney faced, he set his cigarette in the ashtray. "Get out of here, and don't try to return without an appointment."

Hazel smirked and snatched his smoke from the dish, lifting it to her painted lips. "Until next time, Mr. Melling."

***

When Alexander returned home from Mass Sunday, he found Lucy pacing the morning room. Her gown shimmered behind her frantic movements, and the dark, red-rimmed shadows around her eyes gave her a haunted look.

"Lucy, you're trembling." He stilled her with a consuming embrace.

Ushering her to his den, he telephoned Darla. "Darla, could you come? I have Lucy in the den, and she needs you."

Alexander then called the rectory and left a message with one of the other priests for Claudio to come as soon as possible. After opening the French doors to the October air, he settled Lucy on the chaise, arms about her to absorb her fears.

"Can you speak, my queen?"

"Yes." Her voice sounded raw.

"I won't leave you alone again. I'll make sure someone is always with you when I leave the house." He rocked her as he spoke. Her neck was damp with sweat, and he wanted to braid her hair to help cool her but didn't wish to let go. "I'd change things if I could, Lucy, but I'm afraid it's too late. At least your parents are happy. She'll be here tomorrow, and the week will pass quickly."

Lucy remained silent. Alexander started humming "Nearer, My God, to Thee" to help his nerves. Thinking of the way he had sounded singing it with Magdalene and Douglas brought lightness to his heart as worry over Lucy's condition threatened to overcome him. She nestled closer, a hand lightly resting near his throat as though the vibrations soothed her.

"Will you sing it?" she whispered. "I remember you were a choir boy."

How she recalled something like that amid a parish the size of the cathedral, he didn't know. Perhaps Edmund was one at the same time, but he'd skipped half the practices, choosing to hang out in the park when he could get away with it. Alexander began softly but raised his voice on the second verse. Darla and Henry came in during the third, waiting near the door.

Alexander looked to Darla—the one he trusted to save Lucy from any complications—as he sang the final verses. Seeing her reach for Henry's hand and her eyes wet with tears, he hoped Lucy was moved as well. When he finished, a hushed stillness domed the room.

Lucy shifted. Trailing her hands up his chest, they went to his neck like the wings of a dove. She guided his head lower until she could reach his lips with her own. The kiss—pure and full—compared to nothing save their first one across from the mistletoe.

"Promise me, Alex. Promise me you'll sing to him."

His hands went to her rounded middle. "I'll sing to both of you, whenever you wish. Darla's here now. May she come over, my queen?"

"Yes."

Henry kept near the door, but Darla crossed the room with purpose, her complexion rosier than ever. "Alex, that was beautiful. I had no idea you were a fine tenor."

Lucy kissed him once more. "He was a rascal of a choir boy back in the nineties. He and Edmund set someone's robes on fire once."

Henry blurted out a hearty laugh.

"I'd forgotten about that. But yes, I suppose fire has always been a thing for me." Alexander looked to his burned hands.

Darla's smile faded. "Would you step outside with Henry while I see to Lucy?"

He brushed his lips against Lucy's forehead. "I'll be on the patio, my queen. Call to me, and I'll return."

Taking the gold cigarette case and matchbook from the corner of his desk, he nodded to Henry, who followed him until he was outside the kitchen. There he lit up and belatedly offered a cigarette to the younger man, who accepted.

"I didn't know you indulged."

Henry smiled. "Just during social outings with the guys, a few times a week at most, like drinking."

Alexander nodded. "Sorry I can't offer you a drink. Frederick never started with smoking, did he?"

"No, he's all about staying as healthy as possible for the gym."

"And what about drinking? I've never seen him drunk, but I smelt brandy on his breath Monday morning—not the most obvious time for liquor."

"Last Monday was a special circumstance if I remember correctly." Henry took a drag and stared at Alexander but was polite enough not to mention any infractions. "Davenport does drink, though. More so than he did when married to Lucy. Melissa's sophisticated New York taste probably has much to do with that. They've been known to consume a full bottle of wine over dinner."

Alexander raised his eyebrows. "I never would have guessed it of either of them."

"Oh, they don't drink daily, but they like to relax when they're out for the evening. Darla and I have even stopped in on a Friday or Saturday night for drinks after the girls are in bed. Melissa likes to serve olives and cheese with it. Some reek worse than a manure pile."

Alexander laughed. "That has to do more with her European travels than New York."

"All the same, I've learned to sniff everything before putting it in my mouth."

To keep his mind occupied, they spoke of Apollo, riding, and the polo practice Alexander attended the day before.

"And then, as I was leaning over with the mallet," he told Henry, "a mockingbird swooped out of nowhere, and I nearly slid off the saddle. I pulled a shoulder muscle righting myself."

Darla stepped onto the patio. With a slight nod at Henry, he immediately tucked his cigarette into the ashtray on the table. He kissed his wife on the cheek and went into the den to watch over Lucy. Then Darla made Alexander sit with her in the wicker chairs.

He extinguished his smoke and exhaled his final mouthful off to the side.

"There are just weeks to go. Six, I reckon, but if Lucy keeps this up, she and the baby aren't going to make it." Darla took his hand. "Don't worry just yet. It appears the stress is about her sister coming, so that's short-term, but it sounds like she hasn't slept well this past week, and she's lost weight. It's too much stress on her body, and therefore on the baby."

He jerked his hand away from Darla and raked his fingers through his hair as he stood to pace. "I didn't realize. I would never have agreed to help Opal had I know how scared Lucy was of her. She never confided in me about that day. I assumed she no longer worried."

"She never had to worry because the threat was gone, locked away in another county. All that pain she never processed is now running rampant in her over-taxed body."

"Could I bring her to the hotel in Point Clear tomorrow? Would having the bay separating her from Opal make a difference? Maybe send word to Magdalene and see if the Campbells would take her in for the week on the island? If the new house on Seacliff were ready, I'd tuck her away there."

"Alex, she's not fit for traveling in anything other than an automobile for a trip to the hospital. She's wasted away this week, or have you not noticed? When I stopped by to see the girls Wednesday morning, Lucy looked tired. Today she's teetering on the edge of exhaustion."

It had come on gradually, so Alexander didn't see it as readily. Still, he had to agree Lucy's sallow complexion and lack of energy that morning was concerning, though she insisted he attend church. She'd eaten little at meals, but he attributed it to the baby's weight inside her making her feel full. And yes, she was restless at night. Twice he'd woken and found her staring out the window.

He dropped into his seat and gripped the midwife's hand. "What can I do? Darla, tell me what to do!"

"I'm going to telephone Dr. Hughes and ask that he secure a prescription for a sleep aid. She needs to rest fully at night and be as still during the day as possible. She needs someone with her all the time—"

"I already told her that much when I returned from Mass."

"Good. Whether it's Naomi or Melissa or me, it matters not, but she shouldn't be watching the girls, either. I know she'll be upset about that, especially with them going out of town at the end of the month, but she needs complete quiet, at least for the next several days. Depending on how she's doing, she might sit with them Wednesday, along with someone else, mind you. When I call Dr. Hughes, I'll ask to have my schedule cleared tomorrow so I can stay with her while you're at work. I'm sure Melissa will keep the girls home." Darla's blue eyes stared straight at him. "Lucy needs to be in bed now. Would you mind if Henry carries her upstairs? He's not as large as Frederick, but he could manage. You can walk behind him if that would make you feel better."

"Whatever is necessary."

"I know you're intelligent, but I'll say it anyway to ease my conscience. Absolutely no attempts at seducing, lovemaking, or even dancing right now."

Alexander pressed his lips together and raised his eyebrows in sincerity. "There hasn't been much of any of that the past week."

"Are you ready to withhold your own needs? With her being weak and Dr. Hughes liking to advise the final month not include physical exertion, there might not be another—"

"I've gone without as I waited for her after the fire. I'm capable when there's no other alternative."

"I want you to be prepared." Darla stood. "Let her be until I complete the telephone calls, and then we'll move her upstairs."

Darla slipped into the kitchen door to keep from disturbing Lucy. Alexander took a moment to cross himself and complete a "Hail Mary."

"God in heaven, please don't take my Lucy or our child. I'd end myself for real if I lost them. Please strengthen her and forgive my trespasses. In the name of The Father, and The Son, and the Holy Spirit. Amen."

"Alex!"

He ran to the sound of Lucy's voice.

Wide-eyed on the chaise, her thin arms were about his neck. "I felt you leave me. Please don't leave me!"

"Never, my queen. I'll be on this earth as long as you." He held her until Darla returned.

"The sleep aid will be ready within the hour. Henry and I will pick it up once Lucy's settled. And Melissa has no problem keeping the girls the next several days."

"Phoebe and Bethany," Lucy whispered. "I need to see them."

"The girls will come as soon as your strength is back, my queen. For now, you need to go to bed, and Henry, our dashing young friend, is going to carry you there. Please don't be swayed by his strength or indigo eyes. Remember the fragile old man you gave your heart to when you're in his capable arms."

Her smile was whole, her countenance lighter. "I could never forget you, my angel."

Twenty-Three

After Darla and Henry left to secure the medicine, Alexander saw Lucy changed into a modest silk nightgown—elbow-length sleeves and a higher neckline than most. Once she settled in bed, he donned a pair of sleep pants. He laid on his back and wrapped an arm around her, hugging her against his right side.

"Are you tired, Lucy?"

"Tired, but not sleepy."

Hoping to give her something to focus on other than Opal, he kissed her temple. "Did you ever decide where you want to place the bassinet?"

"I'm down to two ideas—by my side table or centered in front of the footboard."

"Do I get a say?"

"Of course. He's your son."

"Then place the bassinet in the center. I'm just as capable of going to the babe when there's crying in the middle of the night, even

if I do nothing more than give a kiss and hand the bundle to you."
He turned toward her.

Lucy's cool hand went to his demonic scars, fingering over
the lines as though they were keys on her typewriter. "You'll have to
share me with another, at all hours of the day and night."

His hand gently cupped her breast in return. "Just be sure to
leave things open, so there's a good view for the spectator. You were
more than generous in that regard with Bethany."

A giggle—that silvery sound he hadn't heard in over a
week—erupted. "I was trying to satisfy you until we could finally be
married."

"It was anything but satisfying, my queen. Arousing,
stunning, breathtaking, inspiring, and spiritual." He kissed her cheek
after each word, slowly moving closer to her lips.

The kiss was slow but deep, hands still on the other's chest.
No frenzy, just the sensation of utmost love between two people
expressed through tiny caresses, gentle movements, and soft lips.

They continued on and on, Alexander never tiring of the
contact with his wife.

Darla stomped into the room. "I thought I made myself clear,
Alex!"

Both arms hugging Lucy to him, he kissed her once more
before answering. "That wasn't seduction. Seduction is a means to
achieve sexual gratification from someone. We were mutually
expressing our love with no thought of physically heightening things.
It was beautiful and filling."

"Whatever it was, I'm glad I left Henry downstairs to make
toast." Darla set the supplies on the side table. "You need to have a
bit of food in your stomach before taking this medication every
night, Lucy. And I want you to drink more to help your strength
return. So, what would you like with the toast?"

"Lemonade," Lucy said with a smile. "Alex makes the best
lemonade."

"I'm learning all sorts of things about Alex today—singing, kissing without seducing, and lemonade-making skills."

"You heard my singing, and you've sampled my lemonade before without knowing I made it, but I'll have to draw the line at kissing you. Poor Henry would never feel adequate again."

"You're a real pig," Darla countered.

Alexander snorted as he fluffed the pillows around Lucy. "I'll be back as soon as possible, my queen."

He was halfway through squeezing a pile of lemons when the doorbell rang. Alexander looked to Henry across the counter from him. "Would you?"

The younger man soon returned with Frederick.

Alexander offered a hesitant smile to the frowning man coming at him. "Did you come to visit Lu—"

Frederick had him by the throat with both hands.

"If she dies over this mess with Opal, I'll kill you."

"If she dies, I'll kill myself." Alexander jabbed his lemon-covered hands at Frederick's eyes.

Frederick shoved him away and went for the sink to rinse his face. Alexander wiped his hands on a towel and went back to the pitcher, pouring the lemon juice into the water before blending it with a wooden spoon.

"I mean it, Freddy. If something happens to her, I'll end myself. There's no sense in Phoebe and Bethany losing their mother and then their father to the legal system. I'm updating my will tomorrow morning. If Lucy and I are both gone, everything goes to the girls, except ten percent to the cathedral." He stopped stirring. "But if we lose the baby …"

Alexander gripped the counter and raged with curses. Henry guided him to a chair and patted his bare shoulder awkwardly.

"I messed things up too much this time, and not just for myself. I'm going through hell and deserve every second of it, but my queen doesn't."

"Why don't you go say hello to Lucy, Davenport," Henry suggested. "Be sure to tell Darla we'll be up in a few minutes with the lemonade and toast."

Once Frederick was gone, Henry thumped Alexander on the back.

"Come on, Melling. Lucy wants your lemonade. If she's anything like Darla, she gets testy if you fail to deliver on time. Am I right?"

Alexander laughed as he stood. "You know me well enough to spur me to action with innuendos."

They finished the preparations and climbed the stairs, Alexander with Lucy's tray and Henry holding the pitcher and glasses with ice for the rest. Darla sat in one of the chairs by the fireplace, and Frederick perched on the edge of the bed, holding Lucy's hand. Alexander tried to keep the tray steady as jealousy burned like he hadn't felt since the night he brought Edmund home from a Dardenne meeting and found Frederick waltzing Lucy around the Eastons' dining room.

He's her best friend. I'm worked up because she admitted she was jealous of Melissa, which means she still has feelings for him. A bit of something more-than-friends leftover from marriage.

"Sorry for the delay, my queen, but your refreshments are now ready."

"I'll stop in tomorrow on my way home, Goosy." Frederick left a kiss on her forehead. "Listen to Darla. She has your best interests at heart. You can telephone me anytime, and that goes for whoever is with you as well."

"Kiss the girls for me." She brought the back of his hand to her lips. "And thank Melissa. She's been so good to them."

"I will, Goosy." His smile dissolved as soon as he turned away from her. He gave a curt nod to Alexander before Darla offered to see him out.

"Now, my beauty, here's your lemonade with a fourth a cup of ice, as you prefer. I may have stirred an extra pinch of love into it. See if you can taste it."

Her smile brightened the room, and he couldn't remove his eyes from watching her lift the glass to her lips. "It's perfect, Alex. Thank you."

"Anything for you, Lucy." He settled cross-legged on the bed beside her with the tray, holding it steady so she could set her glass down to eat.

When Darla returned, she brought Claudio with her. "He was on the front porch when I let Frederick out."

The priest went to Lucy, kissing her cheeks. "You are not allowed to grow weary. Too many people rely on your love and kindness. What can I do for you?"

"Pray for the baby, Claudio. And pray for Alex."

"I would be honored to."

He laid his hands on Lucy's head and spoke soothing words in Italian as he pled with God to heal her and keep her child safe. Then Claudio went to Alexander's side of the bed and prayed over him as well. Alexander understood most of it and was glad the others couldn't. His friend spoke of his mistakes and asked on his behalf for Alexander to be forgiven and allowed a full life with his wife and child.

When he finished, Alexander looked to his best friend and said in faltering Italian, "I do my best. If they die, so will I."

"I will pray for them morning, noon, and night," Claudio replied in his native tongue.

Darla passed glasses of lemonade to Henry and Claudio. Only after she and the priest declared it terrific did Henry brave a taste.

"It's just like my mama makes. How'd you learn that?"

Alexander laughed. "My housekeeper in Louisiana. I was helpless until she showed me kitchen basics."

When the drinks were gone, and Lucy had eaten two pieces of toast, Darla helped her to the bathroom before showing Alexander how much of the sleeping draught to give her. Alexander saw Claudio, Henry, and Darla into the hall.

"Don't give the sleep aide to her until she's in bed, and don't let her get up alone in the night," Darla told him in a hurried whisper. "I'll be over about seven-thirty, but call me if you have questions, or she takes a turn for the worse."

"Thank you, Darla." Alexander wrapped her in a hug.

"Hands off, Melling."

Darla stepped away, giving Henry an annoyed glare. "He's a grateful gentleman, you jealous husband."

"He's half-naked in his pajamas!"

Alexander took Darla by the hand. "But you didn't mind. Does that mean you'd be up to teaching me to Turkey Trot?"

Darla laughed. "In your dreams, Alex. Go to Lucy. We'll let ourselves out the backdoor."

"Would you put a note on the counter asking Naomi to come to see me?"

"Of course. I don't want you leaving Lucy alone until we see how she reacts to the medication."

Alexander nodded in agreement and cuffed Henry's shoulder. "Thanks for being a sport. I appreciate you both."

Seeing Lucy look drowsy when he entered the room cheered Alexander enough for a smile.

"Come to me, Angel."

"You're the only one who ever called me such. Even as a boy, I was a rascal despite my tender years and unmarred face." He crawled over her prone form. "You're the angel, my queen. Your touch changed my life."

"And yours made me a woman." Her eyes closed, lips smiling.

Alexander had to kiss them. She returned the affections for a moment and then was still. Dropping to her side, his hand went to her chest. Satisfied at her rhythmic breathing, he lowered his hand under the covers to rest on her middle. Their child stirred within.

"God strengthen them," he whispered, settling himself beside Lucy's sleeping form.

***

A poke to his shoulder roused Alexander. Naomi's wide stare beside the bed with her blind eye greeted him. Standing, he paused to see that Lucy still slept before taking Naomi's elbow and leading her to the hall.

"What's going on, Mr. Alex? She hasn't been looking good lately, but Miss Darla left a note saying she had to get medicine and she was going to sit with Lucy tomorrow."

Alexander explained the stress on Lucy because of his folly in getting Opal home, as well as the plans for her to rest the next few days.

"I'll sit with her Tuesday," she said. "Wednesday if needed as well. I can do late suppers after you arrive home, no problem."

"Arriving early and staying late won't be an issue for you?"

"It's just dragging these bones across town at a different time."

"Would you want to stay over in one of the guest rooms the next few nights to save yourself the commute?"

"I wouldn't want to impose, Mr. Alex."

"It's no inconvenience. Lucy would insist on it as well." Alexander squeezed her arm. "When you come tomorrow afternoon, bring enough things for a few days and choose which room you'd like."

"I always fancied the yellow one."

"Then it shall be yours. Don't worry about supper tonight. I'm not hungry, but if you could fix something that will be easy for Darla to prepare for her and Lucy's noon dinner, I'd appreciate it." He took the tray loaded with the lemonade and toast remains off the side table and gave it to her. "Just leave a note for Darla about the food. I appreciate it, Naomi."

"You make sure you rest too, Mr. Alex. I'll lock up on my way out."

He kissed her cheek and returned to the bed. Lucy slept on without disturbance, and Alexander nestled against her.

In the middle of the night, he woke to her screaming as she pushed him away.

His arms went around her shoulders, and he pulled her closer. "Lucy, it's all right. You were dreaming." As she quieted, he kissed beneath her ear. "What can I do for you?"

She rested her cheek against his chest, lithe arms hugging him. "I'm thirsty."

"I'm going to turn on the light." He let go of her to reach the side table lamp, but she clung to him, following his movement with her own. He blinked at the brightness and looked to the mantel clock: quarter-past midnight. Lucy had slept eight hours but still needed more. A tray with a pitcher of water and glasses sat on the table by the fireplace.

"Thank you, Naomi," he muttered.

The darkness around Lucy's eyes had lessened, and he trailed a finger along her jaw. "I need to go across the room to get your water. Will you survive without me?"

"I'll try." She tilted toward him and closed her eyes.

He could no more deny her a kiss than he could stop loving her. With tenderness, he cupped her pale face in his palms and brushed his lips across hers. They were dry, so he licked his own before pressing in for more, hoping to relieve some of her discomfort. Her kiss in return was desperate as her cool hands went for his waistband.

Alexander ran his hands down her neck to her shoulders and the entire length of her arms until he gathered her hands in his to still her frenzy. "Lucy, allow me to get your water. Stay here a moment, all right?"

She nodded, and he propped the pillows behind her so she could sit with support. The water in the pitcher must have been filled with ice because it was still cold. After she drank half the glass, Alexander helped her to the bathroom and filled the sink with warm water to wash her face.

"Will it be like this when I'm old and frail?" she asked as he patted her face dry with a fluffy towel.

"I pray it is. I want nothing more than to love and honor you all the days of my life. Forgive me, yet again, for causing you pain."

Hugging her to his chest, he felt her weakening and hurried her back to bed. Lucy swallowed more water, and then the light was off as Alexander snuggled against her.

"Try to sleep again, Lucy."

"Can I do anything for you?" she whispered.

"Sleep tonight and relax all day tomorrow. Will you do that for me, my queen?"

She kissed his neck where Frederick had him earlier by the throat. "Anything to please you."

Twenty-Four

The stillness of the pre-dawn air woke Melissa. It was warm for October, and she felt herself aching for crisp autumn days and early snowfall. It probably had something to do with Freddy's stand-offish attitude since he returned from the Mellings' the day before, but she was homesick for New York.

"How was Lucy?" Melissa had finally asked when she climbed into bed with him the previous night.

"I haven't seen her look that bad since she was hospitalized after the attack." Then he turned his back to her and clicked off his side table lamp.

It was a long, miserable night for her though Freddy's breathing turned rhythmic. Melissa hoped Monday would be better—for both Lucy and Freddy. Her hopes weren't high for herself because the girls had clamored for Lucy when their father said they'd have to stay home with Melissa the next few days. Never had she felt so unloved by the girls than when their tears began to fall, though she knew it was over not seeing their mother rather than being in her company.

She tentatively touched Freddy's shoulder. Nothing. She scooched closer until she nestled against his broad back. Wishing he slept without a shirt, Melissa ran a hand around his pajamas until she had one arm about his chest.

"Beloved," he breathed as he laid his hand over hers.

"I love you, Freddy. Please don't pull away." Her whispered words ruffled the wave of hair on his head.

"Melissa." He turned onto his back, pulling her on top of him and kissing her lips. "I'm sorry."

She tucked her head under his chin, relaxing into his warmth. "You don't need to worry alone. I'm here for you."

"I know you are. I'm sorry for shutting you out yesterday. If I do that again, you have permission to box my ears."

Melissa held her position, enjoying the sensation of being in his arms.

"Goosy looked near dead like she hadn't slept in days. And she's lost weight, which is dangerous at this point in her pregnancy. She was always robust and healthy with Phoebe and Bethany. It scared me to see her like that."

"I'm sure Darla will be able to help." Melissa trailed his biceps.

"Yes, and Alex finally understands what he did inviting that devil home, though it's too late to stop it." Freddy's hands came to rest at her hips. "I nearly strangled him, but I left it as a threat to do so if she dies."

"Surely she won't—"

"She's weak and looked to have nothing left in reserve to call upon." Freddy rolled to the side, releasing his hold on Melissa. They lay facing each other as he gathered his thoughts. "I'd never been scared of losing her until I walked into her room yesterday. Yes, she was lost to me personally when Alex came back two years ago, but we still share the girls. They need her. Even with you around, they need their mother."

"Have hope, Freddy."

"I put on a brave face for Phoebe and Bethany, but this is what I'm dealing with."

Melissa brought a hand to his beard, trailing her thumb across his lips. "Let it out before we open the door to the girls."

"I'm tense and tired over my fears."

"May I help you in other ways?" Her hands went to the buttons on his shirt, releasing the top two. When he didn't stop her, she opened the rest and caressed his chest.

"That feels amazing." Freddy kissed her and brought his own hands around her. "But I don't have anything to give in return. I'm sorry, Melissa."

She nodded and smiled to herself, determined to refill him so he'd have the emotional means necessary to reciprocate. Caressing massages, slight kisses on his face and torso, and all manner of subtle attention were what she showered him with as the sun brightened their room.

Half an hour later, Freddy returned the sensual attention with a firm grip at her waist. Brown eyes intense with an air of need, he whispered, "I'm ready, Beloved."

Passion released, they were upon each other. Shared intimacies revisited as Melissa gave her all to expel the feelings of isolation. Their throbbing desires left them breathless amid tangled sheets, but Freddy continued kissing as though thirsty for her taste.

"Forgive my neglect." His breath was a warm breeze across her sweat-dampened skin. "I'm still getting used to having your support. Your care is a blessing like no other, Melissa. I didn't mean to hurt you by turning away."

"You sure know how to make it up to me."

"I've only just begun, but we may have to continue tonight."

"Don't stop now." She beguiled him with a smile and touch.

They managed another pinnacle before the patter of feet struck the hallway. Clinging to her husband, Melissa initiated another deep kiss.

"Is it just me," he murmured in her ear, "or is this getting better the longer we're together."

An unbridled laugh escaped as she gazed into his eyes. "The practicalities of getting to know each other are past, leaving us free to explore the experience itself. It's like traveling. On your first visit to a city, you see the obvious sights and eat at the well-known restaurants. But each time you return, you dig deeper for those lesser-known places. Their beauty and talent is equal to or surpasses the more talked-about ones, but they've escaped notice until you discover them."

"That's beautiful." He kissed her thoroughly. "You're beautiful. All of you."

His attention brought forth another laugh.

Phoebe knocked on the door. "Daddy! Sissa! We're awake!"

"We'll be out in a minute, Phoebe," Freddy called. With a nibbling kiss at her ear, he hugged Melissa once more. "And, yes, we'll continue exploring tonight, Beloved."

***

After eating their midday meal, Melissa gathered the girls, clean sheets of paper, and a fresh box of crayons at their table in the study.

"We're going to make cards for your mother and deliver them to Miss Naomi."

"I want to give my card to Momma myself." Phoebe crossed her arms.

"I don't think that's possible today, but having Miss Naomi bring them to her will be just as much of a surprise." Melissa handed Bethany an orange crayon, and the girl immediately scribbled across the page with bold motions. "Maybe we could find a few flowers along the way to bring as well."

"Mums! Golden mums for the golden maiden!" Phoebe declared with the flourish of Alex and the sincerity of Freddy.

"I think Mrs. Conner has some in her yard. I bet she'll allow us a few if we ask. Remind me to bring a jar of water with us."

"Yes, Sissa."

Phoebe concentrated on drawing a castle with a Rapunzel-type woman hanging her hair out of the tower window, a knight and horse on the lawn beneath her. Every time Bethany tried to eat a crayon, Melissa gave her a new color so her paper would be cheerful and distract her from chewing on them. The final step was writing GET WELL SOON, MOMMA on a slate for Phoebe to copy the letters onto her page.

They pulled Bethany's perambulator out so she could ride if she grew tired. In the pram, there was room for Pinky, Rummy, and Baby, as well as the jar for flowers and the cards. Melissa tied on the girls' sunhats and a straw hat for herself since she couldn't hold her parasol and push the buggy at the same time.

Down Catherine Street they strolled, Phoebe chatting at every living thing she passed from butterfly to human. When they reached the Conner house near Government Street, Phoebe held the gate open for Melissa and Bethany to enter and then walked up the front steps and knocked on the door while the other two waited at the foot of the stairs.

The maid opened the door. "Why hello, Miss Davenport."

"Good afternoon, Miss May." Phoebe had learned the names of all the neighbors and their help on the walks Melissa took the girls on. "Is Mrs. Conner in? I have a question for her."

"She sure is. Let me get her right quick."

Mrs. Conner came onto the porch in a lace day dress. "Hello, Phoebe. And Mrs. Davenport and Bethany. What a surprise. Would you like to come in for tea?"

She curtsied. "No, thank you, Mrs. Conner. We're on our way to Momma's house to deliver feel-better cards. She's sick in bed with the baby in her tummy, but I know she'd like to see your beautiful mums. Could we please take a few samples for her?"

"Your mother is ill?"

"Yes, ma'am. We can't stay with her for many days."

And by the sweet words of one earnest girl, gossip about Lucy Melling would spread through town. Melissa tried not to cringe.

"Well bless her heart, and yours too. You may pick as many chrysanthemums and anything else you'd like to brighten your mother's day. Be sure to allow Bethany to choose some as well."

"Thank you, Mrs. Conner." Phoebe curtsied and ran to collect the jar and Bethany. She glowed like never before as she prepared the gift for her mother. A blonde angel of a girl with her dark-haired sister at her side, hand-in-hand gathering blossoms.

Melissa smoothed her beige walking suit and met Mrs. Conner at the foot of the steps.

"Thank you for allowing them this moment," Melissa said. "I'm afraid our yard is mostly spring flowers. I'll have to look into planting more things to extend the colors year-round."

"It's no trouble, Mrs. Davenport. My boys want nothing to do with my garden. They aren't allowed in the front because they're prone to tear things up with their play." She smiled knowingly at Melissa. "But I must say you're an asset to the neighborhood. Your family is a joy. The girls are so polite and lovely. You've done well with them."

"All the credit goes to my husband and Lucy. I've only been in their lives half a year."

"Everyone knows Mr. Davenport is a fine father, but their mother never did half as much for them as what you do. She was rarely seen in public and only sporadically since Mr. Melling returned. And usually, it's just the two of them causing a stir, not her with the girls."

Melissa smiled politely. "Most mothering is done in the home, not in the presence of others. Mrs. Melling loves her daughters and has taught them well. Thank you again for your generosity."

When the jar was full, Phoebe returned to the porch to show Mrs. Conner what they'd gathered.

"You have a fine eye for arrangement, Phoebe. That's a good thing for a lady to know. I hope they cheer your mother."

Phoebe curtsied and helped Bethany do so as they both thanked her.

Then the Davenports were back on their way, the jar tucked under the corner of the padding inside the pram. When they reached Government Street, Melissa put Bethany into the buggy. The girl sat peacefully and held her doll. Phoebe walked with a hand on the push bar and the other holding Rummy. They waited a minute for the streetcar to pass and the automobiles to stop. Crossing the wide road, they safely arrived on the south side for the final leg of their journey.

When they reached the Mellings' mansion, they made their way up the driveway to the back gate. They parked the perambulator on the patio and removed the jar and cards before making their way to the kitchen door.

Naomi answered their knock. "What a surprise! I've got some shortbread cookies fresh from the oven."

"We came with presents for Momma." Phoebe held out the jar and her card.

"But they know you'll have to deliver them," Melissa added.

"We'll see about that. For now, you sweet things sit at the table and allow me to get you cookies and milk." When Naomi turned to the icebox, she nodded Melissa to the door and pointed up.

As Melissa neared the master suite, Darla reading something about Mr. Knightley filled the air. *Emma* by Jane Austen, one of her favorites. *Is there no wonder I love Freddy? He's just as honorable as that fictional man.* It took a moment of her standing in the doorway for Lucy to notice her. She was paler than usual, with dark smudges around her eyes, but not as bad off as she expected from Freddy's attitude. Lucy smiled, and when Darla reached the end of the paragraph, she turned in the wingback chair that was pushed close to the bed.

"Melissa, come in. Lucy slept sixteen hours last night and three more today so far, but there's still more catching up to do."

On closer inspection, the exhaustion was more apparent. Lucy's skin appeared dry, her shoulders and collar bones more pronounced.

Melissa hugged her in greeting. "The girls have something for you, but they know they might not be able to deliver it themselves. Naomi is feeding them cookies for the moment."

"Did you walk all the way here?" Lucy's voice was dry.

"Yes, but Beth rode in the pram half the time."

Lucy nodded and smiled. "They've always loved taking walks."

Melissa turned to Darla. "Could they come a moment, or would it be better not to?"

"Just for a minute." Darla stood and took Lucy's hand. "And don't be mad when I shoo them out. But first, let me get your night cream, and you need to drink more, Lucy. Your skin's as thirsty as your insides."

She handed her a glass of water before going to the dressing table. Lucy drank half the contents, and then Darla applied the cream to her face, neck, arms, and hands. "Someone once told me night cream was a good luxury to use on your hands when they're overly dry. I now use it after every delivery because my hands and arms are raw from scrubbing."

Melissa smiled over the memory. "I'm glad it's helped you."

Darla went downstairs to fetch Lucy's tea tray and get the girls.

"Melissa, did Freddy thank you for me?"

He said hardly two sentences to me when he came home from his visit, she wanted to say but nodded instead.

"Well, let me tell you anyway. Thank you for loving our girls and caring for them when I can't be there."

"They're wonderful, Lucy. I'm happy to help you and Freddy."

And then they were there, entering without a bounce or skip like little ladies to the bedside.

Bethany handed her paper first and patted her arm. "Momma, love. Get better."

Melissa lifted Bethany so Lucy could kiss her cheek. Then Bethany went to Darla by the door, and Phoebe approached.

"I love you, Momma. Feel better so we can play here." She handed her the drawing. "That's you and Daddy. Poppy locked you in the tower."

Lucy's laugh wasn't as loud as usual, but Darla seemed to find it a good sign as she smiled at Melissa.

"It's wonderful, Phoebe. And the flowers are for me, too?"

"Bethany and I picked, and I arranged them."

"They're beautiful, just like you both. Would you put them on my side table, Phoebe Camellia?"

"Yes, Momma." She did so and leaned up to kiss her mother. "Rest good, fair maiden. I love you."

Lucy brought a hand to her cheek. "You're as valiant as your father, and that's a wonderful thing."

Twenty-Five

Alexander took his riding time first thing Monday morning, spent the middle of the day in his pathetic office, and then went to the train station—smoking as he paced the platform at three o'clock.

"Melling." Edmund clapped his shoulder with unnecessary force. "Maxwell and I thought it best a member of the family was here to greet her."

Alexander blew a ring of smoke at him. "And I'll never fill that role, will I?"

"You know what I mean. An Easton!"

"The nicest thing about Opal's letters is that she addresses me as a brother. 'Dearest brother' in most cases. Maybe you could learn a thing about politeness from her."

Edmund laughed. "You'll never be my dearest anything. And Opal was always one to play sweet to get her way."

Alexander's jaw tightened. Everyone knew Opal had played him, and he didn't appreciate having an audience when he met her. "Am I still entrusted to bring her to your parents' house, or has that been decided it's best for a *real* family member to do as well?"

"Cool your heels and give me a cigarette. Bringing her home is all for you to glory in. Mother will be pleased. That's why you did it, isn't it? Win the favor of your in-laws after a rocky start with Lucy, both in ruining her and then causing a divorce."

Alexander felt the heat rush to his face as he passed a cigarette to Edmund.

"You think you're sly, but you're an open book, Melling."

"Like I've told you before," Alexander's voice was icy, "we don't all have your smooth, Easton ways. But at least I didn't become a fat, whoring slob for years on end."

Edmund's smile dropped, and he brushed his mustache with the hand that held the unlit cigarette. "You always liked cheap shots, but I bested you, and you know it. Whether it was fighting or winning the hand of the brightest debutante at a ball, I came out on top."

"Your Easton charm served you well over the years. I'll not deny your family is superior to mine in that regard. You're all players in one way or another."

"Even Lucy?" Edmund teased as he took a drag.

Alexander's smile was bittersweet, thinking of the way she was ready to heighten their love affair when they dated. Not to mention the way she played Mr. Noble and his staff with her Southern charm, though it was Melissa who won the magazine column with that name. "She might be the best of all."

The train came in with a thunderous noise. The hiss of the steam and the commotion of the porters clamored about the platform. In her last letter, Opal mentioned she didn't like crowds and planned to wait until the other passengers disembarked before exiting the train. Alexander stepped to the side, but Edmund stayed near the front of the multitude.

When the crowd began to thin, Edmund looked back to him and shrugged. Over Edmund's shoulder, the shine of uncovered brass-toned hair caught Alexander's eye. The navy traveling suit fit her young figure like a second skin beneath her proud Easton chin and eyes shining with intrigue.

Edmund turned back to the train and rushed to his sister. Alexander watched the man behind her. A hand was on the small of her back, his other holding a decidedly feminine traveling case. The man lowered his touch when Edmund was close enough to hug Opal. Alexander discarded his cigarette before advancing.

"What a pleasant surprise, Edmund," Opal's voice was rich, deeper than it was eight years before. "I wasn't expecting to see anyone but Alexander when I arrived. There he is. I'd know those blue eyes anywhere, though you've changed otherwise, dear brother."

She embraced Alexander and kissed his unshaven cheek. "And what of me? Am I not all grown?" She spun, a hand on her shapely hip, and winked an emerald eye at the man behind her.

"You're a lovely young woman, Opal," Alexander said. "It's good to see you."

"I have to get back to the office, but I'll be sure to tell Maxwell we've still got the prettiest sisters in the state." Edmund hugged her once more. "Behave for Alex."

Opal smiled after Edmund as the man behind her slipped her case into her hand and took a slinking step away.

"May I have an introduction to your chaperone?"

The young man froze, and his dark eyes shifted as he lowered his derby over his brow.

"I told you he was clever, Bruce." The man stopped and adjusted his cheap suit. "Alexander, this is Bruce Youngblood. He's an orderly at the asylum. Show him your papers, Bruce."

"That won't be necessary." Alexander took the case from Opal. "But isn't it unusual for a lady of your tender age to be sent alone with a man?"

"In the asylum, we're treated more like livestock than humans. I doubt anyone there sees me as a woman."

Alexander gave Bruce the Melling stare. "I'd have to refute that, Opal. I'm sure there are several appreciative eyes that glory in your femininity."

She gave a light-hearted laugh. "I'd forgotten what a charmer you are. Lucille is lucky to have you. Bruce has relatives in town and was more than happy to travel with me for the express purpose to visit his cousins for a day before heading back to work tomorrow."

"Then there will be no further need for him to see you." Alexander took her arm. "Thank you for bringing her. Good afternoon, Mr. Youngblood."

Opal stepped toward Bruce, shook his hand, and mouthed something to him Alexander wasn't quick enough to catch.

"Where are your luggage tickets?" Alexander asked once Opal was on his arm.

"I only have one. Asylum life doesn't afford the extravagance of large collections. Does Lucille still have oodles of books?"

"More books than dresses, and that's saying a lot." Alexander took the ticket from her, and she pointed out her trunk. A porter brought it to his automobile, and he tipped the worker before helping Opal into the front seat.

"Is Lucy as lovely as ever?" Opal asked once he climbed in beside her.

"Most assuredly."

"The city is busier than I remember, and some of these new buildings are massive." Opal continued to chatter about what they passed on their journey, asking especially to be driven by the cathedral.

"Do you still attend?" she asked.

"Yes, though I typically do Sunday Mass at St. Mary's as it was closer to the old house."

"But your heart is still here." It was more a statement than a question.

"My heart is with Lucy," he replied.

"And you and Lucille attended the cathedral while you were courting."

He saw no reason to reply to her pointed remark.

Opal motioned to his gloves. "I heard about the fire. Are you so disfigured that you hide behind leather and that pathetic attempt at a beard?"

"It's not too bad, but it saves me from stares and questioning."

"Surely everyone knows the story. I doubt it would be a shock, especially with you being so handsome. No one would stare at your marks with those crisp eyes of yours to admire."

He gave her a brief smile, and she settled into silence with a pleased grin.

When Alexander parked in front of the Eastons' home, Opal huffed.

"So Mother and Father were sent to this shack while Lucille got the house."

"It's a lovely home and the right size for them. And Lucy didn't get the house, she bought it at a fair price with her own money, and then Frederick bought it from her when we moved into my parents' house."

"Will I even get a room here, or will I have to sleep in a cupboard?"

"Your mother set the guest room exquisitely. Do be grateful."

"*Our mother*, dear brother. You have no family left, from what I've heard."

"I have out-of-town cousins and the like, but Eliza and my parents are gone from this world."

"Then you need us Eastons as much as we need you." Opal held his gaze with a sharp intelligence before breezing up the front walk, much like Alexander would have pictured Eliza doing.

He followed with her small case and stepped around the Eastons as they greeted their youngest on the porch. After depositing the luggage in the front bedroom, he returned to his automobile. Maxwell pulled to a stop behind him and hopped out of his vehicle in time to help Alexander carry the trunk. He dropped his end in the living room to greet his youngest sibling before rejoining Alexander.

"Edmund was right," he told him as they went down the little hall. "She has the best features of Lucy and the twins combined. I'm glad I don't have to worry about chasing suitors away from her. Susan, Cora, and Emma all out in society at the same time was bad enough. Then Lucy gave Eddie fits when she started stepping out with you."

Alexander held his tongue in regards to Opal's virtue already being in question from her time on the train, not to mention what could have happened within the walls of the asylum. The stories he'd uncovered in his research attempting to find a new placement for her were not kind, especially when female patients were involved—things that made Hazel's stay in jail seem like a holiday.

Alexander followed Maxwell into the front room. "I'll be here at eight-thirty tomorrow to collect Opal for her doctor appointment."

Mrs. Easton held out her hand, and Alexander kissed the back of it.

"Thank you for getting her home to us. There's a family supper party for her birthday Friday night. Don't forget to tell Lucy."

"Thank you, but she's on bed rest the next several days, doctor's orders."

"Anything I can do?" Mrs. Easton asked.

"You enjoy your time with Opal. I'm sure Lucy will be back on her feet soon enough."

"Give her our love," Mr. Easton said from his chair.

"Yes, sir."

Maxwell threw an arm around his shoulders as he held the door for Alexander. "You better take care of Lucy," he whispered.

"Until my last breath, I swear it."

***

"It smells wonderful in here, Naomi."

"Shortbread cookies are in the jar, and I'm prepping for fried chicken."

"You're the best." Alexander kissed her cheek as he removed his gloves to get at the cookies. "How's Lucy?"

"She's looking a mite better and accepted a few callers this afternoon. Don't you get upset," she said when he frowned. "Those girls walked all the way over with drawings and flowers, and Miss Darla wasn't going to send them away. They delivered their presents and were out of the room in two minutes, though Miss Lucy's smile has lasted long past that. I stuffed them with cookies, and then they were on their way with Miss Melissa."

"I'm sure their visit was more of a blessing to her than anything. Frederick will come by some time as well. Be sure to send him up."

Alexander left his briefcase and outerwear in his den before going upstairs. He found Lucy propped on a pile of white pillows, wearing a sky blue gown. Her eyes were closed as she listened to Darla read from one of the romance novels she collected. Ignoring the midwife, Alexander slowly climbed onto the bed, sitting on his knees beside Lucy. She smiled before she opened her eyes.

Darla went for the door. "I'll give you a few minutes."

Lucy immediately went for his necktie. "I love sensing you coming to me. The smell of you, the sound of your breath, the shifting of the bed when you join me, and the vision of your open shirt—it's as thrilling as ever."

"It's titillating to come to you, my queen." He leaned closer so she could open the buttons at his neck easier. "You look happy, and those are some lovely flowers."

"Melissa brought the girls. I tucked their pictures for me into the mirror frame in the bathroom. Wasn't that thoughtful of Melissa to go to that trouble?"

"Very considerate. I'm glad they brightened your day." He kissed her gently, but she wrapped her arms about him, holding him to her as she deepened it.

"You brighten my days and nights." Her breathy voice left a trail of longing across his skin.

He straddled her legs, supporting himself with a hand on the headboard to keep his weight off her. She quickly opened the rest of his shirt, and her hands progressed down his torso. A pleasurable moan escaped his parting lips, and he pressed in to taste her neck as she worked his belt free.

"Alex!" Darla's voice cut through their moment of hunger. "You're incorrigible!"

"It was my fault." Lucy played along the faint line of hair below his navel. "I was trying to see if I could seduce him without moving more than my hands."

"I think we all know Alex doesn't need an excuse. A mosquito could give him the eye, and he'd—"

Alexander fell on his back, laughing.

"You've always been absurdly cruel to him, Darla, but a mosquito!" Then Lucy's silver giggle broke through as well.

Darla crossed her arms over her ample bosom and tried to frown. "If you don't need anything, I'll be on my way."

"I need a shower, but I could bring Lucy with me." He winked.

"She's already had hers today," Darla's voice was firm.

He looked to his wife. "Tomorrow, I'll see to it. Don't let anyone else accompany you."

"I wouldn't dream of it."

"Get in there." Darla waved him away. "And don't step out unless you're fully dressed."

Lucy's bright smile was enough encouragement for him to attempt another kiss before shutting himself in the marble bathroom. After showering, he stood with a towel about his waist before the foggy mirror. Phoebe and Bethany's drawings curled at the corners from the humidity in the room. Swiping a patch of mirror clean, his gaze traveled from his arms to his chest to his face. He leaned closer, rubbing the scraggly beard that was never quite enough to cover the discoloration. With a swift movement, he turned on the sink and pulled his neglected shaving kit from the cabinet.

He expected the razor to hurt, but the shaving cream soothed his face unaccustomed to the action he used to partake of daily. The marks weren't as bad as he figured they'd be—not like what marred his hands and arms. A reddish splotch on his lower right cheek noted the side closest to his father when he yelled for Douglas to take Magdalene out of the house. The worst, a mottled area of white-brown-red, marked his left jaw from where his father flung his burning shirt back at him the moment they were alone.

"I may have your name and house, but I'm not you," he said to the shadow of George Melling he felt standing over him more often those days.

Hoping to sneak up behind Darla, Alexander opened the bathroom door with a smooth motion. Frederick sat on the edge of the bed with a hand on Lucy's cheek as he whispered. Her gaze was one of rapt adoration, and an ache opened beneath Alexander's scarred chest. Catching his breath before advancing, he went for the dresser rather than interrupt the tender scene.

"Alex," Lucy called to him, "come join us."

"I'm sure Freddy would appreciate it if I dressed first."

"He doesn't care, do you?" Lucy touched Frederick's arm. "You are around all those men at the gym. Alex in his towel must be nothing to you."

Frederick's eyes narrowed, and his fists clenched. "It's your home, though I prefer not to see the scars. It reminds me of all the people he's hurt."

"They remind me of all he's overcome."

Lucy's devotion surged through his veins as Alexander stepped into the bathroom to slip on his pajamas. The paisley print set had a loose cut, and he kept the shirt unbuttoned to annoy Frederick.

Lucy's gaze fell on Alexander's face for the first time when he returned. Holding her arms out to him, he boldly stepped between her and Frederick. Her fingers danced across his face and pulled him closer. Kissing his marks, she then trailed her lips along his smooth jaw and cheeks.

"You're as handsome as ever, Alex." Lucy released his chin and kissed him on the mouth, which he happily returned.

Alexander sat beside Lucy on the bed. "Did Darla go home?"

"Yes, after Freddy arrived. She wanted to save herself from your possible exploits after showering."

"Darla is a smart woman." Alexander brought Lucy's hand to his lips to kiss the back of it and then kept hold as he dropped it to his lap. "You are welcome to visit as long as you like, Freddy, but I plan on staying with Lucy until I leave in the morning. Naomi is sleeping in a guest room the next few nights, so she'll be here as well."

"Were you successful in bringing the prodigal daughter home?" Frederick's tone was deadly.

Alexander turned to Lucy. "Would you like to hear?"

Frederick flushed as though realizing he was the means of bringing Lucy stress when it was the last thing she needed.

Her smile was tight. "I'd rather know."

"She arrived not long after Eddie joined me. It appears the family wanted a real member of the Eastons there to greet her. Her chaperone was a shifty-eyed young orderly who I don't trust an inch. They appeared to have some sort of understanding, but Eddie didn't notice because he was blinded by Opal."

"She's pretty?"

"Not as fine as you, my queen, but she has the charm you Eastons possess. Maxwell showed up at the house in time to help me with her trunk. He and Eddie proclaimed they have the prettiest sisters in Alabama. I'd have to agree solely based on you." He kissed her temple with a lingering quality.

"So, what's to be done with her?" Frederick demanded.

"I bring her to a few medical appointments tomorrow to check her overall health. The psychiatric appointment is on Thursday. I think your mother wants to take her shopping and around town on Wednesday. And there's a family supper for Opal's birthday Friday, but I told your mother you were on bed rest and wouldn't be up to it."

"Thank you."

"She sends her love, of course. Your father, too."

Lucy smiled and closed her eyes. "I'd like to rest now."

Whether it was her way of changing the subject or escaping, Alexander didn't know. He squeezed her hand.

"I'll stop in tomorrow, Lucy." Frederick kissed her forehead. "I'm glad you got to see the girls today. We all love you."

Her eyes cracked open. "I love you all as well. Allow me to kiss you so you may send it to the girls. One for each of them, and one for you."

Frederick leaned over her, and she kissed his cheeks and then quickly on the mouth. He jerked back, straightening. "Goosy, you—"

"I'm sorry. I'm not feeling myself." She feigned sleep with a slight smile on her naughty lips.

Twenty-Six

Melissa swung in the gazebo while the girls ran the length of the backyard with their play swords when the rumble of Freddy's automobile came into the porte-cochere. Phoebe led the battle cry toward the returning king. The squeal of the girls being thrown into the air pierced the autumn twilight like lights from the New York City skyline. Just as Melissa was about to stand, Phoebe's voice rang out.

"Sissa is in the castle. She took us to see Momma!"

"So I heard," Freddy's voice carried across the lawn with conviction. "You all made your mother very happy. Give me a few minutes, and then we'll go in for supper."

Freddy paused in the doorway of the gazebo. He looked depleted, body and soul. Melissa went to stand, but he raised his hand and started for the swing.

"Work extra hard at the gym?" she asked as he leaned over for a kiss.

He opened his suit coat buttons and sat beside her. "I had to get them out of my veins."

Melissa leaned against Freddy's side for a hug. His arm went around her shoulders, tucking her closer. After several moments of silence, Freddy spoke again.

"At least she looks better today. I appreciate you bringing the girls over." He lifted her chin and kissed her lips. "Naomi and Darla said that's what brightened her the most."

"It gave purpose to our afternoon. Finding ways to keep them entertained the next few days will be the trouble."

"We'll be on the train in a week."

"I look forward to it." Melissa's hand went to his knee with a caressing motion. "I hope you don't mind, but I asked Sharon to come every day through Friday to cook supper. We'll be at Alex's Saturday, and I'll cover the difference for—"

His mouth went to hers with a searching intensity that drew her to his lap. They indulged a minute, and then both returned to respectable locations as the girls sounded closer.

"I have no trouble paying Sharon. It doesn't matter to me who cooks, as long as I'm eating with you. And as for our vacation next week, I telephoned the hotel today to check our reservations, and one of their suites had a vacancy. I changed our reservations so we'll have two bedrooms and a sitting room. The girls will have to share a bed, but they shouldn't mind. We'll load up Beth's side with pillows so she won't roll off."

"Our own room!" Melissa was back on his lap, arms around his neck. "That makes everything perfect, Freddy. Thank you!"

He laughed as a hand slipped up her blouse. "It was purely selfish on my part."

"I'll never complete my itinerary."

"I wish you the best of procrastination each day, Beloved."

In the place they had married, Melissa and Freddy were heedless of the darkening sky or the girls frolicking in the yard as they expressed their love. Only when Bethany tugged at Melissa's skirt did they separate.

"Supper, Sissa."

Melissa happily took the almost two-year-old into her arms when she stood. "Bethany Iris Davenport, your father is the best man in the world."

Freddy put his arm around Melissa and leaned closer to his youngest. "And your Sissa is the smartest, sexiest woman in the universe."

"Embellishment isn't your thing."

"No exaggeration. Allow me to convince you at bedtime." His hand roamed down her back as they walked to the house.

When they were all washed, they gathered to one end of the massive dining room table. Flounder, rice, and turnip greens— something Melissa had not yet grown accustomed to—were the main fair.

"How would you ladies like to go to the diner for breakfast tomorrow?"

"Yes, Daddy! I like the waffles." Phoebe bounced in her chair.

"Waffles." Bethany smiled.

"You girls get to bed early, and I'm sure Sissa will have an adventure for you in the morning."

Phoebe looked to Melissa with her wide blue-green eyes. "What type of adventure?"

Knowing it was worth the effort for more time that night with Freddy, Melissa would come up with something. "The best city adventure yet."

Bethany's big brown eyes were just as enthralled. "Adventure with Sissa."

"Eat up, Beth!" Phoebe shoved a spoonful of buttered rice into her mouth.

Freddy caught Melissa's gaze across the table and winked.

After supper, Freddy took the girls upstairs for their baths. Melissa settled at her desk with a fresh sheet of paper. She began by marking two columns of five squares two inches in size. Within each square, she did simple sketches of things they could find downtown: an automobile, horse, church, bank, bench, peanuts, hat, gloves, briefcase, and a soda bottle. She fastened the paper to a clipboard along with a pen on a piece of yarn so the girls could check things off as they found the items. When their scavenger hunt was complete, they would go for ice cream.

Melissa left the board on her desk and turned off the lights in the rooms she passed. The dining room and kitchen were set to rights, and Sharon was gone, so Melissa climbed the stairs.

Freddy stepped out of the hall bathroom shirtless, his trousers spotted with water. "They're a bit exuberant over the idea of an adventure, but every ounce of energy they expel in the bath means quicker sleep."

Melissa leaned against his warm skin, a hand exploring his muscles. "I prepared a scavenger hunt for them."

He lifted her off the floor and nuzzled her neck. "Make a list for me to accomplish tonight. Find the spot that makes Melissa moan. Find the place that makes her squirm in ecstasy. Find the tastiest spot to lick."

Melissa melted against him as his tongue worked her earlobe.

"Daddy, Beth's all done!"

Freddy hugged Melissa to him a moment longer. "Get yourself ready for bed. I'll see to the girls and come for you when they're settled."

She trailed her hands over him as he stepped away and then closed herself in their bedroom. Glad for the quiet time, Melissa drew a hot bath in the master suite's claw-foot tub. While she waited for it to fill, she brushed, braided, and twisted her hair into a bun atop her head to keep it dry. Lying back in the bathtub, she placed a small rolled towel behind her neck and closed her eyes, forgetting Lucy, the girls, and even her husband for the time.

"Every minute I watch, more bubbles disappear. I'm trying to calculate how much longer it will be before your gorgeous body is on display."

So relaxed—possibly asleep—she didn't hear Freddy enter. He stood beside the tub in his underdrawers, rubbing his beard in contemplation.

Melissa raised a hand to him. "Help me out and see it all now."

Freddy wrapped a towel about her shoulders when she stood. "Were you sleeping?"

"Possibly."

He carried her to their bedroom, standing her beside the bed as he sat on the edge, his warm gaze studying her as she dried. When she was almost done, he spoke. "You've been tired lately."

"I suppose I'm getting old, or maybe we're expending too much energy in here."

Laughing, he reached around her waist and tugged her to him. There was a spark in his eyes, and—it could have been her imagination—his hand seemed to linger low on her stomach.

He's perceptive. He'll have noticed I haven't claimed my monthly for longer than usual. He's already noticing my tiredness. But I'm not ready!

"We're still rising to our prime, Beloved, but I'll be leisurely tonight if you wish it."

Freddy's lips on her skin sent new vitality coursing through her. "Let's just see where this takes us."

***

Thursday morning, Melissa did nothing more than burrow in Freddy's embrace in the pre-dawn darkness. She wanted to give herself another thirty minutes to see if her mood changed, but she was content to feel his powerful arms about her. Melissa had asked him to sleep without his shirt so she could feel more of him when they lay together, and he happily complied. She was certain Freddy suspected a change within her. His hands were about her waist more than usual, and he asked morning and night how she was feeling. But neither spoke of the possibility of pregnancy. Nor did Melissa tell Darla her worries when she and Henry came over for supper after the men practiced at the gym the night before.

When the sunlight coming into the room proved it to be after six, Melissa tried to turn away from Freddy so she could rise, but he tightened his grip.

"I've been waiting patiently for you to make an advance, not an escape."

She laughed and leaned her head on his chest. "You could have said something."

His kiss felt like a warm cup of tea, and her nightgown nudged higher as his hand trailed up her leg. "I didn't wish to urge things along if you needed more rest."

"That's thoughtful of you." She kissed the hollow of his throat. "I do feel off this morning."

"Shall I make you some coffee? Breakfast?"

Melissa trailed her hands over his torso. "Offering is kind enough."

"Nonsense. Allow me to make breakfast today. I'll go down now unless you need something else from me first."

He managed to look both sultry and sweet, and she wanted more than anything to accept the offer for lovemaking. Settling for a stirring kiss, she absorbed his essence.

"I'm sorry, Freddy. Hopefully tonight."

"I'm happy to be of service in the kitchen rather than the bedroom. The girls and I have more fun than I ever thought possible with you in our lives. I love you, Melissa."

"Even when I've talked you into doing something you didn't want to do?"

He sighed. "It's like you said, Opal coming here when you and the girls are gone can't hurt anything. She lost most of her childhood because of what afflicts her, and it's the kind thing to do."

Melissa recalled the telephone conversation she'd had with Alex the day before. "It means a lot to Alex as well. He's sorry and hopes you forgive him for the pain it's caused, Lucy."

"She's *his* wife. He should have thought of Lucy first, but at least she's on the mend now. I'm glad you're staying with her today. She and the girls appreciate it." He kissed Melissa before picking his shirt off the bench at the foot of the bed.

They managed a quiet breakfast for two before the girls ran the upper hall. She saw to the girls so Freddy could dress for work, and then he dished out the girls' oatmeal while Melissa packed a day bag of items they might need at the other house.

The Davenports let themselves in the Mellings' kitchen door Alex left unlocked for them.

"Poppy! Momma! We're here!" Phoebe's voice carried through the hallway.

"There's my girls!" Alex ran down the stairs and sat on the bottom step. Melissa stared at his shaved face as she had the day before. It gave him an air of innocence that was at odds with what she knew about him. "Let me see Bethany Iris first, Phoebe Camellia. I spent time with you at the stable yesterday afternoon, but I hadn't seen this cherub in days as she was napping when I picked you up."

Though quieter, it was obvious Bethany loved Alex as much as her big sister. She hugged his neck with a grip that looked to rival her father's. Touching his smooth face, she kissed the discolored patches on his jaw like they were wounds needing a healing touch.

"Bad hurt, Poppy?"

"No, Bethany. They're all better."

"Momma?"

"She's sitting in bed until I can walk her down. She wanted me to rush to you first because she knows I've missed you."

"I'll see to Lucy." Freddy climbed the stairs around him.

After Bethany went for Melissa's hand, Phoebe jumped into Alex's lap.

"Knight Phoebe, be sure you tell Momma all about what you did yesterday with Starlight."

"I will, Poppy." She smacked a big kiss on his cheek and disappeared down the back hall.

Alex stood and smoothed the wrinkles from his trousers. "Are things more fulfilling at home, Melissa?"

"I've taken your advice," she said as he stepped closer, "and am enjoying the quick and intense moments, as well as the longer sessions."

He let out a whoop and left a kiss on her cheek. "My protégée has found success!"

Melissa laughed and blushed as Freddy reached the top of the stairs with Lucy. Her blonde locks shone around her shoulders like a halo, and her floral kimono shimmered under the stairwell chandelier. Her improvement was a hundredfold since Monday, and a twinge struck Melissa knowing that those two had made a handsome couple in their time together.

"Sorry it took us so long," Lucy said when they were half a dozen steps from the main floor. "I tried to talk Freddy into braiding my hair, but he refused."

"Good for him," Alex proclaimed. "I don't wish another man to touch your hair, my queen, even noble Frederick. Allow me to see to it. Where would you like to settle?"

"On the patio. I think the girls would enjoy playing in the yard. I'd rather be out before it gets too warm."

Freddy, still holding his ex-wife's arm, lifted Bethany with the other so Lucy could kiss her. "Come with us, Beth."

Alex followed the threesome outside, and Melissa went in search of Phoebe. She was making a pillow fort in the morning room but eagerly went for the backyard, her pink-clad form disappearing into the camellia maze.

Freddy hugged Melissa. "I'm going to go back to the house but will be at the office by ten. Telephone if you need anything."

She kissed him fully. "Thank you."

Alex finished Lucy's hair and patted Bethany's back, who sat in her mother's lap. When he stepped toward the door, he motioned Melissa over.

"Have you started?" he whispered.

She shook her head. "Nothing yet, but I think Freddy might suspect."

"He's been through it before. You should talk—"

"I'll talk to him and Darla when we return from St. Augustine. If things are only off, surely they'll regulate by then."

"One would think." He squeezed her hand and dashed inside.

Alex returned wearing his suit jacket and shoes, but gloveless. Wondering over his exposed scarring, Melissa couldn't help but touch his shaved cheek when he stopped at her chair to bid her farewell.

"Do you like it?" he questioned.

"You're handsome either way. I'm just curious as to the why."

He leaned to her ear. "I thought I'd see if people cringe when they look, but it appears women still wish to touch me."

She laughed and shoved him away.

Not long after Alex left, Bethany went in search of her sister. Traveling the length of the lawn together, Phoebe taught Bethany how to set wickets for a game of croquet.

Lucy lounged on the patio chaise, watching the girls. "I talked Alex and Frederick into allowing me to keep Bethany during the tournament Saturday. Naomi and Sharon will be here so that I won't be alone. Bethany was clingy at the last one, and she can't follow what's going on like Phoebe. I want you to be able to enjoy watching Frederick without balancing her on your lap the whole time."

"That's kind of you."

"And the Campbells and Walkers are coming to town. Maggie might want to stay with me since Simon is so young. Tabitha, too, though Maggie might have shopping plans with Claire. The Campbells stay in the hotel when the Walkers come and take rooms next to each other. After the last visit, I don't think Douglas is keen on having Maggie around Alex much."

Melissa raised an eyebrow, causing Lucy to laugh.

"That's about the look Douglas gives Alex. I think Douglas expected things between Alex and Maggie to tame after a while, but they're still shameless."

"Does it bother you?" Melissa asked with sincerity.

"Not usually, especially when he flirts with a friend, and she knows not to take him at face value. Like with you this morning. He was practically hugging you he was so close when Freddy brought me to the stairs, and you were laughing and blushing. Freddy clenched his fists, but I knew it was nothing. And then you touched his face, and he whispered to you before he left."

"I'm sorry if I was improper, Lucy."

"He craves validation. I give him all I can, but sometimes it's not enough. I don't mind him seeking kind words and admiration from our close friends. It's when he's beaten down and seeks that approval from other sources that it's dangerous. Heartbreaking."

Melissa had never heard Lucy speak of Alex in such a way. While she wasn't complaining or speaking ill of him, there was a vulnerability and depth of understanding in her acceptance of her atypical marriage that was beautiful. It showcased a level of maturity she hadn't seen in Lucy before.

"Should I—"

"No, Melissa. You two have a great bond, and I wouldn't change it for the world."

The driveway gate opened, and Darla came into the yard. She greeted Phoebe and Bethany while they continued to place the wickets.

"Darla gives him attention from her annoyance. I think she enjoys it but would never admit it."

Melissa still laughed when Darla reached the patio.

"Your color is great today, Lucy."

"I feel much better, thank you. Do I need to keep taking the sleeping aid?"

"I think it would be good for you to do so through the weekend, to make sure you stay caught up on rest," was Darla's polite way of letting her know she needed it as long as her sister was in town. She looked to Melissa. "I've got an hour before I need to leave for my first appointment."

"Would you like to play a round of croquet with Phoebe and me?"

"That'd be fun."

"Shall I get a book for you and Bethany?" Melissa asked Lucy.

"Yes. And a glass of iced tea, please. There should be a pitcher chilling."

Melissa returned with the requested items and saw Lucy settled with her youngest before joining Phoebe and Darla on the lawn. Phoebe handed out the mallets, and they began along the back fence, beyond the labyrinth entrance. They took turns—youngest to oldest—whacking the balls toward the house with lots of laughter between the players.

Halfway through the game, Phoebe was ahead a dozen feet. After a satisfying *crack*, her ball went through the designated arch. She swung her mallet in a victory dance before stepping to the side of the playing field for Darla to take her turn. The gate to the driveway she stood by opened. The movement caught Melissa's attention as a young man stepped boldly into the yard. He was dressed in a suit rather than a workman's uniform. The landscapers, grocery deliverers, and such would come unannounced into the yard but no one else. Melissa's intuition set her in motion toward her stepdaughter.

"Who are you?" Phoebe demanded of him before Melissa reached her side.

He grinned, a creeping closed-mouth smile, as he lowered his derby over his eyes. "Are you Phoebe?"

"Yes, but you're a stranger."

"Run to your mother." Melissa's hand went to Phoebe's shoulder with a gentle nudge while she memorized everything about the man she could. When Phoebe ran, his eyes followed the girl to her mother, where his gaze lingered on Bethany. Melissa set her mallet on her shoulder. "What is your business here?"

Seeing her poised to defend, he took a step toward the open gate. The smile left his face as Darla joined Melissa. "I think I have the wrong house. Good day, ladies."

He was gone as quick as he came.

"Did he strike you as odd?" Melissa asked her friend.

Darla shivered. "He reminds me of my cousin Richard's friend who used to hang around my uncle's house—and he was up to no good."

Twenty-Seven

The whole trip from the Eastons' new house to their old one consisted of Opal fidgeting. Whether it was from excitement or anxiety, Alexander didn't know—and didn't want to find out. Opal made it halfway through her week-long visit without issues, and he prayed it would stay that way.

Frederick stood on his front porch when they pulled into the driveway. Escorting Opal, Alexander slowed before the unwelcoming posture of their host.

"He looks intimidating with that beard," Opal whispered.

At the front steps, she released her hold on Alexander's arm and rushed to Frederick.

"Frederick Davenport, how I wish I could call you brother, but unfortunately, I wasn't here for those years." She threw her arms around him, but he didn't move to embrace her in return. "But you were always family, especially within these walls."

To her credit, she kept the smile when she stepped back though no kindness was shown.

"Before I open my door to you, you must agree to the rules."

"You don't need to be so formal. We're family here for a quick visit. Nothing more."

He stood like a mountain, unyielding and stern. "If you wish to enter, you have to follow my rules."

She clasped her hands before her tasteful green walking suit. "I'll listen, though your attitude is alarming. You've not even greeted me."

"I'm not happy to have you here. It was by my wife's urging that I've allowed you to come. The last day you were here, you changed everything."

"I was nothing but a child back then, Freddy. The events of that day that, as you say, 'changed everything' belong to him." She pointed to Alexander. "He was the catalyst, not me. Alexander and Lucille are the ones that provoked. By their sins was I driven to madness."

Alexander froze under the accusation. He couldn't deny it, but the fact that Opal had turned on him when she'd been so pleasant was a shock.

Frederick actually smiled. "You're still blaming others for your bad behaviors when you've claimed to have grown up."

She straightened her posture beneath his stare, adjusting her shoulders and chest in a way Alexander had often seen Eliza do in an attempt to get the man she was hunting to drop his guard.

But Frederick had none of it. "If you want to step a foot inside my house, you must stay in the same room with me at all times. No opening drawers, cabinets, or the like. We will walk through, no sitting, no refreshments, no bathroom privileges. You are to be done by nine-fifteen—then you must leave and never return."

Opal smirked, dead eyes glaring. "Losing Lucille has made you downright hostile, Freddy, but I accept your terms."

He stepped to the side, holding the screen door open for them to enter.

Opal ran her hand over the woodwork in the foyer and stopped in the dining room first. "The Easton table still resides in the space, as it should." She cruised around the twelve-person table and then went for the kitchen.

Nothing was said until she walked into her father's old study. "Now, this is completely different. His and her writing tables and a workspace for the girls, I presume."

"Yes." Frederick crossed his arms.

"I hear she's a writer like Lucille." Opal touched the typewriter. "Lucille was spoiled extra that Christmas."

"My wife is a nonfiction writer, not a novelist."

"Level-headed for steady Freddy. Lucille was too whimsical for you."

In the parlor, Opal spun around, taking in the different furniture and the less-cluttered shelves and tabletops. The mantel drew her over, and she lifted the twin photograph frame of sleeping Phoebe and Bethany.

"How recent is this?" she asked Frederick.

"April, now put it back."

Not knowing if she would listen, Alexander stepped closer in case he needed to take it from her. She replaced the frames and stroked the photograph of Bethany. "She's perfect. Almost two, Mother said. Bethany Iris Davenport, the child born to a fractured family."

"She's well-loved. They both are." Frederick tightened his fists. "What happened between the adults has nothing to do with how we feel for the children."

Opal lifted her chin and caught Alexander's gaze in the mirror—her stare frigid. "Between two sets of parents and doting grandparents in town, those girls must be spoiled."

At the other end of the mantel, she fingered his boxing trophy. She sighed and touched the frame holding the portrait

Alexander had taken before Frederick and Melissa went to the Trellis Room for the first time. "She's lovely, Freddy. Not as stunning as my sister, though she possesses an allure of culture and intelligence. What color is her hair?"

"Red," Alexander responded, hoping to bring the uncomfortable experience to an end.

"A shining copper," Frederick corrected. "If you wish to see upstairs, you need to move along."

In her old room, Opal's eyes darkened. "Does no one live here?"

"It's a guest room." Frederick's voice was still strained. "The girls share Lucy's old room."

"And Edmund's?"

"Another guest room."

Looking in the girls' room, Opal sighed. "Yes, completely spoiled. Having them share a room is a poor cover-up. Soon the oldest will demand her own space."

"That's none of your concern."

She held Frederick's eyes and boldly stepped closer to him. "And how was it when you finally had your way with my sister? Did she fulfill all the fantasies you've had about her since she grew breasts?"

"Opal!" Alexander jerked her out of Frederick's strike zone.

"Alexander ruined her, yet you were polite enough not to care. Then he came back with the story of going through hell for Lucy, and she runs to him like you were nothing to her. Did she at least pretend to love you those years? Did she ever moan 'Oh, Alex' while you were inside her?"

Frederick's face burned red, and his fists strained white. Alexander grabbed Opal's arm, running for the stairs.

"She's still a selfish, spoiled brat!" Opal screamed as Alexander brought her to the foyer. "She doesn't deserve anyone's devotion when she doesn't care enough for her own children to save a marriage! She doesn't deserve her money or anyone's love when all she loves is herself!"

Alexander opened the passenger side door and wanted to shove Opal in but held her arm with a trembling hand instead. When he climbed behind the wheel, he had to sit until his breathing calmed, praying Frederick wouldn't tear out of the house after them.

"I hope you're satisfied with ruining Frederick's trust in me." He started the automobile.

She laughed. "You're fooling yourself if you think he ever trusted you."

"Maybe so, but at least he was hospitable. Never again."

***

Alexander was as tight as one of his mother's corsets and chain-smoking since the ordeal at Frederick's house, but his body loosened a tad when he brought Opal back to her parents after her appointment with the psychiatrist.

Mrs. Easton greeted him with a hug. "When do we hear?"

Alexander kissed her cheek. "I can bring all of you to his office tomorrow at eleven. Dr. Moore is gathering her files and the medical reports from the exams she had this week, as well as contacting several facilities to find the right placement."

"You're such a dear for helping us, Alexander. I do wish you would allow James to pay you for your services."

"You're family. I wouldn't dream of it." *But if Opal ever asks for something more, I'll never agree.* "Shall I pick you all up at ten-thirty tomorrow?"

"Yes, Alexander. Thank you."

"Thank you, brother," Opal cooed before kissing his cheek.

Alexander said goodbye to the Eastons, wishing he could go straight to the riding club, but he had appointments to see to. Hoping to keep his energy levels higher for his later ride, he stopped at a lunch counter and happened across Maxwell.

Taking the barstool next to him, Alexander sighed. "That sister of yours is a piece of work. I told Edmund the other day Lucy was the best player out of all of you, but I was wrong. Opal has her beat by a longshot."

Maxwell laughed. "Come on. Tell big brother all about it."

"She said some unforgivable things to Freddy when I took her over to see the old house. I think the fact that she's female is the only reason she's still alive."

"Details, Alex. Details."

He recounted Opal's biting remarks and Frederick's stalwart control as well as the hasty exit over their roast beef sandwiches. "I want nothing more than to be rid of Opal, but there are four more days. Remind me never to legally help your family members after this."

"Is Lucy doing better at least?"

"Yes, fortunately. She's taking sleeping medicine through the weekend, and we aren't leaving her alone. Melissa and the girls are with her today. It's the first time they've stayed this week."

They exchanged a few pleasantries, and Alexander drove to his office at one o'clock.

Ms. Trigg gave him an anxious look after staring at his scarring a tad longer than polite. "You haven't been in yet today, and I was afraid you weren't going to make it for your appointment," she said to him as he collected his mail. "Mr. Brady is here, but he just stepped out a moment."

"Send him in when he returns."

Alexander sorted his correspondences and was ready with a clean pad of paper when Chuck Brady walked into the room.

He stood to shake the man's hand who nearly won the heavyweight title instead of Frederick last spring. "Good to see you, Mr. Brady."

"Come on, Melling, no need to be formal. Davenport is like a brother to me, and that makes us family." He accepted Alexander's hand and bought his other arm around his shoulder, thumping him on the back with his full strength. "Well, maybe not a brother to you, but you're close. Closer than he'd like to be most of the time."

"And I'm afraid that's even truer today. Be glad you aren't training with him this afternoon."

Chuck laughed. "I already received a telephone call about that at my office. Apparently, he nearly busted a hole in a punching bag this morning and then wore out three boxers in the ring before he called it quits."

Alexander ran his bare hand through his hair. "That was all me, I'm afraid, with a little Easton help." He pulled out his cigarette case and offered one to Chuck.

"I regulate myself to three a day, but go ahead. Davenport tells me if I stop, I'd be able to beat him. Whatever you did to get him worked up this morning, please don't do it Saturday."

Alexander laughed as he lit up. "I promise."

"I befriended Davenport after he married Lucy, and he was a dedicated boxer, but when you returned, he trained harder than ever. He was finally getting over Lucy when Melissa came to town. Perfect timing for a perfect match."

"Frederick suffered the most, and I'm sorry for it. He's the best type of man there is and took care of Lucy better than I ever could." Alexander took a hard drag on his cigarette. "But he and Melissa are great for each other. I'm happy for them, but what can I do for you today?"

"I'm getting married in a few weeks."

"Congratulations."

"Thank you. With the tournament this Saturday, I want to go ahead and write my will. You know, in case Davenport clobbers me."

Alexander laughed. "I already promised I wouldn't rile him that morning."

"I appreciate it, but if something were to happen, I'd like my assets to go to Rachel rather than my parents, either before or after marriage. I'm the advertising manager now at Gayfer's, so I've gotten a boost in income. Not that I have a lot compared to a guy like you, but at least I can afford your services at this firm rather than Lyons, Melling, and Associates."

Alexander slouched under the remembrance of how far he'd fallen on both the social and business ladders. He clamped the cigarette between his lips as he went to the file drawer and then passed Chuck the paper and fountain pen. "Here's a form you can fill out that would give us a good start on drafting a will. You're welcome to sit here or take it to the waiting room. Your choice."

Chuck settled in the chair, and Alexander busied himself with filing he'd gotten behind on while being absent from the office much of the past week. A few times, he paused to look at the new photographs on his desk, compliments of Melissa—Phoebe on Starlight, Lucy sitting atop Apollo, and a sweet picture of Bethany seated in the grass. The matching one of him on Apollo was on Lucy's desk in the morning room. He sighed and took a drag.

"That's your third cigarette since I've been here, Melling. How do you keep such a habit when Lucy dislikes it?"

"How do you—"

"The gym is ripe for discussions of all sorts. And before you ask—because I see the way your mind works and have heard stories concerning you—Davenport never boasts or discusses bedroom practices about his wives, and he's had the most out of any of us."

Alexander smiled mischievously. "I don't discuss my time with my wife either." *Except to Frederick or Claudio.*

"No, Melling, the word is that you discussed everything about all the *other* women when you were younger, including having no shame in people knowing you paid for services."

Alexander took a final drag and put out his smoke in the ashtray on the corner of his desk. "Ah, but those women have told me they felt they should have paid *me* for their time." He winked. "But that was a lifetime ago, before my purging by fire."

"And what will cleanse you after representing Hazel Kline?" Chuck handed over the paper. "It's said she's paying with favors, and you're looking a mite too pleased to be back with a red light woman."

"I've never been with Hazel, nor do I have any intention of accepting favors from her or anyone else. Lucy is all I'll ever need."

"So Davenport says whenever someone mentions stories about you in his presence. Yes, he defends the man who broke apart his marriage. That says a lot about his character."

"I don't see how anyone could ever doubt his intentions," Alexander said as he crossed his arms, "but my past lays me open to a world of scorn."

"And you have no one to blame but yourself."

Feeling as though he'd been struck in the gut, Alexander looked to the clock to count the minutes until he could crawl home.

Twenty-Eight

Melissa was in the morning room with Lucy, Phoebe, and Bethany when Alex returned. He went straight for Lucy's lounging form on the sofa, practically climbing upon her as they kissed. A hand settled on her cheek.

"You look much improved. Having your knights home must have been what you needed."

"It's been a lovely day, except for the man who came in the backyard this morning."

Alex went to his knees and listened as Lucy recounted the tale of the young man who claimed he had the wrong house.

To distract them from hearing the worry in their mother's voice, Melissa gathered the girls. "Let's tidy up so we're ready when your father gets here."

They had the books and toys gathered when Alex stood, leaving a final kiss on Lucy's lips. "Allow me to get comfortable and sort a few things in the den."

After greeting the girls, Alex caught Melissa's eye and waved her to the door with him. Not liking the firm set of his mouth, she prepared for the worst.

"I'm sorry, Melissa." He rested his hand on her elbow. "Opal said a lot of horrible things and ruined the visit. It appears she planned to use it as a ploy to jab at Frederick and release her feelings about Lucy—which are still abominable. He's furious, as am I. Hopefully, he's calmed by now, but I'll speak to him and make sure he doesn't blame you for encouraging the visit."

"Thank you, but he wouldn't—"

"He's human, Melissa. He's bound to disappoint you some time."

"Worry about yourself and Lucy."

"If you insist." He kissed her cheek and disappeared into his den.

Phoebe and Bethany sat with Lucy on the sofa, so Melissa went to the front room to watch for Freddy. His automobile pulled into the driveway a few minutes later, and she stepped onto the veranda to meet him. There wasn't a smile, but his glare softened when he looked at her. The gaze turned to yearning as he lifted her in his arms and walked into the mansion.

"Is everyone all right?" His breath, hot on her neck, sent goosebumps down her arms as he pinned her against the curving banister.

"Yes," her word was a heavy whisper, uncertain what to expect.

Freddy kissed around her neck and up her jaw until his lips were parting hers. He tasted of sweetened coffee, and she eagerly partook more. Possibly it was the thrill of necking in the Mellings' foyer, but Melissa's body surged with cravings of her own. Hands searching beneath his jacket, they dropped to his waistband, fingers teasing. He hiked her skirt to grasp her thigh, his other arm supporting her completely.

At that moment, Melissa didn't care where they were. "I want you."

"Like last week?"

"Anything, Freddy."

Catching movement in the corner of her eye, she turned toward the back hall and caught her breath when she met Alex's blue stare. Freddy followed her gaze.

Alex nodded to the stairs. "Pick a guest room."

Expecting Freddy to drop her and go at Alex, Melissa yelped in surprised as he tossed her over his shoulder and climbed the stairs while Alex laughed.

He chose the green room, and much of their clothing was soon on the floor, but they didn't use the bed. Freddy's strength and Melissa's long limbs afforded them ample means of enjoyment as they clung together in flushed passion.

Afterward, she leaned against him, his left hand hot and low on her back. "You're incredible."

"Melissa." His hands and lips roamed for a minute while she gloried in his attentions. "Thank you for loving me as you do."

They dressed silently, flirting and smiling, taking almost as long as the act itself.

"Shall we return arm-in-arm with the succulent glow of sexuality about us?" Freddy teased.

She accepted his arm. "I feel like we could light the world."

Freddy went to gather the girls from Lucy in the morning room while Melissa waited in the hallway. Hands grabbed her waist from behind, causing her to jump.

Alex chuckled as she turned to him. His shirt was half unbuttoned, shoes long gone. "Which room does Naomi need to change out the linens in?"

"None." Melissa smiled behind her blush. "Freddy can hold me the whole time."

Alex pursed his lips and raised his eyebrows as he digested the information. "That makes me want to start lifting weights. Lucy's legs wrapped around me … grasping her bu—"

"I don't need to hear your plan, but yes, strength comes in handy outside the ring."

"Lucy told me the other day my abdominal muscles were looking toned with all my riding." He rubbed his discolored hands over his stomach and winked. "She loves me the way that I am."

"I know, Alex. And she's lucky to have a man like you love her in return." Melissa touched his smooth cheek to give him more of the validation he sought. "Start working out, and after the baby is born, you'll be able to try new positions with Lucy."

"You have a wicked mind, and I love it." Alex raised his arms as though flexing muscles while gyrating his pelvis.

Freddy came up behind Melissa, wrapping his arms around her as Alex continued his ridiculousness. "Knock it off, Melling. The girls are right behind me."

Alex laughed and went to his knees to hug the girls on their way to the front door, Melissa patting him on the head as she passed.

"You aren't upset, Freddy?" he asked.

"Your offer this evening has almost made up for this morning."

"Then stop in and take her anytime," Alex replied.

"Take who, Poppy?" Phoebe asked. "Where's Daddy going?"

"Your father is taking all his girls home, Phoebe." Then quieter, he added, "But he might be bringing Melissa over the moon."

***

Freddy collected Melissa from the Mellings' Friday at noon. She'd spent the morning with Lucy and the girls, but when Naomi arrived midday, Freddy and Melissa went home so they could pack for their Florida trip. With the tournament and visitors from the island, the next two days wouldn't leave much room for preparation. They ate delicatessen sandwiches Freddy bought before getting to business.

"Do you wish to use a trunk or several suitcases?" he asked over his cup of coffee.

"One trunk for the hotel and a few smaller cases to use on the train."

"I'll bring them into the hallway when I'm done. But I'm afraid we'll have to stay on task until the majority of work is done."

"Make sure I get the new bathing suits for the girls. They're hanging in the hall closet."

"Isn't it on your list? The ever detailed, extremely long packing list you write up before every trip?"

"Possibly." She met his teasing gaze with one of aloofness. "But you'll be a dear and double-check with me because it's nothing I've ever packed for them, and I may have overlooked adding it to the list. And their Halloween costumes, as I'll never hear the end of it if Phoebe misses her dress-up day. I'm sure she'll be able to charm a few treats off unsuspecting hotel guests or workers in her fairy dress."

"She has that way about her like the little Easton she is."

They finished eating, and Freddy neatly stacked their dishes in the sink before running upstairs. Melissa stopped to wash the plates and glasses. When she reached the upstairs hall, Freddy placed a suitcase on a luggage rack he'd set beside the trunk. He wore only a pair of boxing shorts and a smile as he posed to showcase his massive build.

"One private showing for Melissa Stone Davenport."

Melissa jumped into his arms, and they kissed.

"Now it's time for packing." Freddy set her down a minute later. "Where's your list?"

"Still on my desk."

As he hurried down the stairs, Melissa undressed to her undergarments. When he returned, Freddy tucked the paper in the frame of a painting of Mobile Bay in the hallway so they could both read from it.

"Let's put the girls' things in the bottom of the trunk because they wrinkle less," Freddy suggested.

"But they'll need one of the nightgowns and two changes of clothes for the train."

"Shall I gather for Phoebe and you, Beth?" he asked. "The first one done gets to choose …"

"Where the other kisses the winner," Melissa finished.

"Only kiss?" The right side of Freddy's mouth lifted into a charming smile.

"For now."

"Ladies first." He held out an arm toward the girls' bedroom and followed Melissa inside.

Taking the allotted nightgowns, Melissa placed one in the suitcase and the others she folded neatly into the bottom of the trunk. Then she went for shoes and underclothes. Freddy copied her choices with what he gathered for Phoebe, placing things tidily into the correct luggage.

Freddy checked the list. "Do you really think only two fancy dresses?"

"We won't be dining too late with the girls. Surely they can wear the same dress multiple times."

"Make it three," he insisted. "We can bring another suitcase or trunk if needed."

"All right."

He sidled up to her, hands tracing the outline of her chemise. "Or to save room, you could skip *your* nightgowns."

She kissed his biceps. "I'll need something presentable to wear should they need assistance in the night."

Freddy's mouth went to her décolletage. After a few well-placed kisses, he raised his head, smiling. "You're even more attractive when your nurturing spirit shines through. No matter what you think of your domestic skills, you're a wonderful mother."

She felt her cheeks heat and turned to the closet to get the swimsuits before she forgot. Then they were back in the pink room to gather the remaining outfits needed. Melissa had forgotten their game until she saw Freddy run for the door with Phoebe's ruffled gowns in his arms. He tossed them into the trunk.

"Behold your champion!" He flexed his muscles and turned his back to her, showcasing his form from a new angle.

"The finest man in town." Melissa grabbed his tight rear with a caressing hold. "And where do you require your winning kiss?"

He kicked a leg up, foot propped on the door frame to their bedroom at a right angle. "Here."

Freddy pointed to his inner leg, where the hemline of his shorts hit mid-thigh.

Laughing, she rubbed his arm. "You just want me between your legs."

"You're very perceptive."

With one hand, she caressed his knee, and the other trailed down his chest as she lowered her mouth. She left a teasing kiss where he required it, then turned fully to him, wrapping her leg around him as her arms entwined his torso. Lips joined, they breathed each other into their souls.

"Melissa. Melissa, I think…." He nuzzled her neck. "I think we'll need another suitcase for the hotel."

Laughing, she slapped his buttocks. "Then go get one so we can finish this list and see if we have time for pre-training recreation."

His strong hands pressed her to him as he rhythmically bumped against her hip. "I'd skip the gym to spend more time with you."

"Not the day before a tournament."

After packing, they shared their bed for an hour of pleasure.

"Rest if you want, Melissa." Freddy pulled on his clothes. "Sharon is seeing to supper, and it will be a couple of hours before I return."

She stretched, tucking the pillow further under her head. "I think I will. Train hard, Handsome."

"I will, Beloved." He kissed her on the lips. "And I'll make you proud tomorrow."

Twenty-Nine

Alexander watched as the carpet in his bedroom grew closer before pushing back again. *Two. Three. Four.* He huffed, pushing himself past five—as far as he got yesterday. *Six. Seven. Eight!* He collapsed face down on the rug.

"Alex, this is the second morning in a row you've gotten out of bed to do pushups. If Frederick threatened a fight, I'd tell him to call it off."

He stared up at Lucy's lovely face gazing over the side of the bed, loose hair like a waterfall about her enchanting shoulders. "I'm doing this for us, not him."

She reached for his back. "I love you as you are."

"A little more strength and stamina never hurt anyone."

"Then lay off the cigarettes. Freddy swears they drain the lungs' capacity. He says it's the only thing keeping him a step ahead in the ring."

"I have been overdoing that lately." He sat up and kissed her. "I'll cut back, beginning next week."

Lucy straightened, the sheet falling away from her bare body. "It's early yet. Will you join me?"

Her question was a double-edged sword. It had been nearly two weeks since their last act together. Darla had declared Lucy better the previous day—though for her to continue to rest as much as possible—but she never said Lucy was free to return to *all* activity. Looking from his wife's chest to her eager eyes, Alexander decided Darla intentionally left out the part she figured he would be most interested in to spite him for all his jesting. Lucy had slept peacefully through the night, her color was healthy, and the air of yearning about her wasn't one of a sick woman.

Alexander smiled at her shining face, removing his sleep pants before slipping into bed. "It would be an honor, my queen."

Without words, they explored one another, their motions slow and seductive. The desire weighed heavy between them, but the execution was gradual—almost agonizingly so as Alexander's instinct to reclaim her burned hot. Afterward, he lowered his lips to the profile of her womb with a tender touch.

"My family," he whispered. "I love you both."

"And we love you, Alexander Randolph Melling."

Not wanting to showcase his feelings after the intimate act, he snuggled beside Lucy and buried his face in her hair as a few tears rolled out. Her hand went to his chest, then caressed upward until her fingertip found the wet trail.

"You're a beautiful soul, Angel," she whispered. "Don't feel the need to hide. We share everything."

He kissed her cheek and pulled her even closer. "It's more real to me now. If anything happened to you or the baby, I'd shatter."

Lucy tilted her head toward his face. "You please me like no other. Thank you for coming back, for finally allowing me to take your name."

Their kissing grew heated, Lucy near frantic in her touching. As Alexander moved to align them, the baby visibly somersaulted within Lucy.

"Dear God!" Alexander tumbled off the bed.

"Alex!"

For the second time that morning, he found himself staring up at Lucy from the floor.

"Are you all right?" he asked.

"Am *I*?" She laughed. "You're the one who went head over heels off the bed!"

He scrambled to rejoin her, a hand tentatively going to her round middle. "Does that tear you up inside?"

"No, but sometimes it startles me, though not as much as you."

Her curving smile filled him with love and wonder, but still, he worried. "I don't think the baby appreciates our time together. And, come to think of it, it's a little awkward knowing what we're doing with the baby *right there*. You said we shouldn't be intimate around Bethany anymore, but what about this child? Doesn't the babe feel and hear everything we do?"

Lucy's silver laughter filled the space as she fell back on the pillows. She pulled out his old handkerchief and dabbed her eye. "Alex, why don't you ask Darla a few questions while you're at the tournament. I'm sure she'd be happy to help you understand."

"Then she'd know we're back in action, and I'm not sure she'd approve." He curled against Lucy, resting his cheek on her soft chest.

She linked their fingers over her belly. "She told me Thursday I was fine to do as I wished, so long as I'm comfortable."

He playfully nipped at her. "And you didn't tell me, my queen?"

"I waited for the right time."

"I ached for you last night." He knelt over her. "I wanted nothing more than to feel you completely around me."

Her eyes fluttered as his body teased against her thigh. "And I want that for you, but today."

Alexander kissed her lips and then her neck. "Why today?"

Her gaze turned softer, almost shy, before she clung to him. "Because I want to make sure you're completely satisfied before seeing Magdalene."

"Lucy, nothing will ever happen when I have you, I promise. You're my everything. You and soon this child, who appears ready to claw his way out." He kissed her smiling lips. "Now, are you ready for more for your own sake and not for what you think I need to be fulfilled?"

"I want you again, Alex."

"And I'm more than willing to oblige, my queen."

***

After Bethany was dropped off, Alex settled in the morning room with Lucy and her daughter. They took turns reading poems and watched Bethany build a block tower.

Alexander tucked Lucy under his arm. "I'd stay all day like this if I could. You, me, a beautiful child to oversee."

"We'll have our time soon, Alex. Today you need to represent our family at the tournament. You're already missing the lightweights. Be sure you get there before Henry's rounds. And remember to talk to Darla."

"I'll be sure to make her blush."

"Bring along a clean riding outfit in the automobile so you can go to the stables afterward if you have time before the party."

"Should I bring a change for Phoebe?"

"It wouldn't hurt. Talk to Melissa about it."

"I will." He kissed her and stood.

He gathered Phoebe's things and then stopped for a lengthy goodbye. On his way through the kitchen, he greeted Naomi and Sharon.

"It smells terrific in here already. Lucy and Bethany are in the morning room."

"We'll need plenty of cookies for all those kids coming this evening." Naomi wiped her hands on her apron and adjusted Alex's tie. "I've got my eye and ears on your girls. Don't you worry."

"Thank you, Naomi."

The last time he arrived at the tournament, Lucy and her daughters parted the sea of spectators with their beauty. This time, Alexander had to elbow his way through the crowd, receiving shoulder slaps and jostles along the way as old Dardenne brothers called out things like "Ahoy, Melling!" and "The cad's finally arrived!" He nodded in response, and when he got near the front of the aisle, he turned to the stands and searched the bleachers for his group. Claudio waved from across the room, and Alexander caught sight of Phoebe's fair head between Douglas and Kade. He fought his way over, arriving out of breath at the front row on the riser.

Joe Walker slapped his back as he entered their space. "Finally tore yourself away from your wife, did you?"

"Barely. Good to see you, Joe."

He nodded to Joe's boys—Emmett and Abraham—as he went down the row to Melissa and Darla, giving a kiss to each lady. Then he settled between Douglas and Claudio. Phoebe immediately transferred to his lap, hugging his neck.

"Poppy, I'm glad you're here. I want to sit with you and Kade."

Before the middleweight match began, Alexander set Phoebe beside Kade and made his way to the ladies. Darla and Melissa had their heads bent together, talking as best they could in the noisy space. He squatted beside them, a hand on each of their knees.

"Melissa, do you think it would be all right for me to take Phoebe with me to the riding club if Freddy's rounds are over by four? We'd meet everyone back at the house by six. That would give Freddy a chance to get cleaned up and whatever else you two need to do." He winked.

She laughed. "You'd have to stop and get her clothes."

"Already have a set in the automobile along with my own." Alexander squeezed her knee.

"All right, I'll let Freddy know."

"And Darla, I have questions for you." He leaned closer. "How much does the baby feel and hear when the parents are making love?"

Her blush was immediate, and Melissa shifted in to listen.

"Does it harm the baby if things get a little bouncy?" he continued. "If the baby starts moving a lot before, during, or after, does that mean the child knows what's going on and wants to stop it from happening? If the mother cries out in rapture, will the baby think she's being hurt?"

Darla pushed his hand off her knee and stood. "Alex, this isn't the proper location to discuss—"

Claudio pulled Alexander by the collar. "*Calmati, amico.* Darla does not appreciate your conversation."

"But I need to know," he said as Claudio began to tug him to his seat. "Please, Darla, help me understand the limits!"

Melissa chuckled, and then Darla laughed. "Put him down, Claudio. I'll talk to him."

Alexander squeezed between the two women, smiling sheepishly. "Thank you, Darla."

"The infant is encased in a sack of fluid, so any motion associated with *the act* would only feel like a gentle rocking to the baby. Most people—"

"I'm not most people."

Darla rolled her blue eyes. "Don't remind me. As I was saying, most report the baby seems to rest during the act as though being rocked to sleep."

"So the baby likes it!" He felt the wicked grin on his lips and went to adjust himself.

Melissa caught his hand halfway up his thigh. "Control yourself."

Alexander looked from Melissa to Darla's expression and laughed.

"I don't know what I should be more shocked by, Alex's lewdness or the fact that you knew what he was going for." Darla looked away in disgust, but a second later, she grabbed Melissa's arm. "There he is! I knew it!"

"What?" Alexander and Melissa said at the same time, releasing the other's hand.

"The man that came into the yard the other day! He reminded me of my cousin's friend, Otis Youngblood, and he's there with him now. They have the same smile."

Youngblood! Alexander's attention snapped to where Darla looked on the opposite aisle and a chill settled over him in the crowded room.

Alexander jumped to his feet. "That's who came and spoke to Phoebe?"

"Yes," both women agreed.

"That's the orderly who accompanied Opal here from the asylum. He was supposed to return to work the next day."

He started down the row. The announcer called out the first match for the middleweights—Henry versus Sean Spunner. Melissa grabbed Alexander's arm, and he returned to the space between Darla and Melissa.

Sean came on strong, and Henry took several blows before he got his guard up. Darla's hands clasped over her heart, but after a minute of intense action, she grew further agitated. The crowd roared with shouts, including Phoebe, Kade, and the Walker boys.

Alexander laid a hand on her knee, but she snatched it and squeezed. After a few seconds, he sucked in his breath. "Darla, you're hurting me."

She released his hand but then clutched him around the neck, hiding her face on his shoulder. "I can't watch!" Then she let go and turned back to the ring. "But I can't *not* watch!"

If he hadn't been concerned over Bruce Youngblood still being in town, Alexander would have enjoyed Darla's attention, but he couldn't stop watching the men across from them. At least if he knew where he was, the man wasn't out causing trouble with Opal.

Henry narrowly won the match, and it was another twenty minutes before he was in the ring again. By that time, Alexander sat with Claudio and the captains, Phoebe on one knee and Kade on the other with redheaded Abraham beside them. Henry advanced to the finals, and it was half an hour before his match for first place. Alexander looked beyond Douglas to see Darla's death grip on Melissa's hand—thankful to have his stepdaughter bouncing on his knee instead.

Halfway through Henry's next match, Maxwell arrived with Opal on his arm. As Alexander kept a close eye on Youngblood rather than the boxers, he was the first to see them approach.

"God help us all! I promised Freddy and Lucy I'd keep the girls away from her," Alexander told Claudio as he pressed Phoebe to his chest and lunged for the far aisle.

"Poppy, where are we going?"

Alexander ignored Phoebe's question.

Melissa touched his arm as he climbed over her lap. "What's wrong?"

"I can't stay here!" He rushed up the aisle, hugging Phoebe to him in the crowd.

Thirty

Melissa watched Alexander until he stopped along the sidewall, hoisting Phoebe to his shoulders. Maxwell was almost to their row with a haunting young beauty on his arm. She had the same chin as the Eastons, and her hair was a brassy blonde. The curve of her hips beneath her slim-fitting skirt was reminiscent of Lucy, but her stare reminded Melissa of her first meeting with Eddie. Opal Easton—the reason for Freddy's sour mood and bitterness the past two weeks—stood brazen on her eldest brother's arm with a cold fire in her emerald eyes. The captains looked at the newcomers with surprise. Only Claudio understood the seriousness of the situation. He quickly greeted them, but Melissa couldn't hear the words exchanged.

The crowd roared, and Darla let go of Melissa's arm and ran for the ring. Expecting to see Henry on the ground like at the last tournament, Melissa smiled to see him jumping around in victory. A few of the gym regulars lifted Darla to the outside of the ropes, and Henry rushed over for a celebratory kiss. Melissa looked to the Youngbloods and saw the one Darla knew talking to the orderly with a malicious smile.

All joy Melissa felt in expectation of Freddy being victorious washed away with Opal's arrival and the unease the Youngbloods created. Melissa was sure Alex would have confronted the man if

Henry's match hadn't begun, and now he was trapped away with Phoebe.

"Melissa!" Maxwell called her over. "Meet my youngest sister. She wanted to see Eddie in the ring. Opal, this is—"

"Frederick's *third* wife. I recognize you from the photograph I saw on your mantel, though you're even prettier in person." Opal's hand was clammy, her smile forced. "Thank you for allowing me over on Thursday. It seems you're more hospitable than some of my own family members. I don't know why Alex ran away when he saw me. I wanted to meet my niece as they didn't attend my party last night. She looks to be a miniature Lucy, and I wonder if her temperament is the same."

Melissa refused to comment and turned away. Freddy—in all his athletic glory—stood beside Alex and waved her over. When Melissa reached him, she leaned into his bare chest, kissing his neck.

"Stay away from her." His voice was hard in her ear. "Don't speak to her unless it's unavoidable. Alex is under orders not to let Phoebe loose. Not with that man Alex told me about and Opal both here."

Her hands caressed down Freddy's back. "Maxwell said she wanted to see Eddie's match."

"That's an excuse. Alex told me you permitted him to take Phoebe riding, and that's fine. I told him they could go after my first match if they'd like. The stables would be a safe place for Phoebe."

"Safe?"

"I don't trust Opal an inch. Especially after that man showed up in the backyard. But at least they're here because I don't like the thought of Lucy and Beth being alone."

"Naomi and Sharon are with them. Try not to worry while you're in the ring." She gave him a firm kiss. "Focus on your match, all right?"

"And what you'll reward me with afterward." Their lips touched without thought of their audience. With a hand at her waist, he gave one last kiss. "I'll always fight for you and the girls."

Freddy was called to the warm-up area, and Melissa watched him go, smiling over her mighty husband. She still didn't understand how they ended up together, but gratitude flowed through her for their union.

"He's an impressive sight," Alex remarked, "and I see you enjoy the view."

Melissa laughed. "That's my right and privilege, just as you enjoy gazing upon Lucy."

"Nothing compares to that beauty. I'll keep an eye on those needing it, but don't mind us if we leave after his first match."

Phoebe crossed her arms and set them on Alex's head. "I want to sit with Kade and see all Daddy's battles."

"We'll try, but we might need to leave to make sure we have time to ride before going home. Kade will be there for the party."

"But Abe will be there too, and Kade makes me share with him. I don't like that Walker's freckled face. I want as much time with my best friend as possible."

Alex patted her leg dangling over his shoulder. "Kade's a great friend and doesn't want Abraham to feel left out. That's a good thing, Phoebe."

"I'll tell Kade and his father where you are," Melissa said. "Maybe they can come over."

That brought a smile to her angelic face. "Thank you, Sissa."

Darla joined Melissa. "Henry's gone to change, and then he'll be with us. I'm glad he stayed on his feet this time."

As they approached their seats, Melissa leaned closer. "The young woman with Maxwell is Opal."

Darla gasped.

"Alex has to keep Phoebe away from her, so they won't be returning."

Once Darla was seated, Melissa went down the row to Douglas, speaking into his ear of Alex's need to keep Phoebe away. He nodded in understanding. When Kade next asked after Phoebe, Douglas brought him through the crowd. He sat atop his father's shoulders and held hands with Phoebe on Alex's.

Claudio, now sitting beside her, leaned over Melissa. "Are you well?"

She nodded. "Trying not to worry."

"I feel Frederick will do fine."

She looked down the row, where Maxwell and Opal sat on the far side of Joe and his sons. "But the girls."

"We are alert to the danger. Nothing will happen within these walls."

Chuck Brady won during the first match, but Freddy didn't take his turn for over a quarter of an hour. By then, Henry was with the group. After Freddy won the match, Maxwell brought Opal to meet the Adamses. Her green eyes soaked in every inch of Henry's features, from his bare forearms beneath his rolled sleeves to his bulging thigh muscles under his trousers.

"You were magnificent," she gushed like a love-struck girl.

"Thank you, Miss Easton."

"And your eyes, they're the deepest, most exquisite shade of blue I've ever had the privilege of beholding." She placed her hand on his shoulder and angled closer. "Your dear wife is the most fortunate woman in the city. Be sure to let her know if she doesn't show you proper respect that you can find adoration elsewhere."

Darla was on her feet, her usually cheery face hard as she slapped Opal's hand away from Henry. "I don't care who you are or what you've done. No one speaks to my husband like that!"

Opal's curving smile was more sinister than sensual, but it had the same set as Lucy's. "I can't help myself. I am, after all, kin to my sister. She didn't care whose heart she broke along the way or what she did to her family's name on her descent into sin."

The announcer's voice boomed over the din of the crowd. "Next match is Edmund Easton versus Thomas Charles."

Maxwell was back at Opal's elbow. "Come on, sister. Since you can't hold your tongue, I'm taking you home after this match."

Henry pulled Darla into his lap and murmured something in her ear before they kissed. She switched to her seat in time for the bell announcing the start of Edmund's round.

Thomas Charles proved a worthy opponent, but the weight behind Edmund's strikes appeared too much for him. Edmund had trimmed his body in the last half a year, but much of his fat seemed to have turned to muscle as he outweighed his opponent by thirty pounds. Melissa looked to Alex and Phoebe and was pleased to see them cheering on their brother-in-law and uncle, Douglas and Kade, still beside them.

When the second bracket began, Maxwell returned from taking Opal home. Freddy, Edmund, and Chuck all bested their challengers. Melissa pulled her fan from her purse as the room grew stuffier and her head lighter. Douglas and Kade settled with the Walkers and Claudio, telling the others that Alex had left with Phoebe.

The priest patted Melissa's knee. "Frederick is doing well."

She nodded and looked to where the Youngbloods still loitered.

The next hour was a blur of rounds and knockouts. The only thing Melissa could focus on was that Freddy still stood when his opponent went down, and Edmund clobbered poor Chuck. Rachel hung over the ropes in an attempt to comfort him.

"Melissa," Darla said as she knelt in front of her, "you look pale. Are you all right?"

She nodded—or thought she did. "My head is spinning, and I'm incredibly thirsty."

"Henry, we need to get her into the fresh air."

Claudio rose, and he and Henry each put an arm around Melissa. Darla ran ahead to find a drink and met them in the lobby with a cup of water.

Freddy burst out of the tournament room, rushing to the bench where she sat. In his haste to embrace her, water sloshed from the cup onto her skirt.

"What's going on, Melissa? Are you all right?"

His body was hot against her. It would have been heavenly if she wasn't already stifling. "I over-heated, nothing more." She touched his face as she stared into his intense gaze. "You're doing great."

"All for you, Beloved."

"Davenport!" a man barked from the entry. "You've got thirty seconds to report before you forfeit your place!"

He stood but held Melissa's hand. "My wife is suffering from the heat. May she have permission to stand in the warm-up area so she has more breathing room? And Adams and his wife in case she goes faint?"

The man nodded and motioned them back to the room.

"You stay with us if you want, Claudio," Darla told him. "They won't kick a priest out."

"*Sí*, my vestments come in handy at times like this."

A few fights later, the final round for the championship was down to Freddy and Edmund.

"Alex and Lucy should be watching this," Darla remarked. "I wonder who Maxwell is rooting for."

"The Eastons stick together," Melisa replied. "They're a tight family even if they don't agree on everything."

The former best friends in the ring didn't appear to be gentle with each other. Edmund—knowing he had a lot to prove—started heavy-fisted and didn't relent. Freddy blocked and struck with precision, his face set like Melissa had never seen. A minute in, she felt herself going weak. Only when she shifted in an attempt to revive her body did she notice Claudio had moved directly behind her and held her elbow.

"Lean on me, Melissa," he practically shouted into her ear to be heard over the roar of the crowd. "I will not let you fall."

Melissa found herself relying more on Claudio and settled against his chest to relieve her fatigue. How he tolerated his priestly frock in the room where all of the other men had their jackets off, she didn't know.

Freddy faked Edmund with a hook, landing a powerful strike to his jaw with his other hand. Saliva went flying as he crumpled to his knees.

"Davenport!" the howls went up. "Davenport for the win!"

The last thing Melissa saw was Henry's jovial face as he came to help her to the ring. Then the world went black.

Thirty-One

Worry pricked at Alexander—the thought that Lucy needed him refusing to leave. Rather than saddling Apollo after Phoebe's training, he tipped a groom to take care of Starlight so they could leave immediately.

Phoebe snuggled beside him on the front seat. "May we get ice cream, Poppy?"

"Not today, Knight Phoebe. We need to get home and help your momma ready for the party, but Miss Naomi will have cookies for us."

"Could we go see if Daddy is winning?"

Alexander's grip on the steering wheel tightened. "I'm sure he's made it to the finals at the very least."

As he drove within a block of the house, a line of police vehicles and horses blocked his advance. Pulling into a neighbor's yard, Alexander hugged Phoebe to his chest for the second time that day and ran for the mansion. He bound past the officers milling about the front of his house.

"Where's my wife?" Phoebe clutched his neck as Alexander shoved through the detectives in the foyer. "Lucy!"

"Mr. Alex!" Naomi came out of the back hall and took Phoebe from him. "She's in the morning room."

Lucy's pale form was stretched the length of the sofa, red-rimmed eyes staring at the ceiling. He collapsed on the rug beside her, taking her hands. "My God, Lucy, what's going on?"

She nearly crushed his fingers as she stared at him with fear beyond any he'd ever seen on her countenance. "He took Bethany!" she sputtered before sobbing.

"Who?" He looked up to the nearest police officer. "Who did this?"

He flipped his notepad in his hand. "She said it looked like the young man that came in the yard a few days ago, but she only saw him from the side when he rushed out the gate with her daughter. He left instructions with a ransom note for twenty-five thousand dollars."

"We'll pay it! Get our daughter back!"

"She's not your child, Mr. Melling. We've dispatched a team to the tournament to collect Mr. Davenport. We need to speak with the father and plan a course of action to reclaim the girl."

Alexander leaped to his feet. "Like hell she's not my daughter! I've loved her since the day she was born. We'll gather the money and give the bastard what he wants to get Bethany back safely. Now get in touch with the bank president so we can withdraw the needed cash from our accounts!"

"It's not always best to give kidnappers what they want, Mr. Melling," a second officer said. "They could take the money and escape with the girl as well."

"We'll do whatever it takes to keep our girl safe, do you hear me? We'll not allow you to play chess with our daughter as a pawn! Have you taken people of interest into custody?"

"We don't have names or a good—"

"Bruce Youngblood. He's an orderly at a children's asylum and has relatives in town with the same last name, including another young man. A cousin, most likely."

"There's a Youngblood who works in the city records department," a policeman said.

"Get on it!" an officer commanded the other.

"And Opal Easton. She's temporarily residing with Mr. and Mrs. James Easton. If that was Bruce Youngblood, she's part of this as well. Take her into holding as she's to be admitted to an asylum on Monday. She might need to be brought to the hospital to be sedated, so bring an ambulance with you."

"To your in-laws?"

"Opal's not to be trusted, but treat her parents kindly. They're innocent in all this."

He fell to his knees beside Lucy, smoothing her hair. She still cried uncontrollably, her lungs halting beneath her red lace gown. Nestling under her chin, he kissed her neck.

"I'm sorry, my queen. I'll never forgive myself for this."

Seeking to bring her comfort, his surge of emotions allowed him to lift Lucy in his arms. Alexander carried her to his den, where the cooler temperature would be more restful for her. Once she was on the chaise, he covered her legs with the velvet blanket and kissed her wet cheeks as he pressed a handkerchief into her hand.

"Alex!" Magdalene's voice echoed down the hall. "Alex! Lucy!"

She found them a minute later, little Simon swaddled to her chest. "Naomi told me what happened. I've left a message at the hotel for the others."

Alexander stood and accepted her embrace, fighting the urge to fall into her arms with a passion to drown out the hideousness of his mistakes. Before he knew what he was doing, he'd kissed below her ear as a hand roamed her back.

"I'm not fit to live, Magdalene."

"You can't control what others do." Her brown eyes were full of kindness, and he wanted nothing more than to feel loveable.

"Will you help her?" He motioned to Lucy.

"She needs your arms right now."

He'd rather go search for Bethany or cling to one who would hug him back—like Magdalene. Sweet, sensual Magdalene Jones of Seven Hills. He could lay her child aside and cleave to her in his riding clothes she admired. Douglas wasn't there to stop them, and Lucy was too far gone to notice. But he knew Magdalene was correct in saying Lucy needed him, though she could give nothing in return.

Alexander dropped to the chaise and pulled Lucy into his lap, kissing and rocking her. How long he was like that, he wasn't sure, but Lucy appeared to be asleep when Sharon came in with a tea tray. Refusing to move, he kept his arms about his wife.

"Thank you, Miss Sharon, but where's Phoebe?"

"Naomi's got the dear in the kitchen. She's not letting her leave her side. We feel awful about Miss Bethany. One moment she and Miss Lucy were in the yard, and the next, Miss Lucy was screaming for help. We got out as fast as we could, but there was an automobile waiting for the rogue at the end of the driveway."

"And you told the police and gave a description?"

"Yes, Mr. Alex. Of course, we did."

"I mean nothing against you. Everyone knows this is my fault."

Magdalene looked to him from where she paced. "You did what you thought best."

"I was selfish, thinking only of improving my standing with her parents. I wanted to be better than Frederick in their eyes when I've only proved my loathsomeness."

"I love you still," Lucy whispered. Her hand trailed up his chest to his neck, pulling him to her lips.

Sensing her need—or maybe she felt his—Alexander gave to her completely with deep kisses and gentle fondling. They were locked in each other's spell when someone stomped into the room.

"And they continue like nothing happened!" Frederick, still in his boxing shorts with a shirt half-buttoned across his broad chest, stepped forward, fists white with strain.

"No, Frederick." Magdalene stood with a protective arm around her baby. "They've been torn. They're only trying to comfort—"

"He deserves no comfort! Stop hiding behind Lucy and get over here, Melling."

"Don't hurt him, Freddy!" Lucy cried out as Alexander crossed the room. "He's pained enough."

"He'll get everything he has coming to him and more!"

Frederick's hands around Alexander's neck brought him back to the night he went to State Street to claim Lucy. Breaking Freddy's marriage was bad enough, but now his youngest was in danger. Alexander prayed his death would be swift.

"Freddy, no!" Melissa was in the room, pulling on Frederick's arm. "If you kill him, you'll die too. The girls need their father."

The voices began to sound like they were underwater as Frederick's grip tightened.

"Freddy, don't do this!" Melissa pled. "I need you too. I think I'm pregnant!"

With Frederick's release, Alexander went to the ground, gasping. He crawled to the chaise and rested his head in Lucy's lap.

Thirty-Two

After Freddy dropped Alex, he took Melissa's face in his hands, frantic eyes searching hers.

"I've thought you might be, especially when you were overcome with the heat today, but I didn't dare speak it. Creating a child with you has been the yearning of my soul since we first met."

His lips on her mouth felt as natural as breathing. His hands low on her belly, a blessing of warmth and gratitude for having shared the news with him.

"As much as this thrills me," Freddy said as he leaned his cheek against hers, "I cannot enjoy the thought of it until we find Beth."

"I know," she whispered. "I didn't mean to blurt it out, especially now."

"You were right to stop me. Please stay with Lucy while I bring Alex to speak with the police. We need to find out what's being done and what we can do."

Melissa nodded, and he went to Lucy.

"I'm sorry, Goosy." He planted his lips on her forehead. "We need to band together, not fight. I know we're all scared and hurting right now, but I promise not to take it out on Alex."

The pain in Lucy's face as she gazed at Freddy created an ache in Melissa's chest. "Don't take him from me, Freddy. I'd never forgive you. Never! Do you understand?"

"Yes."

"Promise me you'll protect him as you do our children."

"I swear with my life. Have I ever let my maiden down?"

A soft smile curved on her pale face. "No."

Freddy kissed her again and then hauled Alex up by his arms. "Sorry, Alex. I'm too quick to judge. We need to work together."

Not long after they went to the front of the house, Darla and Henry rushed in.

As soon as they heard the news, Henry went for the door. "I'm going to tell everyone. We'll have the whole city looking for Bethany!"

"And Otis and Bruce Youngblood!" Darla shouted after him before turning back to Lucy and Melissa. "Otis tried to get me drunk at my first city party. He was up to no good back then, but it's difficult to believe he'd go so far as to be involved in a kidnapping."

"He might not be, but this relative of his certainly is," Maggie said as she paced.

Though tears continued to fall silently, Lucy allowed Darla to examine her pulse and the baby. Melissa fixed tea and passed around the cups. Minutes ticked agonizingly slow, and Melissa wanted nothing more than to interview the police and be off looking for Bethany herself.

Douglas arrived next. "Claire and Joe are watching Kade and Tabitha. We didn't think it would be right to bring all the children over." He turned to Lucy, taking her hand into his own. "I'm here for you and Alex. Tell me what you need from me."

"Thank you, Douglas. I know you were with Alex through other hard times, and we need our friends."

Edmund burst into the room. "Where is that devil?"

Lucy straightened. "Edmund, who—"

"Your miserable husband! He sent the police to Mother and Father, propelling Mother to hysterics. Opal was supposed to be resting after Maxwell brought her home, but she'd snuck out the window."

Darla caught Lucy's cup a second before she fainted. Transferring Simon into Douglas's arms, Maggie helped Darla with Lucy while Melissa ran for the front room, seeking Alex. He and Freddy were talking to several officers.

"Opal is missing, and Lucy's fainted!"

Alex raced down the hall.

"Opal Easton snuck out of her parents' house and is on the loose," Melissa said to the policemen.

When Melissa and Freddy reached the den, Douglas struggled to hold Edmund back.

Freddy left Melissa by the desk and approached his old friend. "Leave him alone, Eddie."

"This is his fault! He brought her here, and now the stress is going to kill my parents!"

"It's Opal's fault." Freddy's voice was firm. "She tricked a lot of people, not just Alex. If you want to take him down, you'll have to go through me first, and I already bested you once today."

"You won?" Alex asked.

"I'm the two-time heavyweight champion of Mobile," Freddy replied, "but I can't tell you what happened to my trophy."

"Henry has it. And the rest of your clothes," Darla said.

"Go, Eddie." Freddy nudged his shoulder. "Help your parents through this. We have more than enough help and heartache here."

He nodded and trudged out.

Alex, beside Lucy on the chaise as she came to, whispered as he smoothed her hair.

"Douglas," Freddy said, "if Alex and I both have to leave, will you keep watch?"

"Aye, Maggie and I are here as long as you need us." He turned to Alex as he stood and embraced him as a brother. "I left word for Claudio. He'll be here soon."

"Thank you." Alex then kissed Lucy with tenderness. "Try to rest, my queen."

He and Freddy returned to the police officers.

"Follow them, Melissa." Lucy looked pleadingly at her. "Go find out what you can, and then bring Phoebe to me."

Melissa was content to do Lucy's bidding because it gave her purpose. She didn't want to be negated because she was possibly carrying a child. Dressed in a beige walking suit, she blended with the gold tones of the front room. Freddy briefly looked at her as she positioned herself in the front corner, but he didn't bring attention to her by speaking.

"The banker will be here within half an hour. You will both need to write down a note detailing how much money you require from each account, and he will be dispatched with policemen to collect the money and bring it here until the drop time if you insist on giving in to the demands set forth by the letter."

"I already told you we aren't going to see how serious they are if we fail to comply!" Alex raked his hands through his hair.

"And I already informed you, Mr. Melling, this is up to the parents."

"Tell him, Freddy! Tell him we'll give them twice what they want to get Bethany back! I'll not sit by until midnight to drop a bag of money beside the fountain in Bienville Square while they do who knows what to our sweet child!"

"Most assuredly, officer. Alex is just as much a parental figure as I am."

The relief on Alex's face spread warmth in Melissa's soul. Perhaps Freddy said it because she was standing there—that in stating Alex as a key figure in Bethany's life, he also included her role as stepmother equally important. But it was spoken with honesty and respect, as only Freddy could convey.

"Very well, gentlemen. Please decide how to withdraw the exorbitant sum of twenty-five thousand dollars from what I hope are ample accounts."

"That child is priceless!" Alex's nostrils flared with indignation. "There's not enough money in the whole state that could take the place of Bethany Iris Davenport."

Melissa wiped at her eye before tears could fall.

"Save your energy, Melling." Freddy led Alex into the foyer.

"How much can you spare, Freddy? A thousand? Five?"

"Like you, I'd give it all. But yes, five thousand to start with."

"Then we'll take five from Lucy's and the rest from mine."

"Fifteen thou—Alex, I can't allow that. How do you even have it?"

"My parents' interest in stocks and investments. I've tried not to touch it, but there's nothing I'd rather do with the money than give it for Bethany, even if I have to sell the house when all's said and done."

"I can't let you take that burden."

"It's only fitting when it's my fault Opal's here. She's done this on purpose. You remember what she said at your house—that

Lucy didn't deserve her money. She's trying to take it, but I'll not let her bleed my wife dry in her revenge. She can have the tainted Melling fortune instead. I'll fetch paper from the den."

Seeing a good point to slip away, Melissa went for the kitchen, but Freddy caught her.

"Come with me to collect Phoebe from Naomi," she said. "I'm sure she'd appreciate a hug from you before I bring her to Lucy."

Phoebe jumped into Freddy's arms and kissed his cheek. "Daddy, you forgot to get dressed!" She went to button his shirt.

"At least I have my boxing shorts and shoes."

"Use one of Poppy's pants from upstairs."

"It would take both Poppy's pant legs to fit one of mine, Princess."

Melissa smiled, knowing it wasn't much of an exaggeration. "Your mother is waiting to see you, Phoebe," she said.

"May I bring cookies for her, Sissa?"

"Yes, but bring a lot. We have other visitors. Darla, Douglas, and Maggie are here."

"Kade?"

"Not yet, Phoebe," Freddy responded, "but you'll see him before he goes back to the island." He kissed his daughter and set her in Melissa's care before leaving the kitchen.

Thirty-Three

"Where's the note?" Freddy asked when he returned to the front room.

Alexander, half-listening while he wrote his epistle about withdrawing funds from his account, berated himself for not having asked to see it before now.

The lead officer handed Freddy the ransom letter.

"Give it to me next," he said as he signed *Alexander Randolph Melling* at the end of his request for fifteen thousand dollars. He turned to a fresh page and wrote out a note for Lucy, asking for five thousand from her account, and brought it to the back of the house for her to sign. Seeing the empty den sent his heart racing, but a second later, he heard Phoebe's voice down the hall. The group had reconvened in the morning room, a more fitting space for the larger gathering.

He perched on the edge of the sofa beside Lucy and held the paper for her to read. Though weak, her script was bold and flowing.

Lucille Amelia Easton Davenport Melling

Seeing her full name struck him anew. She'd refused to surrender her claim to the Davenport name at the divorce, asserting that since the girls would have the name, she wanted to be linked with them always. But now, the doubt crept in, declaring that part of her still loved Frederick. She'd already reminded all in attendance that Frederick Lionel Davenport had never let her down—that she was still his maiden—when the unspoken words shouted that Alexander Melling had repeatedly disappointed her.

"Freddy and I will see this through. I'll bring your daughter back to you, my queen."

With a nod, she quietly accepted his kiss.

Halfway across the room, he rushed back to Lucy, dropping beside her as he kissed her hands.

"I swear to you, I'll free Bethany if it's the last thing I do."

"Melling Militia is on the move!" Phoebe declared as he went for the hall.

"This is no game, Alex!" Lucy called, but he didn't look back.

With Lucy's paper on top, Alexander handed the pages to Frederick. "Your maiden's request is official."

A smile broke his haggard expression. "I tried to talk her out of keeping all the names. It's no wonder she keeps with *Olive Kent* for book signings."

"I'll always be second to you where the Eastons are concerned, Lucy included. She had your name first."

"Now's not the time to be sore about it." Frederick handed him the ransom note and added the banking letters to his own.

Alexander fell into the nearest armchair and unfolded the page bearing the now-familiar handwriting. "It's from Opal! I'd swear to it in court as we've been corresponding for two months."

The policeman notated the information on his pad, and then the room fell away as the horrifying words registered in his mind.

The unwanted child from a broken marriage is no longer your concern. Knowing how it feels to be unloved at the end of a family, I consider it a mercy to help this girl escape her fate. With broken hearts is where she now resides alongside those who understand her pain. If you decide you need this pitiful reminder of what Frederick and Lucille shared, bring twenty-five thousand dollars to the fountain in Bienville Square at midnight. We will spare her miserable life until then. After that, she's lost to you all forever.

"Damn her to Hell!" Alexander crumpled the words and threw the page on the floor.

"That's evidence, Mr. Melling." The officer retrieved it.

Broken hearts.

Opal never spoke of hearts—of love. In her twisted views, she scorned what others had. What was it she said to me when I picked her up at the train station and drove her about town on the way to her parents? "But your heart is still here."

The cathedral!

He tore out of the house, riding boots striking the brick path on his way to the road.

"Alex!" Freddy shouted behind him. "Alex, wait!"

But he ran on, dodging an approaching streetcar as he crossed Government Street in the dark. Alexander ignored the stares from fellow pedestrians, the honks from the automobiles. Surprised at his swiftness, he cut through the chill night air like an arrow on target until his destination was in sight. He slowed the last block and shoved through the cathedral gate. Bracing a hand on one of the portico columns, he paused to catch his breath.

"God help me," he pled. "Keep Bethany safe, and be with Lucy and our child."

Alexander crossed himself and opened the left door on the portico. A few dozen candles burned, lighting the cavernous space enough for him to check the confessional booths. He walked the marble floor up the nave, pausing amid the pews on the way to the front. An opening in the ground marked by a tiny iron banister held a circular staircase that led to the basement.

Muttering a prayer of forgiveness, he stole a candle lit by an unknown parishioner and went for the stairs stealthily, not knowing if Bethany would be alone or guarded. The gray stone walls didn't hold the splendor of the nave, but the sacred stillness of the space carried through to the bowels of the cathedral.

And then he heard it.

Moans and grunts of procreation.

Opal and Bruce were nearby, but he needed to find Bethany while they were otherwise engaged. He peered in the first alcove, seeming to be a collection of discarded hymnals on wooden shelves. The next space held a jumble of broken pews. The third alcove was closed off with bars, much like a dungeon. Within lay Bethany curled upon a man's suit jacket on the stone floor, behind her a collection of relics from half a century of the cathedral's history. Her face was streaked with dried tears, but she appeared to be sleeping.

Wanting to know where Opal resided before chancing the door, Alexander set the candle near Bethany's prison and crept forward.

Two alcoves beyond, the flickering glow of candlelight glinted off the dank walls. Peering around the arched entrance, he moved an inch at a time. Bruce Youngblood's back was to the doorway, his pants around his ankles. Opal, draped across a bench padded with vintage bishop's robes, had her eyes closed as the man ruthlessly drove into her. If there had been anything in his stomach, Alexander would have announced himself by spewing on the floor.

He stumbled back to his stepdaughter. "Bethany, my child," he whispered.

Her dark eyes opened, and—bless her quiet voice—she replied with a soft, "Poppy."

Alexander brought a finger to his lips. "I'm going to help you, Bethany Iris. Stand up and be ready for me."

He pulled the handle of the door, and it squealed open with an ear-splitting creak.

"Get off me," Opal's sharp voice cut the air. "The brat's awake."

"She's not going anywhere, and you know how I get when we're interrupted."

The sounds of their demented fervor heightened. Alexander held Bethany to his chest and rushed for the stairs, no longer caring about noise.

From the nave above, Frederick shouted, "Alex, where are you?"

There was a scuffle behind him, but Alexander stumbled up the spiral staircase. From below, a hand snatched the ankle of his boot, and he fell forward on Bethany three steps from the top.

"Freddy, take her!"

Frederick appeared in the opening as Alexander was yanked backward. He held to Bethany until her father's hands were reaching for her. Then he grasped the banister to keep from falling. Once Bethany was safely in Frederick's arms, Alexander began kicking, but his legs painfully struck the metal bars more often than made contact with the man.

"Just shoot him!" Opal shouted. "He's nothing to us, and it would pain Lucille."

"I don't have it on me!"

Alexander heaved himself upright and jumped over the curving banister, landing on Bruce. He pressed the man's head into the floor and jammed his knee into his back but was soon flipped and found himself staring at the ceiling as Bruce ran for the alcove.

Opal stood over him in her underclothes, laughing. "You're unfit to defend anyone, let alone your pathetic self."

Alexander grabbed her leg and yanked her to the floor. Taking a dominant stance on top of Opal, he realized he didn't know what to do from there. His body instinctively wanted to advance in a sexual way.

As though she saw the confusion on his face, Opal smirked. "Have you come to take me, Alexander? Did you watch us before freeing Bethany? Am I not as glorious as Lucille now? More so, as my body isn't soft from birthing babies or swollen with child." She arched into him, her firm breasts unpleasantly near his face. "I was made a woman at the age of twelve and would welcome you. What's one more conquest to a man with your history?"

He wanted to press his hands into her face. Pummel her. Kick her until she could no longer speak! But he couldn't. No matter what devil possessed her, Opal's body was that of a young woman, and Alexander couldn't attack.

Being unable to protect those I love from this hideous threat makes me weak, but that's who I am.

Alexander pushed off the floor to stand as a gunshot ricocheted off the walls.

"You idiot!" Opal scrambled toward Bruce. "You could have killed me!"

Springing for the stairs, Alexander shouted upward. "Stay back!"

Halfway up, a shot rang out, and a burning sensation struck his right leg. Alexander gripped the banister but continued up the corkscrew turn. Another bullet hit his left side. Crying out, he collapsed at the top of the staircase, blood pooling on the pale marble beneath him.

A police officer grabbed his right arm and dragged him toward the rear of the cathedral. Near the doors, Frederick had Bethany wrapped in his shirt as he stood in his tournament shorts within the hallowed walls.

Alexander gasped. "Get her out of here!"

"But I promised Lu—"

"Don't let this be in vain!" Alexander sucked in his breath. The pain radiated as he grew light-headed. "Tell her I love her. Always."

The cathedral went dark.

Thirty-Four

Melissa stood on the veranda where she'd kept vigil after Alex and Freddy ran into the night. Several policemen followed them, but a few were still at the house, including one guarding the backyard and two in the front. The air was chill, but knowing Bethany was somewhere without a loved one made Melissa feel selfish to seek a coat or the warmth of the house. The child had been through too much already at her tender age.

Melissa stayed there for nearly an hour before Henry pulled to stop in his automobile.

"Freddy has her! Alex found Opal and Bruce at the cathedral with Bethany!"

Melissa clung to Henry. "Where are they?"

"At the hospital." His voice dropped. "Bethany appeared fine, but Freddy wanted her examined."

Melissa laughed, joyful for the first time since Freddy won the tournament—which seemed like a lifetime ago. "Of course he would."

"But Alex was shot. Twice."

Melissa caught her throat. "No!"

"Fortunately, it's his limbs, not his torso. Will you come when I tell Lucy?"

"Dare we? What would that do to her?"

"She deserves to know." Henry steered Melissa inside.

Phoebe slept on the loveseat, Douglas stood near the back window with Simon in his arms, and Maggie and Darla flanked Lucy in chairs beside the sofa.

Lucy sat up, blonde hair as tousled as the emotions she wore on her face. "What's happened?"

"Alex found them." Henry came forward. "I don't know all the details, but they were hiding in the basement of the cathedral. Alex was able to secure Bethany and passed her to Freddy before they attacked."

Lucy's lip quivered.

"He was shot in the leg and then through the arm. The police captured Opal and Bruce and took all the injured to the hospital. Freddy brought Bethany along to be inspected as well."

Lucy stood up too quickly, and Darla and Henry both took hold of her swaying form. "I must go to them!"

"Easy, Lucy." Darla's calm voice attempted to soothe her. "You need to slow down. Henry and I will bring you and Melissa. Maggie and Douglas will stay with Phoebe, but you must promise to stay calm."

"I will, just take me to them!"

"We need to stop at the Davenport's house on the way. Freddy's still in his boxing shorts, and Bethany could use a fresh change of clothes." Henry kept a firm arm around Lucy.

"And Alex will need something as well." Lucy sighed. "But I don't think I can make it upstairs."

"Tell me where to look, and I'll go," Melissa offered.

Though it was odd to go through another man's clothing, Melissa collected a fresh pair of underdrawers, socks, pants, and a shirt. Remembering Alex had on his riding clothes, she grabbed a pair of loafers as well. Then she did the same for Freddy and Bethany at their house.

Darla secured a wheelchair for Lucy, and Henry pushed her down the hospital corridor until they found the waiting room where Freddy held Bethany swaddled in his shirt. He had a blanket around his bare shoulders that fluttered like a cape as he swayed.

He dropped to his knees before Lucy. "I told you Momma would come, Little Princess."

Bethany clung to Lucy's neck, crying as Lucy kissed her cheek. Freddy took Melissa into his arms, crushing the wardrobe items she held. "It's over. We just need Alex out from surgery. After Bethany settles with Lucy, I'll tell her what happened."

"Your clothes." Melissa raised her arms.

"Bless you, Beloved."

She watched Freddy until he disappeared around the corner, and then she turned her attention back to Lucy and Bethany.

"Sissa got your flannel nightgown and diapers for you, Bethany Iris. Can Momma get you ready for bed?"

"Home, Momma."

"We'll go as soon as I see Poppy, but we have to wait."

"Melling Militia rescue!" It was the most volume Melissa had ever heard the girl use outside of laughter. "Poppy loves me!"

Tears flowed down Lucy's pale face. "I know, Bethany. He was smart and brave and wonderful."

Lucy insisted on rising so she could see to Bethany herself. Using clean washcloths and a pan of warm water Darla secured from a nurses' station, Lucy washed her daughter and fastened her clean clothing. Freddy joined them, looking refreshed though weary. He cuddled Bethany while Darla helped Lucy into the wheelchair and then returned his daughter to her mother.

Sitting beside Lucy, Freddy took the hand that didn't hold Bethany and told what he knew of Alex's battle—his struggle to get Bethany up the stairs, being dragged down, and then his escape when they shot him.

"After the officer pulled him to safety, he told me to get Beth out and tell you he loved you, Goosy. It was the last thing he said before he fainted."

Her green eyes were huge. "From pain or blood loss?"

"I don't know. He's with Dr. Woodslow, and I haven't been updated since we got here."

"I'll see what I can find out." Darla, taking Henry by the hand, went in search of a nurse.

Bethany was soon asleep, and Freddy assured Lucy she'd eaten and drunk fine after her examination and that nothing was wrong with her other than being chilled from her exposure in the damp basement all evening.

"She's resilient, Goosy. There's no need to fear."

Lucy leaned her head on his shoulder and closed her eyes. A prick of jealousy stabbed at Melissa.

Freddy kissed Lucy's forehead then looked to Melissa with gratitude. "I love you," he whispered to his wife.

"I love you, too, Frederick. You're my best friend."

Melissa covered her mouth to stifle a laugh over Lucy claiming Freddy's words. He winked at her and rested his head on Lucy's a moment.

"And you're my goose."

"And fair maiden?" Lucy asked, eyes still closed.

"Yes, though Alex has proven himself worthy of being a knight."

Darla and Henry returned, each of their hands holding a mug of coffee. Lucy straightened to accept hers, and then Henry was gone to collect one more.

"We've been promised to have word within a quarter of an hour," Darla assured them. She quickly drank her coffee and relieved Lucy of sleeping Bethany so she could drink easier.

Bethany settled against Darla's familiar form. Henry returned to the room with a cup of steaming coffee and a cigarette. He settled near the window but watched Darla with a private smile. Thinking the young man yearned to see Darla holding their own child, Melissa hoped he would see his desire come to fruition like she and Freddy were going to experience.

As though sensing her maternal thoughts, Freddy left Lucy and took the seat beside Melissa, a hand going to her middle as he kissed her temple. "How are you feeling?"

"Tired, but all right."

The main detective who had taken all the statements at the Mellings' house came in with another policeman.

"Mr. Melling will be able to see you soon. We still need to get his statement as soon as possible. When the doctor clears him for visitors, we'll give you a few minutes before asking you to leave."

"You cannot keep me from my husband!" Lucy's outrage startled Bethany, but Darla managed to soothe her back to sleep.

"Only for half an hour at most, Mrs. Melling. We know you've all had a trying day, and we don't wish to keep you later than necessary." He scratched his graying head. "I'm not sure what you've heard, but we've been holding Otis Youngblood for a couple of hours. He admits to driving his cousin to the Mellings' house and then taking him and Bethany Davenport to the cathedral. He swears he was told it was a joke between Opal and Mrs. Melling. A prank from one sister to another. He didn't realize a ransom note was part of the plot or that his cousin possessed a revolver. Opal Easton and

Bruce Youngblood were both apprehended in the cathedral after Youngblood shot Mr. Melling. Miss Easton is currently sedated in a room upstairs with a guard on duty. Youngblood sustained a gunshot wound himself and is in critical condition as we speak."

Lucy trembled. "I don't wish to stay here with them—"

"They are no longer a threat, Mrs. Melling," the detective assured her.

Seeing her need, Freddy returned to Lucy's side, gathering her hands in his. "I'll stay with you as long as you need me, Goosy."

Dr. John Woodslow entered, eyeing the crowded space. "Lucy, darling! Don't tell me you need to be seen all decked out in a wheelchair as well."

"It was a precaution to prevent her overtiring herself because of the stress," Darla said.

"Yes, Mrs. Adams. I'm well aware of the precautions you like to take." Seeing Henry's cold stare at the tone the doctor took with his wife, Dr. Woodslow smiled and nodded. "Congratulations on the win today, Adams. And Davenport as well."

"What about Alex, John?" Lucy asked.

"He's out of danger and awake. I cleaned and stitched up his right leg, which was just a graze, fortunately. The bullet to his arm proved more difficult, but he should be good as new in a month or two. And I promise my stitches will be prettier than anything that mars his skin. He's been through the wringer, hasn't he?"

Lucy smiled in relief. "More than I'd wish on him."

"But who could blame him his trials when he ended with the splendid Lucy Easton on his arm at the end?" The doctor leaned forward, brazenly flirting with her. "Did you know it was me who telephoned him at his office the morning you came in after being attacked by your sister?"

"No, I never did."

"He was a wreck that day. I had to hide him away in a doctors' lounge until your family went upstairs, though I never understood why with you two being engaged. But that night, the nurse caught him sleeping on your bed, and I understood why he wanted to hide from your brothers." The doctor was the only one who laughed.

"He didn't do anything besides try to comfort me."

"I know my man Melling from back then. You needn't try to cover for him, Lucy."

"I beg your pardon, Dr. Woodslow"—Freddy spoke through gritted teeth—"but you're walking a dangerous line of compromising a lady's reputation in mixed company."

"My apologies. I was only reminiscing on the old days."

"Of course, but will you bring me to Alex now?" Lucy asked.

"No more than three people at a time, and not in these wheels. It would upset him to see you like this. He needs to be buoyed, not worry over his lovely wife. I'll walk you down. It's just around the corner."

"Frederick." Darla's voice had enough warning to alert the whole city.

"I'll push the chair to his room and help her in," Freddy told the doctor.

"Suit yourselves. Follow me, just three of you."

"Go on." Darla motioned to Melissa. "Henry and I will wait until after the police see him."

"Thank you."

Melissa walked beside Freddy as he pushed the chair down two corridors. Had the doctor forced Lucy to walk that far in her condition, she would have collapsed in the room—if she made it that far.

"He's a miserable Dardenne, though he pretends to be kind," Freddy muttered.

Melissa patted his arm. "Lucy's in good hands with you and Darla around."

"Yes, Freddy. Thank you for everything," Lucy said.

"I'm here to help, Goosy."

Thirty-Five

Alexander shifted in the hospital bed, grimacing as the movement pulled his stitches and sent his head spinning with pain. Wishing he had more than his underdrawers on so the stiff sheets couldn't scratch at his skin, he looked to his brown boots standing beside the door—the only thing salvageable from his riding outfit.

"Blasted Opal," he muttered.

His roommate, an elderly gentleman who was recuperating from a heart episode, grumbled in reply.

The door opened. Freddy came in with Lucy on his arm, Melissa behind them. The worry on Lucy's beautiful face melted briefly as she smiled at him. It seemed like an eternity that he waited, but neither spoke or moved for several seconds as they took in the sight of the other. She had dark smudges under her eyes and held herself as one exhausted. Reaching a hand out to her, he sat up and winced.

She rushed to his side. "You look like you're in agony."

"Kiss me and make it all better, my queen."

It began soft, and her lips gnawed away his discomfort. Ignoring the eyes upon them, he lifted a hand to her neck and slowly trailed down to her chest as he savored the deep, probing kiss they shared.

"My Lucy." His mouth was all over her jaw. "How is Bethany?"

"Good, and it's all thanks to you from what I've gathered." She hugged a little too tight around his shoulders, but he tried not to let it show. "You're a hero, Alex."

The words stabbed his unworthy heart. "Please don't praise me. I only did what I needed to, both for Bethany and to right the wrong I did in bringing Opal here. I am not a hero."

"Your scars prove otherwise."

"They were all begotten because of my sins!" His desperation set him on the defensive.

"Which you turned around and atoned for every time." Lucy pulled the sheet back, kissing his chest scars, then his hands. She kissed above the bandage on his left arm, then his discolored cheek, and moved to lift the bed sheet from his lower half.

"We really don't want to see what's down there, Goosy."

"It can't be any worse than the whole town seeing you run the streets in your boxing shorts," Alex countered as Melissa buried her head against her husband's chest and laughed. "Go on and see to my leg, Lucy. Melissa isn't peeking, though she's welcome to."

"I don't think I'd be able to recover from seeing your magnificence, Alex," Melissa teased.

Alexander laughed and then sucked in his breath so he wouldn't cry out over the discomfort the movement evoked.

Lucy lowered to his right leg. The bandage was above his knee with the most padding on the outside of the leg. Her lips between the wrap and his underdrawers were stimulating, but she quickly straightened as though she didn't wish to arouse him in his present situation.

"Come here, Lucy." He kissed her. "Thank you for loving me as you do."

"You're my essence."

His heart and loins swelled with her passionate words. "I'll have to drop out of polo practice and riding to favor my leg and won't be able to use my arm for weeks."

"I know, Alex, but you'll heal."

"Yes, with your loving attention." His right hand fingered her cheek, and his lips brushed her ear as he whispered. "You'll need to ride me slow and gentle until then. Can you do that for me?"

"It will be my pleasure." Her hand went to his chest, working its way down. "Do you need me now?"

He bent a knee to prop the sheet higher, concealing the power his wife had over him. His voice returned to normal volume. "I don't think now is the time or place. Mr. Cummings, my respectable roommate, is recovering from a heart episode, and it would be too much for him."

"Don't mind me, youngsters. This is the most fun I've had in years."

Lucy's radiant face blushed as the others laughed.

"God knows I love and need you, my queen."

John returned with the police officers. "As much as I hate to pull your gorgeous wife away from you, Alex, the police need to take your statement, and then I'll give you some medicine to help you sleep."

"Darla and Henry are waiting to see him after the officers," Lucy told the doctor.

John took her arm. "I'll be sure they get a chance to say hello before he gets his nightcap. I had the pharmacist's best draught prepared for your husband. Alex will be well-rested in the morning, I promise."

"Then he'll be able to come home?"

John appeared as moved by her anxious green eyes as Alexander was. The doctor patted her arm and smiled reassuringly. "When we change out the bandage, we'll check for infection. If it looks clear, I'll release him, so you needn't spend more than one night alone."

Concerned, Alexander moved to take Lucy's hand, but Frederick stepped forward.

"We'll stay with her, Alex."

"Thank you, Freddy. Melissa. Now kiss me once more, my queen, and go home."

"No matter what you say, you're my hero. Our hero." She held his hand on her round belly until the baby moved.

"I'll try to be worthy."

Alexander gave his statement about the sordid events in the cathedral and answered the officers' questions. By the end of the inquiry, he was beaded with sweat from pain and discomfort. Darla and Henry came in with John, and she was quick to embrace him.

"You've given us all a fright, but we're happy you're alive."

"I always knew you cared." Alexander kissed Darla's cheek. "Please watch over Lucy."

"We're all staying at the house tonight. A few of us will come back tomorrow to check on you."

Henry placed a stack of Alexander's clothing and shoes on the side table. "Take care, Melling. I'll get your family home now."

After they left, John checked his bandages and then poured a shot glass-sized amount of brown liquid into a medicine cup. "Bottoms up, Alex. This will give you sweet dreams."

"I just want the pain to fade."

"You won't feel anything with this mix."

Alex took the whole amount in one swig, flinching at the burn as it slid down his throat.

"I'll see you tomorrow, Brother."

***

Alexander tried to move, but his limbs felt heavy. His head swam with images of Lucy, and it took him several moments to decide they were dreams, not memories. As glorious as she was, Lucy's bare skin on his horse's shining black coat wasn't something Alexander had ever seen. He opened his eyes and moaned at the brightness.

"*Amico*, welcome to the land of the living."

"Claudio." Alexander tried to freshen his pasty mouth with his tongue as he pushed the itchy sheet off his torso, wincing though he didn't use his hurt arm. "I wish I were dead."

"You have had an active morning, even if you slept through it all."

"What do you mean? What time is it?"

"Almost noon. I have been with you since half-past five, though I wish I would have arrived a few minutes prior. I might have been able to spare your roommate some trouble."

Alexander turned and saw the empty bed. "What happened to Mr. Cummings?"

"His heart was over-stimulated with expectations."

A crooked grin found his face. "Don't tell me Lucy came to me."

"If only it were Lucy."

His smile shattered. "Dear God, what happened?"

"Ms. Kline told your roommate if he kept quiet, she would see to him next."

Nausea swept over him such that he had to lay back. "Don't tell me she—"

"She only got as far as pulling off your blanket. I came in, and she tried to say she was checking your bandages. The gentleman did not like her lying to a priest, so he confessed her true purpose and that he looked forward to being taken care of because his wife had refused since his heart trouble began."

Alexander sighed. "Could there be no better way to die?"

Claudio laughed. "You must be well. Your perverted sense of humor has returned."

"I'm not joking, but what else was said and done?"

"You were still as death the whole time, but you spoke in your sleep. 'Ooh, Lucy' and 'faster' were the most often used phrases, coupled with a few—"

Alexander laughed and then groaned. "I dreamt of her the whole time. My wife is magnificent."

"*Sí*, Lucy is wonderful, and I am happy things were not worse from the events of yesterday. Bethany is safe, and you will recover. Allow me to see if a doctor or nurse will be in soon and telephone the house. No one has wanted to disturb you."

By the time the stitches were checked, and bandages changed, Melissa and Frederick collected him. Wearing the fresh clothes brought to him the night before, Alexander leaned on Frederick as he climbed into the back of the giant touring automobile. He lay on the seat and gazed at the blue autumn sky. Images of Lucy above him from his impassioned dreams filled his mind such that he could picture her amid the clouds and canopy of trees he passed under.

"Alex." Melissa turned to face him. "Freddy and I are supposed to take the girls to St. Augustine tomorrow, but we can postpone the trip. Lucy might not want the girls gone so soon."

"She could use the quiet time, especially with Opal and Youngblood being held in town. It might help her feel better if the girls were away from here."

"She brought Bethany to bed with her and held her all night." Melissa's brown eyes showcased her concern.

"That's natural for a mother, as you'll soon learn." Alex grinned. "I'll speak with her when we have a quiet moment, but I think she'll agree with me."

"And if not," Frederick said, "you'll swindle her into it."

"All I would need to say is that I need her undivided attention to heal properly. She couldn't say no to that, especially after calling me a hero."

Frederick shook his head. "There'll be no living this down."

"I don't claim the status, and I told Lucy as much. I'm just a man in love with the most amazing woman in the world."

At home, Alexander settled on the sofa in the front room with his wounded leg propped on top of the coffee table and Lucy close beside him. Darla brought Bethany in first. She immediately ran for him, and he tensed, expecting the impact to jar, but she slowed and carefully climbed into his lap.

"Thank you, Poppy." She kissed his unshaven face with a tenderness only Lucy's offspring could give. "Melling Militia rescue."

His laugh felt more like a choked sob as he gave her the biggest one-armed hug he could. "I tried my best, Bethany Iris. And you were a brave knight. I love you."

Then Phoebe was allowed in, and Bethany switched to Lucy's arms.

"Beth said you saved her, that Melling Militia got her out of the dungeon." She touched his prickly cheeks. "Thank you for saving my sister. I'm sorry you received battle wounds."

"I'd do it again to save either of you."

"You're a true knight, Poppy."

"Time to let him rest now, girls." Frederick took a daughter in each arm. "You'll see him at supper."

Melissa waited near the door.

"Do you wish to see anyone else?" Lucy asked.

"I'd like to rest, but who all is here?"

"For the time being, it's just the Campbells. We have all that food from what was to be the party yesterday. I've asked them to stay for supper. The Walkers are coming, as well as Henry, Darla, and Claudio. Naomi and Sharon are already preparing things. If you aren't up to sitting at the table, I'd be happy to share a tray with you in bed."

He ran his hand through her silky hair. "Let me rest, and I'll see how I feel, but you should be with our guests, no matter what. There'll be time for us later."

"When?" Her eyes were luminous.

"I think Freddy and Melissa should go on their trip with the girls tomorrow. You and I could do with a quiet week to rest and rejuvenate. Spend the afternoon with the girls, and then you can worry extra about me and my wounds beginning tonight."

Her kiss was like velvet on his lips. "Where do you wish to rest?"

"My den, so I don't need to navigate the stairs until bedtime." He looked to the doorway. "Melissa, would you send Douglas to help me? And Maggie. I'd like to thank them both."

While they waited, Alexander initiated a passionate kiss with Lucy that awakened his desires.

Douglas cleared his throat, but Alexander took his time ending the kiss.

"Did ye not wish help?"

"Lucy and I require no help when it comes to lovemaking."

"That we can see," Douglas said with a smile, "but I speak of getting you to a more private location."

"Where the said lovemaking can occur?" Alexander teased as he traced Lucy's curves with his good hand and then extended his arm for Douglas to pull him to his feet. His right side leaned heavily on his friend until they paused before Magdalene.

"Don't you have enough scars already?" she asked.

"I fancied a few more for my collection. Rips, burns, and bullets. I'd say that makes me well-rounded."

"Only you could pull that off, Alexander." Magdalene hugged him and kissed his cheek. "I always said you were a lion."

"And you've always seen through me, Magdalene. Thank you for believing in me and helping this weekend. You too, Douglas."

"Aye, we Seacliff friends stick together."

Thirty-Six

Even though exhausted, Melissa was glad to see all the friends gather around the Mellings' table Sunday evening. She enjoyed spending time with the Campbells and Walkers and loved any hours with Darla, Henry, and Claudio. Alex took supper at the table, Lucy on one side and Maggie on the other—spoiled with affection from both women.

Tired from playing with their island friends, Phoebe and Bethany fell asleep on the ride home. The girls were hurriedly washed and changed for bed.

Arms around Doff, Phoebe snuggled onto her pillow with ease. "Kade still likes me best, even if he plays with Abe Walker," she whispered to her cat.

When Freddy joined Melissa in their bedroom, he took her in his arms. "God's cared for the girls extra this weekend."

"The whole family."

"You must be tired, but at least the train doesn't leave until midday so we can sleep as long as we want in the morning." He rubbed her back in a circular motion. "What do you want to do now?"

"Take a warm bath."

Freddy started filling the tub. "Any salts or fragrances?"

"Surprise me," she called back to him.

He returned a minute later with a smile. "I think your vacation should begin tonight. I'll be back with tea shortly."

Melissa found herself in a bubble bath smelling of gardenias. She washed her hair first and then laid back, eyes closed. Her mind—racing with thoughts of the trip—made it impossible to relax fully.

"Your tea, Beloved." Freddy set the saucer by the sink and handed her the teacup.

"I hate to ask for something—"

"What can I do for you?"

She smiled sheepishly. "I need to make a list of what I need to do tomorrow."

"You and your lists." He kissed her.

When he returned to the bathroom, he had the dressing table stool and her notebook from the bedside table. His shirt was half unbuttoned, the patch of dark hair peeking between the white an inviting sight as he settled tub-side.

Melissa rattled off everything from cat food to camera while Freddy took faithful notes.

"Could you hold it up so I can see everything?"

A third of the way down the list she'd dictated, the additions began: "Wake Freddy with a kiss." Two entries beyond: "Sunrise session of love." And the final entry: COMPLETE ALL WITH THE HELP OF MY HUSBAND!

"The list appears to have everything important."

"I'll do all your bidding."

She passed Freddy her cup, which he set on the sink. "Then join me."

Watching him disrobe continued to be as tantalizing as it was the first time. Melissa released some of the water to add more hot before standing. Then Freddy settled in, and after the water was the right temperature and depth, she lay back against his chest—his arms wrapping around her until his hands rested low on her belly.

"You needn't be afraid," he spoke into her ear. "And don't try to push yourself too much, on the trip or otherwise. Allow me to help. You aren't alone on this journey to motherhood."

The feel of her husband surrounding her and his loving words brought a smile to her lips and relief to her anxieties. "It isn't me alone on this path because it took a man to start me on this journey."

"I'm blessed to have that honor, to share with you the fullness of marriage. I waited my whole life for this kind of love. Thank you for sharing it with me, Melissa."

***

The Davenports arrived in St. Augustine on Tuesday afternoon. Phoebe, eager to stretch her legs after the train journey, begged her father to walk from the station to the hotel. Melissa took the opportunity to ride to Hotel Ponce de Leon with their luggage in the hopes of unpacking before Freddy arrived with the girls.

When the taxi pulled onto the hotel grounds, Melissa looked in appreciation at the sprawling structure topped with terracotta tiles and turrets as spectacular as many buildings she'd seen in Europe. *The girls will think they've arrived at a palace.*

She smoothed her gray traveling suit and entered the exquisitely carved oak woodwork and detailed mosaic floor of the lobby. Under the soaring magnificence of the rotunda, she was greeted by a middle-aged man.

"Welcome to the Ponce de Leon, Madame. How may I help you?"

"I'm Melissa Davenport. Our daughters talked my husband into walking from the train station, but I'd like to get the room settled as soon as possible. The taxi with our luggage is out front."

"Of course, Mrs. Davenport." He bowed and led her to the desk. "We've been looking forward to your family's arrival. I trust your trip from Alabama was pleasant. Sign in at the desk, and I'll have someone show you to your suite. The hotel staff loves *Noble Travels* and is honored to host you this week. I hope you enjoy your stay."

A few minutes later, she was shown to a gorgeous corner suite overlooking the gardens. She directed the luggage to the bedroom she chose for her and Freddy, and after tipping the bellhop, immediately set to opening the windows to feel the warm air. She started unpacking in hopes their supper clothes would hang out properly so she wouldn't need to send them to be pressed.

After putting the last of Phoebe's underclothes in a drawer, Melissa took a moment to look out the window at the tropical grounds. She immediately spied Freddy in his brown walking suit and derby—Bethany a burst of yellow on his shoulders and Phoebe a streak of lavender running ahead of them. He tipped his hat to everyone he passed, and when Phoebe stopped by a group of ladies near the building, all heads turned to him when he came up behind her.

The women were a mass of smiles and flickering fans. One went so far as to bend down and coo over Phoebe.

"Thank you," Phoebe's boisterous voice carried on the breeze, "but I'm a big girl now. I can ride a pony and make my own bed."

The women tittered.

"It's most refreshing to see a man about with his children," a lady in white said. "Did you travel here alone?"

Smooth way of finding out if he's eligible.

"Not at all. I walked with my daughters from the station, but my wife took a taxi to have a head start on settling in."

"Do we get to go in the castle now, Daddy?" Phoebe asked.

"Yes, Princess. If you would excuse us, ladies, we're eager to see our accommodations and be reunited with my better half."

As soon as Freddy and the girls were out of sight, the women reconvened in a tight circle. A few choice words made their way to the open window: amiable, strong as an ox, and handsome among them.

Melissa hurriedly changed into a tea gown and perched on one of the settees to wait.

"Sissa, isn't it lovely?" Phoebe squealed as soon as they were in the door. "It's a giant fairy castle with a magical garden!"

Melissa hugged her back. "Wait until you see your bedroom. Pinky, Rummy, and Baby are on the bed you'll share with Beth."

Bethany stopped for a kiss and then chased her sister.

Freddy leaned over Melissa, an appreciative gaze on the low neckline of her dress. "Does everything meet your satisfaction?"

"The suite is perfect, and the hotel is as fine as any place I ever stayed. I was able to unpack everything, but could you move the luggage out of the way? I nestled the smaller cases into the trunk, and I thought they could be pushed into the corner."

"First, I want to ring for tea to be sent up, something to hold us over until our supper reservation. And then I'm afraid we might need to take the girls swimming. The porter insisted on showing them the gigantic indoor pool before bringing us to the room. Phoebe is more than excited."

"Leave Beth if she seems tired. I'll stay with her."

"Do you need the rest?"

"I'm fine either way, Freddy, though I do think I'll sleep well tonight."

After he telephoned for room service and set the luggage to rights, he joined her on the settee. They listened to the girls playing in their room, and Melissa leaned her head on his shoulder. The next thing she knew, there was a knock on the door.

"Rise and shine, Beloved." Freddy kissed her cheek.

The tea service was set at a table for four by the windows. Enjoying the view and fresh air, the Davenports partook of the sandwiches and sweets. Afterward, Melissa helped the girls into their bathing suits, matching navy sailor style with knee-length bloomers. She passed through the bathroom that connected the two bedrooms and found Freddy looking every bit the athletic man he was in a navy suit of his own. The shorts reached mid-thigh, and the cut of the sleeveless top accentuated his broad shoulders and sculpted arms.

"I don't think it's fair for you to go to the pool. All the other men will feel inferior next to you."

"Only because I have a gorgeous wife and the prettiest daughters."

Melissa shut herself in the bathroom while she changed into her cornflower blue suit. The pant hem hit above her knees, the over-dress half as long. The embroidered detail and piping at the neckline and belted waist coupled with the puffed short sleeves helped her feel feminine in the best possible way. She let down her hair and opened the door.

"Have I ever remarked how wonderful it is that bathing stockings are going out of style?" Freddy took her hairbrush off the dresser and brushed through her copper waves in preparation for a braid.

She laughed. "It's much easier without them, but did you know there are some bathing houses and beaches where swimmers wear nothing at all?"

"Don't tell me you frequented them on your travels."

"I may have gone to a few—for research, you know."

In the vaulted pool room, Freddy and Melissa stayed with the girls near the staircase the first quarter-hour until they were used to the depth of the water. Then Freddy sent Melissa off to swim. After a few laps, she floated on her back, looking up at the second and third-floor balcony openings in the casino where guests could look down at the pool.

The group of women she'd seen in the gardens arrived under one of the arches, and she propelled herself toward them.

One was quick to point out Freddy. "There he is with his girls again! Did I not tell you he was strong?"

"His arms are twice the size of the man next to him."

"Just look at those shoulders!"

"How could his wife leave him alone so much? If my George looked like that, I'd never leave his side."

Melissa smiled and flipped around to swim the length of the pool twice more. The second time she drew near the stairs, she glided to a stop beside Phoebe.

"Sissa, you swim like a mermaid. I want to learn! Daddy says he's going to ask about lessons for me."

"That will be wonderful. Women can compete in the Olympics now as swimmers. Maybe you can be an Olympian someday."

"I'd rather compete on horses." Her mouth was firm, her chin defiantly Easton.

Melissa laughed. "There's plenty of time to decide. For now, climb on my back and hold loosely under my arms."

Melissa pushed off in a smooth glide while Phoebe squealed. A moment later, Freddy was beside them with Bethany, her arms linked through the fabric of his suit between his shoulder blades. They swam and played for almost another hour before they forced the girls out of the water.

Partway through showering, Melissa realized she should have gotten out of the pool earlier to conserve energy. But she survived, and the Davenports arrived in style to their supper reservation. They were seated in a quiet alcove, and even Phoebe kept her voice to a polite level.

It could have been her impending motherhood or the attention Freddy received from the women, but Melissa was near bursting in her role as Mrs. Davenport. She felt beautiful in her emerald peacock gown, and Freddy's attention fed her happiness all the more. While the girls were eating dessert, Freddy tipped a waiter to stand watch at the table so he and Melissa could dance, sharing a Viennese waltz with a sensual grace.

"Will you dance with me once more tonight, in the sitting room?" he whispered on the way back to their table.

"Gladly."

"Daddy, you and Sissa looked as pretty as Momma and Poppy!"

Freddy laughed and lifted Phoebe into his arms, kissing her. "Come, it's time for bed."

He set her down, and she took Melissa's hand. Bethany snuggled against her father's shoulder and fell asleep before they made it to the elevator. Freddy did nothing more than remove the girls' footwear and dresses before tucking them in bed in their underclothes. Melissa waited on the settee, feet bare and hair down.

When Freddy joined her, his shoes and jacket were gone, but the white bowtie was still under his bearded chin, though somewhat crooked.

There was a knock at the door, and Freddy answered. He returned to Melissa with a silver tray bearing a wine bottle and two glasses.

"You didn't need—" Melissa began.

"I didn't. Why don't you read the note?"

Frederick and Melissa,

Please accept this small gift of appreciation on your first true night of vacation. I can never repay you for your love, friendship, and support. This weekend would have been much different without either of you beside me and Lucy. We miss you and the girls already but know you need the time away as much as we need the quiet to heal and rest. Enjoy your adventure, but more importantly, each other. Hugs for the girls from both of us.

We'll see you in a week.

Love, Alex

"He even charms through a letter."

Freddy took her hand and brought her to his arms. He kissed her lips and then the skin exposed by the scooped neckline of her gown. "We have a promised dance to fulfill. Afterward, we'll drink to Alex's health, and then I'm going to carry you to bed and enjoy our time together—as he recommends."

Thirty-Seven

As the clock struck midnight, advancing Tuesday night to Wednesday morning, Alexander lay awake in bed. He'd spent the last two days there with Lucy. While his leg was much improved, the bullet wound in his arm still throbbed several times a day. After the hangover from John's potent sleeping draught in the hospital—and the fact he wasn't awakened when Hazel came to him—he refused any sleep aids or pain medicine. He needed to be alert at all times to protect Lucy. But there was a natural remedy that took his focus away from the pain, and he needed another dose.

"Lucy, my queen, I need you." She made a humming sound and shifted. His right hand caressed over her hip to her backside and squeezed her through the silken gown. "My glorious Lucy, take the pain away."

Turning, she rested her cheek on his chest as her hand roamed down his bare body. "I love you," she murmured.

"And I love you. I can't live without you."

Alexander trailed his fingers across her back as he relaxed under Lucy's rhythmic grip. When he could only think of himself and letting go, his right arm clutched her to him. So sweet and thorough, she brought a warm, damp washcloth to clean up the remnants before she settled back in bed.

He tucked her against his right side, though the position put pressure on his leg bandage. "I hope to repay your benevolence a thousandfold."

Her lips tingled against his neck. "When the baby comes, I'll need you more than ever. Try to sleep, my angel."

And he did.

Waking to the sound of a blue jay fight screeching through the open window, Alexander marveled at the steady movement within Lucy that bumped against his ribs. Five minutes he waited, afraid to move lest he woke his wife, who appeared to sleep through the commotion.

Now I understand that proud look Douglas always had in his eyes when he spoke of his strong babies. But how can Lucy love me when I filled her with this squirming mass that brings discomfort?

Slowly he lifted his bandaged arm to touch the mound that held his child. The thin layer of red silk between his hand and Lucy's bulging womb conducted each movement of the baby as though they were one.

"My child," he whispered. "I'll love you the best I can."

Lucy's head raised, and her luminous eyes opened. Her curving smile brought meaning to his day. "Did you finally sleep?"

"Yes, thanks to you. Your touch is my balm." Alexander parted the curtain of blonde hair that hung around her enchanting face. "My queen, my everything, I don't wish to leave you today."

"You told Mr. Connell you'd be in, but three nights and two days of sharing each moment with you has been heavenly, Angel."

"Your cut, burned, and shot angel, my queen."

"And still you survive, renewing yourself from your torments like a phoenix."

"My poet." Alexander kissed her.

"Susan said it first, that Thanksgiving Bethany was born. When I arrived at our parents' house and spoke of you, she said you returned like a phoenix rising from the ashes of Seacliff Cottage."

"I rather like that image."

"It struck me as well, and I think of it often, especially when you're recklessly brave."

"Or burning with desire?" His hand stroked her cheek and followed the curve of her neck to her décolletage.

She arched into his touch. "Do you need me to give you something to remember me by while we're apart?"

"I'm always ready for you and have learned never to turn you away."

Lucy's laughter lightened his soul as much as her lovemaking. Afterward, he sponge bathed and dressed for work, Lucy helping with everything. They descended the stairs together, her purple gown trailing a wake of lavender.

Naomi had a hot breakfast ready and handed Alexander a gold-tipped black walking stick.

"Thought you might be able to use the help for a day or two, Mr. Alex. And it will give you a distinguished look to boot."

"It's dapper with that charcoal suit." Lucy beamed. "Thank you, Naomi."

"Yes." He kissed the cook and tapped the cane on the tile floor. "It's not something I would have admitted needing, but it's perfect for taking the strain off the stitches in my leg."

After breakfast, Alexander gathered his briefcase from the den and slipped on his shoes. He found Lucy at her desk in the morning room and Naomi dusting the mantel.

"Sharon is coming after dinner to help me give the upstairs a good cleaning. We'll see that Miss Lucy naps while we're up there."

"Invite Sharon to stay through supper if she'd like. We might as well lighten your load and give her a bit extra since the Davenports are gone all week."

"She checks on Doff twice a day, but that's easily done to and from here," Naomi said.

"I do miss that cat." Lucy sighed.

"My queen, I'd give you a cat of your own, but with a baby coming, I do believe you'll have plenty to cuddle. Not to mention I'd be afraid you'd pet me less."

Lucy's deep kiss was accompanied by a snaking hand around his neck. "I'd take you over a cat anytime. Hurry home to me."

He locked the kitchen door behind him and drove to the office. After making small talk with Mr. Connell, Alexander collected his mail and messages before closing himself in his room and picked up the telephone.

"Davenport Allied Accountants," the secretary said.

"Mr. Adams, please."

"Whom may I ask is calling?"

Surprised she didn't know his voice—but then again, he couldn't remember her name—he answered curtly. "Melling."

"Good morning, Mr. Melling. I hope you're doing better after your frightful ordeal."

"I'm on the mend, thank you."

"I'll let Mr. Adams know you're on the line. Just a moment."

Henry was quick to respond. "Alex, how can I help?"

"You're already doing me a favor by seeing to Apollo this week."

"That's no trouble. He's well if that's why you're calling."

"I wanted to make sure you're holding up with your extra responsibilities at the office and then having to drive out to Spring Hill every afternoon."

"It's stress relief, not a burden. Lucy knew what she was doing when she bought you a horse. I might need to beg my father for one, but I don't think Darla would put up with equestrian and boxing hobbies."

"You've already proved yourself with a trophy in your division, twice beating out my old friend Sean. Sounds like a good time to return to the stables."

Henry laughed. "I'll think about it."

At nine, Alexander met with a new client seeking divorce due to an unfaithful wife, followed the next hour by a tedious will of an aging grocer. Only when he was alone in his office again did he realize he hadn't lit a cigarette since the kidnapping. Patting his pocket, he felt the case he slipped in earlier without thinking, but he didn't feel the urge to take it out.

Knocking at the door brought him back to the moment. A defeated-looking priest stood on the threshold.

"Claudio, it's good to see you." Alexander embraced his friend. "What's wrong?"

"Hazel is missing. Apparently, she disappeared for a few hours yesterday as well."

"And she told no one?"

"Sister Prudence didn't think it necessary to tell anyone until today."

"Where did she go?"

"She contacted Rupert on Monday, worried your injuries would make it impossible to help her any longer."

"More like not wanting to because she tried to take advantage of me when John had me knocked out!" Alexander removed the gold case from his pocket.

"I may have been too harsh with my chastisement."

"No! That's the worst thing she could have done. The least I can do for Lucy is to keep myself untainted from other women the duration of our marriage."

"Then you drop Hazel as a client?"

"Yes."

"Then it should not matter to you that she met with Rupert at his office yesterday, and he set up an additional meeting this morning at a different location."

"Oh God, no!"

Claudio put a hand on his left shoulder, causing him to wince. "But she is no longer your concern."

"I wouldn't send my worst enemy off with that man! Where did they meet?"

Claudio looked to the ceiling a moment as if gathering heavenly strength. "Your old duplex."

"He's always coveted what was mine!" Alexander pocketed his unopened cigarette case, grabbed the walking stick, and lumbered to his vehicle.

A few minutes later, he parked in the alley off St. Francis Street by the kitchen door. Claudio went ahead of him up the steps but found it locked.

"Bust the pane," Alexander demanded.

"I am a man of God, not an intruder."

Alexander heaved up the stairs and, with a quick jab of the cane, shattered the rectangle of glass over the knob. Reaching in, he opened the door and stood aside for Claudio to enter first. He did the sign of the cross and stepped onto the tile floor. When Alexander closed the door behind them, he felt the breath of Hell at his back.

Lucy's dishes were on display in the open shelves above the dinette set he'd picked out—complete with his crystal ashtray in the center—as though he'd stepped back in time to the day he chased Lucy to the kitchen and found her in Frederick's arms. He grabbed the back of the nearest chair to keep the room from spinning.

"Are you in pain?" Claudio placed a hand on his arm.

"Agony. Do you not feel the evil?"

"*Sí*, but we are here to check for the safety of Hazel. Let us be done so we can leave."

He motioned to the dishes. "Those were Lucy's. This is the furniture from our engagement."

"Surely they are kitchen castoffs." Claudio inched the swinging door open and peeked through to the rest of the main level. "It is clear, *amico*."

Alexander found himself beside the maple dining table he'd pick out with Lucy at the Eastons' warehouse. He ran a hand over it, the bittersweet memory of wanting to take her on the surface mocking him because it was left unfulfilled. On impulse, he turned to the study behind him and flung open the door. The room where Edmund sullied Eliza was unadorned, just as he'd left it nearly eight years before. Using the cane to get to the front room, tears filled his eyes at seeing Lucy's empty bookshelves between the windows.

"Why has no one changed it in all these years? I set this up for Lucy." He raked his right hand through his hair. "This was to be our home, but it turned into my worst nightmare. A den of sin and folly that's haunted me all this time!"

Claudio placed a hand on his back and urged him toward the stairs. Halfway up, Alexander froze.

"I can't."

A muffled scream sounded from above.

Alexander pulled himself up with the use of his good arm and the banister. "Call the police, Claudio. Get help!"

Alone in the upstairs hall, Alexander steadied his breathing as he looked at the runner beneath his feet that Edmund had helped him place there. It could have been his imagination, but he thought he caught the fragrance of lavender in the air. Another wave of muffled protests sounded, forcing him to the closed door.

He knew it would be a vile scene, but he wasn't prepared. Seeing Bruce go at Opal in the Cathedral and the horrors of what he attempted with Magdalene at Seacliff Cottage were coupled with what he'd done to Lucy clouded his vision along with the current situation.

The dresser that had held Lucy's clothes for a short while and the perfect rotating bookshelf—empty, like his heart the day Lucy left him—still resided. Alexander looked to the four-poster bed he'd bought with the unused whorehouse funds. Hazel rolled off the far side in an attempt to escape her bondage.

"Melling, have you come to join the fun?"

"What the hell are you doing in my house?" Alexander thundered.

Rupert straightened his underdrawers. "I own it outright like I do the law firm. I'll show you the papers if you'd like."

"This house was for my bride! This was to be our wedding suite!"

"But you couldn't wait to take virginal Lucy, could you? You defiled this bed long before I did. I was happy to seize the lease when you walked away from it. We Dardennes enjoyed our time here the night of Eddie's bachelor party. He even had a go with your little sister while you were up here with his."

Alexander's face heated with rage, but he couldn't form a retort.

"Consuela was put out to have missed her opportunity with you that night, but Hazel is our stand-in today. I'm afraid she might be worn out, but have a go with her. She's my client now, and unlike you, I've always been happy to share."

Alexander raised the cane and whacked Rupert on the side of the head. A line of blood ran along his ear, and he staggered to the bed, sitting on the edge.

"I couldn't get a new suit without you buying one like it. You wanted the women I had. You wanted my job. You wanted my house!"

"The ladies always paid you more attention than me with your blue eyes and perfect smile though I was just as powerful as you and your pretentious family. I won your father's office and bought your house when you merely rented it. I even bedded all but two of the women you've had. Well, maybe three. Melissa Davenport stayed at your house this spring, and anything might have happened while your wife was busy writing. I practically had Magdalene Jones, but Lucy Easton always managed to elude me. At least I've used the same bed she did."

Unable to stop the anger, Alexander struck him again. The walking stick continued to *thwack* his head after Rupert fell on the bed. But Alexander didn't rest.

"*Amico!*" Claudio came from behind, gripping Alexander's arms to stop the blows.

Alexander cried out as his stitches pulled, warm blood seeping through his sleeve. He dropped the cane from his good hand, that arm now fatigued from use, and leaned on his friend. Only then did he finally understand Frederick's rages—his righteous anger released in a devastating haze of red. He had been this way with his father after the hurricane at Seacliff Cottage. As then, a vile man spoke of the precious women he loved. *I'm not angry about what's done to me. My fury burns for those damsels trodden by evil.*

Several police officers rushed in, jostling the friends to the side.

"The woman," Alexander said as he pointed to the far wall, "she's on the floor. He brought her here on the guise of helping, but he abused her horribly. Get a clean blanket from the hall closet to wrap her in until you can bring her to the hospital."

Seeing the dark stain spread down the sleeve of his suit made Alexander's head woozy. "Claudio, my arm."

The familiar walls of the duplex faded from view.

***

"—this moment! You cannot keep me from my husband!" Lucy's voice pulled Alexander from sleep.

"You need to stay calm. They won't let you in if you're hysterical." *Darla.*

"Oh, I haven't begun to get hysterical!"

Alexander lay in a bed with scratchy sheets once again. Through an open door, he saw a nurse blocking the way.

"My queen!" The force of his voice made the ache in his arm return. It was heavily wrapped with fresh bandages, and he was shirtless.

"Alex!"

"For Pete's sake, let her in, or I'll sue the hospital for upsetting a pregnant woman!"

She was in a moment later, her purple dress bright in the drab room. Flushed with nerves, Lucy fell upon him, kissing his face.

"Can you please not make a habit of bleeding out wounds and winding up in the hospital? I don't think I can handle another episode like this!"

He smiled at her earnestness. "I'll try, my queen. But this time, it was Claudio's fault."

Darla folded her arms across her blue jacket. "Only you would blame a priest."

"It is true," Claudio said as he entered. "I have given my statement to the police. They will be here in a moment for Alexander's."

"Can we not go back in time to yesterday afternoon, when the girls had safely arrived in Florida and you and me comfortable in bed?"

"Ah, but with this setback, I've earned another day in bed. Halloween with you…." Alexander fingered her neck. "I may dress as Count Dracula and nibble your throat, my luscious Lucy."

The fact that her eyes swam with longing set his happiness and yearnings full force. He guided Lucy's chin to his face and kissed her until the officers arrived.

For the second time in four days, Alex was left to explain his actions to the police.

"Is this a carryover from the kidnapping events on Saturday?" one asked.

"Opal and Rupert are two people I hope never befriend each other."

"Miss Easton was transferred to the asylum this afternoon." The man closed his notebook. "Now, this matter of Rupert Lyons is another issue. He's a respected member of society, and while all men in his position are given leeway to their fetishes, Hazel Kline is in poor shape. She might not survive the injuries. Lyons is still unconscious. You managed to give him quite the beating—possibly crossing a line from when you could have stopped to save the woman. If Hazel dies, he'll be charged with murder. But if he dies, that would fall on you."

The image of seeing his father burn scorched his mind. *Had I gone too far then as well? Am I guilty of murder when I only sought to protect? As long as my father lived, he would have been a threat. Rupert would continue to abuse women as well.* Alexander looked to Claudio, eyes pleading for divine help.

The priest cleared his throat. "Is it not clear that Mr. Lyons's actions were nothing but devilish, an abomination to the Heavens?

How can a man set on stopping that sin be accused of murder? Would God judge him for protecting one of his children?"

The officer looked to his partner, shrugged, and then studied his shoes. "All I'm saying is that it'll look bad if Mr. Lyons dies after Mr. Melling's thrashing. It could turn him into a martyr, like Mr. Wayne. Kate Lyons could seek retribution, send the law after you."

Alexander laughed. "It might be a favor to her. Do you really think a woman as sharp as her didn't notice her husband's philandering ways? I wouldn't be surprised if she thanked me in either outcome."

The second officer hid a laugh behind a cough.

"Thank you for your time, Mr. Melling. We'll be in touch."

Two days later, Hazel Kline passed from her injuries as Rupert recuperated in the hospital with a concussion. The following Monday, Alexander's first appointment was Kate Stuart Lyons, seeking a divorce from her newly incarcerated husband.

Thirty-Eight

Lucy lay in bed with Alexander, trying to ignore the reoccurring pains. It was a Monday night in mid-December, and she hoped for a Christmas baby to go with her Thanksgiving one. She knew Frederick would call her a goose for that, so she kept her wishes to herself as the white bassinet at the foot of the bed teased her every passing day.

Since the fight at the duplex, Alexander had been more subdued. Whatever he faced in the building had shaken him. The only thing he told her was that the house was the same. *Everything was the way we left it.* Reliving the highs and lows of their last weekend there would be her undoing, and she pitied him for having to face it. But Alexander now had his old office back with the view of the fountain he admired. Since Rupert awaited his murder trial, Alexander purchased the tarnished law firm with his inheritance without the least bit of guilt. He found the original *Melling & Associates* sign in a storage closet and had it rehung. After subdividing his father's—and Rupert's—old space into two offices, he gave the true senior associate who had started nearly a decade before himself the other park-view office.

Lucy's fifth book had published in November, and she did a book signing at Mr. Lloyd's store a few weeks before. Reviews for *Under the Gardenia Bush: A Mystery Romance*—which she dedicated to

Melissa—were almost as good as they were for *Winter of My Heart*. The past month and a half had been notable, but it all came down to that night.

Curled on her side with her running thoughts and increasing contractions, she tried to hold out. After eleven, Lucy decided she could no longer wait.

"Alex, wake up." She nudged his bare shoulder.

Instinctively he grabbed for her hips, but his hand skimmed over her taunt middle instead. He blinked in the darkness.

"You need to call Darla and Naomi."

In his haste to jump out of bed, his legs tangled in the covers, and he went sprawling to the floor.

"Are you all right?"

Alexander hopped to his feet and fixed the leg of his sleep pants that had caught in the blankets. "No. I mean, yes. Are you?"

"Yes, but please call them."

As he stumbled from the room, Lucy couldn't help a short laugh, but then she was back to breathing through another contraction. *I should have told him to call Freddy.* During her last pregnancy, it was Frederick who was her rock. Though Alexander hovered nearby, Frederick was the one who had supported her through labor as she brought their second daughter into the world weeks before their divorce was finalized.

It seemed like an hour before Alex returned, but she'd only made it through two contractions before the light turned on.

"Darla's getting Naomi on her way. She called Dr. Hughes so I could call Freddy."

A relieved smile found her lips after the grimace of the contraction faded. "Thank you."

Hand on his scarred chest, he looked about anxiously. "What can I do?"

"Towels. Lots of clean towels. Naomi will see to water when she arrives."

He piled the towels in a wingback chair and then curled in front of her, staring into her eyes with his bright blue ones. "I love you, my queen. Don't hate me because my part in this creation was all pleasure while you carry the pain."

Smiling, she leaned forward to kiss him. "I've had plenty of pleasure with you on this journey, and I've seen the pain when you worry over the baby and me. Our balance is good."

She held him close while they kissed with fervor.

"I should have known!" Darla's tone was indignant. "Here she is about to birth a baby, and you've got your hands and lips all over her like there'll be nothing left to share with the child when you're done with her."

They both laughed, and Alexander playfully fondled Lucy's chest before inching away.

Darla crossed her arms. "Don't make me kick you out of this room before we even begin."

"You can't send me out of my bedroom," Alexander said defiantly.

"Watch me! All I need to do is stick my head into the hall and holler for Henry."

"He came along?"

"I knew I'd need some brawn to keep you inline. Heaven knows you don't respect me."

"You wound me, Darling Darla."

When Lucy sucked in a sharp breath, their attentions turned to her.

"Breathe, Lucy. Remember how you did before. Slow and easy," Darla's calm voice walked her through the pain while

Alexander massaged her lower back. "Now, we need to get you up and protect the mattress."

"I feel damp between my legs already. I haven't moved to keep it from spreading."

"Alex, place two towels on the floor there, and then two more behind her on the bed, tucking them under her backside as far as you can. And no hanky-panky."

Lucy couldn't see what Alexander did, but Darla huffed and rolled her eyes. They helped Lucy turn over and then sit on the edge of the bed before standing. Her long, red nightgown was soiled with the fluid, but Alexander happily removed it. Seldom did she wear under clothes to bed as it slowed things when their loving embraces turned to more, and she blushed under his appreciative gaze.

"I'll remember this glorious sight always. My queen as she carries our child the final night of pregnancy."

"Get her something practical," Darla snapped. "Something with buttons on the front. Cotton, not silk."

Alexander returned from the closet with one of his shirts and helped Lucy slip her arms into it.

"That's the best you've got?" Darla spread fresh towels on the bed as the clock struck midnight.

"All her nightgowns are silk and lace." He rolled the sleeves to her elbows and then snuck a kiss at her chest before he buttoned a few holes closed above her protruding belly.

Just as Lucy was enjoying Alexander's sandalwood scent on her body, the wave of another contraction crested.

"Hold her, Alex!" Darla came to their side to make sure Alexander had a firm grasp on Lucy as she went limp to ride beyond the discomfort. "Don't let her go until I tell you."

Dr. Hughes arrived, and he and Darla examined Lucy. When she was covered, Henry entered with buckets of sterilized water and other supplies. Word came that Freddy arrived, but Lucy didn't see him.

Alexander held her hand or held her in his lap off and on the next hour, wiping her face with a cool cloth between the tough times.

"By God, you're brave, my queen," he whispered.

Dr. Hughes stepped out of the room to update the rest of the household.

Darla returned to the bedside after washing. "You're good to push whenever you're ready. And I've got a modified position since we can't do what we did at Bethany's birth."

"Why not?" Alexander demanded.

"Because you can't hold Lucy's full weight for an undisclosed amount of time," Darla said. "Freddy held her for an hour, standing with no supports."

"Well, bully for him. I can make her clima—"

"You better shut your trap if you want to stay in this room!"

"Alex," Lucy whimpered. "I need you."

He smoothed the loose hair off her forehead. "Anything you wish, my queen."

She was still a moment and then lurched upright. "He's coming!"

Between Alexander's awkward movements and her nervous distraction, they managed to position themselves with Darla's help. Alexander perched on the edge of the bed, supporting Lucy with his upper legs and arms as she squatted between his knees. Dr. Hughes and Naomi entered not long after.

"Do you still have what I gave you?" Darla asked Naomi.

"In my pocket, Miss Darla."

The pushing went quicker than with the previous births. With her final effort, relief enveloped Lucy.

"It's a beautiful boy!" Darla said as she caught him.

Lucy leaned her head against Alexander, giving him a clear view of the birthing space.

"Don't look!" Darla's warning came too late. "Naomi, the smelling salts!"

Lucy felt Alexander's arms go limp and braced herself on his thighs. As soon as Naomi held the potent aroma under his nose, he shook himself back to alertness, leaning his head on Lucy.

"A boy?" he questioned, and she nodded. "I have a son! You were right all along."

"Keep her there a few more minutes, Alex, until the afterbirth passes. I'll hold him up for you to see when I clean him up a bit."

"You mean more of that bloody mess will come out? Is that safe? Is something wrong? I'll sue—"

Dr. Hughes laughed. "I think I need to implement a no lawyers in the birthing room rule. I'll go tell the others the news."

Darla washed and checked the infant. "He's a mite smaller than Bethany was, but everything looks good."

"The odor!"

"Stuff it, Alex. The remainder of the things will be removed soon." Darla gently rubbed the baby's head. "It's drying fair. The poor boy will be like his father, handsome and full of himself."

"Did you hear that, Lucy? She called me handsome."

Ignoring his remark, Darla turned to Naomi. "Would you hold the young Melling while I clear the floor? Then we'll get Lucy cleaned up and in bed while the *handsome* father shows his son off."

Still leaning on Alexander, Lucy called Naomi over so she could kiss her son's fuzzy blond head. "Momma's still here, little one."

Moisture dripped onto her shoulder. She looked back at Alexander's awed face and fell more in love with him as he marveled over their child.

"We did it, Lucy! We made this amazing baby together. When can we do it again?"

Darla's hands went to her hips. "Don't you dare touch her until her healing time has passed! Besides which, I think it'll be several years, if ever before I could stomach being in a birthing room with you again. You keep all your parts to yourself, you hear?"

"Yes, ma'am."

Once Lucy lay back on the towels, Darla and Naomi slipped out of the room with what needed disposing of. Alexander sat beside her, their child in his arms.

"In a month or so, I'll want that ride on Apollo with you," Lucy said with a smile.

"Maybe a St. Valentine's Day picnic would do well. I have our secluded spot picked out. And there's another surprise I've been working on, having to do with all those pushups I started back to after my arm healed." He gave her a flirtatious grin that brought color to her face before he turned serious. "But he's wonderful, Lucy. Thank you."

"You're just as much part of him as I."

They shared a tender kiss, and Alexander straightened. "Now, what shall we call him? Not Alex or George."

"Phoenix, the new beginning of the Melling family."

With a smile as radiant as the heavens, he caressed her cheek. "You and your beautiful mind. Do you not think it too unconventional?"

"Since when do we worry about convention?"

His laugh warmed her though she was still in nothing more than his shirt, damp with sweat.

"But what middle name would suit that?"

"Asher. We can call him Asher or Ash if you prefer. An ash tree to go in our garden with the camellias and iris."

"It's perfect, my queen. You're perfect. He's perfect." He carefully kissed Phoenix Asher's forehead. "I love you, my son, and I'll do my best for you."

Darla and Naomi returned, and Alexander went for the door.

"Keep him away from drafts, Alex," Darla warned. "Give us at least twenty minutes."

Lucy watched with pride as her husband took the white blanket her mother crocheted from the bassinet and wrapped it around the towel already encompassing their infant. He stopped by Darla on the way out.

"Say hello to Auntie Darla, Phoenix Asher. Be careful. She can give a scolding like no other."

She smiled until Alexander clipped her cheek with a kiss.

"And Miss Naomi's the best cook in town." He left her with a kiss too, and then he was in the hallway. "Freddy, come meet my son!"

"Freddy?" Lucy straightened. "I need to—"

"You need to get cleaned up first," Darla reminded her. "Alex will keep him company until then. Henry and Claudio, too."

"What about Melissa and the girls?" she asked as Darla helped her to the shower.

"Freddy thought it best to keep the girls home until you're settled."

Once showered and propped in the bed wearing her most functional silk gown, the door was opened for visitors. Frederick rushed in, a smile on his gallant face and brown eyes shining.

"He's wonderful, Goosy. And Alex is over the moon about him. I never thought I'd say it, but he'll do well as a father."

She laughed. "And the girls will love Phoenix Asher, won't they? A baby brother for the knights of Kingdom Davenport."

"And another member of Melling Militia." Alexander strode into the room. "Your turn with him, my queen."

"Is his diaper soiled already?" she teased as she opened her arms.

Frederick pressed a kiss on her cheek. "I'll come back later with the girls and Melissa. I'm happy for you both." He turned and embraced Alexander. "I know you'll care for them, but enjoy these moments. Time passes much too quickly."

Henry and Claudio came in next.

"He's a handsome fellow, Lucy," Henry said as he held her free hand. "I'm going home, but I'll be back after work to check on you and Darla."

She thanked him for his help, and Darla walked him out. Then Claudio knelt beside her.

"I wish to give my congratulations and ask if I could bless you and the child."

"And you'll do the baptism when it's time, won't you?"

"*Sì*, it would be an honor."

She looked at Alexander's expectant face. "In the cathedral, like we both were."

"My queen." Her husband kissed her, eyes shining with moisture.

Claudio's uttered prayers in Italian relaxed Lucy such that she was grateful he left immediately after. She dressed Asher in a white layette gown and brought him to her breast. His little mouth suckled only a minute before he fell asleep.

"My queen, my lover, my wife, the mother of my son, my everything. You know what today is, don't you?"

She looked to the mantel clock. After five in the morning. "Tuesday, December...."

"Seventeenth. Eight years ago tonight was the Christmas party. Eight years ago, I kissed you for the first time in these very walls, and my lust turned to love—or most of it anyway. I still harbor those base cravings, but my love continues to grow deeper roots."

Phoenix Asher was successfully transferred to the bassinet, and then Alexander arranged the pillows on the bed so Lucy could recline easier. With his scarred arms about her, she fell into a deep sleep.

Epilogue

The Mellings' house brimmed with love and laughter on Christmas Eve 1913. Lucy and Alexander hosted the Davenports, Adamses, Campbells, and Claudio for a supper party. A fire burned cheerfully in every hearth, and the children scampered about the main floor, spilling into the yard.

Henry and Darla's Horatio was the youngest member of the group at two months of age, and the baby never lacked caring arms about him. Bethany and Tabitha were sweet enough to allow Simon and Asher to toddle after them, but the oldest two had their own games.

"Try and catch me, Kade!" Phoebe called as she sped across the patio, blonde hair streaming behind her like a flag. In a flash, her red dress disappeared into the camellia maze, followed by Kade's sturdy form.

Frederick snuggled his red-haired six-month-old under his clean-shaven chin, breathing in the lemony scent Louisa Constance Davenport picked up from being held by her mother. He walked back to the morning room, where most of the adults gathered.

"Is it all right if I declare those two aren't allowed in the maze once they strike the age of thirteen? Maybe even twelve."

"Who's that?" Douglas asked.

"Phoebe and Kade."

Lucy stood, hands on her shapely hips in her crimson evening sheath. "Frederick Lionel Davenport, just what are you saying about my daughter?"

"Our daughter, Goosy. And at that age, I knew I loved you. With two romantics as parents, there will be no helping the poor girl. A beau will possess her heart long before I'd like to admit."

"Aye, Kade speaks of nothing but Phoebe for days when we return home." Douglas scratched his ginger beard.

"They're children." Conviction dripped from Lucy's voice as she righted the white camellia behind her ear. "Let them run wild while they can."

"Allow them freedom in their innocent years." Alexander started Tchaikovsky's "Swan Lake" on the gramophone, bowed before his wife, and offered his arm. "The forbidden fruit will appeal even more if you try to restrict them too much."

"And you know all about the temptation of forbidden fruit," Frederick's sarcastic tone mocked.

Melissa and Magdalene entered, and Alexander's gaze followed the women as he waltzed his wife around the parquet floor.

"Yes." His smile was coquettish. "I'm well acquainted with temptations because of the rainbow of beauties surrounding me in life. But I hold all I need in my arms."

He dipped Lucy back and tasted her neck. It took all his self-control to keep away from her décolletage—more pleasing than ever—before their audience.

"Shall we rendezvous in my den?" he whispered as his hand snaked around her waist.

Her curving smile was all he needed for response. Scooping her into his arms, he went for the door.

"Not with my baby under this roof!" Darla's eyes burned.

Alexander laughed. "You should be used to us by now."

"And be warned if you ever accept an offer for a weekend at Seacliff with them, you'll not wish to tarry in the kitchen after hours as it's right below their bedroom," Douglas said.

Darla scowled. "As if I'd ever go there."

Phoenix Asher hurried into the room, his first tuxedo adorning his pudgy, year-old self. "Momma! Poppy!"

Alexander set Lucy's bare feet on the floor while Darla gloated in what she perceived as a victory in thwarting their unruly passion.

"What is it, Ash?" Alexander asked as he lowered to a knee, gazing at his blue-eyed son.

"Cookie!" He bounced—albeit unsteadily—much like his oldest half-sister.

"Uncle Claudio is sitting by a cookie platter." Alexander pointed across the room and kissed his son's blond head. "He'll help you get a snack."

Darla huffed. "Setting a man of God in charge of your child while you ravish your wife on Christmas Eve with a house full of guests is—"

"Exactly like Alex," Magdalene said. "He's changed, but he's still Alexander Melling, and we love him for it."

With a flourishing bow, Alexander smiled at his guests before taking Lucy back in his arms. "May we all be blessed to cleave to our first love affair."

THE END

Bonus

"Natural Selection in Life and Love"

The Possession Chronicles #6.1

Sean Spunner removed his hat as he entered the Davenports' foyer on the first Friday in December, 1912. Welcomed by the party's hostess, he smiled at the attractive redhead and bowed over her extended arm to kiss her hand.

"Thank you for the invitation, Mrs. Davenport."

"You're most welcome, but please call me Melissa. I've been with Freddy over half a year. We can dispense with formalities."

"In that case…." Sean's hand slid to her elbow and he kissed her cheek. "You look ravishing in that peacock gown, Melissa."

"I am glad you're here, Sean." She smiled and placed his hat on the credenza. "There's a friend of mine I want—"

"Spunner!" Chuck Brady hollered.

Sean looked from Melissa to the younger man making his way through the crowded hall. He stepped to the side to greet Chuck, bracing for the hefty thump he knew would come from the heavyweight boxer. Not a weakling himself in his middleweight division, Sean held his own with his average height and toned physique. Chuck, on the other hand, flashed his stature and strength with youthful exuberance as he clapped Sean on the back so hard he would have stumbled into Melissa if he hadn't taken a solid stance.

"Spunner, my Rachel's got a cousin in town for Christmas and wants to introduce you. She's a cute girl."

Sean pressed his lips together, trying to think what to say to get out of the matchmaking scheme. He had no interest in a woman labeled "cute". At thirty-two, he craved maturity and substance. An ample bust wouldn't hurt things either.

Melissa stepped between the friends. "I'm sorry, Chuck, but I counted on Sean to help with one of my friends tonight. I'm sure Rachel's cousin would be better-suited to one of the men closer to your own age."

Chuck's laughter blurted through the din of chatter. "Davenport got himself a fine one, didn't he? I'll leave you to the aging population, Spunner. If you decide to flirt with a lady without a cane, let me know."

Melissa's warm brown eyes followed Chuck's retreating form before looking back at Sean. "I hope I didn't overstep my role as hostess."

"Not at all. Thank you for saving me."

"I welcomed Rachel and her cousin when they arrived with Chuck." She tucked her arm through the crook of Sean's. "The young woman is pleasant, but based on what I know of you, she wouldn't be to your liking."

"We've only met a dozen times, Melissa."

"But we've talked at length at the last two parties and I'm a keen observer. Investigating people goes hand in hand with being a travel writer."

Intrigued, he led her into the nearby dining room where the furniture had been set aside and the gramophone played lively tunes. He settled beside Melissa in chairs lining the wall, doing his best not to look at Henry and Darla Adams as they Turkey Trotted across the hardwood floor.

"And what do you believe about my preference in women? For all you know, I could be happily set in my bachelorhood."

"You never pay any attention to the twittering ladies who flock to contestants after a tournament, you seem more than impressed with the Adamses relationship, and I learned you were once engaged last decade. The young woman you were pledged to shared several likenesses with Darla Adams, but I think it goes beyond her looks. Darla is mature for her age—a career woman. You admire that over the flounces of the females your younger friends surround themselves with. You want a woman with a strong mind that will challenge you in the evenings, not to mention a solid figure to keep you satisfied in bed."

Sean laughed. "Are all New Yorkers as outspoken as you?"

"I know how to speak my mind without worrying about offending Southern sensibilities, if that's what you mean. But it's not just New Yorkers."

"Davenport is a lucky man."

"I'm glad so many came tonight. Freddy loves parties."

"I've never seen him happier than he has been since you came to Mobile. Where is he?"

"In the parlor, last I saw. Now about my friend—"

"I'd like to give my thanks to the host before being paired off." Sean squeezed her hand and stood. "I *am* looking for a match, Melissa, but I won't settle for anything less than what Frederick found in you."

He stopped at the credenza and helped himself to a tumbler of whisky before making his way to the parlor. All the Davenports' friends were there save one couple—the Mellings—but Frederick's ex-wife and her husband were probably watching his daughters while he and Melissa hosted the party to kick off the month of Christmas.

Sean slung back his glass and refilled it before scanning the crowded parlor for Frederick. Edmund Easton and Thomas Charles were across the room. Both were boxers and former Mystics of Dardenne brothers, but had settled into married life well enough. After his first months back at the gym, Edmund appeared to have thrown off his whoring habit, but maybe it was more of reduced circumstances than a complete turnaround. His roaming eyes settled on anything with shapely proportions, even with his wife standing two feet away.

Frederick Davenport was with a group Sean knew by sight—a few newspaper reporters and shopkeepers. All their attentions were upon a woman that a reporter's shoulder blocked all but the top of a brunette chignon from Sean's view.

"Marie Curie sharing the Nobel Prize in Chemistry must be seen for what it is—an advancement for women in science. We've come too far in recent years to allow men to shove us back into Victorian parlors and petticoats." The voice was soft but firm and very much Yankee, though not like Melissa's New York accent.

"Well stated, Ms. Fernsby," Mademoiselle Bisset said. The robust form of the French dress shop owner turned to Frederick. "Mr. Davenport, pray excuse me, but I must find your wife. I heard she's in a most exquisite gown that did not come from my store."

Frederick laughed. "I hope to speak with you again before you leave, Mademoiselle."

Sean stepped into the vacated space to see who captivated the group. Though petite in height, the outspoken woman was curvaceous in all the right places. Fresh faced but mature, Sean assessed her to be in her mid-twenties. She wore not a flashy gown like the society wives in attendance but rather a functional azure dress. The buttons down the side of her bust further drew his attention to her shapeliness, but it was her arresting sky blue eyes as they narrowed at him over her glass of eggnog that he focused on.

"Spunner, you made it!" Frederick shook Sean's hand and motioned around the circle. "I think you're acquainted with everyone except Mobile's newest resident, Ms. Fernsby. She began teaching

Science at the Girls' High School this fall. Ms. Fernsby, Sean Spunner with Finnigan and Spunner Law Firm."

She smiled up at him and offered her hand. "Hello, Mr. Spunner."

"Welcome to Mobile, Ms. Fernsby." He kissed the back of her hand.

She withdrew, frowning. "I'm afraid I'll never get used to the liberties Southern men take in the name of chivalry. I offer my hand as an equal and expect it to be embraced as one. Any lips on my skin are to be there by direct invitation only."

Sean reddened and the others chuckled.

"And how many men have been lucky enough for that invitation, Ms. Fernsby?" the reporter asked.

She offered a sardonic smile. "More than you need to worry about, Mr. Powell. Please excuse me."

The other men watched her walk away with amused grins, but Sean wasn't ready to lose her company.

"Ms. Fernsby, I beg your pardon."

She turned to him in the hall, the blue of her dress brightening her almond-shaped eyes under the electric light. "Yes, Mr. Spunner?"

"Forgive my unfamiliar manners. I assure you I meant no offense."

"But offense was taken. As a lawyer, surely you respect that actions have consequences and justice must be served by those victimized." Her impertinent chin lifted.

Sean managed to keep his mirth to a slight curl of his lips. "And what can I do for the scales of justice to be leveled between us once more, Ms. Fernsby?"

"Prove you can be a gentleman without taking advantage by dancing with me." Her sly smile cut almost as deep as her sharp tongue—and he craved more.

***

Hattie Fernsby couldn't help but tease the man Melissa praised. Happy to have found him before an awkward introduction could be orchestrated, Hattie relished the control it gave her over the presumed match by her friend. Melissa often spoke of Sean's quick wit and she eagerly tested it.

Sean bowed, golden eyes mischievous under his wave of brown hair. "Ms. Fernsby, would you do me the honor of sharing a dance?"

"You may have *one*, Mr. Spunner but I'm afraid you'll need to wait until a traditional tune is played. I don't Turkey Trot or know any of the new dances," she admitted as Darla and Henry Adams pranced across the room.

Sean smirked as he looked down at her from his half-foot advantage. "That's rather depressing, Ms. Fernsby. A modern woman should be well-versed in the newest dances, especially when females are losing their jobs for doing them in public dance halls during their time off while their male partners suffer no consequences. That's not fair, is it? Where is *their* justice?"

"I'm surprised a man like you takes notice of the lack of freedom women have."

"I assure you I am *very* interested in women, though only one at present."

Hattie bit back a smile as a new song with a Latin beat began.

"Your dance education begins now, Ms. Fernsby. Follow my lead and keep moving." Sean took her right hand and his other went snug around her waist as the length of his firm body pressed against her front.

A gasp escaped Hattie as the sensual dance began and she looked away from Sean's smug grin. The host and hostess entered the room and the Adamses were shown up by the Davenports' tango.

"With a bit more practice, you'll be gliding as easily as Melissa, Ms. Fernsby."

Hattie stumbled and Sean pulled her even closer, her chin jutting into his chest. Over his broad shoulder, she caught Melissa's gaze, who flashed a smile of encouragement. Soon the dizzying tune stopped and an old-fashioned waltz began.

"You survived the first lesson, Ms. Fernsby. Would you honor me with this next dance as well?"

She took a half step back and nodded.

He settled into a stance for the waltz. At ease with the familiar pattern, Hattie relaxed enough to recognize Sean's elegant moves. Remembering Melissa told her Sean was a friend from Freddy's gym, she understood he needed to be light on his feet in the boxing ring. Curious to the state of his form beneath his suit, Hattie's left hand roamed from his shoulder to feel the thickness of his biceps.

"Why, Ms. Fernsby, I'm offended." Sean brought them to a halt amid the other couples. "I did not ask you to dance to be groped."

Caught off-guard, her face heated as the other dancers had to alter their course to prevent bumping into them. "I meant no harm."

"Still, an offense was made. You owe me restitution." His mouth was set in a sensual pout but his eyes were merry.

Playing his game of revenge, she looked up at him with a humble countenance. "What may I do to set things right?"

"Come to the porch with me."

Happy to escape the curious stares of those in attendance, she hooked her arm through his. "Lead the way, Mr. Spunner."

"Please, call me Sean."

"All right, Sean."

His triumphant smile served to make him look younger than what Melissa informed her was his age of thirty-two. A six year difference wasn't too much. It could even be said it was the perfect difference between a male and female as men matured slower.

On the porch, Sean saw her seated on the bench swing before taking the other end. He tilted toward her to converse easier over the dance music coming from the open window.

"Now, Ms. Fernsby, I—"

"You may call me Hattie if I'm to call you Sean."

"Miss Hattie, no matter where things go from here, you have brightened my evening."

"After I called you out for kissing my hand?"

"Especially for that. Not to mention your suggestive touch while we danced. I'm happy to settle your curiosity." He made quick work of the buttons on his jacket, slipped it off, and held his shirtsleeve to her. "Touch all you want."

"*This* is your restitution? For me to do what you found so offensive?"

"Only if yours is the same." He winked.

"I merely wished to feel if you were muscular. There appears to be a large ratio of boxers to businessmen here."

"But many are both, Hattie. Boxing is a great hobby. Use your scientific powers to deduce how strong it keeps me." He lifted her right hand onto his arm. "Explore away."

Never had a man been so forthright. Usually a line or two was exchanged, and then the man moved along to a woman who offered more of a physical show. "But then you will expect to kiss—"

"No, though I hope you will request my lips pay a return visit to your delectable skin at some point in the future. What is your scientific guess for that happening?"

His eyes gleamed in the shadowed porch light like the purest amber, playful as a cat.

She spread her fingers around the thickness of his forearm before traveling over his elbow and biceps. "The data is showing favorably for you."

"Was that before or after you felt my muscles?"

"Before." Hattie managed to speak as her laughter quieted and she clasped her hands in her lap. "Your company is refreshing."

"And you, besides pricking my soul with your cleverness, are the first woman to touch me like that since—well, in a long time." They stared at each other, a soft smile on his lips that Hattie felt reflected on her own. "I'm afraid I need to return to the party. Our lovely hostess wanted to introduce me to a friend of hers, hoping I'd entertain her. A great loss for me because no one can be as good company as you, Hattie."

"Unless Melissa double booked your companionship for the party, you may stay here. She's been talking you up to me for weeks and was pleased to finally introduce me to you tonight, though Freddy unknowingly took that honor."

Sean crossed his arms. "You've had the advantage over me from the beginning, haven't you?"

"It appears that way." Her smile brought his back around. "But you should be pleased to know you've kept up with me like no man before."

"Are you keeping score?"

"Always. Men interest me very much, though only one at present."

Sean's chipped-tooth grin was infectious. "I could spend weeks like this and never tire. Tell me of yourself, Hattie. Where did you move from and why?"

"Boston, born and raised. I needed a change of pace after my mother died. My father's family has been in Boston for generations, but my mother's parents were Irish immigrants during the famine."

"My mother's family was Irish. I was raised by uncle and aunt after my parents died. All of us our Catholic, and you?"

"Baptized, but not much of anything these days. It's been nearly a decade since I've attended Mass." Noticing the downturn of his mouth, she pounced. "Don't tell me a sharp-witted lawyer like yourself attends regular Mass and confession."

"I try for Mass at least bi-weekly—even when I was a scoundrel—and need confession as much as the next man."

"Or woman." She raised a challenging brow. "I would have loved to have crossed paths with you in your scoundrel days."

"Those times are far in the past, though a sharp woman like you brings it all back to me." His face softened as memories clouded his vision.

Hattie laid a hand on his knee. "What was her name?"

"Eliza," he whispered without pause. "Next month will be seven years since she died."

Hattie noticed the moisture glistening in the corner of his eyes and squeezed his knee. "Melissa told me you were once engaged. I would love to hear about her if you want to talk."

"She was the Fourth of July, Mardi Gras, and New Year's in one explosive package—all reckless passion and fantastic dreams." Sean gave a dry laugh. "I thought my experience over her eighteen years readied me for her, but Eliza Melling bled me dry. I gave her everything within my power, but it wasn't enough."

***

Sean closed his eyes, embarrassed to look upon Hattie after spilling his heartache in the first hour of their acquaintance. He rarely spoke of Eliza. Why would he break that silence with someone he just met?

Within the Davenports' house, a ragtime tune poured from the dining room window. Hattie's warm hand remained on his knee, a friendly gesture—bold and comforting.

"Forgive my reminiscing. I'm sure you would rather be with your friends. Allow me to escort you inside." Sean shifted to stand.

Hattie tightened her hand on his leg. "Yet more chivalrous ideals from a Southern gentleman. I assure you, Sean, when I want to return inside, I will—with or without you."

There was something about her—the smallness of her stature and the clarity in her blue eyes coupled with the elvish smile—that created the illusion of frailty. Sean's instinct was to protect her, but he knew she would resent him for attempting anything.

Sean placed a hand over hers. "I'm glad to hear that, Hattie. Your company is most enjoyable."

Smiling, she released her hold on his knee and turned to clasp her fingers through his. "Do you mind?"

"Not at all." He stroked her dainty wrist with his thumb.

Hattie shifted closer, allowing their hands to settle between them on the swing. "Thank you for bringing me out here. It's much easier to talk."

"And my thanks to you for accepting an invitation to join me in a secluded location."

"Will my reputation be sullied?"

"You will not be gossiped over for this rendezvous. I've been known as an old wallflower for years."

"Good." She sighed. "I can't afford to lose my job. I used most of my savings to relocate and don't wish to return to my father or beg one of my brothers for a place in their households while I scrounge for work. Teaching jobs in Boston are scarce. There are too many teachers and not enough classrooms, especially for science."

He gave her hand a gentle squeeze. "Why science and not literature or history or—"

"Something more suitable for a woman?"

"Don't put words in my mouth, Hattie." *I'd rather have something else in there.*

As though she heard his thought, she blushed. "I've been fascinated by the natural world since childhood. I was not welcomed to play with my brothers and spent hours observing any wildlife I could find. Things like how wind affected water, the subtle changing of the shadows, and nature in general, but no one took my questions seriously. Girls shouldn't be dismissed for their curiosity."

"Your ideals are admirable, your search for justice commendable."

"And how were you as a child? Did you bar girls from playing boys' games?"

"I welcomed them. Both at home with my cousin and during events at this house. The Eastons lived here back then—all ten of the children. Davenport was a close friend to one of the middle sons. They hosted the best battles in the yard. Come see!" He stood and drew Hattie after him, hurrying down the front steps and across the lawn to the base of a live oak. "Can you make out the board between those branches?"

"Yes."

"Sometimes the Easton sisters would play with us—Lucy most often. Whoever it was became a scout. I always made sure she climbed up first so I could see her knickers."

"Why you little cad!" Hattie dropped his hand.

Sean laughed. "I told you I was a scoundrel, but I wish I could say that was the worst of my infractions."

"Tell me the worst," she whispered.

"I was a member of Mystics of Dardenne for seven years," he trustingly declared.

"And what's that?"

"The most notorious Mardi Gras society—secret, of course. All bachelors with too much money, alcohol, and drugs but little in the way of common sense or decency."

"Scandal for the scoundrel?"

"I never got caught and confessed every vice at each opportunity."

She stepped before him, her buxom chest nearly brushing his middle. "And what would you do to me if we were alone like this a decade ago?"

"Are you welcoming my lips?"

Before she could fully nod, he cupped her face with a hand while the other reached around her back to steady her as he pressed in. He felt her smile and trailed his hand from her jaw to neck. Whether he was on his second or third kiss, Sean didn't know. It all blended into a heady rush of desire he hadn't felt in years. Her lips brazenly parted with a welcoming flick of her tongue. Hands trailing her back, he tried not to devour the deliciousness of her rum-infused mouth.

Hattie was right there with him as he brought them into the shadow of the oak, lowering her to his lap on a wrought iron bench. He continued to caress her as their heaving breaths mingled while they tasted each other.

The front screen door snapped shut and they broke their kiss.

"I thought Spunner was out here," Chuck bellowed.

"Try the kitchen!" another voice replied. The door slammed again.

Hattie kissed Sean once more before standing. "You've proven to be no wallflower, Sean."

He put an arm about her waist, gently tugging her against him. "I'm sorry if I went too far."

Hattie fingered his lips and smiled. "Never. I just can't be caught in a compromising situation. Against my better judgement, I pledged a code of conduct for my personal life when I signed on with the Girls' High School. I need this job."

"There aren't any school officials at the party." He accompanied her across the lawn.

"I've learned this city loves gossip. I like you, Sean, but I have to be careful." She stopped at the front door and turned to him. Sean did his best to memorize the tender look on her countenance. "Please stay with me the rest of the evening. Give me as many dance lessons as you'd like, but keep me out of dark corners. Will you do that for me?"

"I'll do anything you ask, Hattie."

****

A week later, Hattie sat at her school desk during lunch and nibbled a sandwich. A crisp breeze blew through the open window, nothing like the cold in Boston that time of year. She was alone by choice because she needed silence to better recall the magnificent hours she'd spent with Sean the Friday before. They had danced and talked until they were the last guests, then took a final cup of eggnog with the Davenports. She had informed Sean she would contact him, but she'd kept silent all week. Having lost her head over a man before, she couldn't risk that with her job in the balance. It was best to stick with daydreams when it came to Sean Spunner and his delectable lips.

On Sunday, she almost went to the Cathedral of the Immaculate Conception for late Mass. Not keen on revisiting the rituals of her youth when all she wanted was a glimpse of the man, she instead telephoned Melissa and they took a meandering stroll along the bay.

Another week passed much the same as the previous— dreaming about Sean whenever she wasn't teaching.

On Thursday, December 19, Hattie readied for her final class of the day. The students filed in and took their seats. She barely had a decade on her students age-wise, but Hattie took charge and lifted a shoebox of fossils she brought from home.

"Ladies, I have a special treat for you today. As I stop by your seat, reach your hand in and retrieve one of the items nestled in the cotton padding. I want you to quietly study your specimen and record as much about it as possible in your journal—size, shape, texture, and so on. All the scientific data you can muster from an observation. Then everyone will report to the class what they have in their possession before you exchange them among yourselves to see the variations."

"Oh, Ms. Fernsby!" The curly haired brunette in the front row clutched her fossilized shell to her chest. "It's a—"

"Please hold your enthusiasm, Rosella. Take notes and there will be time to talk later."

With all fourteen girls on task, Hattie settled at her desk with a shark tooth in her palm. She ran her thumb across the serrated edge while thinking of Sean's chipped tooth that had heightened their playful kissing session. Few things in life brought her greater joy than giving her students what she was denied—an authority figure who loved science and believed each student was capable of success with the subject—but Sean's attentions were high on her list as well.

When observation time was over, Rosella begged to go first. She spiritedly shared information about the fossilized spiral mollusk. Twenty minutes later, the students completed sharing about shells, conifer cones, and shark teeth. Then Hattie reminded them about their lesson from the day before about how fossils were formed before sharing the history of the specimens.

"I collected these when I was your age. My family used to camp on Martha's Vineyard each summer. We'd travel all over the island, but my favorite part was Gay Head. It has the most beautiful clay cliffs and aqua water, not to mention a plethora of fossils."

"Aren't fossils what led Charles Darwin to believe in evolution?" Rosella's dark eyes shone.

Surprised that some her age would know about the controversial figure, Hattie smiled. "You're exactly right, Rosella. Darwin studied fossils, rocks, plants, and animal samples that he collected during his global journey on the HMS Beagle when he was only twenty-two—younger than me."

"Who's Charles Darwin?" another asked.

"He was a famous British naturalist during the previous century. His scientific studies led him to believe in evolution of species—that nature causes plants and animals to adapt to the world, that only the strongest survive. Natural selection."

"He thought humans evolved from monkeys," Rosella declared.

A few girls giggled but more gasped. Then the whispers began.

"That's blasphemy!"

"My brother looks like a monkey."

"God created man—my Sunday School teacher says so."

"Please settle down." Hattie stood silent until the room quieted. "Charles Darwin had his opinions, as we are all entitled, but now is not the proper forum to debate the merits of his theory. Be sure to finish reading the chapter on sediments tonight. I look forward to showing you my second collection tomorrow. Please return the specimens on your way out, ladies."

Rosella stood by Hattie's desk, looking over each item as it was added to the box. "Thank you for showing them to us, Ms. Fernsby."

"Stay after a moment, if you can."

"Yes, Ma'am."

As the last student filed out, Hattie motioned to the opened box. "Pick one to keep, Rosella. I know you will take good care of it. I want you to have something to remind you about discovery."

Rosella smiled and bent over the open container. "You're the best teacher, Ms. Fernsby. I can't talk about Darwin's theories with anyone at home."

"Or in class, I'm afraid." Hattie sat in her chair behind the desk. "Darwin's concepts have the potential for trouble."

Rosella looked up. "I'm sorry."

"Don't be. Whenever you wish to talk about evolution or anything else, take lunch in here or stay after class. I'm happy to discuss topics beyond our textbook with willing students."

"I'll remember that." She pulled the mollusk shell from the box and cradled it in her hand. "I'd like the one I chose. Thank you, Ms. Fernsby."

"I'll see you tomorrow, Rosella."

Hattie closed the box and collected her coat. Crossing Government Street, she walked south until she reached the boarding house on the far end of a residential area. She switched out the fossils in the box with ones from her display case, preparing for the next day's lesson before settling with a book about the Amazon while waiting for the dinner bell.

The supper table was usually interesting with the mix of the house's inhabitants—teachers, sailors, and sales clerks. On any given night, there were as many as a dozen souls around the table, including the landlord couple, Mr. and Mrs. Grimes. That evening, there were only five: two other female lodgers who occupied the first floor rooms next to Hattie and the owners. Not wanting to be lumped into spinsterhood with the aging teachers across from her, Hattie made up her mind to telephone Sean after school the next day.

"Thank you for another good meal, but I'll be taking supper out tomorrow, Mrs. Grimes," she said after dessert.

"Another party invitation, Ms. Fernsby?"

"No, I am ringing up an acquaintance."

"Remember the rules, dear. You were out much too late the other week, though the Davenports are respectable. Take special care of who you associate with."

Rules.

Codes of conduct.

I'm a grown woman in charge of my own destiny!

"Yes, Mrs. Grimes."

After a restless night, Hattie buttoned on her nicest blue linen day dress and donned her gray capelet. She journeyed through the chill morning to Barton Academy with her box of fossils. Pleased with the thought of finally talking to Sean, she hummed the tune that had played when he taught her to Turkey Trot, hoping he wouldn't be sore over her prolonged silence.

As soon as she was through the front doors, her name was called.

The secretary stood in front of the office. "Mr. Gentry needs to speak with you."

"Allow me to place my things in the classroom and—"

"He said it was urgent, Ms. Fernsby."

Hattie sighed and knocked on Mr. Gentry's door. She balanced her things in one arm as she turned the knob at his sharp call of "Enter!"

"Ms. Fernsby, have a seat."

Not a fan of the man who over saw both the girls' and boys' higher education, she managed a tight-lipped smile and carefully sat in the chair before his desk.

He met her gaze with brown eyes hooded by fuzzy eyebrows. "Ms. Fernsby, you have been released from your contract with the school. You can pack your bags and head north because I doubt any school in the state of Alabama will hire you after your outrageous behavior."

"I don't understand. What have I been accused of, Mr. Gentry?"

"Accused? No, there are more than enough witnesses to prove it happened. You may return after the close of the school day to remove your personal items from the classroom, but you must leave the property before students arrive."

"What is it people say I did?"

"You taught about evolution in your final class yesterday, Ms. Fernsby. Darwinism is not allowed in our schools, as you well know. Three of your students went home and spoke of this progressive education you are forcing on their impressionable minds and I fielded telephone calls all evening from angry fathers. I thought the first must have been mistaken, but after the others, I had no choice but to promise your expulsion from the school system."

"I didn't teach evolution, Mr. Gentry. One of the girls brought up Charles Darwin an—"

"There is no referencing that man under this roof! Now please leave, Ms. Fernsby. Do not return until after four o'clock or I will call the police."

Hattie strode from the room with her chin up. Numb with the encroaching weight of her predicament, she headed for the only place she could think of.

***

"Mr. Spunner, there's a woman here to see you." Ms. Keller said from his open doorway.

Sean looked up from his morning coffee and half-read newspaper. After seeing his secretary without glasses for over a year, Sean had to admit the new specs somehow improved her appearance—correcting the unfortunate squint that had marred her otherwise unremarkable face. "Does she have an appointment?"

"No, but she looks distraught. I think she might be in trouble."

Disappointed his lazy Friday was interrupted, Sean's second thought was maybe it would quicken the passing of time that had all but came to a stop two weeks before. "Send her in."

"Yes, sir."

Sean stood from his padded chair behind the mahogany desk, buttoned his suit jacket closed, and made sure his tie was straight. As he crossed his office, a burdened Hattie accompanied the secretary into the room.

"The door, Ms. Keller," he snapped in his eagerness.

His secretary closed it when she left. Before questioning Hattie's worried countenance, he swept her box and bags onto the nearest chair. Then he took her in an embrace that squeezed the breath from her.

"Hattie, dearest! I was beginning to think you came to your senses about me and I'd never see you again." He kissed her forehead. "But the concern on your face shows you're here for help."

"I'm sorry for not telephoning. Over supper last night, I made up my mind to do just that after school today."

"There's nothing to forgive now that you're here." He lifted her chin and planted a kiss on her lips. Seeing the unease in her typically glittering eyes, he smiled. "Now quit being a stoic feminist and tell me your troubles so I can help."

Sean saw the flash of annoyance before she began crying. Arm about her, he led her to the leather sofa along the far wall where he sat close and rubbed her back.

"Hattie, you're safe here." He leaned his head to hers, inhaling the marvelous scent of soap and woman as he nuzzled against her neck. Coming to his senses, he removed a handkerchief from his pocket.

She accepted Sean's offering and wiped her nose. "It's already too late. I've lost my job."

Hattie's sobs returned. Sean's first thought was no more blasted code of conduct. He wanted to show her how he felt about her without fear of repercussion, but settled on offering a sympathetic ear.

"Start from the beginning and tell me what happened."

"There's no point. I'll still be out of work."

"Hattie, dearest. Look at my office. I can't furnish an establishment like this without being a successful lawyer. I may have been a scoundrel in my youth, but I brought my uncle's firm out of obscurity the past few years. I'm well versed in the law and backroom deals. If there's a loophole in what happened to you, I'll find it."

She sniffed and her gaze lingered on the carved trim of the shelves lining the opposite wall, the collection of law books that filled them. The Turkish rug met her stare next as she fingered the soft leather of the sofa's arm beside her.

"Why on earth are you interested in me, Sean? You should be with society's elite, not a teacher living in a boarding house."

"Because you're the most extraordinary woman I've ever met. Yes, I loved two others before you, but they were girls. You, Hattie Fernsby, have gained my fondness for the woman you are. I haven't stopped thinking of you since the party. The only reason I didn't rush to you the next day was because you asked me to wait for your outreach. You've tortured me severely, but you haven't lost my affection in our days apart."

A blush covered her cheeks and she smiled so that it reached her eyes a moment. "I've also thought of you every day, but it will do no good with me being forced to leave town."

"Have faith in me, dearest, and tell me everything."

Her chest heaved with a sigh. "Mr. Gentry wouldn't listen to my story, he only spouted off what he'd heard and dismissed me, saying he would call the police if I returned before the students went home."

"Don't tell me he found out about our time at Freddy's house?"

"Worse."

"What is worse than a code of conduct breach?"

"Charles Darwin." She narrowed her eyes. "And if you have the nerve to ask if I'd been kissing him, I'll call off every daydream I've had about you."

Sean laughed. "Kissing a corpse? Do think better of me than that. Darwin has been dead decades now. I may not be a scientist, but I am well-read. You must know it's against the law to teach Darwinism."

"Yes, and I didn't. I brought in a box of fossils I've collected to go along with the lessons in the textbook on sediment and fossil formation. Rosella, my brightest student, mentioned Darwin collected fossils and the others wanted to know who he was. I briefly explained how he got his start as a naturalist and the most basic of his theories so the others had a point of reference. Nothing more. I even held Rosella back after class and let her know we could not discuss Darwin or his theories in class and she apologized. But apparently a few girls mentioned to their families what was said and their fathers telephoned Principal Gentry. He promised them I would be dismissed from the school system."

"Franklin Gentry?" Hattie nodded and he laughed. "Leave it to me."

"How?" She asked as they stood.

"Loopholes, Hattie, and you're coming with me. But first, I need to do something before you're officially under a code of conduct clause again."

Sean took her in his arms, gazing down at her for a signal of acceptance. Her eyes widened, bright blue above her rosy cheeks before nodding. Caressing her back, his hands roamed to her hips as he leaned down to meet her enchanting mouth with a deep kiss. Hattie fervently returned the attention and he lowered her to the sofa, a knee next to her middle and an arm braced on the cushion beside her head.

He tasted her lips and kissed the swell of a glorious breast atop her dress. "It's been so long," he breathed the words.

"For me as well," she whispered, holding his gaze without embarrassment as though she tested his reaction. "It was one man, several years ago."

"I don't need names or dates. You in my arms right now is enough."

"I better be the only woman you've laid down in this office. I wouldn't be able to sleep at night knowing this was a habit for you."

"You're the first and the last, the most perfect example of 'endless forms most beautiful.'"

A flicker of surprise crossed her face—whether it was over him declaring his lasting affection or quoting Darwin, he wasn't sure. Sean kissed her once more and straightened, raising Hattie from her wanton pose. He draped her outerwear over her shoulders and took up his own coat and gloves before collecting her box.

"Ms. Keller, I'm out for the morning. Ms. Fernsby's case is my top priority. I'll check in with you this afternoon."

At his automobile, Sean stored Hattie's box on the floorboard of the backseat before helping her into the front. He drove the few blocks to Barton Academy and parked on the side street next to the three story building.

Taking her hand in his, he kissed her fingers. "This will only take a few minutes. Sit tight, dearest."

"I wish to come and speak for myself."

"No offense to you, but Franklin Gentry needs a man to show him the error of his ways."

At the corner of Government Street, he turned and smiled at her elvish face watching him through the windshield. Hattie's returned grin empowered his mission tenfold. Sean strode through the schoolyard and straight to the secretary.

"Solicitor Spunner here to see Mr. Gentry." Sean removed his leather gloves with the air of a man bored. "And no, I do not have an appointment, though you may assure your principal that it is in his best interest to see me promptly."

"Solicitor Spunner, his schedule is quite—"

"I will give him five minutes before I head to the courthouse to file my complaint."

"Ye-yes, sir!" The secretary scurried for the principal's door and knocked. She disappeared inside, then the door flung open a minute later and she raced out before the portly man a decade older than Sean.

"And to what do I owe the pleasure of your visit, Solicitor Spunner?"

"I make a point never to discuss business in doorways, Mr. Gentry."

He reddened and a bead of sweat rolled down his temple. "Of course. Do come in and have a seat."

Sean pretended to sit. As soon as Franklin Gentry's cumbersome backside was lowered into his chair behind the desk, Sean straightened and glared down at the man.

"Hattie Fernsby will be restored to her science classroom in January."

"Ms. Fernsby? How can she afford a lawyer and secure one so quickly?"

"What you need to be worried about is whether or not you want the entire city knowing what the principal of the high school did at the Mystics of Dardenne masquerade in 'ninety-three."

Mr. Gentry's countenance went ashen. Moisture trickled from his forehead.

"I see we are on the same page now, Mr. Gentry. Send Ms. Fernsby a note of apology for your too hasty dismissal by the afternoon post and all will be well."

"But she broke the law!"

"No, Mr. Gentry, that's what you did at the masquerade. Ms. Fernsby did nothing more than respectfully field the comments and questions of curious students. Had you taken the time to listen to her side of the story, you would understand she handled the situation with utmost decorum."

"It's beyond my control. Ms. Fernsby's file has already been sent to the superintendent, along with the authorized letter of her dismissal."

"A one-sided account, which did not include her signature and statement. That is, unless you forged it."

The man went red once more. "It's the last day before the break and—"

"Ms. Fernsby's classroom will not be altered, nor will she collect her personal items this afternoon. Come January third, you *will* welcome back the best science teacher ever employed at the Girls' High School with graciousness."

"But Superintendent Hill will—"

"He will fully agree with me. Promise to do as I instructed and I will have no need to see you again."

"Yes, Solicitor Spunner. And the superintendent's agre—"

"Do not doubt it will be done." Sean pulled on his gloves and turned for the door. "Now pray I do not need to seek another moment of your time."

***

Hattie's clasped hands began to cramp. She stretched her fingers and smoothed her blue dress. Only ten minutes, but it felt like hours before Sean emerged from the school. With a jaunty spring in his step, he rounded the sidewalk.

He patted her hand before starting the engine. "It's going to take another stop, but never fear."

"He refused to—"

"Principal Gentry is ready to welcome you back after the holidays, but I have to follow the paper trail. In his haste to clear things out before Christmas, your file was immediately sent to the superintendent's office. Lucky for you, Mr. Hill and I are members of the same Mardi Gras society."

"The one from your youth?"

"No, my current one, but the Dardenne connection came in handy with the principal."

"That old badger?"

"One and the same. There was quite a report in the society minutes about Franklin Gentry's antics at the masquerade in 1893. It made this backroom deal my easiest yet."

"What did he—"

"A Dardenne brother never spills secrets. No one will hear of his fetishes unless he fails to welcome you back."

"Fetish—Sean! What did you do? It sounds a lot like extortion."

"But it's made possible by his sins, which was all his doing."

Stomach hardened with fear, Hattie laid her hand on Sean's knee. "Couldn't someone hold similar power over you one day?"

"I've never done anything half as bad as *that*. Besides, only Dardenne members serving as president or secretary have access to the locked minutes. I did my time taking notes so I could peruse the past." He parked outside the district office and gathered her hands in his strong ones. "Listen well, Hattie, for I'll tell you this once. My first love was a sweet, pure one. I was seventeen and she fifteen. After a few months of our acquaintance, she died from yellow fever. The following year, I took up with Mystics of Dardenne while studying law. At their parties, I drank too much and acted a fool like many of the others, but I never participated in anything lewd in a common space—if you understand what I mean."

Hattie's face heated, but her heart softened more. "Go on."

"I did, through the years, indulge in the red light district during Mardi Gras. You'll be hard-pressed to find a man raised in this city that hasn't—Davenport is the only one I know of. But all that came to a stop when I began wooing Eliza Melling the spring of 'o-five. She was young but experienced. Not to mention completely uninhibited. Once we were engaged that fall, we held nothing back. When she died the following January, my passion did too. As I told you the other week, she bled me dry. I've focused on my career since then. Using my secret society knowledge and contacts helps with success on the business front, but my personal life has been dead. I've buried myself in books, a habit from my youth. No one has stirred an ounce of my interest until I heard you proclaim Madame Curie's Nobel Prize as the turning point in women's role in science."

His intense stare—amber in the sunlight—caused her to look away.

"When I saw you, Hattie, I wanted nothing more than to bare your curves and lick every inch of you." He took her chin and gently turned her to meet her gaze. "You gave me back my passion. I'll not let you go without doing everything within my power to turn the tides in our favor. If that makes me selfish, so be it. I'm not letting you leave Mobile."

She managed a blushing smile, but couldn't speak.

He kissed her cheek. "Think all that over while I meet with Superintendent Hill."

Think? Hattie could hardly breathe as she watched his steady stride disappear inside the building. Never had a man been as brash, but at the same time tender. He laid his shadowed past bare, though he revealed a future of resplendent colors. Fearing she craved him as much as he did her, Hattie wrestled it over with her liberated lifestyle.

How can I allow him to manipulate others as a means to secure my future while I wait for him in the automobile like an outcast?

One backroom deal and loophole at a time, it appears.

Sean returned a minute later, lips pursed in his thoughtful way. "Apparently he left town this morning to spend Christmas in New Orleans. He will, however, be back in time for our society's ball."

"I'll have no closure until then? What will I do?"

"Shop, of course. You need to be outfitted for the Order of Mayhem's New Year's Eve masquerade."

"But my students!" Frustration over Sean's easy dismissal of her joblessness and his blithe attitude about shopping and parties reminded her of their different stations in life. "Rosella was counting on me."

"And she'll not be disappointed. You will be there with your fossils and enthusiasm the day the students return."

***

The next week and a half was a rush of excursions for Hattie, all revolving around Sean. Two trips to Mademoiselle Bisset's shop for a New Year's Eve gown and fitting, with the bill—at Sean's insistance—sent to him. Dinners together, as well as Christmas Mass at the cathedral. Plus, a chartered boat ride to Dauphin Island with the Davenport family so Hattie could see the Indian Shell Mounds and explore the beach.

Looking back, it was the simple outing of midnight Mass that brought the largest impact. Hattie expected to feel like an outsider within the cloak of the church, but instead saw the beauty of the architecture and felt the peace of the hymns. Sean's warm body beside her and his whispered words after the service as he linked their fingers brought an unexpected rush of joy.

"I feel your peace, Hattie. There's enough good from your childhood for you not to cast it all aside. Leave at least one pinky holding to your faith—enough to allow for a wedding Mass and baptism for any babies we might be blessed with. That's all I'd ask of you." Then he'd kissed her ear beneath her hat and flashed his chip-toothed smile that made him look every bit the young rascal he claimed he once was.

No matter his journey, Sean was an educated gentleman who could quote the likes of Keats, Darwin, Thoreau, and constitutional laws like they were old friends. He was at ease with people of all walks of life and constantly made her feel like the most adored woman in the world—whether he treated her with the respect due a queen or the lusty banter befitting a bar wench. And she loved him for it.

Now, she stood in the middle of her boarding house room in a splendid purple silk gown as she awaited him to escort her to the New Year's Eve masquerade.

A knock sounded, followed by Mrs. Grimes calling through the door. "Mr. Spunner is here!"

Hattie collected the silver beaded reticule that had arrived by delivery that afternoon along with a note proclaiming it a last minute thought over which Mademoiselle Bisset telephoned Sean, saying Hattie needed it to complete her attire for the evening. And the ensemble was stunning—silver shoes, gloves, wrist bag, and mask against the royal purple of the provocative square neckline and short sleeves on the floor-length gown.

"Oh, my dear, you look like a princess!" Mrs. Grimes exclaimed when Hattie opened the door. "Mr. Spunner is most charming. You could do no better, Ms. Fernsby."

Ignoring the baited statement, Hattie went for the receiving room. Sean stood before the fire in a flawless black tuxedo with purple accents and mask that matched her dress.

"Hattie, you look even lovelier than I expected, which says a lot." He took her hand and kissed her cheek before turning to Mr. and Mrs. Grimes. "Thank you both for your hospitality. Happy New Year's."

Surprised to see a hired automobile before the house, Hattie clung to Sean's arm on their way down the walk.

"It's tradition to have a chauffeur for Mardi Gras balls." He helped her into the back of the limousine and settled beside her. "That way the revelers can enjoy every bit of company before and after, as well as not worry about driving home after indulging in too much drink. May I taste a sampling of your offerings, dearest? I've waited weeks to see such a display. I promise not to leave a mark or rumple your dress."

He motioned to her breasts with his gloved hand and she laughed, which caused her cleavage to jiggle. His eyes widened with pleasure beneath the mask and she laughed all the more.

"Oh, go on, you cad."

His smile was soon buried in her décolletage. Lips and tongue explored each swell and the valley they created before he trailed kisses to her mouth.

After he settled back, his hand went for his tuxedo pocket. "I love you, Hattie Violet Fernsby. I want to feast on you every day for the rest of my life. No matter what happens with the superintendent, I want you to consider me for your husband as an option in your future."

He brought forth a purple silk handkerchief and unwrapped it to display a stately diamond ring. Hattie's eyes immediately misted over, a lump forming in her throat.

"We might have met a month ago, Hattie, but it feels like we belong together. I want to continue to get to know all the wonders that make you special as we share a life. Will you at least consider it? Take as long as you wish to answer."

She took several deep breaths, ever aware of his watchful gaze. "I love you too, Sean," she finally managed to say. "I want to say yes, but I feel I must satisfy my critical thinking by forcing myself to mull it over. Will you give me the evening to think on it?"

"Only the evening?" Sean laughed. "I was expecting to wait a year, dearest."

"It will be if I wait until after midnight." She took his cheeks in her gloved hands and kissed him squarely on the lips. "Don't fret. You have more than enough going for you."

Never had Hattie experienced such splendor as when they walked into the ballroom at The Battle House hotel. The chandeliers, silks, jeweled tiaras, and masks created a treasure trove for the eyes. Sean made several introductions, but she could sense him searching for someone.

Superintendent Hill.

He stood twenty feet to the right, along with a lady who appeared to be his wife and another couple. Sean angled directly for him.

As soon as the others turned away, Sean inserted himself. "Superintendent and Mrs. Hill, it is a pleasure."

He kissed the back of the woman's glove and grinned.

"Mr. Spunner, my favorite gentleman." Mrs. Hill beamed like a schoolgirl though pushing fifty.

"You are too kind, Mrs. Hill. May I introduce the young woman whom I am fortunate to escort tonight? Ms. Hattie Fernsby."

"It is good to see you with a companion, Mr. Spunner. I do worry over you. Ms. Fernsby, you said?" She turned to Hattie. "Any relation to the Fernsbys of Moss Point?"

"No, I'm afraid not. I'm newly arrived from Boston."

"Boston! How exciting."

"It is indeed." Sean winked. "And there has been a bit too much excitement these past days. I was hoping your husband could help us. It would only take a minute of your time this fine evening, Superintendent Hill."

"Hmmm?" The man looked up from his champagne.

"Mr. Spunner needs your help," his wife urged.

"What is it, Spunner?"

"Hattie is a teacher at the Girls' High School." Mrs. Hill's hand went to her chest in shock, but Sean continued. "There was a mix up at the school the Friday morning before break. Miscommunication of sorts, as you know happens from time to time. As it turns out, the secretary sent Ms. Fernsby's file with a false letter of dismissal to your office. I am sure you can imagine what a damper it has placed on her Christmas and now New Year's to worry that her file sits on your desk awaiting your stamp to destroy her hopes of ever teaching again in our fine city."

"And you've discussed this with Mr. Gentry already?"

"The following hour, Superintendent, but his staff was so efficient, the paperwork was already sent. I told Principal Gentry I would see to it myself and be sure the teacher and her file were returned to his school in time for her first class in January."

He grunted. "Very well. Come to my office Thursday morning and I'll give you Ms. Fernsby's file."

"Thank you, Superintendent. I do believe our New Year's is off to a great start."

"Yes," Hattie said, "the perfect time to celebrate our engagement."

Mrs. Hill brightened with the news. "Why, Mr. Spunner, where have you been hiding this delightful creature?"

"In the science department. It's been grand, but we need to find the Davenports. I will see you Thursday, Superintendent. Enjoy your night."

As Sean led her across the room, Hattie felt lighter with each step.

He brought them to a dim corner where he stared down at her. "Did you mean it or did you accept my offer to improve Mrs. Hill's opinion of you?"

Her eyebrows pinched together behind the mask. "Sean Spunner, you're a prig if you think that of me."

"And the same to you, Hattie Fernsby, if you think I was serious." He fished the handkerchief from his pocket and retrieved the ring. "Slip off your glove and let's see if this piece of coal fits."

Both laughing, Sean managed to place the ring on her.

"It's perfect," she whispered.

"Thank you for making me the happiest man alive. Now we need to find Freddy and Melissa so they hear it from us rather than the gossip I'm sure is being spread about the room like wildfire. They did introduce us, after all."

Hattie pulled on her glove and took Sean's arm, hoping to stay within touching distance of him all night.

***

Two mornings after the Order of Mayhem's ball, Sean collected Hattie from the boarding house. She was prettier than ever in a wool walking dress with the engagement ring on full display. After a decorous kiss, he helped her into his automobile so she could accompany him to the superintendent's office. Hattie waited in the automobile when he went inside.

The secretary showed him into Mr. Hill's office where the superintendent looked through Hattie's file.

"Spunner, I hope you know what you're getting into with this woman. Mr. Gentry's note mentions Charles Darwin. You know what an offense that is."

"I do, as does Ms. Fernsby, and it will not happen again. I'll see this file returned to Barton Academy."

"Very well, Spunner. I hope to see you at the Aethelwulf Club soon. Your court stories are the most amusing to hear."

"You can count on it."

On his way down the hall, Sean flipped through the file, slipping the contract labeled CODE OF CONDUCT into the front space.

He swaggered to the automobile.

"You got it?" Hattie asked.

He nodded when he sat behind the wheel.

"Now what do we do?"

"Stop by my house, if you'd like. We can light a fire in one of the hearths, using this as kindling." He presented the contract of behavior standards with a flourish. "Then we may do whatever you wish, Hattie. My housekeeper has the day off."

"Sean, we couldn't burn it, could we?"

"A dismissal over lewd behavior would be difficult without a copy of the signed code of conduct." He kissed her forehead. "Do you want to pussyfoot about when we have so much desire between us? It's all up to you."

Her blue eyes went from his face to the papers and back several times. Then a devious smile spread across her alluring face.

"I do feel a chill, Sean. A fire sounds like a good idea."

"Allow me to see you to your future home, dearest."

Hattie tucked beside him and they blazed a path across town because, as Charles Darwin said, "A man who dares to waste one hour of time has not discovered the value of life."

THE END

Author's Note

Thank you for hanging out with The Possession Chronicles this far. There are two more books in the numbered series to go, plus all the side projects (short stories, novella, and spin-off novels.) Part of the fun of creating detailed stories is the connection with the characters—both for myself and the readers. A huge shout out to the members of Dalby's Darklings for their encouragement and support—plus the comments about favorite and least favorite characters. (LB, I hope you're pleased with Opal's return in this book.) The members of Darklings are my sounding board and consist of the loudest cheering section an author could want. If you would like more of the inside scoop to the series and my other projects, including Mobile history and character insights, find us at: https://www.facebook.com/groups/2113892472031891

Many thanks to Candice Marley Conner for all the years of being an excellent critique partner. I hope the occasional dark chocolate treats are enough for you to continue to cringe through the Alexander scenes. (I'm glad he's slowly winning you over, even if you won't admit it.) Much appreciation goes to beta reader Jennifer Lamont for her eagerness to read early and for loving the characters as much as I do. Plus, Sandra Buford, for being willing to listen to all my thoughts and reading the snippets I send your way as I travel this journey, even when you aren't active in the official critiques. My family continues to be central to my creative process for both emotional support and loving me even when I'm hyper-focused on a project and other things fall to the wayside.

Thanks to Cassandra Fear for her editing efforts—including all the grammar fixes, among other things. And to Ashley Byland for her assistance with the cover art from the first edition.

About the Author

While experiencing the typical adventures of growing up, Carrie Dalby called several places in California home, but she's lived on the Alabama Gulf Coast since 1996. Serving two terms as president of Mobile Writers' Guild and five years as the Mobile area Local Liaison for the Society of Children's Book Writers and Illustrators are two of the writing-related volunteer positions she's held. When Carrie isn't reading, writing, browsing bookstores/libraries, or homeschooling her children, she can often be found knitting or attending concerts.

Carrie writes for both teens and adults. *Fortitude* is listed as a Best History Book for Kids by Grateful American Foundation. She has also published *Corroded*, a contemporary teen novel about friendship and autism, several short stories that can be found in different anthologies, as well as a multitude of Southern Gothic novels for adults.

For more information, visit Carrie Dalby's website:

carriedalby.com

www.ingramcontent.com/pod-product-compliance
Lightning Source LLC
Chambersburg PA
CBHW060949190726
48286CB00005B/1489